The Dancer moved through that light, his body a darker gold, yet also light; he moved in a dance of Praise that was as much beyond description as it seemed beyond the reach of human movement.

For several moments the Dancer continued as if he were unaware of Nov's arrival. Then he bowed to Nov and wheeled through an eccentric spiral to the empty altar, leapt on it, and sat cross-legged, his hands on his knees. "Pan Nov," he said, his voice multiple yet soft as a whisper. "What do you want of us?"

Nov hadn't forgotten how his comrade had died; he hadn't forgotten the Dancer freezing him in place with a gesture. And behind his growing fury at the Dancer's lack of action was a knot of fear colder than the wind off the mountains. "Give me a day so I can get ready to move. Name a day, Dancer."

Eyes like butter amber stared at him unblinking. Nov felt sweat beading on his face, and fought to breathe normally. "A day," the form said, the multiple voices stronger. "Let it be so. On the fourth day of the Nijilic month Sarpamish, I will send men to you from the warrens of the South."

Nov bowed, relief making his knees shake. He wheeled, walked briskly from the chamber. Two weeks. It was just enough time to plan the attack.

"Let it be so," the Dancer whispered once Nov was gone. "The Sacrifice begins. . . ."

Jo Clayton
Serpent
Waltz

THE DANCER
TRILOGY #2

DAW BOOKS, INC.

DONALD A. WOLLHEIM, FOUNDER

375 Hudson Street, New York, NY 10014

ELIZABETH R. WOLLHEIM
SHEILA E. GILBERT
PUBLISHERS

DEDICATION

Many, many thanks to Linda R. Fox for all the
weaver's talk and to Judith Tarr for horse lore.

First Printing, March 1994

1   2   3   4   5   6   7   8   9

DAW TRADEMARK REGISTERED
U.S. PAT OFF AND FOREIGN COUNTRIES
—MARCA REGISTRADA.
HECHO EN U.S.A.

PRINTED IN THE U.S.A.

Contents

What Has Gone Before:

Awakened from the tree dream, SERROI finds herself uneasy in the world where she once fit. From the moment she was herself again, the magic force that had faded from the world when she slept uses her as a focus to flow back from wherever it had gone.

And the enemy comes forth. The Fetch troubles her sleep, calling her, calling like a calf to its dam.

As she joins a Company from the Biserica going on Ward to Marnhidda Vos of Cadander, that flow increases, turns to a flood as she heals. She spawns a vast array of new life, nixies for the rivers, dryads for the trees, ariels, fauns, lamias, kamen who are souls of stone, sirens, and many many more. Children are born with new talents. Old forces that had shelled over and lay dormant wake again, arise to walk the earth.

They reach Dander the night that Ansila Vos, Marn of Cadander is killed in a bomb blast. K'VESTMILLY VOS, her daughter, becomes Marn in her turn. With the help of the Company from the Biserica, she takes firm hold of the rule and things seem to be going well enough, but raiders in the hills and an army of attackers advancing across the southern plains complicate her life. And the Enemy is busy in the cities. While her forces are busy in the south fighting the invaders, the Cadander Pans (barons with assorted holdings, some economic—as in control of all shipping—some land based) turn on her; PAN NOV (the leader) seizes and imprisons her. She escapes with the help of ADLAYR RYAN-TURRIY (gyes of the Biserica, shape-shifter, mind speaker), ZASYA MYERS (meie of the Biserica, Fire-born chosen, mind speaker), and her consort CAMNOR HESLIN, and rides south to join the army and the General she has chosen, VEDOUCE PEN'S HEIR.

Camnor Heslin is a descendant of Hern Heslin who was Domnor of the Mijloc and Serroi's lover in her first life. This Heslin is a big, clever man with a wonderful, deep voice and an equally deep understanding of the way minds work. K'vestmilly Vos chooses him as her Consort although, at that time she is in love with Vyzharnos Oram, a poet and rebel against his class who doesn't like her much and has no idea of how she feels. She wants Heslin's intelligence and strength for her daughter; she likes him, but at first he doesn't attract her—it was a choice of the mind, not heart or body.

As K'vestmilly Marnhidda Vos rides from Dander, Vedouce Pen's Heir goes into battle with the invaders, wins a great victory at a cost that would have been higher if Serroi weren't there to heal even the most savagely wounded. As the Marn nears the army, the Enemy strikes at it, Taking over half Vedouce's men; they turn on the others and try to slaughter them. He rallies the remnants of the army, drives the Taken off in time to get K'vestmilly Vos safe in camp, then the Enemy breaks off the battle and draws the Taken back to Dander.

After consultation, Vedouce Pen's Heir decides to pull back to Oskland in the mountains and rebuild his forces before he marches on Dander.

On the morning of the departure, wearing the Mask of the Marn, K'vestimilly Vos speaks to the weary, angry men, telling them they have fought well and will fight again, not only for her and the life they've known, but also for the future of Cadander since she is carrying a daughter, the next True Marn.

Prologue—

Weary from the dreams that haunted her sleep, Serroi sat in the Summer Garden at OskHold, watching the dryads dance and flirt with the gyes Adlayr Ryan-Turriy who lay stretched out by her feet, his hazel eyes half-closed, his hands laced behind his head, his long black hair loose, the breeze fluttering the fine ends; he was as relaxed as the huge feline that was one of his alterforms.

Zasya Myers sat in the shade of a tree, a pile of clothing beside her, clever fingers making quick work of alterations and repairs to bits of their meager wardrobe, most of it provided from the bins and coffers of the Hold. Zarcadorn Pan Osk had offered sewing women to do that work, she'd relinquished some of it, but kept a part for herself; having her hands busy rested her better than idleness. The breeze blew her shoulder-length fair hair about her face. When the tickling annoyed her too much, she stopped to tuck it behind her ears, then went back to her work, as contented for the moment as Adlayr.

The sprite Honeydew flitted from tree to tree, her face, arms, and hair butter yellow with the pollen she was eating, sticky with the nectar she drank, the sun turning her translucent wings to stained glass glories.

K'vestmilly Vos pulled in her stomach, flexed the muscles in her legs, annoyed and bored with the bargaining that seemed to be going on forever between Zarcadorn Pan Osk and her General Vedouce—no longer Pen's Heir

but Pan Pen since word had come of his father's death.
Vedouce was himself again, worry dropped for the moment; his wife and children had reached OskHold alive
and well, Heslin's warning catching them a breath before
Nov's men came for them.

The Grand Hall was filled with light streaming down
from windows high in the walls, painting patterns on the
long table from the lacy lead tracery that wound between
eccentric glass shapes. Intricately embroidered banners
hung from galleries that ran around the upper part of the
walls, drafts keeping them in constant motion, patches of
red and blue, green and purple and an abundance of gold
thread glowing as they caught the light, darkening as they
retreated into shadow.

In and out of the lacework of light and shadow on the
shining red-brown wood of the council table, there was a
scatter of bowls of sliced fruit, wine jars, glasses, cha pots
and cups, pads of paper and stylos, jars of ink, and towels
and bowls of warm water to wash off ink and juice.
Hedivy was standing by the wall, half lost in the shadows
from the banners. Camnor Heslin sat at K'vestmilly's left
hand, slouched and silent. A short distance along the table,
the Mine Manager Kuznad Losyk and Osk's High Judge
Chestno Dabyn sat saying nothing, their faces carefully
blank as they listened to Vedouce Pen arguing with their
Pan.

Arguing. K'vestmilly touched the Mask. Two months
ago there would have been no arguing about support.
Law, custom and the Marn's Guard were more than
enough to guarantee that. Now there was a false Mask, a
False Marn with thousands of the Taken to serve her. Her
own army counted only five hundred weary, worried men,
she had no money (though, as far as she could tell from
reports out of Dander, the Marn's Treasure was still hidden, waiting for her return), no base to move from, and a
faceless, frightening Enemy.

She didn't count Nov, he was only a tool. If he were
the one behind this, she could call in Osk's men and
Ank's men, add them to her own, sweep down on the cities and boot Nov and his minions to the strangling post.
But she couldn't be sure of anyone any longer; the Enemy

could put out his hand and Take others and start a new massacre. She didn't know why the Free were still free, what key explained the Taken. And until she knew, she didn't dare move against the cities. The Enemy. Mother Death to the Dancer. The Fetch according to Serroi. Like a disease you picked up just breathing the air of a place.

She glanced at Heslin.

He saw the Mask turn, shook his head quickly, then looked down.

Heslin was right, of course. He always was when it came to people and their reactions. Zarcadorn Osk was a Pan, loyal in his way, but he didn't like foreigners on his homeground, he didn't trust them, dug them out as soon as he could in courtesy, and sent them down to Dander, traders and fugitives alike, whoever came into his mountains. His people took their cues from him and even K'vestmilly Vos was looked at slant-eyed; the anointed Marn she might be, welcome she wasn't.

>><<

Treshteny came into the garden, eyes on the baby faun dancing before her, a tiny bright green creature whose curly horns reached only to her knee. The faun saw the dryads and ran to play with them, Treshteny made her unsteady way through her time ghosts and sat on the bench beside Serroi. "Healer."

Serroi touched the woman's arm. Out of curiosity she let the manyness of the timeseer's vision continue without fighting it to a solid whole.

The dryads showed no change even in the timesight, perhaps because as they themselves had told her they had no dark seeds in them. She looked down. Adlayr was a weirdness so complex that she could make out few details except for a brief flash when he was a dolphin curled in a great leap. She blinked, turned away and saw the trees, seed/sapling/maturity/death, saw a portion of the wall, there/not there/blurred with crawling patterns of moss and erosion/a ruined heap of stones, saw Zasya as a palimpsest of infant to crone, saw Ildas as a firestreak . . . she concentrated and brought everything to oneness, held it

there until she felt Treshteny's arm move. She took her
hand away and smiled at the woman beside her. "Interesting."

Treshteny looked fondly across at the faun who was
chasing one of the smaller dryads across the grass; she
was giggling and tossing handfuls of broshka petals over
her shoulder at him, darting behind trees, vanishing into
zhula bushes in a shower of dark yellow flowers. "It is
better now that I have my son Yela'o." Her eyes widened.
"Your new children come."

>><<

Camnor Heslin sighed and tapped his wineglass on the
table. "Pan Pen. Pan Osk." His deep voice broke into the
tense silence between the two big men. "There's something you should consider. How long can the Steel Point
mills keep going without more coal, more ore from the
mines?"

Vedouce frowned, looked down at his hands. "Two
weeks. No more than that. There's enough steel stacked to
fill orders for a while, but if they let the fires go out,
they're going to have one zhaggin' miserable time getting
those pizhes cooking again."

"And the sand for the glasseries, some of that comes
from pits in the Merrzachars, doesn't it? Along with the
minerals for coloring and the different sorts of glasses."

The annoyance at the interruption washed from
Zarcadorn Osk's face. He moved to the head of the table,
pulled out the Pan's Chair and settled in it. "Heslin," he
said. "Marazhney said a thing or two about you. I see that
she was right. How soon do you expect them to march on
us?"

"It depends on what Nov knows about running a man-
ufactory. Pan Pen?"

"He's got Sko to tell him. If he listens." Vedouce wiped
his hand across his face and looked sleepy. "He never did
before. We probably have a month or so grace before he
realizes he needs to get busy or destroy a good part of
Cadander's wealth."

>><<

The wall bulged, a long section of stone separated from the rest, took a crude manform and came across the grass, the legs seeming to move, the arms to swing, but the whole process so strange it made Serroi's head ache—as if the creature's image moved forward, then its substance shifted into the image with a ratcheting flux almost like the timeseer's palimpsest visions, layer upon layer laid down, thickening the form, the process repeated over and over, a hundred and a hundred times a breath.

Adlayr scrambled to his feet, came to stand beside Serroi, his hand resting lightly on her shoulder.

She twisted her mouth, shook her head. "No need, gyes."

He watched the stoneman advance for another two breaths, then he shrugged and dropped to a squat beside her.

Behind the first stoneman, the wall was whole and un- changed as if he had simply waded through it. It bulged again a few breaths later, another stoneman oozed free, then another and another. They crossed space in their pe- culiar way and squatted lumpily in front of Serroi. In voices like the rock groans of an incipient landslide, they said, *Mama, claim us, too. You claimed the nixies. Claim us, too.*

So I do. What do you call yourselves?

Kamen, Mama.

Kamen, my men. She bent forward, extended her hand. The first kamen closed his stony fingers about hers, the same phase-jump flow inside form. Though the hand looked clumsy, it was gentle and even warm. The kamen bowed, loosed her, and moved away to make room for the next.

>><<

K'vestmilly tapped her glass on the table; when she had their attention, she said, "Nov has the Enemy to provide men for him and the traitor Pans to squeeze for coin and kind. Have you talked to Treshteny?"

"Mad Treshteny?" Zarcadorn Osk had very pale eyes, gray-blue, with little more color in them than the winter ice that lay about the Hold half the year; they narrowed into a measuring, skeptical squint.

"Useful Treshteny, my mother would have said. And Jestranos Oram. Never mind. What we need is information, not guesses. Hedivy, come here."

He came into the light reluctantly, his face shut down, his eyes dull and half closed. "Marn."

"We came away with all the communicators?"

"As you know, Marn."

She smiled behind the Mask, spread her hands as her mother had in a translation of that smile. "You've seen the Taken, so you know what to look for. Do you think you could slip into the cities without getting your head collected?"

He shrugged. "I've done harder."

"Zdra zdra, is it possible some of Oram's agents went to ground and escaped Nov's thugs?"

"Could be. You want me to set up a network?"

"It wouldn't have to be elaborate. Just to let us know what's going on and warn us if there's an ingathering of fighters. Something like you did with the Govaritzer army." She set two fingers on the base of the wine glass, moved it slowly about on the table top, blurring wet circles one into another. After a moment she sighed and settled back in her chair. "So. Are you willing to do that, Hedivy Starab?"

He snapped thumb against forefinger. "When do you want me to start?"

"As soon as you're ready. I'm going to use you hard, Hedivy. Oram called you his best agent." She let her hands smile once more. "You'll regret that before we're done. When you get back, I'm going to send you out again, to finish the job hunting down the Enemy."

>><<

A dappled gray horse with a creamy white mane and tail leapt over the high wall, clearing the top with his hind legs tucked tight, landing so lightly that his hooves barely bent the grass. Snorting and whuffling, he walked to Serroi, nuzzled her hands, then moved off, tail switching, ears flicking, to graze on the blossoms on the zhula bushes and the tender new growths at the ends of the twigs.

Zasya set down her sewing, got to her feet, and angled obliquely toward him, making soft tongue sounds; he twitched, snorted, danced sideways, went back to grazing, ignoring her as she edged closer and finally touched his shoulder, moved her hand lightly up to his mane, digging her fingers in, scratching as hard as she could, working clawed fingers down the curve of his neck. "Ah, you beauty, you love." She chuckled as he leaned into her, hooking his head over her shoulder. "Yes, you are, yes. . . ."

He shook loose and danced away; at a comfortable distance, he turned his head and looked at her, his slate gray eyes knowing and strange.

Zasya laughed at him. "I know you, Pook, do you think I wouldn't, after watching you jump a twenty-foot wall? Hah!"

Ariels drifted overhead, golden-winged fliers sculpted from air and sunlight, teasing Honeydew, swooping low to brush past Serroi's head. Unlike the dryads and the nixies, even the kamen, they had no voices, but they didn't seem to miss them.

Abruptly they rushed together into a fluttery knot, then were gone.

The dapple-gray snorted, back off a few paces, and went running at the wall. He pushed off from the grass, rising as if he had wings, cleared the top, and vanished.

The dryads melted into their trees, the faun trotted to Treshteny and huddled against her leg, Honeydew fluttered to Adlayr and settled on his shoulder, clutching at his hair.

A swaying figure came from the trees and stopped on the edge of the sunlight, an immense serpent at least thirty feet long with a woman's torso and a woman's heavy head; her powerful arms were folded beneath large breasts. At times she was solid, at times a translucent near-hallucination. She stared at Serroi for a long, tense moment, then she, too, was gone.

The room high in the guest tower was filled with sunlight shimmering across tapestries bright with color and onto simple furniture whose beauty lay in the handling of the different woods it was made from. K'vestmilly Vos stood at a window, Mask in her hand, looking down on the walled gardens filled with bloom in this brief mountain summer. Behind her, Camnor Heslin sat at a table writing in a diary, his stylo scratching without pause across the pages.

K'vestmilly turned from the window. "Thanks," she said.

Heslin looked up from diary and smiled, his dark blue eyes nearly lost in laugh wrinkles. "Timing is all," he said.

She crossed to him, rubbed the back of her hand down the side of his face. "Talking about timing, I want our daughter born in a Pevranamist surrounded by peace and prosperity."

"We'll do our best, Milenka. A little luck and a lot of planning and maybe that can happen."

1. In the Skafaree

Serroi wrung water from her skirt and grimaced as the cloth slapped against her legs when she dropped it, the sound lost in the murmur of the surf and the hiss of wind-blown sand. A patchy fog swirled round her ankles, lit into ghostwater by the Jewels of Anish low on the western horizon. It was only an hour before dawn and cold enough to start her teeth chattering.

Adlayr crouched atop a high dune a step away, blending with a mix of tall grasses and tangled brush, Honeydew snugged into a shirt pocket, protected by his cloak from the foggy damp. Hedivy was further on, standing in the shadow of some scrub growing beside a rutted track that paralleled the shore.

The triangular black sail of the fishermen's boat that had slipped them into this shallow cove on the north end of Jelepakan was a low blot on a horizon turning pink with afterglow when Hedivy came back, a Skafar behind him leading a bony vul hitched to a cart.

The Skafar climbed on the plank that served as a driver's seat and sat there staring at the ground while Adlayr pitched their gearsacs into the cart. Serroi stepped onto his hands and he threw her up, then climbed in after her. As soon as they were settled, Hedivy took his place on the plank beside the driver. "Let's go."

The man nodded, his ragged turban bobbing unstably; he slapped the reins on the vul's bony rear, muttered, "Muh j'h j'h j'h."

The cart started off along a road that was mostly ruts

and short, wiry grasses, the vul's hooves eerily silent. The only sounds audible above the rising wind were a few clunks of wood against wood and a creak or two.

Serroi drew up the hood of her cloak and pulled the front panels around her legs; she sat hunched over, her arms folded on her knees as the cart swayed along. *Traveling again, and who knows where we'll end this time. This has to be a smuggler's cart, those hooves are muffled and he's got the axle greased to a whisper. Fetch. You haven't been bothering me since I left OskHold. Does that mean you're too busy? It gives me knots in the stomach when I think of what you're probably doing.* She dropped her head on her hands, thought about the weirdlings who were her children. From the moment her reconstituted feet touched the stone of that cliff, the magic that permeated this world before the Sons' War had used her as a conduit to flow back from wherever it had gone. It was getting stronger; at first she'd only felt the energy come into her when she rested after a healing, now each time she put a foot on the earth, she felt a faint tingle, like touching metal on a frosty morning.

She wrinkled her nose. *A little more of that and I'll be skittering around like a surce on a hot griddle. Saa! Wonder what Zas is doing? I suppose Hedivy's right, it'll be hard enough for the three of us to slip and slide, more would be a shout. And the Ward is with the Marn, so someone had to stay with her. I'll miss her. All these men. . . . Hedivy about had a fit when K'vestmilly told him I was coming. Ei vai, I don't care what he thinks, this needs doing and I'm part of it.* She blinked, startled at how much she'd changed in just a few months.

For two years she'd clung desperately to the Biserica and the meien, despite the tension she caused there and the dreams that started again, Ser Noris getting at her, raging because she was free and he was still trapped in treeform, and the Fetch whining at her night after night.

She smiled. It wasn't all so different from the world she remembered. Some things may have changed in those two hundred years, but not people. Nay, not people. And it no longer hurt to face the truth; she wasn't going back to the Biserica ever again. Like a snake shedding her skin, putting off the old life, emerging into the new.

The day was still young when the cart reached the B'roj'n Heath north of P'lubakat, a stretch of fairly level ground dotted with mires and groves of sar'z, a scatter of ragged bamboo plots and attendant hovels with stinking pens of b'ba and k'ji, flocks of oajams scratching grubs out of the brush, the source of the hams, veal, and eggs that fed the port city.

The Skafar stopped the vul by a gloomy grove of sar'z, the foliage so dark and clotted it seemed painted with ink, the pools of ooze under the root pyramids like more ink spilled across the spongy ground. He turned his head, nodded at Hedivy, then sat staring down at the reins dangling between his knees.

Hedivy dug in his belt, dropped a coin on the plank, and jumped down. "We walk from here on."

The winding streets were beginning to fill with the usual mix in every wharf quarter Serroi had seen in the other Lands she'd visited—Sleykyn in darkly glittering velater armor guarding Assurtilan merchants, Sankoyse rug peddlers and their dull-eyed bondservants, black-eyed Minark traders, Fenek sailors, Karpan mercenaries, Shimzely seamen, traders, porters. Lots of Shimzeys, almost as many as there were Skafars.

The stark black and white buildings were flimsy structures; the walls were mats woven from the tough grasses that grew in Jelepakan's sea marshes, plastered with white stucco, braced with poles from the bamboo plots. At intervals, as Hedivy led them deeper into the quarter, buildings on both sides of the street creaked and swayed for a breath and a catch, shed plaster dust and fragments, then settled again, while the walkway wiggled as briefly underfoot. The strings of round bronze bells that hung from many of the doorposts tinged musically. No one paid any attention to the bells or the shaking walls. *Little quakes. They must get a lot of them here. Hev was right, once we get settled, there's no reason to pick us out of this melange. I wonder if there are any Taken here, or was*

*that only in Cadander? Shimzely's next . . . has access to
Oram's spy reports, I wonder if any of those agents are
still alive? Or the ones here. Maiden Bless, this is not going to be easy.*

Hedivy turned into a stinking sidelane with an open
drain down the middle, went past a few houses, turned
again into a narrow dirt pathway between two of the mud-
wattle storehouses, led them through a gate in a fence of
bamboo stakes held together with thick wire, a fence that
looked like a heavy breath would blow it over.

Inside, there was a paved yard, a stable to one side with
four draft vuls standing hipshot and half-asleep under a
thatched roof and a pair of macain licking grain from a
manger. At the back of the yard was a two-story building
with a covered porch running the length of the front wall,
wicker chairs scattered along it, several of them already
occupied by wizened elders whose rheumy eyes followed
Hedivy and the rest of them as they came across the yard.

Hedivy clumped up the three sagging steps, crossed the
porch, and pushed the door open.

Behind a table near the end of a short, wide hall, an old
man sat sipping at a mug of kava and squinting at a sheet
of coarse paper printed on both sides. He looked up when
he heard Hedivy's boots on the tile floor, let the paper fall
beside the mug. "Hev-tan. When you get back in town?"

"This morning, Djuran-tan. Got some rooms?"

The old man peered past him at Serroi and the two
gyeslar. "How many you want?"

"One of those with a daughter's cubby. How much you
going to soak me for 't?"

"Daughter, prh?"

"None of your business, tu'or. Price it."

"A teb a night a head."

Hedivy clicked his tongue. "Going up in the world,
prh?"

"Times change. We don't change with them, we end up
sunk in a B'roj'n mire."

"Baik lah, I'll pay you a week; if we leave before, the
extra's yours."

"Keep it soft, Hev-tan?"

"Like usual, Djuran-tan."

* * *

"So far, no problem." Hedivy stood by the window looking down into the yard. The shutters were open and the casements pinned back; like many of the others Serroi had seen on their way here, instead of glass the windows of the inn had parchment scraped thin and oiled to let light through, another concession to the constant quakes that shook the islands. Glass had to be imported from Cadander and only the richest could afford to replace all the panes broken when the land shook. "Carter Hink wasn't nervous and Djuran's price was too low to mean that rumors have reached him." He scowled at the yard. "Unless he's been paid off to keep face with us."

Serroi pulled her feet up and sat cross-legged on the bed. She glanced at Adlayr who sat in a chair tilted against the wall, his hands laced behind his head, eyes half shut. Hmm. Waiting for them to decide what the day held so he could get on with things. "How do you want to deal with that?"

He shrugged. "If Cambarr's in port, or a few others I bring to mind, won't matter, we'll be off with the tide. If not, hmm." He glanced out the window, his round face going still. "Problem. Boy down there in a hurry to be somewhere else."

"Djuran knows you're here, Hev. If it's something funny, why would he send his messenger where you could see him?"

"No choice, Healer. We backed against a warehouse. One way out."

"Vai, I'll believe that when I see Nov kissing babies. You wouldn't be here if it were true, nor would you bring us."

He didn't respond to her attempt at teasing, just continued watching the boy until he was out of sight. She'd noticed that he had little humor; he was a stolid man with loyalties rather than beliefs, a sharp but narrow intelligence.

"If there's trouble when I'm gone," he said, his voice little more than a whisper, "get to roof, cross to warehouse. North end. There's a way to climb down and a maze to get lost in." He started for the door.

"Hev."

"What?" The word was a growl, but he paused with his
hand on the latch, turned his head so he could see her.

"If you need to, you can trade my services for passage.
Say you've got a healer and . . ." she grimaced, memories
of her childhood training still an angry ache inside her,
"and a windwitch. It's been a long while since I've called
a wind, not since I was eight going on nine, but it's not
something you forget even if you try to. It'll pin us for
the Enemy, remember that in your bargaining. And there's
no way I can fight it directly. I'm not strong enough."

Serroi stood in the doorway and watched Hedivy go
clumping down the stairs. *I don't think you really understand what not strong enough means. You're devious and
sharp enough to prick yourself, but. . . .* She shut the
door, tapped Adlayr's shoulder.

"You think you could go trax and follow him?"

"You don't trust him?" Adlayr pushed the chair down,
stood, and began stripping.

"Nay, not that. I just have a feeling. . . ." She shrugged.
"Anything happens, send through Honeydew." She turned
to the sprite who was sitting on the windowsill, swinging
her feet and fluttering her wings. *Honeydew can do?*

Honeydew giggled, the sound beyond the ears of everyone except Adlayr who winced as he picked up his clothing, folded it and left it on foot of the bed. Honeydew can
do.

Honeydew lay stretched out on the windowsill, her
wings flattened, her chin resting on her fists, passing
Adlayr's report to Serroi. Adlee say Hev walking along the
wharf road looking at the ships . . . not moving fast, just strolling
'long . . . he's stopped a minute by a pile of crates . . . talking to a man . . . a drunk sailor . . . something worrying him . . .
he keep sneaking looks back along the road . . . like he think
something's following him . . . not me . . . someone on the
ground . . . don't know this place well enough to spot what's
bothering him . . . he moving on now . . . head turning side to
side . . . what's he looking for? Ah . . . I think that's it, a pilot's

cat ... he's walking faster ... trying not look like he's hurrying ... he's good at that, you wouldn't see it down below ... saaa, there's a bunch of men coming down an alley ... ahead of him ... dressed in black, black turbans, sabers ... guards of some kind ... another lot, coming out of a warehouse behind him. ...

Honeydew, tell Adlayr just to watch, don't mix in any trouble. Hedivy doesn't need warning, but he might need rescuing, so we have to keep loose.

Honeydew wiggled round as she sent on the message, ran her tiny hands through the thistledown fluff on her head. Adlayr say asha, he watch ... Hev sees the men behind him ... he's running now ... got his knife out ... heading for that cat ... here come the other bunch ... trotting toward him ... he's got a start ... might make the boat ... if he does, they lose ... murd! they shooting ... yelling at him to stop ... he swerves, almost makes the water, means to dive in, Adlee thinks, a Skafar trips him ... now they're all over him, the guards ... giving him a hard time ... kicking him ... using their sticks ... now they're strapping his hands behind him and hauling him off ... moving inland ... you should see the street clearing ahead of them ... like they're a moving plague ... up the hill to that place with the pointed domes all different colors ... BerkHouse ... so this is government business for sure ... Adlee says Hev didn't say he had a problem here, did he? Never mind, we'll talk about that later ... wall around the place, good thirty feet high ... wonder how they cope with all these quakes ... don't see any big cracks, maybe they dug down to bedrock to set the base ... he in through the gate now ... they marching him into the main building ... that's it, he inside. Adlee want to know if he should stay a while, see if. ... Honeydew glanced out the window. Serr, men are coming, men like them Adlee tell about. Look out there, more than Honeydew can count.

After a swift scan that showed her black turbans crossing the yard, Serroi caught up the packet that held their money and papers. *Honey, go on up to the roof, I'll meet you there soon's I can. Tell Adlayr what's happening and to stay clear. As long as he's loose, we've the Biserica to bargain with.*

* * *

Serroi wriggled through the trap, moving cautiously along the rain-bleached shakes.

There was a sharp crack and half a dozen men rose to their feet on the roof of the warehouse, longguns pointed at her. "Go in," one of them yelled. "Go back in or the next shot is in your head."

2. The Reign of the False Marn Begins

Greygen Lestar checked to make sure the shades were drawn, then he wrapped his hands round the arms of the wheeled chair and pushed himself onto his feet. Using a section of pole destined for a table as an awkward cane, he forced his shaking legs to move, one step, another, another until he'd crossed the room. He leaned on the low workbench he'd built to accommodate his chair's wheels, caught his breath, then shook and thumped his way back. He made it three times across and three back before the quiver in his knees warned him he'd hit the floor if he didn't sit for a while.

When he got himself settled, the blanket over his legs, he poured himself some cold cider and raised the glass in a toast to absent friends. After that he sat sipping at the tart drink, musing on events in the double city.

Hus, old friend, it's harder than you thought. And worse. And you not here to give us a shove the right way. Zhagdeep with that spojjin' notney. Pan Nov!

Greygen spat into the waste bucket, gulped down the rest of the cider, refilled the glass.

When Foskit the Beggar passed the word ... zhalazhala, I was knocked sideways. Haven't got m' wind back yet. And the legs are maybe fixed, but till I get some muscle built, I'm weaker than a three-month tatling. Way it is, Hus, we've got to wait till things settle out to know how to move. Then, I promise you, we'll make that notney sorry he was ever born.

Sipping slowly, he emptied the glass again, pushed up, and carried it and the pitcher into the kitchen, walking with slow care. The lamp was turned low; the bright red kettle seemed to collect all the light. Though she was rather ashamed of her taste and struggled to keep it in bounds, Sansilly loved bright, crude color. He liked that in her, though he never found the words to tell her; it was all part of the life that burned so strongly in her, life he warmed himself against.

He built up the fire in the stove, filled the kettle and set it to heat, then went back to the workroom to wait for his wife to get home from her meeting.

When he heard the front door shut, he rolled out of his workshop into the narrow hall. Sansilly was shaking fog droplets from her cloak; her face was red with annoyance, her fine brown hair flying.

"No good?" he said.

She tossed the cloak at the peg, exclaimed with annoyance when it missed and fell in a heap on the floor. She scooped it up and forced it onto the peg with such violence she nearly tore the material. "That Myzah, we supposed to be there to plan sick-visits and clothes for the poor and all she does is rip and smear. I swear 'f I hear that squeany voice one more time sayin' 'oh, isn't it too bad' and all the time she lickin' her lips, I'm gonna slap that spesh so hard she be talkin' from the back of her neck 'stead the front." She stopped her rant when she heard the kettle whistling. "Ah, Greg, you're a luv. A strong cuppa cha will wash that Myzah out my throat."

Greygen watched her as she bustled about, setting the cha to brew, peeling the small greenish pocher she'd saved for a treat after the meeting, washing her hands, a whirlwind of energy despite the long hard day she'd just been through and the one she faced tomorrow. Fifteen years they'd been wed and he never tired of her fits and starts, especially since the accident that pinned him to the chair; it was as if she moved for him. He hadn't told her yet about the healing, because he didn't know how this new thing would change what they had and he was a little afraid of that change.

She pulled apart the pocher sections, divided them into

piles on two saucers, set one in front of him, strained the cha and poured a mug for each, finally perched on the edge of her chair, her small square hands cupped about the hot mug. "Ahhhh, it's good to sit a moment."

"So tell me about the meeting. Not Myzah, the rest of it."

She sipped at the cha, popped a pocher section into her mouth, chewed and swallowed, wiping her lips with the dishrag she'd used as a potholder. "Setra Snestil, she din't say a word the whole time, just sat there looking like a three-day wet, zdra zdra, she's never been the bouncy type, but she was a real piece of misery tonight. Been gettin' worse since the Preörchmat Masked Nov's daughter, zdra zdra, who can blame her, everyone knows Nov forced it, claiming the Marn's dead, tsaa! Maybe so, but if she is, we know who did it."

"You didn't say that?"

"Saaa! Greg!" She saw his grin, shook her head. "You! Well, Setra Vynda she din't leave time for chatter, she had our namelists writ out and what the fam'lies needed, names of storekeepers who said they'd give a little this'n that and papers we was s'posed to hand 'em so they knew we was the ones to get it. Then there was baby nappies to hem and Setra Vynda she said there'd be cloth for shirts next meeting and the Chitzeny brought in wafers and cha and we sewed and talked, most of it ..." she reached over, touched Greygen's hand, "you wouldn't want to bother with, just gossip, girls keep getting babies, don't matter what else goes on, and boys keep trying to slide. Thing is Nevycha, Zrushyn, and Sledova didn't show up, no one said anything till the Setras left, but while the Chitzeny was showing them out, Myzah got her teeth in them, she said they'd gone over to the House because their men got the word, if they didn't show the Glory sigil, their jobs were gone. She was going on about traitors and apostates and ev'ry big word she c'd dig up and a couple the others were looking sick, I think their men were getting the same word, they hated the thought, but their families have to eat. Greg. . . ."

"No one's said anything to me. Yet."

Sansilly wrinkled her short nose. "Yet. Mad's Tits, Greg."

"I know." He drank his cha, played with a pocher section, smelling the tart/sweet perfume rising from it, staining his fingers with the yellow-orange juice. "Sansy. . . ."

She looked up, her brown eyes wide.

He dropped the section, took her hand, held it between his. "Nik, Milach, it's not a bad thing. Just somethin' I was . . . waitin' for a good time to tell you . . . seems like there's no good times left . . . zdra, here it is. A couple weeks before that spojjin' notney Nov had Hus . . . you know, Husenkil the potter . . . had him dragged to the Pevranamist and shot dead, Hus brought the Marn's Healer here. It was your meeting night, Sansy, I think he picked it because of that. She was a little woman, hardly bigger than one of our boys. And green, Milachika, would you believe it? Sort of olive colored, actually. 'Greg,' he said, 'want you to do something for me. Times are bad and they gonna get worse. The Healer here, name's Serroi, she'll fix your legs for you so you can walk, but I want you to keep it quiet. Time could come when the Marn needs someone she can trust, someone no one else would suspicion. I'm thinkin' that could be you,' he said." Greygen grabbed the edge of the table, braced his arms, and stood. "Can't do much yet, I'm still working on it."

Laughing, crying, knocking her chair over as she jumped up, Sansilly ran round the table and caught him in a hug that threatened to break his ribs.

He smoothed his hand over and over her fine curly hair, strands of it clinging to his fingers. "Now now, Milachika, hush now, hush, and let me down."

Sansilly bustled about the small kitchen, pouring more water in the kettle, stirring up the fire under it, rinsing pocher juice off the plates and setting them to drain. She didn't look at him the whole time. He waited, a knot in his belly, while she made up her mind how she was going to deal with this.

She sat down across the table from him, clasped her hands and still didn't look at him. "Weeks," she said, her voice shaking. "Weeks and weeks. You din't tell me. Why? Din't you trust me?"

"Sansy. . . ." He stopped; it'd just make it worse if he said anything more, besides, he didn't KNOW what to say.

She started crying. "You're gonna get killed, I know it, you're gonna get killed like Hus."

"You see how it's goin', Sansy. This keeps up, who'll buy my work say I get shunned? Then we crawl or starve. You want that?"

She twisted her hands together, turned her head away. "Noddy and Mel, what about them?"

He sighed. "If you want, you can take them to your cousin Yorinn up in the Harozh, stay there yourself if it pleases you."

"You trying to get rid of me? Now you can walk? 'Cause I'm country Harozh and not town-bred like that sister of yours. And that sneak Pelousa who comes round making those goo-eyes at you?"

"Sansy!"

She dropped her head on her hands, her shoulders shaking, her voice coming muffled, "I don't know, I don't know."

He chewed on his lip, the knot in his stomach bigger and colder, then he levered himself up and shuffled around to stand behind her, smoothing his hands over her shoulders, kneading the tension out of her neck. He wasn't good with words. He didn't trust them. They were slippery things, seemed to change their meaning between mouth and ear. His hands had always spoken for him; he was sure of them, they said what he wanted and there was no mistaking the message.

Sansilly lifted her head, leaned back against him. "Zhalazhala, Greg, it's a shock, that's what it is." She coughed phlegm from her throat, wiped it away with the dishrag. "What a mess I am, don't look at me. Zdra zdra, let me up, luv, I need water on my face. Sit you down, sit you down, Greg, I'm all right now, I'm all right."

As he shuffled back to his chair, propping himself on the table, she bustled to the sink, washed out the dishrag and hung it on the rail he'd made for her, poured cold wa-

ter in a basin and splashed it on her face, then patted herself on both cheeks with wet cold hands. He sighed and
eased into the wheeled chair, grunting as his leg muscles
cramped; it would have been nice to have it all back, one
day a crock, the next, running like a racing man. That
didn't seem to be the way it worked, at least, not for him.
He sneaked a glance at Sansilly, relaxed as her face
emerged from the towel reddened by the rubbing, but
calm again.

When the kettle started whistling, he pushed the chair
back, meaning to let her get herself together.

"Nik, nik, Greg. Be still, I like making cha, it's a quiet
thing. Settles me." She bustled about, humming one of
her offkey songs.

He closed his eyes and pretended nothing had changed.

Still humming, she strained the cha into one of
Husenkil's gift pots, then started for the table, holding the
pot by the handle, with a finger of her other hand under
the spout to help balance the weight.

There was a sudden burst of shots outside, screams, the
pound of feet, slams, more shooting.

Sansilly started, nearly dropped the pot, splashed boiling cha down her dress. For a moment, she just stood
there, shaking, then she ran to the table, set the pot down
with absurd care so that it didn't even click against the
wood; she gazed at her scalded, reddened hands, touched
her dress, and burst into tears.

Greygen didn't try to stand this time; he wheeled the
chair round to her, lifted her onto his lap and sat there
with her, holding her, rocking a little, saying nothing, letting her cry away the fear, anger, hurt.

The noises in the street stopped as suddenly as they'd
started and the warren settled back into the tense quiet
that had been the chief quality of every night since the
False Marn was Masked.

>><<

Lisken squeezed his watch from its pocket, clicked
open the cover. "Zach, I'm getting antsy about this."

The kavarna was dark and smoky, almost empty since

it was long past midnight; there was a man sitting alone at a table, hunched over a small glass, several pairs in the booths built along the walls; the man behind the long bar was polishing glasses, his eyes drooping, his movements slow. The sole waiter sat at the end of the bar, leaning on folded arms, talking in low tones with a tired whore on the stool next to him.

Zachal dug into his short gray beard. "Tomal was Hus' best source and he hates Nov worse'n poison. Kostan says . . ."

"Wait, I think that's her."

The door swung shut behind a slight figure, a woman in a dark cloak, the cowl pulled forward to hide her face.

The two men slid from the booth. Zachal stood beside the table, Lisken went to the bar.

She crossed to Zachal, shook her head when he motioned to the bench. "Sit first," she said. Her voice was low and husky, hardly more than a whisper.

He shrugged, slid down, making room for her. A moment later Lisken was back with three glasses of beer.

The woman sat turning the glass between her fingertips. Her hands were long and slender with a curiously unused look, the fingers bending back as if the bones were elastic, the fingernails buffed and pointed. "I want protection," she said in the same low husky voice. The stubby oil lamp in the center of the table lit her chin and a trembling lower lip. "I want you to get me out of Dander."

"Why?"

"Because I can tell you what's going on, how it started, who the focus is." She hesitated, hushed her voice yet further. "For Mother Death. Tonight, promise me, you'll get me out tonight."

"If you're in that . . ."

"I'm not in it, I loathe . . ." Her voice rose, then went back to a whisper. "I was his . . . I watched Her eat him . . . there's nothing left but a shell."

"We'll get you on a boat, upriver to the Harozh, that all right?"

"It'll have to be. I can't stay here, the shadow that's

left of him, he needs me, and She'll feed him as long as she has to. Prak, here it is." Her voice sank to a thread of sound, the lamplight touched her eyes as she leaned forward, they glistened deep blue and they were ringed with white. "My name is Fialovy, I was dancing partner to Treshtal, you know, him who danced for the Marn. He hated the Families. He had reason, more than most, but there was a kind of crack in his head that made it worse than it should be. I don't know the first time that thing he calls Mother Death touched him, but I watched him change." She slapped her hand on Lisken's arm when she saw his face shut and his eyes glaze over. "Listen to me, this is important, you have to know it all, if you're going to live through it." She sucked in a breath, let it out in an explosive sigh and went on, her whisper hurrying faster and faster. "After the Marn's death rites, he stopped dancing, zdra, his knees hurt him, but that wasn't it. That Thing crawled inside him and began eating away everything he was. I didn't know what was happening in the beginning, but I could see he was changing. He had hazel eyes, almost green, but they turned yellow as butter, and when I touched him, it was like touching, I don't know, a fish maybe, cold and not exactly unpleasant, but different. . . ." She shuddered. "I couldn't bear to stay with him, I left him, but he followed me, he put his hand on me and I couldn't move, I sat there in that chair, I could hear and see and smell, but couldn't feel anything, I couldn't shut my eyes or move my head to look away from him, and he said to me, you'll never leave me now, I'll find you wherever you go, then he sat down in another chair and he looked at me a long while without saying anything and then he told me this: I am the vessel; Mother Death dwells in me and She will take this Land and make it Hers. I will be one with the Land then and I can lay down and sleep and you will lay down beside me. Then he took my hand and I could move again." She swallowed, Lisken could see the working of her throat. "He . . . he makes love to me and she watches, the girl in the Marn Mask. She's part of it now, that Thing has laid its eggs in her." She straightened, pushed the cowl back, and smiled triumphantly at them, though her eyes were dark with terror. "You have to do what you promised and do it quickly. He'll come for me soon and if he finds you with me, you're dead."

>><<

"Spider one to Northman." Greygen glanced at Sansilly who was standing watch in the door to the bedroom, then focused on the com in his hand.

"Northman here. Go."

"Sending you a hot package. A woman. She's on her way, be there by tomorrow night. Talk to her, you need to know what she has to say, but get rid of her fast, for your own sake, pass her on. Go."

"Pushing your problems on us? Why shouldn't we just shove 'em back? Go."

"If you want her blood on your hands. And our blood, too, probably. Go."

"She that important? Go."

"Could be. Wait till you hear what she has to say. Go."

"Prak. Anything else coming our way?"

"Not at the moment. Both sides are still shaping up here, I'll let you know the minute there's movement. Out." He touched the com off. "That's it, Milachika, nothing to worry about, is it?"

"Unless Nov's sprocherts find that thing. Or follow you back when you meet those others ... nik, don't tell me, I don't want to know who they are, that way I can't say anything, you know me, I talk too much. Just be careful, Gregishli. Please?"

"I will. The boys are still asleep?"

"Yes. Mel snores a little. I can hear him."

"One more call, then that's it. We can sleep, too." He woke another light, murmured into the grill, "Spider one to Mountain."

"Mountain here. Go."

"A bit of luck here. Spider three reports he's got the name of the Enemy, nik, that's wrong, not the Enemy herself, but her Carrier. The Dancer Treshtal. According to his source the Enemy used Treshtal to spread the infection. He's nine out of ten sure that's accurate. What do you want me to tell him? Go."

"You're on the ground. Could the Web get at him? Go."

"Maybe a sharpshooter with a longgun. I doubt any one man or combination of men could get close enough for anything else. If you want us to try, we need to watch a while to work it out. Problem is, It's infesting more than just Treshtal. Spider three says the source says It's in the False Marn, too, Maiden knows who else, so the Web'd be sacrificing a man for probably not much gain. Go."

"Prak. I'll pass it on. Tomorrow night, same time, unless there's trouble. We'll have someone watching the com. Out."

>><<

The dapple gray leapt over the wall again and trotted to Treshteny's side. He nuzzled at her shoulder, then turned his side to her. Yela'o jigged on the walk beside her, his tiny hooves clicking on the stepping stone; he lifted his arms and waved them urgently.

Treshteny brushed at her eyes. "It's a long way up." She sighed as he made little whining pleas. "Zdra zdra, if it's all right with the horse." She lifted the faun to the dapple's back, smiled at the picture he made, little green boy with his hands buried in the creamy mane.

The horse knelt, turning his head to gaze at her, his slate gray eyes filled with a meaning she couldn't read.

Yela'o slapped at the broad back behind him.

"You want me up behind you? I don't know how to ride."

The dryads came crowding around her, their delicate translucent hands patting at her, urging her onto the dapple's back.

"Zdra, I'll try it." She arranged her skirts to leave her legs covered but reasonably free and straddled the back. As soon as she was settled, it changed, muscle and gray-haired skin moving up around her, locking her in place.

The horse stood, walked in a slow circle until she'd fitted herself to the motion, then he moved near the entrance to the garden, paused a breath, and began running; half-way across the lawn, he gathered himself, left the ground with a great surge.

As he cleared the wall, Treshteny felt a need to look back.

A number of Osk's Guard burst into the garden, spread out to search among the trees.

The horse landed lightly and began trotting south along the mountainside. Before long the trees closed over them and she could no longer see OskHold. She stroked Yela'o's downy cheek. "So we go. Somewhere. I suppose it doesn't matter where. I wonder why they're annoyed, do you know, Yela'o?"

The faun leaned back against her, a small warm armful, and the horse glided along, his motion smooth as if he ran on clouds. She relaxed in the cradle of his flesh and watched the land pass by.

3. Trading

When the Berkwast's Jagals brought Serroi into one of the lesser reception rooms in the BerkHouse, Hedivy was standing to one side, in front of a long panel of embroidery whose shimmering jewel colors made him look shabbier and loutier than ever. There were manacles on his wrists and ankles; chains clinked as he moved his hands. The Jagals prodded Serroi into place beside him, then went to stand at attention against the back wall, dividing into two groups, one on each side of the door, black turbans and black uniforms stark against the intricately carved screens of sea ivory whose joins were so skillfully done there wasn't a shadow of a line where the bits were mated.

The Berkwast tented his fingers, the row of lamps behind his backless chair glinting off the diamonds in his rings, shining through the polished ruby teardrop large as a modary's egg hanging from his left ear. "You wanted them, there they are."

The man kneeling on one of the cushions tossed in a line before the dais turned his head and stared at Hedivy and Serroi. "There's another one," he said. "The shapechanger."

"He wasn't around. What do you bid for these, Ajilan Novat?"

"Bid? This is the Marn's Writ." The Nov Cousin held up a sheet of paper rolled in a tube and sealed. "It is a request for the return of traitors, not a purchase order."

"Hmmm. One of your Marns. We've heard there are two now."

"You've heard wrong. The Old Marn is dead, the New has been Masked and is the only true source of Rule in Cadander."

"Tjela-tjelat, the pacts we've signed are all with the Old Marn. So we start with the ivory polished or we finish this now. If you are Marn's Zast as you say, what do you bid, Ajilan Novat?"

Serroi spoke suddenly, her voice ringing out before anyone could stop her, "Be sure you get a good price, Berkwast, you're attacking the Biserica by these acts."

The Berkwast dropped his hands on the carved arms curving up from the velvet cushioned seat. He didn't look at her, but he was scowling as he leaned forward, eyes probing the Cadandri's face. "You didn't mention the Biserica, Zast."

"I don't answer liars, Berkwast."

"We see. Good day, Ajilan Novat. Go and think over your answers carefully. We will speak to you again tomorrow noon."

Novat opened his mouth to protest, but the Berkwast's eyes were closed, all expression drained from his face. The Zast stood, glared at Serroi, then stalked from the room.

When the clump of the Zast's bootheels had faded, the Berkwast straightened and turned to contemplate his two prisoners, stroking his long forefinger over the thin black mustache and short beard that bracketed his mouth. "You we know to our sorrow, Hedivy Starab, your snooping shot us down the last time we bargained with the Marn. We'll send you back with no sorrow at all ... if that randung skent meets our price, if not, we'll have you carved for zark-bait." He smiled, tongue sliding along his rouged lips. "When the word gets out, we'll have less interference with our will. Now you, woman ... hmp ... if it weren't for your shape, we'd think you were a child. Who are you?"

"I am a healer from the Biserica. The shapechanger that flea spoke of is a gyes and my minder. If you'll look through the papers your Jagals took from us, you'll see I speak truth."

"Why are you with the spy?"

Jo Clayton

Serroi hesitated; she didn't know this land or this man and had to pick her way by the little she'd seen of him. The lavish, somewhat overdone decor of this room and his royal plurals suggested that a bit of pomposity would serve better than blunt speech. "Our Ward is with the True Marn; we act on her orders which is our lawful duty. Whatever that man tells you, we left her very much alive." A muscle twitched by his mouth. She returned the sketch of a smile with twist of her own lips. "Which I think you know quite well, Berkwast-tan, though it may not suit to you acknowledge it." *That went down sweetly enough, look at him preen, thinks he's so impenetrable, but a baby could read him, so let's finish, oracular to the nth degree.* "Consider what you do, O Man of the Skafaree, and remember what I say, that the gyes is out of your hands and I think will continue to be, that the Shawar watch over their children, meie, gyes and healer, and the Biserica protects its own and avenges them if necessary, that even were the Shawar fooled somehow, secrecy is a leaky pot."

When the cell door slammed shut behind her, Serroi wrinkled her nose, then picked her way across the mucky floor to the plank bench which with a bucket was the only furniture in a room little bigger than a closet. They were in a wing on the east side of the BerkHouse, so the rising sun was painting a small round image of the funnel-shaped window set high in the outer wall on the greasy planks of the door, the window-grill black lines across the whitish circle.

Behind her she heard the clank of the door as Hedivy went into another cell, the tunk-clunk of the turning key. She wrinkled her nose, walked the few steps to the bench and sat down. It was not quite as filthy as the rest of the chamber.

There was a flicker in the circle of light, then Honey-dew came fluttering down to perch on Serroi's knee. Eech, Serree, stink! The sprite wriggled around till she was comfortable, her tiny, bright eyes darting here, there, taking in the cell, the door with its heavy planks, iron bands, and studding, and the small barred opening, chin-high for

most men though it was several inches above Serroi's
head. Adlee is perching on the tower, one of the flat ones that
goes up on the edge of this place. Her miniature features
squeezed into a grimace of distaste that matched the dis-
gust she packed into the word place. She kicked her feet
against Serroi's skirt, moved her shoulders so her wings
jerked up and down. Adlee say what you want he should do?
He can't stay there long, he get awfully hungry when he a trax.

*Tell him to get away, find someplace to go to ground
where he'll be out of sight for a while. Until we can get
out of here, Adlayr's being loose is about the only thing
keeping us alive. The Berkwast believes firmly in the silence of the grave, but as long as Adlayr's free, he can
start the Biserica moving against the Skafaree and that
does scare our happy tyrant.*

Adlee say Maiden Bless and see you later, he taking off now . . .
eeeehh, it make Honeydew's skin crawl when he drop like that,
Honeydew expect he going to hit the ground splat! But he
don't, she added with a three-cornered grin that made
Serroi chuckle.

She sobered quickly. *Asha, Honey, be very very careful
no one sees you and go exploring for me, if you will,
please? See how the cells are laid out, where the keys are,
where the guards are, anything you can think of to help us
get out of here. Honeydew can do?*

Honeydew fluttered to the hole in the door and knelt
there, peering out. Honeydew can do. She twisted around,
waved a hand, then slipped through the bars and flitted
away.

Cells of various sizes lined three of the walls of the
huge, rectangular cellar. There were individual cubbies
like the one where Serroi was; then came larger, two-man
cells—they marched down both walls to the long cage
built across the back where a number of men chained to
the wall lay in filthy straw, some moaning, some silent,
one of them screaming an unintelligible word every few
minutes.

The central space in the cellar had a rack, other instruments of question and a line of whipping posts; it was lit

by a single smoking oil lamp hanging on a chain from the high ceiling.

There were no guards, only a jailor—and he spent most of his time in his quarters at the head of the stairs leading up to the first floor of the Servant's Wing. Through a doorway with no door in it, there was a small office with a table, lamp and chair, a locked chest in one corner where the property of the prisoners was kept, and keys on a ring hanging from a peg driven into one wall.

The day passed slowly, hour on hour of nothing happening.

The jailor brought water and bread about midway through the afternoon, but Serroi had trouble forcing them down. The windows slanted upward to open on a ditch; when the wind changed and blew from the east, the stench from the stagnant rainwater collected in the bottom of the ditch spilled down the slope of the window into the cell so that the taste of it was in the drinking water and on the bread.

Waiting like this was the hardest bit: wondering if the Berkwast would send for her or Hedivy, what she should do if they were separated, what deals the Berkwast was making with Nov's agent.

The hours crept past, the light in the room fading slowly until she sat in dim twilight, her legs tucked up under her, her head back against the wall, her mind lost in memory, some of it sweet, some terrible.

The jailor drunk 'n snoring, Serree, eeeeh the stink, worse'n aaanything down here, he wet himself and he look like he an't had a bath for a year. Honeydew pull his hair. She giggled, flutter-danced in vertical circles, then sobered and went back to hovering. He didn't even feel it, Serree. He wouldn't hear it if a bull orsk roared in his ear.

Serroi tied the last knot in the line she'd made by tearing strips from her skirt. *This should be long enough now; take the end and fly it along unless I tell you to stop; that'll mean it's still too short and I have to add another strip. Honeydew can do?*

Honeydew can do.

>><<

Honeydew took the end of the white strip and flew down to the floor with it, then trudged along the filthy stone, sweating with the effort it took to drag the cloth behind her. When she reached the stairs, she drove her wings, working harder than ever to lift herself onto the step, then did it over and over until she reached the landing and sat drooping, sweat rolling down her body. It had to be done. There was no other way. The metal keys were far too heavy for her even to think of moving them.

She used the end of the strip to pat herself dry, wincing as the coarse cloth rasped her skin. When she had her breath back, she hauled the strip through the doorless entry and over to the wall where the keys were. No word from Serroi, so that meant she still had strip to spare.

Honeydew knelt, her eyes closed, her breath coming slowly as she prepared herself for her last effort. When she felt ready, she wrapped the end of the strap about one arm and drove upward with every bit of strength she had.

She lifted slowly, slowly, eyes blurring, her body burning, especially the long muscles that powered her wings—but she kept rising, inching up until she edged past the bottom of the ring. She slapped her hands about the ring, pulled herself over till she was straddling the metal, then she collapsed, her body pressed against the slippery tarnished bronze.

She rested like that until her shaking stopped, then she maneuvered the strip around the ring twice and tied it off with two half hitches.

She rested again for several breaths, then launched herself into the air. Honeydew done, Serree. Give it a jerk and let's see if the knot holds.

The cloth strip tightened, tugged at the ring. The keys jangled faintly as it slid up the peg. It fell with a crash, began snaking rapidly out of the office.

Words came faintly to Honeydew: *Honey, see what the jailor's doing, will you? We don't want him waking up.*

Honeydew can do. Honeydew fluttered through the half-open door into the living quarters.

The jailor hadn't moved a hair; sodden and snoring, he was stretched out facedown on the bed, one arm hanging over the side, limp fingers curled round the neck of an almost empty bottle. He don't know nothing, Serree. Wouldn't hear the ceiling falling on his ugly head.

She sniffed and flew out, following the ring as it bounced down the stairs and traveled along the stone to the door.

A moment later the door opened a crack and Serroi slid through, a thumbnail prying at the half-hitches as she moved, working the knots loose. She looked up, smiling. *That was splendid work, Honeydew. What would we do without you?* She sighed. *Show me where Hedivy is, mh?*

>><<

Hedivy raised his brows at her skirt which was hitting her at midthigh now, the rest sacrificed to fetching the keys. "We'll have to find you better before we get out of here."

"I'll settle for getting out."

"Not I. I'm leavin' here with supplies and coin. Reparations for harassment and false arrest if you need to calm your conscience, Healer."

"I'll find my own rationalizations, thank you."

Once again he didn't respond to her tone with its attempt at humor, just looked at her a moment with round eyes like river pebbles, dull gray-green and empty of warmth, then he moved past her, his booted feet noiseless despite the grit on the floor.

Scowling at the stench, Hedivy tore a sleeve off one of the jailor's shirts, wrenched his hands behind him, and looped the strip of cloth around his wrists, ignoring the shapeless grunts and squeals from the sodden man. He used the other sleeve as a gag, then came out into the office and knelt beside the chest. He turned the top back and began lifting out their gearsacs. "Most of our stuff seems to be here." He opened his own pack, pulled out his moneybelt, swore as he checked empty cavities. "They cleaned us, prokkin' sprocherts."

Honeydew sat on the table, legs crossed, head turning as she watched what was happening with bright interest. Serroi had the table's single drawer open and was taking out whatever caught her interest. "Mh?"

"Our coin. In some sproggin' jagal's pocket."

She looked up from the knife she was inspecting, a fine steel blade barely wider than a needle that folded into the ivory handle. "I thought you'd decided to do a little cleaning out yourself."

"That's different. They owe us."

"Adlayr's gear there, too?"

"Waiting for us to hump it out to him." He pulled the lid down, piled the gearsacs on the chest and crossed to stand beside her. "What's that?" He jerked his thumb at a leather folder beside a heap of coins.

"A very neat little burglar's kit." Serroi flipped it open to show him the lock picks snugged into their pockets and sections of a small steel lever with screw threads on them.

"Mind?" Hedivy didn't wait for an answer, but folded the kit back and tucked it into a pocket.

Serroi slid the knife and coins into a pocket, scraped the rest of the debris back into the drawer, and got to her feet, pushing the drawer shut with her hip as she stood. She looked down at her skirt remnant, decided not to re-place it with one from her sac since there seemed to be a good chance she was going to have to run hard before they were out of here. "Ei vai, it's only about an hour till dawn, let's get moving."

Hedivy led them through the dark and silent corridors of the ground floor, lit at every corner by small, sputter-ing night lights. Serroi could feel vague stirrings around them; it was very early, but this was the Servant's Wing and servants rose with the sun to get the work of the house completed before their employers left their beds. She thought about saying something about this, but they were already moving as fast as they could and Hedivy wasn't going to change his mind. He was right, of course, despite the danger. They hadn't a chance without the money to buy passage.

With Honeydew flying scout ahead of them, they reached the Bursar's Office without seeing anyone or being seen.

Hedivy lifted a night light from its bracket. "Hold this for me, will you?" One after another, he inserted the keys from the jailor's ring into the lock. The fifth one turned stiffly but threw the wards. He pulled the door open and went inside, crossing the waiting room with a few strides. The same key opened the door to the inner office. By the time she'd followed him in, he had a small, iron-banded chest on the worktable and was choosing a pick from the burglar's kit. He glanced at her, frowned, then went to work on the lock.

>><<

Honeydew perched on the lintel of the office door, watching the shadows cast by the night lights dance on the drugget as the hall drafts blew the flames about. She was tired and aching, impatient for this ordeal to end.

She heard the clump of feet, fluttered to the corner, and saw two young men in black with white and black striped turbans coming down the hall; she pressed herself against the wall and as they turned the corner, sent a warning. *Serr reee, guards coming, hush hush.*

She heard quick footsteps, saw the door eased shut, heard the clink of metal on metal as the key turned in the lock. *Good work, Honey. Take care, mm?* More footsteps moving away.

". . . Mad's Tits, I'll kiss Tampin's toes when this Turn's done, Mata. Jetji boot me out her bed yesterday, sh' says all I do's snore, sh' says 'm wastin' good silver and borin' her with it."

The guard Mata patted a yawn. "Ia, ia, so you keep sayin'. Me, I say 'tis easy work, Ol' Tamp goes light on the spit'n, you know what I mean. Next round it's Dakan. Jetji'll be complainin' y' hands take her skin off, after Dak the Scrub's got you polishing Jagal leather, day on day off. Look a that, Tip, the night light's gone. There by the Bursar's door. Stand back, I'm gonna try the door."

Mata put his ear to the wood and listened a moment,

then he tried to turn the knob and rattled the door. He shrugged and rejoined his partner. "'S locked, all right. Din't hear anything. What you think we should do? That's Bursar's Office. If there's anything wrong. . . ."

Tip scratched his crotch, twisted his mouth as he considered the door and the silence around him. "Twenny minutes left our Turn, we c'n report it when we hit t' barracks, let Tampin do the worryin'."

Honeydew watched them walk away. The guard called Mata kept looking back until they vanished around a corner. They gone now, Serree, but they going to report the light missing when they finish Turn, one of them said twenty minutes so you better hurry.

>><<

"They're gone." Serroi repeated what Honeydew'd told her. "Maybe we'd better take the box with us."

"No need . . . I think." His eyes went blank as his hands moved delicately with the pair of picks. "Nik! Got it." He withdrew the picks, slid them into their pockets and put the kit away, then lifted the lid of the box. "I thought so, payday tomorrow." He began lifting small leather pouches from the box. "As many as you can carry, Healer, shove them in a pocket or down your shirt. And warn Adlayr we're on our way, he should be ready to take out the guard on the Workgate."

It was still night outside, quiet, no wind blowing, a few horsetail clouds and no moons, just starlight to let them see where they were going. Overhead, Adlayr was a patch of darker shadow circling above the guard tower.

When they reached the wall, he swooped down, shifted to manform and opened the door to the guardcage. A moment later he was out again, the guard draped over his shoulder. He dropped the man to the ground, went inside, and the gate began creaking upward as he worked the winch. Serroi dived under as soon as there was enough room for her. She straightened, dug into her gearsac, found her spare skirt, and slipped it on. The morning wasn't cold, but she pulled the cloak on anyway. She was

too different from the tall lanky Skafars and the less they
saw of her, the quieter the going would be.

As soon as Hedivy had rolled under the gate, Adlayr let
it slam down and took to the air as a trax. With him flying
over them as advance scout, Serroi and the others hurried
down the hill and into the city.

Hedivy strode up the gangplank; Serroi followed behind him, amused by the swagger he'd put on—that sort
of thing was as alien to him as humor, but he played it
well enough. Adlayr followed silently behind, carrying
the gearsacs as if he were a porter hired for the moment.

"Phindwe, you got room for passengers?"

"Eh'ha, Hev! Long time, where you been? Whatcha
mean passengers?" The small, wizened Shimzely Shipmaster pulled at his spindly beard, peered past Hedivy at
Serroi. "Hix forbid, Hev. You forgot I don't take women,
bad hanla all round."

"This one is a healer and a windwitch. Good hanla."

"Gonna cost you, if I make a big exception like that."

"Gonna cost you, time comes you want a good wind or
a break healed."

Phindwe ripped a rag off his thumb, extended it toward
Serroi, exhibiting a ragged, angry tear that went nearly to
the bone. "Show me."

Serroi came around Hedivy, took the hand on one of
hers, set the other over the wound; it was ugly but trivial
and her hands barely glowed as she knitted the flesh together. She took her hands away and stepped back.

Phindwe blinked at the smooth skin she left behind.
"Not even a scar. Good hanla for sure. You know we
leaving right now?"

"What I thought."

"What about him?"

"He's coming, too."

"Three. Hmm. Got one cabin, you sort it out. How far
you want to go?"

"Bokivada."

"Ten silvers, twelve if it's local coin. Berkwast, he's
been lowerin' the weight." Phindwe looked past Hedivy

at the dock. "No time for bhumbul, Hev. Take it or leave it, and if you take it, I want to see the coin right now."

"You're a zhaggin' pirate, Phin. We'll take it." He dug into his belt, counted the Skafar peks into the Shimzey's hand.

In the dark and smelly hole that Phindwe called a cabin, Serroi sat cross-legged on a bunk, Adlayr sat on the floor, and Hedivy was hunched over the porthole, watching as the *Tengumeqi* followed the pilot cat past the breakwater.

He relaxed as he saw the tip of the cat's sail slide away as the pilot began tacking back home.

Serroi smiled. "We jumped through that hoop well enough. Maiden grant the luck continues."

4. Friction in Cadander

"Spider one to Northman."

"Northman here. Go."

"Web wants to know about the woman. Go."

"She got here, told the tale, enough to freeze the bone. We sent her on, like you said, put her with one of the tribes who weren't Taken, zdra, two of that Clan were, Taken, I mean, but the Majil Stiny cut their throats and burned the bodies, so they're still clean. They're headin' as far west as the Windrunners will let 'em, won't come back till this is settled. Don't want nothin' to do with that Mother Death. Tell you something, Spider, I had a strong yearning to ride out with 'em. Go."

"Zdra, I know the feelin'. Something else. Three boat-loads started north 'bout 'n hour ago, some Taken, some Nov's thugs, keep your eyes open. Go."

"Thanks, Spider. Any more good news? Go."

"That's the budget, Maiden Bless. Out."

"Spider one to Mountain."

"Mountain here. Go."

"The woman got clear, was passed on to a Free Tribe and 's ridin' west. We been watchin' False Marn and the Dancer. 'S almost funny because Nov's helpin' us in a way, though he don't know it. He been tryin' to make distance round him, bringin' in women from the Shipper's Warren who hadn't gone over to Glory. The Web has touched in with some of them, got 'em to keep eyes open and pass on what they see and hear. We gettin' lots of reports of him and the Dancer quarrelin', zdra, that's not exactly true, it's Nov doing the shoutin', the Dancer just listens and does what he wants. Sometimes it's what Nov says, sometimes it ain't. Nov been tryin' to get the Taken to march on OskHold, sayin' coal's getting low, iron's almost gone, he's gonna have to shut down the mills if he don't get supplies fast. And Sko is gettin' antsy about the Glasseries, he's havin' to close down and he don't like it one bit. Dancer don't care spit about any of that, just keeps sayin' in a little while, in a little while. Neither Nov nor us know what he's waitin' for.

"Nov and his lot are tightenin' down on the Warrens and the Nerodin. All stores and businesses have to have licenses to open, have to buy them from the Pevranamist, answer all sorts of questions, and swear a loyalty oath by Glory and Maiden both. Had to do it m'self. Didn't like swearin' false, but I figure Maiden knows why and will pass on this'n. You have to have a job or a business to live in the Warrens. If you can't show a license or a jobpaper, don't matter why, you get booted out, shoved in a barge and sent south to work the fields, I suppose they want new bodies to stand in for them that got killed in the gritz war.

"Lots of rumors from the South . . . about Ker and Ano Rodins, cousins and younger sons, folk say they're takin' farmer's land any excuse they can think of, or just takin' it if they can't think of one, makin' farmers work like hired hands on land their families has had since Cadander was birthed. All those Rodin need is favor of the Pan. I don't know how much to believe, but Nerodin passin' through, headin' for the Harozh, they tell us that some of those Rodin are gettin' over handy with the whip, more than one Nerod has died at the post, we have names. I don't know if you want them, there's no confirmation.

"The Web is pickin' up word of more charnel houses every day, the kind Hus and his Peacemen were reportin' before the Marn left. There's no way of tellin', the pieces left an't big enough to show who they be, but Spider three says he thinks maybe not all those pushed out of the Warrens make it South.

"There's a new thing maybe connected to that, a line of men or women, they usually not mixed, they'll start formin' up, Maiden knows what sets 'em off, go dancing down the street, swinging macai quirts, whipping themselves and anyone else they can reach, tearin' their clothes, chantin' this one word, kazim, same two notes over and over and over, then when all of 'em are good and bloody, they stop, 'bout as little reason for stoppin' as they show for startin'. Lines get longer every day, first it was only two, three, now it's up to twenty.

"The Nixies are goin' after the Taken, pullin' them into the river and drownin' them whenever they get a chance, capsizin' boats, settin' merfolk to chewin' the wood, startin' leaks, ruinin' what they can't steal, not just here, but all along the river. We'd cheer them on 'cept food's gettin' tight and expensive, if there's some way the Marn can get to them and say leave the food alone, we'd appreciate that. Go."

"I'll pass that on, no idea what'll happen. About the names, keep a list, I'll ask if they want 'em. Anything more? Go."

"That's about it for now. Maiden Bless. Out."

>><<

In the Setkan where she'd called a meeting, Motylla Nov sat in the Marn's Chair, her small hands on the carved arms, the False Mask sickeningly warm where it touched her face. The part of her that was still free was unhappy; she felt dwarfed by the massive chair, miserable at the sullen faces of the Warren Chitveks looking up at her from the ranks of the visitors' chairs. She knew they were measuring her against K'vestmilly Vos and it made her feel low as a worm. *She was twice as old as me, she could do what she wanted. Do you think I can? If you do, you're fools.*

The eight Treddeks on the Treddekkap stools drawn up about the table sat silent, their hands folded. She'd put her thumb on them and they'd vote aye. She wanted to shout at them all *get away, get me away, too, I hate this, I HATE THIS!*, but she knew there was another thumb held over her, ready to smoosh her flat.

As long as she kept these notions to herself, she was

free enough, so most days she wasn't frightened as she had been in the beginning—but every time she saw the Dancer, her stomach twisted with the sick certainty that the same thing would happen to her, that her *SELF* would be pushed into a smaller and smaller space until it was altogether gone.

The Mask heated up. Hands clasped in her lap, Motylla fixed her eyes on Tecozar Treddek Nov as he rose for the formal greeting.

Pinned into that receptive posture by what the Dancer called Mother Death but she thought of as the Black Thing, she couldn't squirm or interrupt, just wait for the stinkbag to wind down, enjoying in the free bit of her mind the increasing restiveness of the chitveks and the other treddeks as he droned on and on, having his say at last. K'vestmilly Vos always interrupted him before he could get going and made him waste all the flowers he'd polished for her; she'd heard him grumbling about that, scratching at her father, trying to get him to complain to K'vestmilly about such disregard to the Treddek Prime because it undermined his position on the Treddekkap. She swallowed a sigh. Maybe so, but it looked to her like he was undermining himself with all that wind.

He finished at last and stood flushed with pride, waiting for the praise he expected.

"Splendidly spoken, O Treddek Prime." She listened to the words coming out her mouth and wanted to be sick; she'd rather kick him where she saw Vassy the maid kick the drunk, but her mouth wasn't her own now. "I have called you here, O Treddeks and Chitveks of Dander and Calanda, because I wish to speak of something that troubles me. There are spies among us and saboteurs, some of them in the most delicate of places. The Headmistress of the Sekalarium has been discovered to be working against us and all sekalaries are suspect. To leave the health of Rodin and Nerodin in such hands would be the act of one indifferent to the well-being of her people and I will not do it. The sekalaries are at this moment being collected and brought to the Pevranamist for examination by Inquisitor Ravach Zypam. Those that he declares clean will be returned to the clinics and their work, the others will be re-educated and sent to tend the health of the farm-workers in the South. I ask the Treddekkap to declare this Law of Cadander, that the clinics will henceforth be over-seen by the Servants of the Glory."

The Black Thing retreated. Motylla relaxed, though she didn't dare let the change show much.

This was stupid. It wasn't mean and silly like a lot of the things that the Black Thing made her do, it was just out and out stupid. She could see the anger in the stolid faces of the chitveks. They didn't dare say anything either, but she knew what they were thinking. The sekalaries were good people, everyone knew that, most everybody had been tended by them one time or another. Her father couldn't know about this or he'd have stopped it. Or tried to, anyway. She winced inside as she remembered arguments with the Dancer, her father shouting and red-faced, the Dancer moving all the time, making light-patterns in the air with his fingers, listening or not-listening as he chose.

Tecozar was on his feet again. He was pale and there were beads of sweat under the square-cut black fringe that he affected to hide the narrowness of his brow. "The Treddekkap thanks the Marn for her tender care of her people." He got the words out, but it sounded like he was biting their tails off. He cleared his throat, swallowed. "The Marn has spoken, it is for the Treddekkap to con-sider her words. Are there any among the Treddeks who wish to speak, be it for or against?" He waited. The si-lence stretched so taut, Motylla felt it'd break if she plucked it. "That being so, I call the vote." He lifted the box. "On the left, black tiles for nik, on the right white tiles for aya. Let each put a hand inside and declare him-self or herself in secrecy and silence."

When the box came back to him, he thrust his own hand inside, then opened the hatch. Eight white tiles slid onto the table top. "So it is spoken and so it shall be."

Motylla Nov walked in the Marn's Garden, waiting for her father to answer her summons. She walked alone, as she'd been alone for months now; her father refused to let her see her sisters or his new wife and none of the Treddeks or Pans brought their children to visit her.

The Mask was in her bedroom. She didn't look in the mirrors anymore, but she knew its scars were there on her face, white patches like some sort of disease. Her father didn't like to look at her with the Mask off. Zdra, he was going to have to today whether he liked it or not. *I told him to come, I told him I NEEDED to see him.*

I will NOT live like this. I WILL not! She touched her face, drew a fingertip across one of the dead spots as she scowled up at the sun, her eyes squinted against the glare that hurt her more and more each day she wore the Mask. He was supposed to be here by now, her father was.

She walked faster until she was speeding through the trees, her robes flailing against the trunks, gathering thorns and bits of bark, tears burning in her eyes, her breath coming in harsh gasps. He wasn't coming. She was Marn, she ordered him to come, but he wasn't coming.

She flung herself on the grass beside one of the garden fountains, brushed impatiently at her eyes, and set herself to brooding over what she was going to do about the cage she was in. And how she was going to punish her father.

When this thing began, she was scared but excited. At last she was going to get out, get to do things. All her life her father had kept her and her younger sisters penned in Nov House with nurses following them everywhere; hers was a tall Harozhni woman with a face like macai, a rigid sense of duty and no humor in her, not a crumb. He wouldn't let them go to school or have friends to play with; they had tutors and dance teachers and sewing teachers and art teachers and riding teachers—lessons and lessons and lessons. . . .

Back then, at least, she'd had her sisters; they made up games, sneaked away from their nurses, and had play parties in the attics—and they could look at each other when things got bad and know there was someone to stand with them. There was no one to stand with Motylla, not any more. She had the Mask and Mother Death and she hated both. And her father wouldn't come see her, not even when she asked.

>><<

K'vestmilly Vos twisted her mouth behind the Mask,
but kept her silence as Pan Osk scowled at the Harozhni
guard who was standing before the tribunal, his mouth in
a straight line, his eyes unfocused, not-listening to what
was being said with a passionate ferocity.

". . . and he came up to her and showed her money and
said things to her I won't foul my mouth with." The big
woman glared at the guard. "And she came running to
me, crying her eyes out, poor baby, him strolling along
behind her, grinning all over his ugly face, and he tried to
give ME money. Zdra, I tell you, I yelled for Sov, my
houseguard, you know, and he put a handgun in that
pizh's back and held him till the landguard they come,
and that's the truth, all of it."

Pan Osk settled back in his chair. "And you, what's
your name?"

"I am the Trivud Throdal Ankar." He stood at attention,
looking past Osk's left ear; he had a light tenor voice that
went badly with his battered warrior look.

"Harozhni."

"Yes, tuhl Pan." All inflection had been leached from
the words; they had a surface smear of courtesy, but his
anger was close to bursting free.

K'vestmilly chewed on her tongue, her mind scrambling for a way out of this impasse; she wanted Heslin at
her side, but that was out of the question. Her position
was delicate enough without putting extra strain on the
fragile bonds that held Osk and his people with her. This
was the start of trouble, the first charge against her men;
there'd been irritations before, but with a lot of talking
and showing the Mask to remind these people that they
were all Cadandri and facing a common danger, she'd got
the rough spots smoothed over. If this thing exploded as
it showed signs of doing, it could blow them all out of
here.

Osk glanced at her, giving her a chance to interfere if
she chose to do so, but she wasn't ready, so she gave a
slight shake of her head. He turned back to the Harozhni.

"You're a visitor here, guard, and you're an officer; you should have the sense to keep your cod tied and your mouth shut. Mad's Tits, what did you think you were doing?"

Heslin, Heslin, what would you do? Something sideways, that's what, something to defuse the situation. Turn them into jokes, those provocateurs, get people laughing at them, that's what you said when my mother died and the liars were whispering I did it. Get people laughing ... but how? Not at Throdal or that harpy, but at the situation. Nik. Laughter's too tricky and I haven't the touch. He has ... was he born with it or ... saaa, this isn't the time. So what do I do, what in Zhag do I do?

Throdal pressed his lips together, glazed his eyes, and set himself to take whatever injustice was heaped on him.

K'vestmilly swallowed a groan. His thoughts were so obvious they might have been written on his forehead; he'd probably keep hold of himself this time, but the first Merrz who snickered at him would have his head handed to him. Think, woman! Time's running out. She glanced from one man to the other, then scanned the hostile crowd. A notion came to her: We haven't seen the girl. What about the girl? She sat up. Sideways. That might be it.

As Marn she was supposed to hold dominion over every part of Cadander, Family landholds, city, village, but her seat was more than a little shaky now. Make a note, woman; you'd better talk this over with Heslin soon as possible. I need to be strong, not stupid. Courtesy now, zdra, I don't know anything better.

She leaned forward, the light streaming through the high windows sliding off the Mask and onto her hands. "Pan Osk, may I speak?"

"Certainly, O Marn."

Keep it light, woman; he's not liking this, not at all. She beckoned to the large woman whose name she'd forgotten for the moment. As the woman waddled over and lowered herself to her knees with some difficulty, she scrambled in her head, trying to retrieve that name; she didn't need Heslin telling her that saying the name would buy a smear of good will which she might need. Prak!

Got it! Maiden Bless. "Jam' Vana Zabraneh . . ." she let
her hands smile at the woman, her lips smiling behind the
Mask as she saw the flush of pleasure in the Merrzin's
broad face, "events have piled themselves in such a tangled heap, I had no chance for the Masking Journey; this
is my first visit to the Merrzachars and I find you have
more jewels than those in your mines. Introduce me to
this gem who has bewitched a fighting man like that," she
waved a hand at the Trivud, "a man who's killed more
gritzers than leaves on a tree."

Vana Zabraneh's mouth tightened. She wasn't about to
be tickled out of her complaint. "You should talk to me,
O Marn, Shera Dulmineh is in my care and I won't have
the child made a mock of. I saw and I heard and that's all
you need to know what sort that is." She turned, spat at
the Trivud's feet, just missing the toe of his boot.

K'vestmilly heard a thread of fear in that hoarse voice
and knew she'd touched something important. "Pan Osk,
I have no wish to interfere; though the Trivud Throdal
Ankar is my man and thus mine to punish, this is your
landhold and your court, it is for you to say who comes
and who goes. But I ask as a favor, send for the girl. In
order to judge the severity of the punishment, I wish to
hear the story from her own lips."

Pan Osk examined the woman's face a moment, then
flicked his finger at a landguard. The guard touched his
brow and left. K'vestmilly could hear the slap of
bootsoles on stone as he broke into a run the moment he
left the room.

A girl came hesitantly through the rows of benches, her
shoulders rounded, her head down. She was the image of
the shy young girl, small and pretty, with an abundance of
black curls bubbling over her shoulders. K'vestmilly
watched her, watched the reaction of the Merrz to her,
and groaned inside, then cursed the Harozhni for a fool
who just might have wrecked everything for them.

She glanced at him, saw his nostrils flare, his lips go
even thinner. *Whaaat?* She examined the girl more
closely and saw a dimple flicker, an eye black and shining
as polished coal slip sideways between narrowed lids,

come hurrying back. "Lift your head, young Shera,"
K'vestmilly said, a hint of laughter in her own voice.
"There's no one blaming you for this. Tell me your side. I
want to hear it from your pretty mouth."

Shera touched her tongue to her lips, then, suddenly,
her dimples danced as merrily as her black eyes. "You
know, don't you." She shrugged her shoulders, the shift
of the thin white blouse bringing audible sighs from her
audience. "I told her it was a fool's game. I don't want
none of it and that's the truth. M' Da 'prenticed me for
m' dowry's sake and 'cause m' mam died and he thought
I sh'd have a woman carin' for me; he's a good man and
it's only 'cause he's down mine that SHE had the zhluc to
try this on. SHE told me I'd get half, but I don't think
so." She lifted her hand, the loose sleeve of the blouse
falling back from a fine white arm. She opened the hand
wide. "That'd be her half and this'd be mine." She
pinched thumb and forefinger together.

"Nonetheless young Shera, tell me exactly what
happened—for your sake and his."

Shera winced away from Vana Zabraneh's glare. "Zdra,
it was washday at the Inn, so I was out back haulin' tubs
of sheets to the drylines. SHE hires washerwomen for the
scrubbin' and whitenin', but me," she wrinkled her nose,
flounced her hair, "I'm good enough for hanging things
out. I come staggerin' out with this tub and him," she
turned, smiled at the Trivud, "he comes along and gives
me a hand. We talk about this'n that while I hang up the
sheets and zdra zdra . . ." she shrugged, tossed her head,
"there comes a mention of coin, very polite and he don't
push it when I say nik, I'm workin' for dowry, not my old
age, he says prak, that bein' that, what about me comin'
to sup with him so he can make good his takin' me wrong
and I was thinkin' that over when HER, SHE pops out the
bushes with ol' Sov, the houseguard SHE keeps round to
bounce troublemakers. SHE yells at him over there and
ol' Sov, he has his gun out and his eyes squinnied like he
only wanted half'n excuse to blow him over there his
head off. SHE yells he's tryin' to rape me and I said
Gahhhh, no such thing, and SHE said you too silly to
know what you talkin' about and anyway your Da he put

me 'n charge of you and you gotta do what I say. And
SHE tells me to go inside and shut my face and so I do,
'cause that's true anyway, Da he told me to do what SHE
said. But I din't go fast and I heard HER pitchin' at him
that if he don't pay HER some golds SHE gonna have his
hide and he told HER some stuff that I am not gonna say
'cause Da he'd have my hide if he heard. But anyway,
him over there, he made a little mistake, but that din't
hurt nothin' and anyway he was polite about it and I was
gonna get a good supper for once 'stead the slop SHE
gives me. And SHE told me to stay inside after that and
SHE take this wet cloth and ol' Sov he holds me down
and SHE pulls my skirt up and SHE beats me on my bare
behind till all I can do is lay on my face and squeal and
SHE locks me in that closet where I sleep and I have to
yell to landguard who come for me just now and tell him
where SHE keeps the key so he can let me out. So tuhl
Pan, I think you should let him over there go and give ol'
Vanchik there a lick or two to teach HER what m' Da
taught me when I climbed Kolevak's broshka tree and
stole his prize broshks."

K'vestmilly let her laughter ring out. "I thank you,
Shera Dulmineh," she said when she sobered. "I'd like to
meet that father of yours, seems to me he's one in a thousand."

A broad glowing smile spread across the piquant little
face. "Oh, yes, he is, he is. A graaaaand man, O Marn.
Oh, yes, he is."

K'vestmilly spread her hands and settled back in her
chair. "I thank you for your courtesy, Pan Osk."

Camnor Heslin poured a glass of chilled broshka juice
and brought it to her. "That was a hit to be proud of, calling for the girl. What brought her to mind?"

"You. I thought about all you did after Mother was
killed." She lifted her feet onto the daybed and lay back
sipping at the juice. "Every time I couldn't see how we
could untie a knot, you'd go sideways and somehow it'd
untie itself. Osk was getting set to hammer the Trivud
and I couldn't let that happen, we need every man." She
drew her fingers across her brow, wrinkled her nose at the

sweaty dust staining the tips. "I thought mountains were cool."

"It's summersend, Kimi. Hot everywhere."

"What's wrong, Hes?"

He walked to the window and stood looking out across the mountainside toward the valley buried in heat-haze. "I'm not used to idleness. Or confinement. I'm bored. I want out."

"I need you."

"Nik. This afternoon's proof of that. Besides, I'm an irritant, more so than your men; if they're not Merrz, at least they're Cadandri." He turned and looked somberly at her. "And you don't need me in your bed. You've got what you wanted. I've watched you looking at him."

K'vestmilly flushed, wrapped her hands around the glass and stared down at the thick yellow-orange liquid. "Don't be silly, Hes. Who've I had time to know here?"

"Doesn't take time. Shall I name him, your Poet?"

"That's nonsense. He doesn't think of me like that. He has Tingajil."

"I wondered if you knew."

"It's reasonably obvious, all you have to do is see them together. . . ."

"Yes, I thought so. I'm going down to Dander tomorrow." He said it quietly, nothing but weariness in that rich deep voice. "If you feel like helping, you could use the com to send word I'm on my way."

He left without saying anything more.

She got to her feet, stood a moment staring at the door, then swung around and hurled the glass against the wall. It shattered and fell to the floor, leaving behind a smear of yellow juice and few glinting fragments of glass.

5. Going South

Treshteny sat on the dapple's back with the sleeping faun cradled in her arms; she blinked down at an old woman who was solid as the stones, no palimpsest of possibility, only a bit of shimmer around the edges—as if she were born as she was and would continue that way long beyond the end of Treshteny's timesight. The boy holding her hand shared that solidity, taking it from her by the contact.

"Mad Treshteny," the old woman said. It wasn't a question. "I am Mama Charody and this is Doby. I think we are both going to the same place."

"It's the horse who knows. I don't." Treshteny looked down as the fan stirred, but he didn't wake, just tucked his little hoofs into the crook of her arm.

"That's not a horse."

Treshteny moved her shoulders in a sketch of a shrug, so she wouldn't wake Yela'o. "If he wants to be something else, then I'll call him that. It's his business, not mine."

The horse shook his head and snorted.

Mama Charody chuckled, a deep rumbling sound that shuddered through her big body. "You're wiser than I, Treshteny Falladin. We'll walk with you, if we may."

The dapple sidled to her, nosed at her, then bobbed his head up and down, whuffling his acceptance; he moved back to the winding game trail and waited there for Mama Charody and the boy to join him.

>><<

Serroi fought her way to the quarterdeck and stood clutching the rail beside Phindwe. She pushed the hair off her mouth and laughed up at the dark face not so much higher than hers. "If there's one thing you don't need, it's a windwitch."

The Shipmaster twitched a long nose with a hook in the off-center tip that would have been at home on a jesser's leather beak. He scowled and pointed at the dark gray clouds churning high along the horizon. "Might need those laid not riz."

Out against the clouds she saw black flukes flip up and slide into the sea. "I don't think so. We have an escort. Look there."

He watched the ring of maremars form about the ship and the sea smooth out, the wind drop to a steady blow. Silkar children came arching up the bow swell, laughing and waving at the sailors aloft and on deck as they vanished back into the sea. "What's goin' on, Healer?"

She combed her fingers through her hair and bent over the rail to watch the Silkar play.

Phindwe reached out to take hold of her arm and pull her around, then he saw the spot on his thumb that was still paler than the rest of the skin and snatched his hand back. "What's goin' on?" His voice was louder, rough with anger and a touch of fear.

She was leaning on her forearms, getting into the rhythm of the ship, riding the dip and sway; she turned her head, the wind blowing strands of hair across her face. "Friends of mine," she said. "I didn't know they'd come, but I was hoping. We'll have a sweet trip south. Now."

>><<

Adlayr stood at the bowrail watching the silkar children play, Honeydew comfortable in his shirt pocket, only her head visible as she stared around at a new and exciting world.

"Hey! You!"

Adlayr swung round, Honeydew pulling her head down

to peep through a buttonhole. She made a face as the Shipmaster came charging toward them.

"You lot, who are you? What's going on?"

Adlayr hesitated, then smiled, spread his hands. "What you see."

"What I see is spooky. Bad Hanla. First port I hit, you goin' ashore."

"Vai, Master, if they have the say," he jerked a thumb at the maremars, "first port you hit's gonna be Bokivada. Which is no hardship since that's where you're headed anyway."

"Who told you that?"

Still smiling, Adlayr shook his head. "Doesn't matter. Cool down, man. I'm gyes. Got nothing to do with you."

"Biserica? What you doing with that Hev, then?"

"Ward, Master."

In the pocket Honeydew giggled silently. Adlayr's mild answers had taken the steam from Phindwe's wrath.

"And her?" Phindwe jerked a thumb at the quarterdeck where Serroi's head was just visible.

"Biserica, too." Adlayr waved a hand at the sparkling sea, the boiling black clouds that surrounded them but couldn't touch them and the escorting maremar. "Relax and enjoy, you've a free ride. No storms, no pirates and the fastest trip you've ever made. What's to worry you?"

"Everything I don't know, gyes. What can come outta the dark and chew ass. Free ride, duokhmi. An't ever been anything pricefree in this world and never will be." Phindwe sniffed and strolled off, shoulders rounded, hands clasped behind him.

Honeydew popped her head up. Why's he so mad? This is a good thing.

He's a wise man, Honey. You just remember what he said. When anybody wants to give you something, look for the strings. It could cost you more than you want to give. On the other hand, friends do for friends, that's a good cost and one you pay with a free heart.

Saaa, Adlee, so booorrring, come, tell me about them there, they're so pretty, playing in the water like that, it looks like fun.

They're called Silkar, Honey, and they live in the sea like you live in the air.

She heard the yearning in his mindvoice and it made her hair itch; if the wind hadn't been blowing so hard, enough to blow her tumbling head over heels for miles and miles, she would have gone somewhere else. And if there was anyone else to talk to. Hedivy couldn't and Serroi wouldn't. And the sailors weren't supposed to know about her, besides, they couldn't understand what she was saying so it was like talking to poles, not very satisfying. She sighed and worked her wings until they were tucked in more comfortably, then settled in to ply Adlayr with questions and wring as much information out of him as she could.

The long swells told Phindwe of the power of the storm outside the charmed circle, their cloud masses a wall all round him, seething and climbing so high they almost obscured the small round of blue directly overhead; it was as if the eye of that storm went with him, however he turned, an eye unlike others, with a steady wind blowing across it that kept his sails taut and his ship scudding along at full stretch.

He counted seven days in the Eye, then he went to Serroi. "Are y' doing this, woman?" he said. "If y' are, don't. You robbin' the land and the islands of rain and wind, and they'll be needin' it. This is the growin' season. If you're Biserica, you know the Balance. You know the need."

"Nay, man. I've kept my hands from magic since I escaped my trainer, which is longer ago than you've any idea. I'll not touch it now, except for the healing."

"Ahwu? And your promise to windwitch if I needed it, you meant to break it?"

"Nay. I was taking a chance it wouldn't be needed."

"What is going on, Healer? What's all this about?"

"It's better you don't know."

"I'll tell you like I told your man. The only thing I'm afeard of is what I don't know."

She looked at him a long moment, then she nodded. "Ei vai, this has to do with what's happening in Cadander. We are hunting the Enemy and It fights back."

"It?"

Serroi shook her head. "Bad hanla for you to fall into this tale. I'll tell you this, though, it might have been worse for you and yours if Hedivy had found another ship. The Enemy does not acknowledge neutrality."

"Why?" He hunched his shoulders, then waved a hand about to say all the things he had no words for.

"I'll ask It when we find It."

"Hev, y' owe me. Who'n shog is that woman?"

"No one to mess with."

"I KNOW that. An't what I asked."

Hedivy stood balanced on the balls of his feet, the wind blowing his sandy shag into eyes with all the expression of water-polished pebbles; he hadn't shaved since boarding the ship, so a smudge of faded reddish beard concealed the contours of his jaw and a mustache altered the line of his lip. He wasn't happy about being questioned, but he knew better than to burn bridges he might need to use again. "Prak. Couple hundred years ago. Sons' War. Know about it?"

"I am not ignorant, Spy. I have been taught."

"Good. Have you heard the tale of the Two Trees, the ones that stand above the Biserica?"

"Aye. Kwa?"

"That is her. The Lacewood. Serroi the Healer. Something woke her. That's what I was told. How true it is . . ." He shrugged. "What I know, best let her be."

"She tellin' true about Cadander?"

Hedivy's mouth pinched together, but the same constraints held. "Yeah."

"Ahwu, I'll do my tradin' south say we make Shimzely still afloat. Good hanla, Hev. I see you doin' what y' have to, I'd appreciate the favor y' did it with some other phut's ship after this."

The days that followed were without change, crisp and cool, with the mage wind driving the ship, night turning to day, day to night, over and over, a pleasant monotony that grew less pleasant as the weeks slid behind them.

Serroi watched the cloud wall and wondered what was waiting for them. Phindwe had spoken of Balance and the word had woken in her the same frisson she felt when she acknowledged to herself that the nixies were as much hers as the dryads, the dark and the light, both necessary. Balance there, too, all-light was as cruel, as punishing in its way as all-dark. It was like this place, a crystal jewel in a matrix of cloud; boring, unchanging, the soul gone with the Silkars.

They'd left days ago, only the maremars were still in place, there at the boundary of dark and light.

Dark and Light and boundaries. Why so important?

Such a sketchy, abstract concept with no ties to flesh that she could see—or how it might help her deal with the Enemy, but she had a strong feeling that the forces propelling her had set up this situation to grind that idea into her soul.

She sat in the bow of the ship, out of the way of the sailors, watching the clouds and the glittering blue of the sea and brooding, day after day on the long journey south.

>><<

As shadows lengthened and the sun started to slide behind the peaks, Horse stopped, knelt.

Treshteny slid from his back, set the faun on his feet, and laughed aloud as he ran around the small flat, patting the trees, trying to tease out dryads he expected to be there, drooping sadly when he found that the trees were just trees.

"Saaa, saaa, luv," she crooned to him. "We're just early, that's all. I can see they'll be there sometime, just not now."

He came trotting back to her, danced in front of her, whining for her to lift him.

She laughed, caught him up, and carried him to a down tree at the side of the clearing, settling there to hold him cuddled against her.

Mama Charody patted Doby on his shoulder, tapped the hatchet strapped to his back. "You see about wood, michi, I'll tend to supper. Remember, down wood only." She

watched him move off, then crossed to sit beside
Treshteny. "What have you been eating, zhena?"

"Whatever comes." She looked up, smiled as ariels
came swirling overhead.

They dipped down, dropping a rain of seeds for Yela'o,
fruit, leaves, stalks, mushrooms of all kinds (some edible,
some not), a few wriggling fish, even a loaf of freshly
baked bread.

She clapped her hands; they flipped and twisted
through a spate of visual giggles, then fluttered away.
Yela'o jumped down and began gathering the offerings
for her, eating the seeds as he found them and heaping the
other things on a clump of short, wiry grass.

Treshteny nodded at the growing pile. "Take what you
can use," she said. "If I need more, they'll bring it."

"Zdra, michi-micha, it's my time to provide. The fish
I'll take. Though I'm sad to say it, I have no trust in your
cooking, Teny."

Treshteny giggled. "Wise woman."

"'Tis my calling, chichi." Mama Charody grunted onto
her feet. "I have my suppliers, too; let's see what they can
provide." She clapped her hand, called, "Brothers, come."

Kamen bulged from the ground, moving in their peculiar way with their arms full of roots. They laid them at
Mama Charody's feet and sank back into the earth that
they moved through like fish through water. As a kind of
afterthought, a depression appeared in the middle of the
flat and rapidly filled with water.

Mama Charody laughed. "That's my babies. Doby,"
she called. "You almost finished out there?"

The boy didn't answer, but he appeared a moment later
carrying a large bundle of wood. He set it on the grass beside the new pool, gave Mama Charody a quick nervous
smile and went back into the dark under the trees.

Treshteny looked after him, then turned to Mama
Charody.

"He talks well enough," the old woman said, "he just
doesn't feel like saying anything. It was the gritz war, you
know—or maybe you don't. Zdra zdra, he saw his kin
shot down and his village burned. And I talk enough for
the both of us." She lowered herself beside the pile of

wood and began snapping the smaller branches over her knee, setting the larger in a pattern that pleased her.

Treshteny pulled a fine curved fishbone from her mouth and tossed it into the scatter of bark fragments and dead leaves piled against the trunk of the down tree. She patted a yawn, got to her feet, and curled up on the grass.

A hairy beast like a long-haired cat enormously enlarged came from the trees and curled about her, its silky dappled gray hair falling over her to protect her, keep her dry and warm. She snuggled against him. "Zdra, Horse," she murmured drowsily, "you must have more Names than a summer cloud. A new one every night . . . don't get . . ." she yawned again, ". . . bored that way." She eased around, began scratching his belly. "Like that . . . mmmm, yes, you do like that. . . ." She scratched and rubbed at him a while longer, then settled in to sleep.

Doby helped Mama Charody douse the fire, hunting down the last sparks and drowning them with fierce satisfaction, then grinding the blackened ash into the dirt.

The old woman squeezed his shoulder. "Tan't fire done your kin, boy, 'twas the one we're heading for who set the gritz stirring." She got to her feet, undid the blanket roll, and snapped the canvas out on the grass. "Come now, wash your hands and face and dry them good, michi, then we'll sleep till the morrow and be on our way again."

A little later Doby crept into the blankets and nestled against her, shivering with cold, his hands and hair wet from the pool. He warmed slowly and his breathing quieted. "Mama. . . ." His voice was low and rusty, hardly more than a thread of sound.

In the darkness Mama Charody smiled; the healing had begun at last. It was a long time coming, but she'd never doubted it would. "What, michi?"

"Her. . . ."

Mama Charody chuckled softly, her body shaking the blankets. "She is a little odd, isn't she."

He snuggled closer, tucked his icy feet under her leg. "Yela'o, too."

"It's all magic, michi, it's coming back faster every day. Me, I'm part of it. You're part of it now, want it or not."

He made a contented little sound, sucked in a long breath, sighed it out. "You, Mama?" he murmured.

"Me, michi-micha. I was sleeping in the ground like a big old bremba root. . . ."

"I dug bremba. . . ." There was a giggle in his voice at the thought of the wise woman in the ground like a tuber, all wrinkled and hairy and covered with dirt. The joy died out of him as he remembered what happened, the gritzers tromping through the field, shooting his cousin and his brothers and burning down his village; he turned his head against her, put his thumb in his mouth, and cried.

After he'd cried himself to sleep, Mama Charody settled herself into the half-coma that was rest time for her, slow memories eddying in her complex brain. . . .

The shot of force like lightning slicing through the dirt, stirring her from her shriveled sleep. . . .

The slow and painful stirring. . . .

Unfolding. . . .

Pushing up through the earth to reach the sun again for the first time in two centuries. . . .

She sank deeper in the coma, no longer thinking or remembering, simply listening to the songs of the earth, the stones.

6. The Web Working

Camnor Heslin knelt at the window, looking over his shoulder at the dead-eyed boy who'd brought him. "You'd be safer on the street."

Tomal was squatting in a corner of the small dusty room, his brown rags and dirty face merging with the shadows. He shrugged and didn't move.

"Your choice." Heslin unclipped the longglasses from his belt and snapped on the shields to keep the lenses from catching moonlight and shining it back. He scanned the river for several minutes, then slipped the com from its belt case, laid it on the sill by his left hand and tapped it on. "Valk here. Go."

"Spider three here. Gleaners in place and waiting. Go."

"River's quiet, not many barges tied up. There's a squad of wharfliks moving along the Lade Road, they're just about at Shipper Mikkel's Wharf, same time as yesterday, give or take a few minutes. Looks like you're clean, no ferts about. Snipers should move in now."

He lowered the glasses, took out a handkerchief and scrubbed the sweat from his face, tucked it back in his pocket, and began watching again. "Hah, good. Spider four's in and no trouble. Not even the wind's stirring. There goes two. Now seven. Cover's in place. Six just left the alley. He's in the barge." He cleared his throat, swept the river again. "Lot of nixies around. There's a clutch of them up by the Glasserie Wharf. Now what . . . it's rocking and bucking almost as if it's trying to break loose and head downstream. Looks like they're taking it apart. Wharfliks are coming from everywhere; they're

starting to shoot, the thrunts. About as much use as shooting the river. Get the Web moving. I don't know what
stirred the nixies up, but it's a distraction we can't waste.
Go."

After a moment, the answer came back. "On their way.
Go."

Heslin knelt, scanning the river and muttering into the
com as he watched dark forms moving in and out of the
warehouses, pushing loaded barrows, emptying them onto
the expropriated barge.

More and more nixies were gathering around the
northend wharves, jeering at the wharfliks and the other
defenders trying to drive them off, swirling around the
piles, worrying at them.

". . . still quiet down our end. Hah! Nixies have pulled
a pile, there's another . . . another few minutes the whole
thing'll be going. Murd! that could mean trouble . . . unless we use it. Spider three, tell the Gleaners to get out
now. I'll mark for you, you send it on. They should go
with the wharf, anyone around'll just think it's another bit
of nixy malice. Go."

Again a short silence.

Heslin saw half a dozen shadows come from the warehouse, loaded down for—he hoped—the last time; they
ran the barrows into the river and vanished into the shadows on the deck. He nodded to himself as he saw the
snipers emerging from the alley and joining the others on
the barge.

"Gleaners in place. Go."

"Wharf is shaky now, it's tilting . . . shuddering . . .
someone with more sense than most is pouring some kind
of liquid in the river, the nixies don't like it, they're starting to clear out, I don't know if . . . ah! the wharf's torn
loose, it's on its way downriver. Tell them to cast off
now. Go."

"Zdra." A pause. "They're off. You'd best get out, too.
Need cover? Go."

Heslin glanced at the boy. "Got all the cover I need.
Out." He twisted off the lens shields, snapped them on
their carry buttons, clipped the longglasses to his belt, and
slid away the com. Hand on the sill, he pushed onto his

feet, worked his knees a minute to get the stiffness out, then turned to the boy. "Zdra, Tomal, let's get the zhag out of here."

>><<

"What do you mean cooperating?"

Ravach slitted his eyes at Pan Nov. "What else would you call it? They started tearing the wharf down the minute the krysh hit the warehouse, covered 'em. Every wharflik in the Quarter was up at Glasserie's trying to drive the nixies off."

"What'd the krysh get?"

"All the longguns stored in Mikkel's warehouse. Twenty barrels, gunpowder, lead, casings, five barrels blackpowder explosive, forty sacks shem and ryzh, ten baskets bremba tubers, ten sacks salt. And a barge."

"No one saw the barge go?"

"Zdra, they did, but the krysh were out of sight, lettin' river take barge, so they thought it was just nixies doin' it again."

Nov swore and began pacing the room, muttering and beating his fist against his side. After a few moments he turned. "Get what you can. They took food, they're going to be giving it out, buying traitors with it. Keep your spies nose to ground, get me names." He filled his chest, roared, "Bring me a krysh bigger than a minnow!"

Ravach grunted. "Workin' on it."

>><<

The Dancer moved about the Grand Chamber of the Temple, bare feet silent on the cold, stripped stone. Fugitive footprints glowed behind him, melted into the air. Around him, workmen labored silently, stone cutters from the Travasherims, glass-setters, carpenters, tilemen from the Potteries, changing the temple from Maiden to Glory. A woodcarver was at work on the Maiden image, changing the face. The arms were already cut off, the new ones laid out on the stone of the altar where the Glory would shine once the changeover was complete.

A runner from the Pevranamist came through the pointed arch of the doorway, stopped just inside, and stood looking nervously around. He ran his tongue along his lips, straightened his shoulders, and moved stiffly toward the Dancer. When he reached him, he bowed, holding out a note folded over and sealed. "Tuhl Dancer, the Marn sends this."

The Dancer took the paper, letting his fingertips run over it.

The runner shivered as the letter glowed a heartbeat, then was dull again, a brownish white as if it had gotten too close to a fire, but hadn't burned.

The Dancer held it out. "Take it to him who gave it to you. I have answered."

The runner bowed again and left more quickly than he'd come.

>><<

Nov was in the Tradurad, in conference with Ashouta Pen (the Treddek he'd appointed to Steel Point after he had Ashkolias strangled), Oppornay Treddek Ker, Sabbanot Treddek Ano, and Zhalatzos Treddek Sko, setting up supply networks, getting an assessment of what it'd take to get the mills and glasseries on line again.

When the runner slipped inside and stood by the door, waiting to be noticed, Nov jerked his head to the doorwindow. "Wait out there, I'll be with you in a minute." He gathered up the papers in front of him, tapped them into a neat pile and stood. "I have to see about this." He tugged at a bell cord. "If you'll adjourn to the Setkan, you can continue this discussion without me or take a break. I've ordered a spread to be laid out there; if you need anything more, the Domcevek will be waiting for you."

Hand over his mouth to hide his sneer, he watched them file out, their bodies shouting worry and fear. Except Treddek Ker, prokkin' pizhla, strutting like a kokh bitch in heat. *Better watch out for her and her Pan. She looks like she knows something I don't. Have to get*

Ravach on her tail. Vych! One more thing I have to fool with.

A knock on the door interrupted his angry thoughts. "Come."

A maid edged inside with a tray loaded with a cha pot, a cream jug, a bowl of berries, and a plate of waffle wafers. She was a thin woman with gray-streaked, brown hair drawn into a tight bun at the back of her head. Nov watched her lay out the things on his worktable, something about her niggling at his mind. "I know you, don't I?"

She lowered her eyes, dipped into an awkward bow. "Yes, tuhl Pan. I was nursery maid in Nov House."

"Zdra, from the Shippers Warren."

"Yes, tuhl Pan."

"And do you like your new place?"

"Yes, tuhl Pan." She flushed, then went pale, stood with her head bowed, her fingers fiddling with her apron.

He smiled; she was obviously so impressed she couldn't speak. He found that soothing. "Is there anything you need?"

"Nik, tuhl Pan."

"Zdra zdra, you can go."

Nov poured cream over the berries and began spooning them up, savoring the sweet-tart taste, alternating bites of wafers and sips of cha.

When he finished, he was relaxed and feeling good. He got to his feet, went to the window, and beckoned the runner into the office.

"Zdra?"

The runner bowed and handed over the folded paper. He saw Nov's frown at the unbroken seal and said hastily. "The Dancer took it, ran his fingers over it, gave it back to me; he said the answer's inside."

"I see. You can go."

When he was alone, he broke the seal, read the words burnt into the paper.

IF YOU WANT TO TALK, COME TO ME.

Cursing, he tore the paper into bits, dumped them in the berry bowl, and dropped a match on them. He sat be-

hind the worktable, leaning on folded arms, and watched
them burn. He'd like to do the same to the Dancer, but he
couldn't, not yet. His grip on the heart of Cadander
wasn't tight enough and there were still two landholds
loyal to K'vestmilly Vos, Oskland and Ankland. Bar and
Sko were restive, but they were negligible, he could kick
them into line as soon as he could find time for it. *Ano's
something else ... watch him ... he'll cut my throat first
chance he gets ... and the new Pan Ker ... I don't know
him ... if he's anything like his father ... Oppornay ...
the way she acts, he could be treacherous as Ano ...
Marn ... Zhag! I hate that bitch ... if I had the men, I'd
... we've got to get the ore trains going ... Ravach ...
I want assassins on her ass ... and Osk, prokkin' chert
... dance on his ashes ... the Harozh ... Ank, curse him
... stinkin' worm ... nose in books ... what'n Zhag he
think he's doing?*

He dumped the cold remnants of the cha in his cup into
the bowl, watched the fine flakes of ash sink into and
muddy the brown liquid. He had to give in to the Dancer.
For the moment. Let those krysh get dug in and it would
be like trying to uproot a struzha bramble to get them
out again, especially if the nixy attack wasn't a coinci-
dence, if they'd really made a pact with those pests....
*Oskliv', it doesn't bear thinking ... I'll go to temple to-
night ... don't want the world to see me licking that
sprochert's toes ... fool's game, Nov, all this scratching
in the head ... time to get back to work ... put my hands
on all the twists in this idiot city ... pek!*

Clouds were scudding across TheDom's crescent and
there was a hint of rain in the night air as Pan Nov
walked into the Temple; as he entered the main chamber,
he stopped, startled.

Pale, nacreous light shimmered through the chamber,
sourceless light filling the room like water. The Dancer
moved naked through that light, his body a darker gold,
also light; he moved in a dance of Praise that was as
much beyond description as it seemed beyond the reach
of human movement.

For several moments the Dancer continued as if he

were unaware of Nov, then he bowed to Nov and wheeled through an eccentric spiral to the empty altar, leapt on it, and sat cross-legged, his hands on his knees. The yellow glow crept back inside his skin and Treshtal's features were once more visible. "Pan Nov," he said, his voice multiple yet soft as a whisper. "What do you want of us?"

"The nixies are working with the rebels now. Get rid of them."

"Rebels or nixies?"

"Both."

"The rebels are your business, not ours."

Nov shrugged. "Prak, I'll deal with them. What about the nixies?"

"If we touch the water, everything dies. Do you want that?"

"What do you mean everything?"

"The river will be dead."

"No fish?"

"More than that."

Nov moved his shoulders. His Holding was the Shipper's Quarter; the Dan was part of his life. He knew its moods and changes, knew it in flood and low water, thick with mud in the Spring and frozen over in Winter. The image of a dead river rang warnings in his head. "Nik," he said. "Nik! Do something else. Keep your promise, Dancer, give me my Land. Alive, not dead!"

"The time is wrong. We have not reached Fullness."

"What'n zhag does that mean?"

"Ignore the nixies. They play, they don't conspire. That is truth, Zavidesht Pan Nov; I know it. Rub smerch oil on the piles and keep cruses of it ready to pour in the water. That will drive them off."

"Drive everyone off. Tchah! What a stench." He shrugged. "Prak, it's better than killing the river. Listen to me, Dancer. I need men." He spat the last words out, putting heavy stress on each of them. "The mills at Steel Point are down to the last possles of coal and they're out of ore, the Glasseries will be running on empty next week. We've got to get hold of those mines. And that bitch!"

"Soon. You've work to do here. Clean your house before you leave it."

Nov put his hands behind his back, closing them into fists. This creature was all promise and very little performance. The problem was he hadn't forgotten how Ker died; he hadn't forgotten the Dancer freezing him in place with a gesture. Behind his growing fury was a knot of fear colder than wind off the mountains. "Give me a day so I can get ready to move. Name a day, Dancer."

The glow was seeping out again, painting a second skin over the body. Eyes like butter amber stared at him unblinking.

Nov felt sweat beading on his face, closed his hands tighter, and fought to breathe normally. He couldn't talk, which was just as well, he didn't know what to say.

"A day," the form said, the multiple voices stronger. "Let it be so. On the fourth day of the Nijilic month Sarpamish, I will send men to you from the warrens and the South."

Nov bowed, relief making his knees shake. He wheeled, walked briskly from the chamber. Two weeks. It was just enough time to plan the attack and get supplies in place.

"Let it be so," the form on the altar whispered once the man was gone. "The Sacrifice begins."

>><<

"Spider one to Mountain."

"Mountain here. Go."

"Things are starting to move here. There might not be time to work to schedule. Be ready for a call any time. Go."

"Prak. I'll pass that on. We'll have someone on watch day and night from now on. Go."

"Nov's getting ready to march. Could be any day now. Like I told you before, for the past two, three weeks his agents have scoured the Zemyadel for supplies and mounts; his warehouses are stuffed to bursting. This morning the pastoras of the Glory began moving through

the warrens, putting their fingers on men, ordering them
to the Temple. Mostly men who've gone a lot to the
Glory Houses. They stay in the Temple about an hour and
when they come out, they're Taken and they go straight
to the Pevranamist barracks. Twenty barges started South
before daybreak. Spider three's sources say they're going
for more men. Nov himself is meeting with that chert
Ravach and the rest of his oslaks, he's clamped down
harder on the warrens, shut down the glasseries and the
mills. The only things left working are Vyk's Paperies,
and even there, only one shift and you have to be Glory-
called to make it. Zdra, that's wandering, sorry. He's still
some way from being ready to march, there'll be the men
coming from the South, there's training and getting the
supply lines set. The Web has organized a relay watch on
the Pevranamist and they're beating the rounds of the
sources. We'll let you know what's going on, I'll pass it
on the minute I hear he's showing signs he's goin' to start
movin' out. Questions? Go."

"Not at this moment. Get back to you tomorrow on
schedule, if you haven't called earlier. Prak? Go."

"Prak. It should be at least another two weeks before
Nov gets his army together, more than that if he's thor-
ough as Vedouce was, but we can't be sure, so expect the
move any time. Out."

7. Shimzely

Chaya Wilish glanced at the owlclock clicking noisily away on the wall, then eased the oven door open and checked the color of the bread's crust, smiling with satisfaction at the high round top and even color. It was coming out perfect, everything had been perfect all day—so far, though it was still early. She shut the door with the same care, straightened with a sigh and a brush of her hand across her face, pushing back the dark brown wisps escaping from her slicked-back hair, wisps the heat had twisted into tight small curls.

A slight young woman with skin the color of kava heavily laced with milk, a generous mouth and brown eyes so dark they seemed black in some lights, she was easy on her feet, quick and graceful as she crossed the kitchen to the cooler well.

The pulleys squeaked as she hauled on the rope and she reminded herself to give them a touch of oil when she had a minute. Her father had dug the well the year before she was born, so the pulleys were older than she was, but he had a Gift at making things. He'd been a woodworker and important in the Wooders Guild, so they were only a little worn and with care would outlast her daughter. If she ever had a daughter—the way things were going. . . . She shoved the thought back as she cleated the rope and took the milk can from the platform. "Saucer, where's that saucer . . . ah! Lavvie, come come, I'm putting your milk by the stove, it'll be warm in just a little while, come and drink it before it turns."

The house snake poked his head from his hole, then

hurried across to the saucer, an undulant red-brown streak.

Chaya laughed. "Lavvie, Lavvie, I should call you Run-for-the-milk. You're just like your namesake, he can smell food fifty miles off." She went out the back door to pick greens for the salad.

When she came back, Sekhaya Kawin was sitting at the table, sipping at a glass of water, a plump, middle-aged woman with slightly darker skin and greenish-brown eyes in nests of laugh wrinkles, abundant light brown hair sprinkled with gray and a few white hairs that caught the light and shimmered like silver wires.

Chaya dumped the greens in the sink and ran to hug her name-sponsor. "Thazi, thaz, it's so good to see you. . . ."

Sekhaya returned the hug, kissed Chaya on both cheeks, then pushed her back. "You're looking splendid, kaz. What a glow you've got!"

"Ahwu, I've worked hard and waited a long time for this." Sighing happily, she freed herself and went to start washing the greens. Over her shoulder, she said, "Lavan's coming by tonight. Now you'll be here, too; it makes my celebration complete."

"Tonight? I thought. . . ."

"My private celebration, thaz. To make Lavan come to the Guild dinner and watch me get my journeyman certificate. . . ." She shook water from a handful of wefi leaves, dropped them in the strainer, then began washing dirt from crunchy yellow homboes, nipping off the roots and tops with a paring knife, tossing the homboes on top of the wefi. "I mean, it would be like rubbing salt, wouldn't it."

"Ahwu, I'm pleased he'll be here, I might have good news about that." She hesitated at Chaya's exclamation, then said, "Kaz, that bread smells done, want me to check?"

Chaya dropped the knife, ran water over the small cut. "What? Yes, why not." She pressed a dishrag against the cut, inspected it, pressed some more. "Good news?" Her voice cracked in the middle of the last word.

"Mh! Perfect." Sekhaya tipped the loaf from the pan,

set it on the rack to cool. She took the pan to the sink, ran water into it, went back to the table. "Yes. I hit Valafam on my rounds, couple weeks ago, I've got a cousin there, Lova Nyezan, no relation to you, Chay, she's on my father's side, his sister's husband's sister's granddaughter, she told me that a cousin of hers called Kubalm, he was apprenticed to this silversmith in Hubawern, that's outside my territory, only a long breath from Bokivada. Naka naka, Kubalm caught a nejuba fever and went off, snap snap, before anyone could do anything, not that one can do much unless one catches it before the yellows show, naka naka, he died and the smith, Casil Kinuqah's his name, Clan Qithu, he was lonesome and looking around for another apprentice, but he's old, old, old, no one wants to go with him and chance him dying on them like Zok did on Lavan. Naka naka, I went over to talk to him, told him about Lavan, about him being a journeyman silversmith and almost ready for his masterwork and certification, and what happened to the Master he was articled to and he said, tell Lavan to come see him and if they could get on, he'd waive the fee for the sake of the company." She slapped the table with both hands, hiccuping as she tried to laugh and catch her breath at the same time.

"You think he's a good man?" Chaya kept her eyes on the solz she was peeling, watching the dark blue-green skin curl back from the paler green inside.

"I think Lavan would be taking a chance of being died-on again, this Qithuin's spry and sharp, but he's older than the stones of Gaph. Thing is, it's the only possibility I picked up and I asked every fam I hit."

The cut opened on Chaya's thumb again; she sighed, washed the blood off the slices of solz and dumped them in the strainer. "I'll let you tell him about it, thaz; he wouldn't take it right, coming from me. I'll go to the kitchen to see about something, tell him then."

"Trouble, kazi?"

"Not trouble, not ... exactly. Put some water on to boil, you know where the charcoal and matches are." Chaya doused the strainer again, shook the water off the greens and took them to the well, where she lowered the platform to the dark coolness below the house. She came back chewing on a stalk of gatsha. "Are you hungry, thaz? I could make some toast, there's honey and butter. I bought some trobel berries for a dessert tart, but there's more than I need."

"Cha's enough for me. I'm getting too fat."

"Tsa! Not the last time I saw Dolman Fippaza looking at you."

"Old men like a lot of flesh, it makes them feel warm." Sekhaya clicked her tongue. "And you're slip-slipping sideways, sly little yeni. What's up, kaz?"

Chaya sat down, folded her arms and stared at a knot in the wood she'd stared at a thousand and thousand times before. "Nothing's right between us now."

"Mmm?"

"You've been south a long time, thazi, so you wouldn't know how this has been working out." She sucked at the cut a moment, pushed her other thumb down on it and went on, the words tumbling out of her as they always tumbled out of Sekhaya.

"It's just that, ahwu, when Zok's heart went, Lavan took it all right. He was upset, he liked Zok and the man was only fifty, it wasn't something you'd expect, but it wasn't like he was kin or anything. Lavan figured he'd have no trouble finding another Master, he's the best there is in the journeymen of his year, everyone knows that. He expected he could pick and choose among Masters, that messages would come from lots, only none of that happened, so he went looking, but the Masters he talked to had all the students they wanted. No one wanted him except for a huge fee which he not only couldn't pay but didn't think was fair. And that was three years ago." She paused as the kettle whistled and Sekhaya got up to set the cha to steeping. "The trouble is, his clan's just about died out, so there's no one to stand behind him."

Sekhaya opened the cupboard, took down two cups and two saucers. "And your uncle won't let the two of you marry until Lavan straightens himself out, which is another slap in his face."

"Yes, and you wouldn't know this, but he barely gets enough work to feed himself, no way he can buy things for his Masterwork. And all the time this is happening to him, here I am, just humming along, no problems, I'm making journeyman tomorrow and I'm a year younger than he was when he did, and he tries not to let it rub at him, but it does, and he takes his hurt out on me when I'm around, not with his fist, Maiden Bless, but with nasty cutting words, and he goes with other women, my cousins make sure I get ALL the news. He's not a strong man, I know all the cracks in him, but I love him. Once this gets straightened out, it'll be all right, I KNOW that." She sighed, lowered her head onto her arms.

Chaya pushed the door open with her hip, eased through the opening with the big round tray. It was heavy with the dessert tartlets, a bowl of whipped cream and the cha pot and the things that went with that, but her arms didn't tremble under the weight, one benefit from years of work at the loom. In a strained hush that tightened knots in her stomach, she set the tray on the low table in the parlor and began shifting the pot and plates.

Sekhaya broke the silence with a laugh. "After that dinner, you expect us to eat some more?"

"Lavan has a hollow leg; he could eat a horse and not gain a pound." Chaya glanced at him and saw the muscle tic beside his left eye start its warning twitches. *Please please, Maiden Bless. I can't tease him anymore. He used to laugh when I called him a hole in the ground. I can't say ANYTHING at all without him blowing up at me. Not in front of my thaz, please, Lav, not tonight.*

Sekhaya read the strains and once again broke in before Lavan could say anything. "Talking about eating, I saw the weirdest thing, I don't really know what to think about it." She took the cup from Chaya, sipped at the cha, smiled.

Setting cup and saucer on the arm of the chair, she leaned forward, greenish-brown eyes moving from Lavan to Chaya, commanding attention. "I saw a line of marchers moving through the center of Bekyafam, almost a hundred of them, must have come from dozens of fams around there. Dressed in white, head to toe, men and women, even children, white robes, high in the neck, long sleeves, hair slicked down, eyes sort of dazed, this goofy smile they put on in between the times they were singing . . . na na, not singing, chanting. Kazim, kazim, kazim, like big white bees following a queen, but it wasn't a queen, it was a cow, a white yearling heifer with white silk ribbons tied to her horns and white daisies sewn on her lead rein. I started to follow to see what was happening, but a man pulled me aside and said, 'you don't want to do that, you don't want to see what they're going to do.'' Ahwu, you know me, if there was anything that would MAKE me follow, it was that, but I wish I hadn't, he was right, I didn't want to see it. There was a field with wheat all around it, growing thick and yellow, but the field was empty, the dirt trodden hard around a raised stone platform. They made the heifer jump up onto the platform, then they swarmed over her. She screamed, went down under the weight of them. They were tearing at her with teeth and fingers, throwing bits of her to the children and the others who couldn't get onto the platform. I fed my dinner to the wheat and went back to the fam. I wanted to know what was that was about and why someone didn't stop it, but the man was gone, the doors of all the houses were shut. And barred, I got that feeling, naka naka. And the windows were shuttered. So I left. If the local folk were that afraid, I didn't want to be around when those others came back.''

Hibayal Bebek, Master Scrivener, was taller than most Shimzeys, though that wasn't apparent as he sat at his desk except in the length of his arms and the long shapely fingers that played with the stylo as he listened to the arrogant young man sitting in the client chair. Like all of his clients, they belonged to important clans—he was, after all, assistant to the Guild Master and first in line for election when the old man died—and the fees he was going to charge them would add considerably to his savings, but there were times like today when the violence he kept hidden rose near the surface and it was all he could do to listen and make the notes he had to have.

"So." When the young man ran down, Bebek ticked a check beside an item on the list. "If I have mistaken anything you said, please correct me. If the child is a girl, she will be accepted into your wife's clan, name-sponsored from that clan. If the child is a boy, he will be name-sponsored from your clan. The totems are to be determined by the sponsors. Have you decided who these will be?"

The young man stroked his little pointed beard, glanced at the silent girl beside him. "Our parents want to do that. They won't say anything until the baby comes."

"You understand, the sponsors' names must appear on the certificates when the seal is impressed, which must be done within one day after the birth. And the child must be presented to the Scrivener with at least one parent, one grandparent, and a witness to the birth to attest that the child is indeed the one born to you."

"Yes, yes, my father told me all that."

"Good, a careful man is a good example to all around him. Have you any preference as to the printer for the certificates? You understand, there will be seven copies and they all must have the guild seal on them along with the attestation seal."

"Seven? Why so many?"

"There is your copy, of course. Three will be sent to Fundalakoda for the Arbiter's Archives. One will be sent to the archives of the child's clan. One to the clan of the other grandparent. One copy will be kept in my office, that is for the protection of the child that is coming; accidents do happen and your certificate could be destroyed or mutilated. It isn't as if you were merely rabble in the streets. You'll want no blot on your child's history."

The young man blinked, then looked affronted. "Who would dare. . . ."

"At the marriage contract, you'll see who'll dare, my young friend. Think back to your own. The more careful we are, the clearer and cleaner the clan lines will be." He ticked off another item on his list. "I will have the form drawn up by my writers and ready for the printer . . ." he glanced openly at the girl for the first time, "in three days. If your families have cognates in the Printer's Guild and want to use them or, as I said, if you have some other in mind, send me the name tomorrow and I will have everything ready for your approval before the end of this sen'night. When the child comes, send for me, I will bring my seal and make the attestations immediately. Are there any questions? Good. Peace to you and yours."

He rose, bowed, watched them stroll out, youth and girl alike sure they owned the world and all they had to do was walk through it. His stomach knotted. "Blot," he muttered, "Blot, blot. . . ." His mother's face floated in front of him, frozen in fear, a red line across her throat that might have been a ribbon but wasn't; there was a scar in the same place on his neck, which was why he always wore a silk scarf about it, neatly layered and folded into the top of his tunic. He pushed his sleeve up, licked the head of a match, lit it, shook away the flame and pressed it against his skin, his lips drawn back from long yellow teeth, eyes closed. When the heat faded, he broke the match in half, dropped it in the waste basket and rubbed a drop of ointment on the burn. He sucked in a long breath, lit another match and touched off a small cone of incense. When he had his sleeve properly in place, he rang the small bronze bell at his elbow and sat with his fingers laced, waiting for his aide to send in the next client.

8. Going South—
Serroi and Treshteny
on Their Separate Paths

The Fetch was a gray ghost towering over the ship, cloud among clouds, the vast mouth opening and closing, the words lost, deflected by the protecting maremars. Serroi smiled, sank deeper into sleep.

The northernmost of the Shimzelys was a speck of rock that barely broke the surface, but supported a colony of racha birds who flew up to circle in the stillness of the eye as the *Tengumeqi* glided past. They squawked wildly as a maremar swam close to the ship, flipped its flukes, and dived.

Serroi turned and ran from the bow, up the ladder to the quarterdeck, reaching the Shipmaster just as the flukes vanished. "Get your men ready," she panted, "the maremar are leaving and that storm's going to hit us." She waved her hand in a ragged swoop to stop his questions. "I'll deflect as much as I can, but I can't do it all. Send someone for the gyes, I'll need holding down and I can't spare the attention to do it myself."

The wall of clouds circling them tried to slam shut.

Fumbling in memory—back and back to her seventh year—back and back to the Sorcerer's Isles when Ser Noris was training her—back and back to ancient unused patterns creaking and stiff, Serroi drew into herself the WORDS of command and the WILL that went with them and as the *Tengumeqi* reeled, close to capsizing, she spat them out. . . .

The winds divided a shiplength before the bow, as if

sliced by a blade; they flowed around the ship and joined in frenzied, freakish turbulence behind it. The water heaved and jolted in cross waves that tossed the *Tengumeqi* about like a cork in a crossrip.

The jarring stopped when they slid into the Sleeve, the long narrow passage between the coast of the Zemilsud and the long spray of the Shimzelys—a sprinkling of rocky dots followed by larger bits of land with two or three families on those that had fresh water, then Shimvor, which was a roundish island two hundred miles in diameter with a spine of small mountains running down the middle, then Shimzely, much larger than all the rest, shaped like a velater with its fins outspread, a thousand miles across, six hundred down, then more small islands that called themselves the Shimtichin or sometimes the Pharelin, the Pearl Islands, ending in another spray of rocky tors covered with a thousand and a thousand species of sea birds.

In that channel there was peace of a sort; a brisk wind blew north, stirring up the waves and whipping the high clouds along the sky. Phindwe started a vigorous house cleaning, changing sails, splicing broken ropes, tieing his cargo down again, getting the bilge pumps set up and working, chousing Serroi into healing every scratch or bruise on his men, yelling at cook and carpenter—he was here, there, everywhere, bouncing about the ship so fast that at times he seemed to be in more than one place at once.

The wind gentled after two days, the sea settled to its usual rhythm, and Phindwe slowed down. As day folded into day they began to meet other ships heading north, one, then two, then more and more of them.

Mother, I see you coming to me. Closer and closer you come. You fill me with delight and joy. I wait for you. I am impatient to embrace you, to take you into me. Why take so much trouble, sweet Mother? Why? When all you need is to reach out your hand, call to me, let me touch you. Come. . . . The Fetch was ripe and beautiful, bending toward Serroi, extending a shapely arm, the glow about her form thick as golden syrup.

Serroi groaned in her sleep. Her mouth moved, shaped the word *nay* again and again, the repetition of that denial slowly, painfully erasing the image from her mind.

On the twenty-seventh day after leaving the Skafarees, the *Tengumeqi* dropped anchor outside the harbor at Bokivada, Phindwe waiting impatiently for the stream of departing ships to clear away so she could get in and unload her cargo.

>><<

Shadows followed Horse, men flitting from tree to tree, more and more of them gathering, elusive and angry. It was late in the day; the sun was low in the west, the darkness curdling under the thick growths of blue-green bovries and a few shivering varch.

Treshteny swayed, dropped into a premoaning fit.

"Blood," she whimpered, "blood and fire . . . they come and they die . . . the boy . . . the boy . . . we die . . . you die . . . I bleed . . . I burn . . . the Horse eats . . . the Horse fades . . . it's gone, it's gone . . . it's all all gone. . . ."

Mama Charody caught hold of her arm, jerked her over and slapped her face, then shoved her upright. "Remember and report, Timeseer."

Treshteny blinked, touched the red handmark; it was rougher treatment than she'd had for a long time now. "Why?"

"Weakness is a lure, Seer. I don't want you bringing that lot down on us before we're ready. Horse, move along. We can talk while we walk."

Horse stared coldly at her from his slate gray eyes, stone eyes.

She sniffed. "Stone don't worry me, Horse."

His ears twitched and he shook his head, his long creamy mane flying into Yela'o's face.

The faun squealed and kicked, his sharp little hooves pricking Horse's hide.

He snorted, humped his back halfheartedly, then seemed to sigh; without fuss he started walking on.

The shadows moved with them, silent and ominous.

"Zdra, Tena, tell me what you saw."

Treshteny frowned down at the solid old woman, prodding at memories already dim. The premoaning visions always melted away, leaving nothing behind except a faint sickness in her stomach. "They did not ask me anything before," she said, "I don't know if I can. . . ."

"They were fools. I'm not. Don't be silly, just do it."

She swayed in the cradle of Horse's hide and flesh, then settled into her usual calm, the images gone pale and distant. "I saw men black and burning, other men with fountains of blood bursting from their chests and out their mouths, Horse drinking the blood and changing to a beastshape I have not yet seen. I saw Doby lying broken, a great hole in his chest, men around him eating his heart. I saw you in a pool of blood, wrinkled and empty and at the same time you stood there tearing up great gobbets of earth and throwing them, dust in a cloud around you. I saw you centered among ariels, burning and throwing fire. I saw my body lying beside Doby's, broken and empty. I saw the forest burning all around us, but we were moving through it untouched. I saw us moving as we are now, but no one under the trees. I saw these things like playing cards painted on glass, part of each overlaying each. That is what I saw."

Mama Charody walked for several minutes without saying anything, her eyes fixed on the narrow, winding gametrail. When they passed beneath a red-leafed varch that grew like a changeling among the blue-green bovries, she said, "I did nothing before the attack?"

"I don't remember more than ghosts now, but I think that was not in the possibilities that I saw."

"So if I act before they do, none of that holds?"

"The old Marn used to do that all the time. If you change the starting point, you change the outcome."

"For better or worse."

"Yes."

Her hand on Doby's shoulder more to comfort him than for support, Mama Charody plodded on.

The boy was shaking, old memories come back. Clutching at her skirt, his small grubby fingers buried in the heavy cloth, he walked beside her, quieting after a while, trusting her.

Mama Charody stopped at the edge of a clearing with a stream burbling along one edge. "This is the place you saw?"

Treshteny blinked. "I don't know. I've forgotten."

"What's the use of ..." Charody clicked her tongue. "Never mind. I know what I know. Stay here. Doby, stay with her." She pried his fingers loose, moved them to Treshteny's ankle, and strode into the clearing.

When she reached a large flat boulder by the stream, she stepped up on it, clapped her hands sharply together.

"Chovan! You there under the trees. Listen and learn." She clapped again.

"I am Mama Charody. You know me, hear this. Brothers of earth and stone, COME!"

The ground around her churned and humped up, then kamen began to squeeze up out of the soil to stand clustered around her, their angular gray forms like the boulder reborn, reshaped and multiplied.

Charody smiled at what she'd called, cried out, "Disturb us at your peril."

Under the trees, Horse knelt. When Treshteny stepped from his back, he sprang up, rubbed his nose along the side of her face, shook himself and *changed* to the beast she'd seen in the premoan. Hairy and brown with tusks the length of a man's hand in his upper jaw and claws that tore at the turf, the beast loped across the wiry grass, reared up beside Mama Charody and ROARED.

Doby giggled, then scrambled for shelter among the tree roots as the shadows closed in around them.

Treshteny wheeled, seeking a way to run.

She was surrounded by a ring of men, battered, bearded, dressed in rags, wilder than the sicamars and mevveds that hunted in these mountains. One of them lunged at her, grabbed her.

She screamed and struggled, his rancid odor nearly strangling her, his horny nails tearing her skin.

The Beast ROARED again and came galloping toward them.

Ariels came dropping through the leaves, golden and shining; they flitted about the chovan, brushing against them, starting small fires in filthy hair, blowing in their faces, pinching their ears.

Seven kamen oozed in their peculiar way across the grass, toward the trees, their stone growls the only sounds they made despite their fearsome mass.

The chovan set a knife against Treshteny's throat. "Back off," he roared. "Or this'n 's meat." He began retreating from the clearing, Treshteny held in front of him as a shield.

With a whining cry of anger/fear Doby rushed from the shadows, flung himself at the back of the chovan's knees, hitting him in mid-step, catching him off-balance.

As he fell, dragging Treshteny down with him, Yela'o hooked at him with his curly horns, tearing at his arms and head, drawing blood. The chovan howled and flailed about, trying to drive off the invisible monster nipping at him.

Treshteny wrenched away from him, went scrambling in blind terror to meet the hairy beast that had been Horse.

The would-be ambushers took a look at their leader being slashed and ripped by a demon they couldn't see, at the kamen crashing toward them, at the roaring monster with the woman lifted in his forelegs; in seconds they were gone, vanishing into the thickening night.

The kamen kept coming and when they'd passed over the point where the chovan was struggling to get to his feet, the only signs left of him were some splashes of blood and greasy smears.

Eyes closed so she wouldn't be distracted by his manyness, though he was back in his familiar shape, Treshteny leaned into Horse's warm, resilient shoulder and drove her fingers along the curve of the neck, scratching and crooning to him, laughing as he curled his head around and blew in her ear, whuffled at her hair. After a while she stepped back, shaking her sore arms. "That's all for now."

He danced a little, bobbed his head, then went trotting off into the darkness.

Doby broke a brittle branch into sections, added it to the fire, then went to curl up beside Mama Charody, his head on her thigh, a roast tuber tucked up against his stomach for its heat; when it cooled enough he planned to eat it.

Treshteny watched the flames dance, laughing as Yela'o danced with them, snatched at them, the red light shining through his small body. She'd worried the first time she'd seen him play with fire, but Charody said leave him be, like the sun, it's his food. He's only a baby and babies play with food.

When he'd settled against her again, she dallied a while with his wiry curls, then sighed with pleasure and regret as he snuggled closer and sank into the state that was sleep for him. She was exhausted, too, but she was afraid to sleep. The noise of the wind in the conifers, the rattle of dead leaves from varch and daub, the soft sounds of small lives invisible in the darkness, these faint noises at the edge of her hearing had never bothered her before, but then she hadn't realized there were people in these mountains. Now . . . every rustle was a reminder and a threat.

She closed her hand on the deep scratches in her upper arm. "Will they come for us again?"

Charody sipped at the cooling cha in her mug. "Not tonight," she said. "Tomorrow night we maybe chase 'em again. Tomorrow and tomorrow, till we leave 'em behind or they leave us alone."

Treshteny wiped her hand on her skirt, dragged it across her eyes, pressed her palm against her temple. "MY head hurts. Why are we doing this?"

"You tell me."

Treshteny shook her head, gasped as pain struck behind her eyes. "Guards came for me, Horse came first. That's all. I didn't ask the reason. I never asked why they moved me around. Things were as they were. It was easier to float, there was no reason to fight the flow."

She held out her arm. In the flicker of the firelight the irregular brown blotch that ran along the inside of it was like a berry stain on the pale skin. "When I was little, my brother pushed me into a table and the cha kettle fell by me; the water scalded my arm. It wouldn't stop hurting. For days and days it wouldn't stop hurting. I'm afraid like that now. I can't stop shaking inside me."

Charody tapped her short blunt fingers on her knee, impatience in the click of her tongue. "Such a tender flower, Tena. Tsaa! Who wouldn't be afraid? Those chovan, if they went down on the flat they'd dangle from the nearest stranglin' post." She wiped her hand across her mouth. "Fear's a good thing, it keeps you lookin' round. You got your own wisdom, Tena, but that wan't part of it. Use your fear like you use your visions. If y' let it stop you, they've won." She chuckled, the sound warm as the fire. "There now, that's enough of that. Horse and me, we'll watch. Zdra, he's out there doing his night business, but he'll be passin' by here, time to time, keepin' his eye on you. So you get some sleep."

The harbor at Bokivada was a deep, circular bay facing south, protected from southern storms by the Shimtichin Islands that curved off Halanzi Point, the end of one of the Shimzely velater's fins. As the sun rose on the day, the *Tengumeqi* poked her nose into the narrow channel between the Point and Cacani Isle, the first and largest of the Shimtichins. That bay was still packed with ships, bad-tempered Shipmasters and fratchety crews, kept there by the fringe winds and freaky weather driven by the storm aimed at Serroi; even those bound south or east, away from the storm, had been pinned in there because water and wind were too rough to let anyone move.

To stay clear of the traffic and wait for a pilot, Phindwe was forced to drop anchor at Kudla Qig, one of the dozens of arid rocks covered with guano and rotting seaweed that speckled the outer rim of the bay.

He paced back and forth along the port rail, dividing his glares between Serroi and the ships creeping past. "I told you so," he flung at her each time he moved past her. "Wind don't stay put, rain don't stay put."

She ignored him and brooded over the little she'd managed to coax from Hedivy. His reticence might be partly
a matter of pride (he was heavy in pride) because he
didn't KNOW much about the Shimzelys; for whatever
reason he ignored most of her questions about the people
and how they ran their lives.

What he did say wasn't all that comforting. *You and the
gyes, you're bait. We separate the minute we hit the
wharf, you go to Vusa Ikala's Inn, get rooms and stay in
them. Me, I'll find Nehod. And nik, I won't take that
spoggin' sprite with me, where I go and what I do is none
of your spoggin' business.*

By the time they tied up, it was after sundown and the
boil along the wharves had settled to a slow seethe.

Hedivy slipped off the *Tengumeqi* as the unlading began and vanished in the crowd. Serroi and Adlayr (Honeydew huddling in his shirt pocket, only the top of her
head visible, her eyes tiny shines) left half an hour later
when Phindwe could spare a sailor to act as guide.

They left the wharves and plunged into a maze of
streets and cross-streets, their guide counting off the turns
on his fingers, whispering a mnemonic to pick his way
through buildings like a child's toy blocks, painted neutral colors, dark gray, green drab, and browns. He was a
short, bowlegged Shimzey, with his black hair braided
into dozens of six-inch plaits, interwoven with copper and
silver wire, a silent man intent on doing his job without
unnecessary chatter.

Serroi drew her cloak tighter around her. With the
ragged clouds overhead, scattered splatters of rain, the
wind scouring between the walls, the lowering night,
she found this place repellent. The few windows visible
had iron grilles on them, the lowest at least fifteen feet
from the pavement. Though the narrow, angling streets
were clean enough to show they had to be swept regu-
larly, a faint stench hung over the area, a staleness with a
urine bite. And there wasn't a touch of green anywhere,
at least not here in the heart of Freetown. Every stretch
like the one before. No street names. It was no wonder
the sailor had to count on his fingers to find his way.

He stopped finally before an anonymous arch, closed by a two-leaved door fitted flush with the wall and painted the same color, muddy brown with a greenish tinge. He slapped the door. "This is it. Vusa Ikala's Inn." He scratched at his chin a moment, slitted black eyes sliding round to Serroi. "Bay's t' west a here. Y' get lost, get t' harbor, c'n hire a guide there. Don't pay 'n 'fore y' get where y' goin'." He touched a finger to his brow, then went marching off.

Serroi looked up and down the street, empty and silent, filling with webs of shadow. "Does anybody get the feeling they don't like foreigners much here?"

>><<

Hedivy felt eyes on him as he moved through the empty clueless streets. It wasn't a new feeling here and it didn't mean he'd already been spotted by the Enemy; anyone in the street was game for the taking if he looked ripe. He had a good memory, so he made the turns without hesitation and the watchers kept watching.

Nehod's room was in a rookery built up against the wall at the inner edge of Freetown, no questions asked as long as you paid the rent on time, with a mix of banned Shimzeys, predators down on their luck, seamen whose drunks lasted too long, travelers trying to scratch up the money for the next leg onward, and a sprinkling of drab, bland types with no visible interests or occupation. Unlike most transient lodgings in Freetown, there was no door in the entrance arch, no concierge in his cage, keeping a minatory eye on entrances and exits. Hedivy went in, ignoring the key-clerk sleeping beneath a broadsheet by his ranks of hooks and holes, and took the stairs at a steady pace, deliberately making noise as he walked; most of the clients of this place would be far more interested in a stealthy creak than an unconcerned tromp. Those he passed on the stairs, going up or going down, paid him as little attention as he gave them.

When he reached the fourth floor, he turned onto the landing and tromped off down the wrong corridor; there was an intersect a hundred feet down that would take him where he wanted to be.

>><<

Like all the rest, Nehod's door was painted a thick, ugly brown, chipped in places, showing the layers of older paint, ugly on top of ugly. Hedivy knocked quietly, a double thump, then a wait. He didn't expect anyone to be there; in his pocket he had a note with a time written in Cadandri glyphs—the hour after midnight, the time when he meant to return.

There was movement in the room, footsteps coming to the door.

Hedivy frowned. He started away, but the door slammed open and he heard a shot, felt a blow in his left thigh. His knee folded and he went down as men with guns emerged from another room just ahead of him.

>><<

Frowning uneasily, Serroi followed Adlayr up the stairs; there was something about the concierge that bothered her, the way his eyes had moved over her before he took their money and tossed Adlayr the key, the tension and queasy expectation she felt in him.

Halfway up the second flight of stairs, she stopped. "Wait," she said.

Adlayr turned. "What is it, Serry?"

"I don't know. Adlayr, give me the key, go on up high as you can, see if you can get on the roof."

Honeydew wriggled out of the shirt pocket and launched herself, dipping until her wings were stretched and working, soaring to the ceiling of the corridor. *Honeydew watch, send on. Serree will be too busy to send, yes?*

Ei vai, Honey, but you be careful. We like having you around ... She looked at the muddy green/brown walls, wrinkled her nose. .... *a lot more than these folk seem to like anything.*

They waited in silence while Adlayr went on ahead,

Honeydew perching on Serroi's shoulder to save her strength for later.

Vai, Honey, let's go see what's waiting for us.

Honeydew do. She fluttered up until she drifted in the shadows above the shoulder-high hall lamps, so nearly invisible that anyone who didn't know she was there would miss her entirely.

The Inn was eerily silent, the corridors as empty as the streets outside; when they reached the third floor, she stepped onto the landing, the knot in her stomach getting tighter and colder.

She matched the sigil on a door with that on the key, unlocked it and pushed it open.

"All right, you, just stand there, don't move."

Serroi swung round.

A man stood in the door of a room across the hall, a burly man, nearly as wide as he was tall, a leather sack pulled over his head with eyeholes cut in it and a heavy shortgun in his hand. "Ahwu, now do as I told you, woman, you won't need knees to answer questions."

>><<

Treshteny glanced to the east as Horse moved round the side of a mountain and she saw the ocean for the first time.

She stared at the speck of jewel blue.

It expanded, unfolded, closed around her until she dropped into a vertigo more terrifying than any she'd known in her thirty years.

She woke cradled in Mama Charody's arms, the wise woman crooning to her, rocking her as if she were a child. Doby squatted beside them, patting Treshteny, humming along with Charody's croon. Horse stood nearby, watching, Yela'o clutching at his mane, eyes huge and worried.

Mama Charody smiled down at her. "That's a good girl. Can you sit up?"

Treshteny took a deep breath, swallowed, nodded. With the wise woman's help, she eased onto the dusty track, her back to the east, opening her arms for the little faun as he jumped down and came running to her. "South," she said, smiling as Yela'o nestled against her. "I saw a mountain burning like a candle. We have to go there."

"Zdra, at least that's useful. What set you off this time?"

Careful not to look, Treshteny reached awkwardly backward, waved her arm up and down. "That."

Mama Charody got to her feet, scanned the horizon. "The ocean?"

"I suppose that's what it is." She smiled down at Yela'o, snuggling against her, then sighed. "Unsteady. No center, nothing to hold to."

"It doesn't bother you if you don't see it?"

Treshteny rubbed her fingertips across her temples. "I think . . . I think that's right."

"Then that's easy enough to fix. Doby, bring me my kerchief."

She folded the thin white cloth into a triangle, refolded it until she had a bandage about two inches wide. "Out the way, Yela'o, let me try this." While the faun teetered impatiently beside the track, she tied the kerchief over Treshteny's eyes, inspected her work, then helped Treshteny to her feet. "Comfortable?"

"Odd, but not worrying."

"Zdra zdra, let's turn you around. There, you're facing the ocean again. Any problems?"

Treshteny's fingers twitched, then she shook her head. "None."

"Then we'd better get moving. We need to find a boat going south as soon as we can."

Treshteny frowned. "Boat. I hadn't thought . . . how will we pay?" She reached out her hand, stroked Horse's warm shoulder. "And what about him?"

"I'll take care of the pay and he'll take care of him."

9. Dander's Up

The pounding on the door jarred Greygen Lestar out of exhausted sleep; before he thought, he sat up, started to swing his legs over the side of the bed.

Sansilly caught hold of his arm, her fingers digging into the muscle. "Chair," she whispered urgently. "Don't know who's lookin', Greg."

He nodded. "Bring it round. Pek! Listen to 'em. What time is it, anyway?"

Sansilly glanced at the line of small holes cut into the tops of the shutters. "Still dark out." Her nose twitched. "Smells like dawn's about due." She shoved her arms into the sleeves of her old worn robe, pulled the belt tight; as she talked, she was bustling about the room, tossing him robe and blanket, bringing the chair from the corner and ignoring his attempts to help himself. "Act right, Greg. You know how we do this. Get your slippers on and don't argue me about keeping that blanket tucked tight, you gettin' muscle back, and it's startin' to show. And calluses. They see those, they gonna start wonderin', even those thrunts who never had a thought since the day they was hatched."

Sansilly opened the door and scurried round the chair to stand at Greygen's shoulder. He looked up at the men who came surging in, Pusnall and his Purgemen, some of them unwilling to meet his eyes, others glaring at him to emphasize their authority. "What do you want?"

"Why'd you take so long to get that door open?" Pusnall didn't wait for the obvious answer, but jerked a thumb at Sansilly. "You. Show us your kitchen and your food stores."

Greygen drove the chair against Pusnall's knees with one powerful shove, grabbed his wrists, and jerked him down till they were nose to nose. "My wife's name is not You. You will call her jama Lestar." He let go, wheeled himself back, and waited.

Pusnall smoothed his sleeves and the red went slowly from his eyes. "I don't fight cripples," he said. "Take the Lestar woman to the pantry. Keep him here." He looked at Greygen. "We'll be watching you."

Sansilly slammed the bar home. "Good riddance!" she whispered; she wouldn't answer Greygen's questions, just wheeled him into the bedroom, made him let her help him into bed as she had all the years since the accident. She poured a glass of water, looked at it, and started crying.

Greygen lay quiet until the outburst calmed, then he said, "What was it, Sansy, what did they want?"

Sansilly drank the water, set the glass down with a sigh, and came into the bed. "I had to tell them where every grain of anything came from," she rubbed at her eyes, "what shop I bought it from, how much I had."

She curled her fingers tight against her palms. Greygen turned on his side, closed the small fists into his hands and held them.

"That proggin' Pusface told me after this I had to have receipts for any food I bought, because they were gonna check again and if I had more, either I was hoarding or in with the traitors and I'd be dumped in a dungeon or left to rot." Her nostrils flared. "Then he ate the bit of tart I was saving for your lunch, just stared at me, daring me to say anything."

"Pek! One thing after another." Greygen twisted onto his stomach, danced his fingers over the squares of wood set into the bedstead; what looked like decoration was a puzzle lock and opened a small cavity in the post. He took out the com, tapped in the call sign. "Spider one to Valk, come on, man, wake up."

"Valk's not back yet, this is Spider six. Go."

"Ravach's Purgers, they're hittin' this warren, checking

food supplies, writing down everything in the chest. Pusnall was in here fifteen minutes ago. We're all right, but if you can, get the word out to the other warrens that the ones who got it should cache the extras. If the same thing's happening everywhere, get the cut-outs away fast as you can, won't take the Purgers long to spot the food and find out who passed it on. We've got to keep the Web clean. Go."

"And stuff Valk down a hole. I'll tell 'em. Out."

Greygen slipped the com back, clicked the panel in place. "It's going to get tougher, Sansy."

She lay beside him, her head turned away.

"What is it, Sansy?"

"Don't leave me out of it this time. I'm not stupid. This is my home, too."

He reached round, cupped his hand under her chin, turned her head toward him. "It isn't a game, Milachika."

She caught hold of his arm, dug her fingers into the muscle. "You DO think I'm stupid."

"Nik, it's just that I don't know what to say." He freed himself and lay staring at the shadows on the ceiling, his fingers laced behind his head. "How many women do you know you'd really trust? I mean, if it meant . . . um . . . the boys were going to live or die." As he watched Sansilly's mouth twitch and her eyes start dancing, the tension flowed out of him. "I know what you're thinking, chika. Nik, not Myzah."

She nestled against him, giggling. Then she sighed, her breath warm against his ribs. "More than you know, Greg. I've been turning this over and over in my head since they started pressing men into the army." She giggled, her body jiggling softly beside him as she pushed away the hand that was teasing at her. "I'm serious, Greg. Maybe it's 'cause I'm Harozh and things are diff'rent up there, but seems to me you're wasting good people just 'cause they women." She caught his wrist. "I mean it. Next time, get us into the warehouses, let us stow the food and see it gets passed around. And there's some who'd do more if they had a little teaching. Like Jasny." She slid her hand along his, held his fingers against the side of her face. "She lost her husband in the gritz war, the Glory people are talkin' 'bout takin' away her rooms, sendin' her south 'cause her girl was one of the sekalari they purged, and her boy, he run off to Oskland." She let his hand go and began stroking the stubble on his chin, her hand drawing a soft rasp as she finished in a whisper, "She'd strangle a Taken without breathin' hard. Or Bakory, or Pabasha, or Fletty, they'd do as ... ooooh ... much. Ahhh ... Grey. ..."

Sansilly went bustling out with the boys as she did every school morning, brushing at their shoulders, scolding them for getting their boots scuffed, giggling at a joke Mel made. Greygen sat in his chair doing the final rub-down on a lamp frame for a House of Glory. The usually busy court outside his window was deserted and the warren itself was like a sick animal crouching down to die. He laid on a streak of wax mix, began working it into the golden wood with a shemmy; it was an uncomplicated business, something he'd done a thousand and a thousand times before and therefore comforting, though it didn't stop him worrying about Sansilly. He'd tried to talk her into waiting until she could meet with Heslin and get his help organizing her women, but once she got an idea in her head, she went at it full strength. He couldn't fault that, it'd saved first his life, then his sanity, but she was going against something now.... He winced and fixed his eyes on the wood, shining and smooth, grain flowing in a darker dance over pale yellow, smiled with satisfaction as it responded to the movements of his hands, the shine sinking deeper with each pass of the cloth.

A shadow fell on the wood.

He looked up, kept his face blank. "Pusnall. What do you want?"

"Just watchin', crip. Just watchin'."

Hot angry words piled in a lump in Greygen's throat and stuck there; under the tarp spread across his lap his legs tensed. He forced his eyes back to the wood and kept polishing, ignoring Pusnall, the work once again taking hold of him and easing out his fury. After a minute he heard the scrape of a foot, then the door slammed. He didn't look up, just kept smoothing the shemmy over and over the wood.

>><<

As Motylla looked at the food her maid Vyspa was laying out on the table in her sitting room, her stomach knotted and her throat closed up. She pushed back from the table and ran from the room.

"What is this!" Her father's voice was harsh and when she didn't answer, his hand came down hard on her shoulder. He jerked her up and around, took both of her shoulders and shook her hard, shouting at her. "What are you trying to do ... spoiled brat ... ruin me ... you'll do what you're told and like it...."

Breathing hard, he dropped her. She thought he was going away, but he went only as far as the nearest young javory, wrenched a small branch from one of the limbs and came back to her stripping away twigs and leaves. Without a word he hooked a hand in her belt, lifted her off her feet and hauled her to a bench. He bent her over the back of the bench, pulled up her skirt, tore her pantlets, and brought the switch whistling down on her buttocks. She screamed, sobbed, begged him to stop, but the beating went on and on until she was hoarse.

He broke the switch, threw it away and left her there.

Motylla hiccupped to silence, trembling more with exhaustion than hurt; she caught hold of the slats of the bench back, pushed herself up, gasping as every movement sent pinches of pain nipping through her.

She stood a moment beside the bench, swaying, holding onto the back, her skirt falling down, the pantlets falling about her ankles like hobbles. Her mind was numb, all kinds of hurt pushed way out there so it couldn't get at her. Stepping carefully out of the ripped pantlets, skirt brushing against her, sticking to her where the switch had made her bleed, she hobbled across the garden to her rooms.

When Vyspa tried to help her, she twisted away. "Spy," she said, her voice a monotone. "Traitor." She went into the bedroom with the maid fluttering behind her, trying to explain. In the door to the bathroom, she turned to face the maid. "Go away. You make me sick."

>><<

Zavidesht Pan Nov washed his hands, dried them, trying to rub away the memory of the past hour; he didn't understand what had happened to him, why he was so furious at the girl. And what he couldn't understand, he couldn't control. That was bad.

When he walked into the sitting room, Ravach was waiting with a stack of folders by his elbow, the weasel look on his face that meant he had bad news, but was going to try to finesse it.

Nov dropped into a chair, lifted his feet onto a hassock, his legs crossed at the ankle. "Zdra?"

"The Purge of the warrens is finished. Caught three in the Glasshouse warren with food they couldn't explain, two in the Mid-Dander, one in Mid-Calanda. Questioned them. One died on us, bad heart I think. Two of 'em wouldn't open, even when we brought in a wife or one of their kids and made them watch what we did. The rest talked, but when we went after the sources—they were all different, by the way—they'd dived down a rathole. No sign of them anywhere. All outsiders, lone men without families, two of them farm hands, one from the Zemyadel, one from the Bezhval, the third was from Halland,a miner what the people round him said, one of those the Mar . . . um . . . her, she brought down just before the gritz war got hot."

Nov laced his fingers over his stomach, tapped his thumbs together; he could see that Ravach expected to get chewed out, but he didn't have the energy or the will for it. "There's a gamer's mind behind this, three moves ahead of us all the time. I know him by his smell. Heslin."

Ravach straightened. "How? He's in OskHold with Her."

"I don't think so. I take it you haven't managed to get a nose in that place."

"Not yet. What little my men can get out of the Hold say it's that meie; she's sniffed out every spy I've tried to plant on 'em."

"What about bribes?"

"I'm not saying Oskers can't be bought, just that we havena found the right one yet. I'll keep Darbik on it. They don't like that Woman's army much more'n they like us; we find a man with a fresh enough grievance. . . ." He shrugged. "Darbik could talk a man into buying his own wife. So we'll see."

"Prak. And put one of your best noses looking for Heslin. He's here, I know it." He got to his feet. "About Ker and the gritz—anything new?"

"Seems like it's true there's talk going on between the new Pan and the new Val Kepal—and visitors from Karpan aNor, all very secret, embassages exchanged, even weapons. Knife in the back for Cadander. But I'll have more than rumor by nightfall. Zajic is due in tonight, the message he sent by jesser said he'll be bringing papers."

"Bring him here. I want to hear it direct."

Kojeth Novarin got hastily to his feet as Pan Nov strolled into the Tradurad, bustling his papers together.

Nov waved him back. "Give it to me short form. What're the problems and what do we need to fix them?"

Novarin sat, took a paper from a folder, glanced at it, folded his hands. "Ker is complaining about the head tax, he sent one-third the assessment in food and animals, no gold, excuses for the rest. Ano hasn't answered at all after the last food levy. Coal's just about gone, even in the Pevranamist stores, but by winter there'll be enough from the Halland coal mines to heat this place and the cities. It's poor stuff, not suitable for the mills or the glasseries. We need the Merrz mines for that. The barge trade along the Red Dan is beginning to pick up a little, but the increase is slow and the traders are nervous. Tuku Kul is not friendly; all trade with the Fenek has stopped, but they're not actively blocking travel. The nixies continue to be destructive, though the smerch oil is keeping them off the wharves; the ladesmen complain, we tell them live

with it or they can find work somewhere else. Since they
need their job papers to stay in the warrens, we don't hear
any more from them. The Steel Pointers keep slipping
away, the fools are loyal to Vedouce. The warren is nearly
empty and there are only a few workers left in the Mills,
all of them Glory men. Even if we had the coal and iron
we need, it would be hard to keep the mills open. There
are not enough skilled steel men left to run them. The
Glass Houses and the Paperies can stay open for another
month or so, but they are low on materials and even they
are starting to lose workers. I have petitions from Sko and
Vyk asking you . . . um . . . the Marn to go easy on their
warrens and their workers, Ravach has arrested a number
of their best men, sent some of them south and . . ." He
shrugged. "You know. The Leatheries are producing well
enough, with all the vul and orsk being slaughtered for
the army. Paper, glass, and leather are what's keeping our
trade alive. That is the overview, tuhl Pan. Is there anything . . .?"

"Not much change from last week."

"Nik, tuhl Pan."

"Hmm. Any activity from the Biserica?"

"Nik, tuhl Pan. One of the traders did mention that the
Mijloc is getting restive because they haven't got word
from the Vorbescar they sent with the meien. Something
about a letter for him waiting in Tuku-kul."

"Zdra, we'll worry about that when we have to and not
before. Do what you can to find other sources of coal, it
may be a while before we can tap the Merrz mines . . .
maybe something in the Zemilsud. If you need some men
to do that, see me fairly soon, the army should be marching within the week."

"You'll be going with it, tuhl Pan?"

"I haven't decided yet. I'll let you know by tomorrow."

Zavidesht Pan Nov climbed the spiral stairs to the room
at the top of the Marn's Tower, leaned in the window
looking down with some satisfaction at the court where so
many traitors had died. The question Kojeth asked came
back. Going with the army. If he did, he left the city dangling like a prize before the noses of the other Pans. But

the army was a prize, too, a bigger one. Didn't matter what happened in Dander/Calanda. When he marched back with that army the double city would be his again.

He moved his shoulders, tension flowing out of him at the prospect of action. He'd never liked the fiddling paper work that came with running a holding, even a small one, a section of Dander, not the broad stretches of the Zemyadel and the rest of the rural Lands. The business of getting firm control over Cadander bored and irritated him, though he recognized the necessity. He trusted Ravach to a degree because the man knew his limitations and liked the job he had, trusted Kojeth for much the same reason; the man was good with papers, miserable with people, satisfied with the power he had and the insulation from anyone who made him feel inadequate. That pair wouldn't turn on him, though they'd run like rats if he showed signs of falling.

He looked across the river at the swarm of tents where the army was growing larger and larger each day, tents half-lost in swirls of dust from the training grounds where his navstas and vudveks were marching the men up and down, sending them through obstacle courses, teaching them to come near hitting what they aimed at, getting them as ready as they could before starting for Oskland. He couldn't see any of that, the clouds of dust hid it from him, but he willed them to be ready. "Five days," he said aloud. "That's all you have. That's when we move."

Byssa Klidina looked up as the Domcevek Novo Pato came into the small hot room where she was ironing table linens. "He wants you," he said. The brackets were drawn deep around his mouth, his eyes narrowed and malevolent. Each time Nov called for her to do the serving at one of his meetings, Pato's jealousy increased and the petty reprisals he took grew more vicious. She never complained. It was important to stay inconspicuous, scuttling about like a gray mouse, blushing carefully whenever Nov looked at her and refusing to gossip with anyone.

She set the iron on its stand, folded the napkin into neat quarters. "Now?" she said. "Or should I finish this first?"

He hesitated, but he didn't quite dare lie to her. "You're to go to the Setkan now, everything's ready. Wait until He signals you, then serve the meeting."

While he fussed at her, she closed the linen bin, doused the coals in the heat box. She took a clean apron from the pile, tied it around her, smoothed her hair, and stood in front of him, waiting for him to move aside so she could leave.

The guard outside the Setkan let her pass, nodding to her. He was very young, a boy from the Shipper's Warren; she'd met him several times when she was visiting her parents.

There was no one in the Setkan yet; she moved to the table at the back, lit the brazier under the cha pot, drew corks from the wine bottles, replaced them in the ice buckets, took the cloths from the plates of sandwiches and wafers. She smoothed her hair down, replaced the starched kerchief on her head, brushed her hands down her apron and brought a chair to the corner behind the table but didn't sit, just stood quietly waiting.

The men started coming in, faces she knew from other meetings, the leaders from the army. As they separated, pulled chairs up to sit at the long table, she kept her own face blank, her eyes down. *So many of them this time. Could mean ... zdra, Byssa, get set, remember everything. ...*

Zavidesht Pan Nov came strolling onto the dais, flung himself into the Marn's chair and leaned forward, eyes on his General, elevated from being the head of his enforcers. "Prak, Mern, how ready are you?"

"Got a lotta fodder out there. No fire in 'em, but they go where you tell 'em, do what you tell 'em and they've got so they c'n hit a target size of a man." Mern looked round at the trivuds and vudveks, getting nods from each of them. "Supplies is gettin' low. Ammo, fodder for the horses and macain, somethin' to stoke the men with, even if it's just porridge."

Nov straightened. "You'll have wagons across there tomorrow, orsks to pull them, supplies to fill them. Can you be ready to march out day after?"

"It'll be ragged, but yeah."

"Shape them up on the go. Here's what I want. Soon's we hit Oskland, we do what gritz did, raze that place to bedrock, anything that moves is dead. It's not harvest yet, so even with warning they won't be able to get in the crops, no way to resupply once we put the Hold under siege. I want mounted navstas scouring the countryside ahead of the army, smelling out and shooting spotters. As many as you can get from the not-Taken. She's got those sproggin' coms. I'll give a thousand gold to any man who shoots a spotter and gets one of those things in working order so we get the message same as them. . . ."

Behind the table, Byssa sat with her head hanging, pretending to sleep as she listened to the talking droning on and on, details hammered out about the advance parties, who'd lead them, an old plan of OskHold that Ravach had dug from Oram's files passed around, discussions of possible ways of breaching the walls, the gates, weak points, on and on until her head felt dizzy from all the information she was trying to stuff into it.

Nov got to his feet, clapped his hands. She let out a gasp, lifted her head, put a hand to reddened cheeks, then began loading her trays again. He was a fool to leave her there, but she knew why he did it. It was vanity; he wanted to strut before someone uninvolved, show off his power and his wit to someone who could never threaten him or even understand fully what was happening, who would just blush and adore. She could provide the blushing, let him assume the adoration.

She went about her work the rest of the afternoon, ignoring Pato's jabs and persistent attempts to find out what went on at the meeting, amused but blank-faced when a pair of Ravach's spies hauled him off to find out why he was so curious about what didn't concern him. When they were gone, she risked a smile. Her silence had pushed him harder every time and she'd known he'd go over the line and the way things were, spies in every nook, he'd tumble into a trap and have no way of crawling out.

An untasty mix of fear and satisfaction on her tongue, she set down the fork she was polishing, lifted another, and went back to work; she could feel eyes on her neck, knew other spies would be watching every breath she took. Heslin had warned her about that when her cousin Lisken took her to meet him so she could tell him direct what she'd learned about the meeting with the Treddeks. *The more access you get, he said, the closer they're going to watch you. It's a dangerous job you're taking on, jam' Byssa. Your only protection is freedom from suspicion. If you've got urgent information, hang a towel to dry in your window, go to the lavatory at the end of the hall at midnight. If there's no one waiting, come back an hour later. Put nothing in writing ever. Do you understand what you're getting into?* She'd smiled at him, told him, *Nov likes to see me blush at him, all the more because I'm not a pretty woman and he can revel in that adoration without anything expected of him. It'd take a lot for him to give that up. Maybe so, he said, but you'll be walking a tight wire over a sicamar's cage. So any time you want out, just let us know.* She shook her head and he laughed at her, deep rumbling laughter that knew and responded to all she hadn't said. It still warmed her when she thought about it.

There was a boy in the lavatory, crouched beside the basin cabinet. She knew him. Tomal. She ran the water and let all she'd memorized flow out of her in a long uninflected mutter, did her business, and left, dropping into a heavy, dreamless sleep the moment her head touched the pillow.

Mask in place, hair streaming, pulling a robe about her nightdress, K'vestmilly Vos came running into the small room. Face grim, Zasya followed, eyes flicking about warily, Ildas roving ahead, checking shadows, sniffing at the others in the room, coming back to stand beside her, panting lightly.

Vedouce was already there, crouched beside the com listening to the deep voice finish recounting the information the Web had got from one of their best sources. Zarcadorn Pan Osk was a shadow in one of the corners.

Vedouce stood, muttered to K'vestmilly, "Heslin, patched through Spider one."

". . . plans are to raze Oskland to bedrock, kill everything that moves. Estimates are he's got about two thousand men, most of them Taken, the rest Nov's thugs, his so-called enforcers. If they do get off day after tomorrow, they'll be coming fast and you'd better be ready. Most of the Web and I are pulling out of here tonight along with some volunteers who have reasons to loathe Nov and his lot. Spider one will stay in place and he's got a new Web in the process of setting up. We'll be leaving three of the coms with him, the others have been collected and we'll be bringing them along with us. As to the Nov's reward, have the meien show you how to set up the coms to scramble messages, in case we do lose a spotter and his com gets taken. The scrambler eats power, so don't do that until you have to. Questions? Go."

"Let me." K'vestmilly bent over the speaker. "Come here before you start the other thing. We need to see you. Go."

"Nik, there's not time. We have to get out and ahead of them, get their setup on the march, identify the roving bands if we can, see how well they work together. Any questions you have we can answer by com . . ." There was a short pause. "You're well? Go."

"Yes, barring a little morning sickness. Take care. Go." She straightened, stepped back. "Anyone else?"

Vedouce nodded, took her place. "As much detail on the order of march as you can, Valk. Don't attack them, I don't want them tightened up when they hit Oskland. Watch and report, that's all. You hear? Go."

"I hear. We'll do that. Anything more? Go."

"That's it. Keep clear and keep clean. Out."

10. Divergences and Diffusion

As dawn came, cool and dew-damp, Chaya stood at the hedgerow that marked the edge of Hallafam and watched Sekhaya's caravan go rattling off. For the first few paces, Lavan was riding beside the Herbwoman, but before they reached the turn around the othile grove, he'd kneed his horse into a faster walk and was pulling ahead. He didn't look back; he hadn't even bothered to wave to her, all she'd gotten was a quick kiss on the cheek as they left the house, a kiss that slid over her nose—he was already turning away. His mind was throwing ahead of him toward Hubawern, willing the old man to be alive and waiting for him.

She smoothed her hand over her hair and started back along the street, her clogs clattering on the wooden bricks of the pavement.

Sidak the Waterman waved to her. "Good hanla, Weaver," he called. "Happy years." He pointed his hose up and tapped the lever so the wind blew a gentle cool spray into her face, then he went back to wetting down the street and brushing it clean.

"Good hanla, Waterman." She shook off her melancholy. It was going to be a lovely day, her first as journeyman. She grinned, danced a few steps, beating a rhythm with heel and toe.

"Good hanla, Weaver." Chocho the Baker was out with his apprentices, loading up his cart with buns and cakes.

The smell of hot bread, sugar, and cinnamon woke the appetite she hadn't had for breakfast. "Good hanla,

Baker." She searched her pocket, found a copper, held it up. "Let me beg a bun," she tossed him the penny.

He caught it, laughed, tossed it back. "Na na, Weaver. To celebrate the morn, let it be my gift. Catch."

Nibbling on the bun, she walked past houses and shops, waving at friends and cousins, answering greetings, now and then breaking into a few dance steps, her spirit soaring—until she realized why she felt so liberated and some of the joy drained away; Lavan was gone and she didn't have to cope with his moods, wouldn't have to for months if the interview went right. She sniffed the clear clean air, popped the last of the bun in her mouth, and laughed when she'd swallowed it. It didn't matter, next time things would be right between them, like before. Until then, enjoy the day, day by day.

She opened the door to the guild hall and a sack of flour fell on her head. The other apprentices grabbed her and danced her around the looms, whapping her with brooms to keep the cloud rising, giggling, laughing, whirling her about, yelling the hairy old jokes she'd yelled with them when Wensay got his papers, finally pushing her into the shower room when she was totally filthy and covered with sweat, rushing in with her to get themselves clean.

When she emerged from the shower, the others were gone already, her old dress gone with them. A new one hung from the peg, made of cloth they'd woven and gotten Matha the sewing woman to make for her. She came out, danced in circles to show the apprentices and journeymen how well it fit, then took the pitcher from Duzelly and went round to the saucers, pouring milk for the House snakes, chirruping to them, stroking her favorite on the head, a dusky black snake with yellow circles about his eyes which gave him a comically grave look. By the time she was finished, the work bell had rung. She hurried to her loom, checked it hastily to make sure there were no tricks there waiting to startle her, then began work, the clack clack of the other looms busy about her. Foot on the treadle, shuttle flung across, back, clack clack, sway and hurl. As a journeyman, she was finally going to be paid for daywork, but her quota was increased again by half. The guild was going to get its due from her one way or another in ells of guildcloth. But once she was done, she could go home and work on her own projects now, the damasks and silks that would be her chief source of income, and start planning the masterwork that would free her completely from the guildwork.

Hibayal Bebek knelt naked before a low table in the attic of his house, swaying back and forth, moaning.

It was a tall, narrow house deep in the Vitifunder District, its facade contiguous with all the other houses in the row, one room wide and three stories tall, not counting the attic he'd furnished as a study, with a kitchen and two rooms attached behind where his cook and maid lived, a minute yard and an equally tiny stable. The door was an elaborate affair with the eels of his totem wound in a sinuous twist, heads curving apart about a small round window filled with pieces of amber glass set in lead canes that formed the Scrivener's sigil, a quill above a scroll.

The table was a rectangle of polished wood, a shining light yellow with a darker grain dancing through it, the legs only a hand's width long, six of them, one at each corner and one in the center of each of the long sides. On the table was a block of obsidian, polished into a black mirror; centered on the stone was a rough egg-shaped geode with the end cut out, exposing crystals of yellow topaz; buttery glows flickered from crystal to crystal, pulsing to Hibayal's moans, building form and body until the Glory shone above the cavity.

"I dreamed last night, I dreamed, I dreamed," Hibayal moaned. His skinny, naked arms were scarred from wrist to shoulder with burnmarks, his thighs still wet with sweat and blood from the scourge that lay by his knee. The scars on his back were much older, from the time his uncle was forced to foster him and whipped him for every bit of mischief and malice his cousins did; he was the bad example, the bad blood, the evil had to be scourged out of him.

He shivered with cold, though the small room under the

rafters was like an oven. He was always cold, only the Glory warmed him.

Tell me, the Glory whispered in him, the sound sliding like blood through his body. *Tell me your dream, Belovéd.*

"It was the old dream, the BAD one. My mother is putting us to bed, my sister and I, singing to us . . ." his voice went to falsetto, "little fishies in their beds, waves going splish splash o'er their heads. . . ." His voice changed again, still high, a little boy's voice. "And Daddy came in, his eyes all funny. He grabs Mummy's hair and jerks her head up and there's this knife and he hurts Mommy with it and her blood gets all over us and Thally screams and he grabs her and hurts her and I scream and I try to get away, but the blankets get wrapped round my legs and I try to kick them away and he grabs me and hurts me. . . ." He shuddered, started swaying again, his eyes squeezed shut.

Give me your hands, Belovéd, lean into me and let me comfort you. Come to me, Belovéd, come.

Arms curled about the geode, head on the table, Hibayal shuddered with pleasure as the Glow moved over him and through him, cleansing away the poisons of the dream, relaxing tensions, feeding him strength.

Belovéd, behold. The light hovered, thickened, flowed away, leaving a dark, dusty, cobwebbed bottle behind, repeated the process till a half-dozen bottles were lined up across the table, three on each side of the geode. *It is brandy, Belovéd, the finest Santakean vintage, finer than all the rest because it has my essence warming it.*

"I see, O Glory. What is the purpose?"

To make brothers for you, Belovéd. Midsummer nears and brings the Guild Gather; when the Guild Masters meet, their Aides meet, too, do they not? And is it not your turn on the cycle to host the Aide Dinner on the next to the last day of the Gather?

"That is so. It is a great expense, but necessary."

Money well spent, Belovéd. When they leave you, they will be true brothers. Soul-sharers. You'll never be alone again. Or hurt, my Heart.

"What do I do?"

Take the brandy to the Guild Hall, tell them a grateful client gave it to you as a bonus that you're passing on for their pleasure, make sure each one has some, at least a sip. And beyond that time, when the Wandermonks come from Fundalakoda to collect the documents for the Archives, give a sip to each of them. And take what you wish to warm yourself. As I have said, Belovéd, the brandy has ME in its heart. All who drink of it will be your brothers, your true brothers, not of the flesh, but of the soul.

11. Sea Changes

"I know about you, Healer. You take one step t'ard me or start any chantin' business and you lose a knee. I c'n shoot the left leg off a gnat and this trigger's filed, so mind yourself."

A small, weasely man with a ragged kerchief tied across his nose and mouth opened the door and hastily stepped back out of reach, sliding along the wall until he was more than an arm's reach behind her, his gun steady on her. The other hooded man left his doorway and two more followed him into the hall; he began backing away in the other direction, also watching her. The new pair moved quickly ahead, using the longgun stocks against any door that started to open.

The concierge was gone from his chair, the paper dropped in a crumpled heap beside it, and the small lobby was deserted. Serroi expected their captors to point her outside, but they didn't. They opened a door beside the desk and started down another flight of stairs.

The basement was a huge vaulted cavern extending under the whole length of the Inn, with bins and racks of staples and wine, pyramids of barrels, with piles of broken furniture and other discards; it was cold and dusty, surprisingly dry, lit by long slanting light tunnels and mirrors. Her captors moved confidently through the debris and the stores, never losing control of her, keeping the sandwich intact. She could sense Honeydew flying in the shadows overhead a few paces behind them; it was a comforting presence. The sprite might be tiny and fragile, but her heart was without measure and her value proven many times over.

"Stop, Healer. Stand there till I tell you to move. And don't y' even breathe hard. Get the door open, Munt."

They were being very cautious. Serroi turned her head slowly, looked over her shoulder at the speaker. The little man tensed, his gun shifting to a point only a few inches from her hip. She turned back.

Two of the men were hauling open a heavy iron door. As soon as the gap was wide enough, all but the Weasel slipped inside; for a short while she could hear their feet on a metal ladder then silence.

"After them, Healer. Move slow and careful."

The room behind the door was no larger than a cramped closet, a square hole in the floor, light coming from below showing her the worn, black iron rungs of a ladder. There was an impatient shout from outside. She shrugged, lowered herself into the hole, and began climbing down.

>><<

Honeydew hovered up in the support beams; several times she'd started to swoop for the door, but the light was too bright, those hooded men too alert, especially the one with the gun on Serroi.

As the Weasel followed Serroi, Honeydew swooped down . . . and squealed with terror, driving her wings hard to carry her back as the massive door slammed shut, so close to crushing her that she went into something like blind panic and didn't stop her retreat until she was sitting on a massive beam, sweating dew from every inch of her tiny body, too devastated to do more than shake and whimper.

>><<

The wound in his thigh crudely bandaged, hands tied behind him, led along by a choke rope about his neck, Hedivy limped down the dank, stinking tunnel, the uneven footing and the dim light from the lantern carried by the lead man making it difficult to do anything but concentrate on staying on his feet. The first shock had worn off long ago and the wound was throbbing, his knee shaking and threatening to fold under him. He forced himself on because he knew if he went down, they'd simply cut his throat and leave him where he fell.

It was the Enemy doing this. It had to be. Shimzely wasn't that kind of place, people didn't disappear down holes; there might be bodies left in the streets from fights and muggings, but that was individual enterprise, nothing to do with the government. There was no central government, too many centers of power balancing each other. That being so, why was he still alive? Questioning? Bait to catch Serroi? There were too many unknowns. Whenever they got to where they were going, he'd probably get some answers. Not something to look forward to.

After a wearisome time of turning and twisting through the old sewers, they pushed him against an iron ladder, looped a rope under his arms and hauled him into the daylight once more.

He emerged from a tumbledown shack and found himself on a small island in the Ixapho Swamp south of Bokivada. A large outrigger was pulled up on the reedy beach and a group of figures stood by a bow carved into a chain of fleshy floral shapes, black robes covering them wrist to ankle, cowls pulled forward to hide their faces. One of them came a few steps forward, stood with his arms folded, hands hidden in his sleeves, waiting for Hedivy and his captors to reach him.

No words were spoken. The robed shape passed over a heavy purse, the Bokivaders pushed Hedivy toward him and left with a haste that sent a chill down Hedivy's spine. He looked around, but with bound hands and a leg that was barely supporting him, there wasn't much he could do. He composed himself as the small figures closed around him and began tugging him toward the outrigger.

>><<

Adlayr burst into the cellar, ran across it. *HONEY, WHERE ARE YOU!*

She pushed off the beam, spread her wings and glided down to him, landing on his shoulder, scrambling to his neck, pressing herself against it. Honeydew almost got caught in the door, Adlee, Honeydew almost got crushed and mangled.

Ei vai, Honey, you didn't, it's all right. What door?

The black iron thing. She wriggled around, still huddling as close to his neck as she could, her tiny hands closed on his hair. There. Straight ahead. In the wall. The bagheads, they take Serree inside and go down.

Hang on, Honey. He trotted the short distance to the wall, found the hole for the latch chain, but no chain; he touched the hole, ran his hand along the hairline crack between the door and the jamb. Not even room for a needle, iron on both sides. He let out the breath he was holding. *Can you feel her, Honey? I can't, but your range is longer than mine.*

Honeydew's trembling had stopped and she'd unplastered herself from his neck, but she held onto his collar and made no attempt to take to the air again. She drew herself into a dense little knot and focused.

With a small spitting sound, she kicked her feet out, shook her hair into a wild tangle. Honeydew do. She going away and away.

Ei vai, let's collect the gear and see if we can follow her.

The huge black trax flew through the wispy clouds above Bokivada, weaving back and forth about a line that trended southeast until Honeydew squeaked with distress.

What?

Gone! Serree is not there. Honeydew lose our Serree.

Dead?

Honeydew don't think so. Like they bang Serree on the head. But not really, no hurt.

Then we're going to have to do this another way. Do you think you'd know at least some of those men if you saw them again?

Honeydew wriggled on his back, her hands tickling his

neckhair. Baaaad men. Honeydew smell them, 'f Honeydew get close enough. Mmmm, true, Honeydew can do.

Honeydew better do. It's about the only chance we've got. The black furred wings shifted and the trax swept in a long curve, heading back for the Inn.

Hedivy lay in the bottom of the outrigger, rolled in canvas, icy sea water knifing over the sides and pelting him in his exposed face and gradually soaking into the canvas. At first he was chilled beyond anything he could remember, even on the coldest mornings when his father booted him from bed and sent him to fetch the vul in for milking, then a fever took him and he was mumbling through delirium, shivering, burning, aching with a dull pain that raked even to the inside of his bones.

There was darkness, light burning in his eyes, darkness again, flickering from one to the other . . . somewhere in there his head was lifted, foul tasting liquid hot enough to burn his gums poured into his mouth, he vomited it out, more was poured in, less of it this time, he kept that down and sank into a nightmare sleep that went on and on. . . .

In a thin fog that clung to the water and barely reached past the sides, the outrigger slid past a line of barrier islands that were little more than sandspits with some grass and brush on higher points, into a south facing bay where there was almost no swell. The smell of rotten vegetation permeated that mist and reached through Hedivy's delirium, bringing him into semi-awareness.

His leg throbbed to the beat of the rowers' oars, his head to the slatting of the limp sail against the mast. He was lying in his own stink, the canvas still rolled about him, soggy, clinging to him like a second skin. He drew his tongue along cracked lips and tried to lift his head, but he was too weak and the effort sent him spiraling into darkness.

He woke in a green twilight, swaying almost as if he were back in the boat. After drifting a while, he under-

stood he was in a rope cradle slung beneath a pole; he
could see the padded yokes fitting over the shoulders of
two men a few spans from his feet and assumed there
were two more behind him. They were walking with a curious hip-hop that kept the pole steady but took them
from root to root in the dank twilight under immense trees
dripping with graybeard and vines. He wondered vaguely
where they were taking him, but hadn't the strength to
hold onto the thought and sank back into the darkness
that had swallowed him before.

>><<

Serroi woke in a cage rocking and rattling in the back
of a stake-wagon drawn by two large vezen, local beasts
that looked like cousins to the draft orsk in Cadander. The
cage was tied down with thick ropes so it wouldn't topple
over, but they did little to stop the grinding, squealing,
and creaking as it twisted and slid over the planks of the
wagon bed, bounced with bumps and potholes in the road,
jolting her about, knocking her against the bars. She had
bruises developing along her arms and legs, green-black
patches under her skin, sore places in her head and shoulders that told her just how much of this rough treatment
she'd undergone while she was still unconscious from
that cloud of powder one of her captors had puffed at her.

Serroi caught hold of a bar and levered herself up.

All she could see of the driver was a shapeless lump
huddled in a heavy canvas cloak, its hood pulled forward.
The cart was alone in an empty land, moving down a road
of beaten white dirt, rutted and narrow, that meandered
around rocky knolls, patches of low, gnarled brush, sparse
grass rustling, dry, yellow spotted with brown, seed pods
with white whiskers.

"Driver! What's happening? Where you taking me?"

No response.

She considered yelling more, kicking the bars, rocking
the cage, creating such a fuss that the driver would have
to do something, but she didn't like fuss and there was a
fair chance the driver had more of that sleep-dust. She

eased down, wedged herself in a corner of the cage to minimize the jarring, and began puzzling over what had happened. Why was the Fetch doing this? What did It want? What was going to happen to her?

After a while the dust, the jolting, the headache from the drug, and the uncertainty wearied her so much she closed her eyes and slept.

>><<

Treshteny felt bathed in sound, the water slapping gently against the piles and the ship sides, the patter of voices from fishermen working on nets, their women gutting fish and hanging them on smoking racks, the creaks and groans of the boats. The smells of the seashore were rich and strong; she reveled in them and in the stability the blindfold gave her. Such a simple thing but no one had thought of it before, not even her.

She missed the Horse as horse; the silent manshape walking beside her frightened her a little—perhaps because for most of her life she'd lived in a world of women. Men had always represented danger and stress, even her own twin brother. Her mind shied away from Treshtal and his life/non-life; thinking about him disturbed her.

The boat was a small one, a yawl steeped with the stink of dead fish. They'd have to live and sleep on deck, sheltered only by a kind of canvas hutch the owner had improvised for them, but there wasn't much choice. Treshteny let Doby lead her into the hutch. She settled on a folded blanket, smiled at the boy she couldn't see. "Thank you."

"Nata, Jam'. An'thing else?"

His voice was still rusty, but he was talking more easily every day; the blindfold wasn't only a help to her, it brought out a tenderness in the boy that grief had buried before this.

"Hmm. I've never seen a ship set sail into an ocean, so why don't you go watch everything that happens and tell me about it."

"Yeh, Jam'." He rushed out.

She heard the excitement in his voice and smiled again. Yela'o's horns jabbed into her arm.

She cuddled him. "Jealous? Bébé, don't be that way. No one can take my son's place." She felt him relax against her. "That's good, luv. It's going to be a hard time, these next days; we're going to be cold and uncomfortable, dirty and bored before we reach Shinka-on-the-Neck. But this is the only way, my bébé. South and south we go."

12. Waiting for the War to Start

The Pastora Harep turned the lampframe in his hands, inspecting the flow of the grain, running his thumb over the joints. He took up each of the three frames, inspected them with the same intensity, set them back on the bench. "It is good work." The yellow grew thicker in his eyes. "If you were a true man of Glory, you would give your work for the good of your soul."

"I am a man with a family to feed, Pastora."

Harep glanced out the window. "Two sons. And your wife seems to be a woman of great energy. That is your family, isn't it?"

Greygen rolled his chair to the window, smiled at the boys coming through the arch into the court, Sansilly following them, blown through on winds of laughter. "Yes."

Sansilly came bustling in, kissed his cheek. "I saw Ol' Longnose leaving. Did he actually pay for the frames?"

"Didn't want to, but he did. And ordered half a dozen more."

"What about the wood? Where we gonna get it?"

"He'll send it from the temple stores, knock off half the price."

"Saaaa! Into his pocket."

"Give him this, I don't think so. Taken."

She shivered. "I hate being round them. It's like they dead but don' know it."

He took down the box he'd clamped early yesterday. "Zdra, how'd it go?"

Sansilly crossed to the window, leaned her elbows on

the sill where she could see the court and be sure there
was no one in listening range, shook her hair loose, and
looked back at Greygen. "The meetin' went fine, tell you
later what we decided." She wrinkled her nose. "Zdra, it's
cover, but washin' sprotish sheets an't the sweetest way t'
pass a mornin'." She winked at him. "I told y' no one
looks close at women doin' dirt work like that." A sigh,
a glance out the window. "There's another charnel house,
down south of Calanda, on the way to where the army
was. Thing is, there was a finger with a birthmark on it.
A boy's finger. It was Bakory who found it when she
went down to where she fishes, wasn't hardly light yet,
but she smelled the place and she went and looked. The
finger was right by the door, she wouldna noticed, 'cept
she sneezed right then, you know Bakory's sneezes, her
foot knocked the finger and it went rollin' away outside. Said she nearly lost last year's breakfast lookin' at
it. Zdra, she's a friend of Jasny's and she recognized it.
Jasny's son. They all thought he'd run away, but the Eat-
ers got him. Zhalazhala, Bakory came to the clinic and
she told us and we all went to see Jasny, almost had to
tie . . ." She broke off and leaned farther out the window,
"Pusnall, what you think you doin'? Take your proggin'
hands off my boy."

She pulled back in, her face red with anger, ran across
the workroom, and out the door.

By the time the front door slammed, Greygen was at
the window, his fingers digging into the sill as he watched
the Purger shaking Mel, slapping his face. Noddy was
curled up on the pavement, whimpering and clutching his
middle. Staying in the chair was the hardest thing
Greygen could remember doing, but he did it; white and
sweating, his teeth grinding together, knees jammed
against the wall, he stayed where he was.

Sansilly flung her solid body into the Purger, almost
knocking him off his feet, clawed fingers going for his
eyes, missing but digging furrows into his cheek. She
struck again, screaming and cursing him.

Women hung out the upper story windows shouting,
"Shame shame, leave the boys alone." Others came hurrying from doors all around the court, shouting the same

thing. Some picked up Noddy, handed him through the window to Greygen, some caught hold of Mel and marched him through the Lestar door, others separated Sansilly from Pusnall, pushed the Purger out through the court arch, hustled Sansilly away, patting her, making soothing sounds,

As soon as she was through the door, they vanished back into their own homes.

Greygen rocked Noddy, the small body shuddering against him as the boy cried himself to sleep. He looked up as Sansilly came into the workroom. "You goin' to have a black eye, Sansy."

She giggled, pressed her hand to her eye. " 'Twill be worth it, Grega. Did you see his face when the women came?"

Greygen grimaced. "I saw trouble, that's what I saw." He freed a hand, scraped the sweat from his face. "Don't you ever do that again, Sans. Don't you ever. I near had a stroke."

She came around behind him, cradled his head between her breasts and stroked his temples. "Beda beda, micha mine, don' think 'bout it any more. It's over, gone away. . . ."

A while later she smoothed her hand over his hair, then came around. "Can you turn Noddy without waking him? I want to look at his middle."

"Mel! You get in here, I want to know what happened and I want to know now."

"Aaah, Mum."

"I mean it. Your father and I are waiting." She glanced at her younger son curled up in Greygen's lap sliding back into sleep, an herb plaster on his stomach where he'd been kicked. "Greg, you want to put him down?"

"Nik, he's fine. Sansy, the way things are . . ." He broke off as the door opened.

Mel came reluctantly into the room, looked from Greygen to Sansilly. "It wasn't my fault," he burst out.

Sansilly sniffed. "So tell me."

"Sta-sta, we were playing kick-ball, Noddy 'n me, you SAID we could till supper."

"That I did. Go on."

"Sta-sta, there we was, playin' nice, not makin' too much noise, you know we wasn't, Mum. Or you woulda yelled at us. And Ol' Purger he come through the arch and he catch hold m' arm and he pull me around and he start mutterin' at me, wants to know who been in the house and all kinds of stuff I dunno and he says I shouldna sass m' elders, but I WASN'T, Mum, he don't got no business askin' me that kinda stuff and I told 'm that and he slap me and Noddy kicks him and he kicks Noddy and I start yellin' and he shakes me and you look out the window, and that's what happened."

Sansilly smiled at him, tapped a finger against his head. "You right, Mely, wasn't all your fault. What you do now," she nodded at the sleeping boy in Greygen's arms, "you teach Noddy to duck for cover when there's trouble round. And you, my big Mel, you're the oldest, it's up to you to keep your eyes open and spot that trouble. You un'stand?"

He nodded.

"Prak. So you take Noddy from y' da and you take y' bath and do your homework and I'll be in with supper in a little."

Sansilly went back to the window, checked the court, turned to Greygen. "Grega, we have to send them North. After. . . ."

"Yes." He smiled wearily. "One thing come of this business, we got a good excuse for 't."

"Another stinkin' cover. Zdra, never mind. How soon?"

"With the Web pulled apart like it is, I don't know. After dark I'll see if I can get hold of Lisken, find out what's moving. Pull the shutters, Milachika. I'm too shaky to work anymore."

>><<

Rain dripping melancholy about him, Heslin sat in an improvised shelter making notes in a bound book as he listened to reports coming in from his spotters.

". . . count five hundred Taken in the second lot. Walking along steady, a herd a sheep'd have more expressions on their faces. I'd say they're making about seven, eight stades a day. Carrying packs, a longgun, belt knife, coil of rope. Two supply wagons, double orsk hitch on each. Twenty macain being herded with them, riders not Taken, three of 'em. Chovan. Make Nov's thugs look like schoolkids. Here's a thought. If Nov's getting recruits from the chovan, Osk better have a look to his backside. That's all I got now. Go."

"You still clear? Go."

"Even the chovan don't look antsy. No one's sniffing around my tree or even looking in my direction. I'll be moving on in a few minutes, get set up again in the morning. Go."

"Watch for strays. They're getting close to the border, there'll be noses sniffing around, looking to get Nov's reward. Out." He switched channels. "Spider seven. Go."

"The fourth barge string passed me ten minutes ago, heading north, food, horses and men. Three barges. Bezhvali this time, from the clothing and the gear I can see, so Ker is being squeezed and lying down under it, covering his backside most likely. I have counted around twenty men per barge, not including the bargeveks. Five horses a barge. There are some bales on the decks, fodder for the horses, a few sacks, lumpy, I would venture they contain tubers, bremba or kedlak. I do not know what is in the hold, but all three barges are riding low. Go."

Heslin frowned, flipped back a page, drew his finger down the notes written there. "Last report was the second string of barges. You skip a number or did we miss one? Go."

"It was not possible to talk at that moment, there was a file of men riding through the grove. No real problem, they were not looking for eyes in the sky. Chovan, armed to the teeth . . . hum . . . don't like that phrase, used to tell my students it was a failure of the imagination to fall back on such worn out expressions, but it gets the job done. Twenty-seven chovan, armed as described, mounted on racing macain which I have no doubt they stole. The chovan and the third barge string went by about an hour after sunup, Zemyadel farmboys, perhaps a hundred in sum, stores stowed on deck and below. The barges were also riding very low, so their holds must have been nearly full. Spider two should be able to give you a better accounting of just what's there when she views the unloading. How much longer do you want me here? Go."

Heslin laid his stylo down, gazed past the canvas front drop into the rain dripping steadily down. "Finish out tomorrow and the next day, then come north and join Spider two. The two of you touch home with Spider one, feed us what's happening in the cities. Questions? Go."

"I hear and obey, O mighty Valk. Out."

Heslin chuckled, set the com down and sat a moment, hunched over, the heels of his hands pressed against his eyes. That was the last of the reports, for the moment anyway. He'd been listening for nearly three hours as the spotters sent him what they were seeing, now he had to organize it into a coherent report to OskHold. And that brought K'vestmilly Vos to mind when he'd rather avoid thinking about her. He remembered his jealous words to Serroi, calling her Hern's grand passion. She'd laughed at him, but he understood old Hern better now. *We Heslins seem to keep coming up with them, these quirky, driven women who get a hold on you that even their indifference won't pry loose.*

He scrubbed at his face, tore a page from the book, leafed back to the morning's notes, and began writing.

>><<

"Chovan." Zarcadorn Pan Osk cleared his throat, spat into his cup and pushed it away. "Losyk, the miners, how many are still out?"

In the drafty meeting hall the tapestries blew in and out of lamplight, throwing shadows over the faces of the silent folk standing against the wall, watching the men and women seated at the table, listening to what was being said. Tingajil sat in a pool of light from one of the lamps, drawing soft, unobtrusive sounds from the strings of her lute. Vyzharnos stood beside her, his hand on her shoulder.

Kuznad Losyk the Mine Manager was a broad, square man with blue eyes glaring from a mass of face and head hair, curling hair like black moss, even his beard was a nest of knots as stubborn as his knotted fists. He cleared his throat, picked up silver rimmed spectacles, and curled the temple pieces over his ears. "We've been shutting the outliers first." Each of the names brought a thump of his spatulate middle finger on the table. "Harn Omota, Harn Melky, Harn Lavit, Hel Pract, Hel Zesla, Hel Podlah, Hel Helny." He coughed, looked up. "Shut down, tools and ore, heavy equipment, that sort of thing, put down mine, pit, gates locked, supporting farms cleaned out, everything useful hauled in, the folk settled with relatives and in the halls, it's crowded, but we're not getting complaints, not yet." He squinted at the paper. "Word's been sent to Harns Snehov, Ramvy, Spalt and Oddany, Hels Tesset, Cluna, Douft, Dulass and Devchah, that the Redits should close them down and bring their people in, with as much food as they can haul and any canvas that's around to help with shelter." He sat back, folded his hands over his small hard paunch. "Be in, all of 'em, by tomorrow week."

K'vestmilly Vos smoothed her forefinger along the side of the Mask as she looked from face to face along the table. Valiva Zarcadorn's wife, Speaker for women, hard to read because she didn't say much, but she seemed reasonably neutral. Chestno Dabyn, the head Judge—he'd resented her from the beginning. Spodrah Najit, Speaker for the farmers. Half a dozen district reps whose names she could dredge up if she had to. She didn't have to have the Healer's senses to feel the anger and resentment in these Osklanders, some of it focusing on the meie standing silent in the shadow behind her, but she wasn't quite ready to call them on it, or lay any stress on the idea that she needed a bodyguard in the House of Osk. She turned to the man seated at her left. "Vedouce," she said. "Your dispositions."

"Five raskas, sixty men each, deployed along the border, each of them half miners, half gritzer veterans; three of them will be taking care of the raiders, two held in mobile reserve with the supply wagons and the best of the

Osk riders. We have nine hundred thirty-seven semi-
trained men with veteran leaders on the training field. We
can add three extra men to each navsta up to twenty five
total without seriously distorting the training and we'll
need them." He looked at the closely written pages on the
table in front of him. "Unless unforeseen events pre-
clude." He looked up, smiled, a wry twist to his mouth.
"Unforeseen events always appear. We simply have to
plan with what we know and hope to ride out the storm."
He tapped his thumb on the papers. "At the moment I intend to rotate newly trained navstas into the raskas at the
border, bring back the seasoned fighters, and use them to
whip the new men into shape. We cannot stop Nov's army
with the men we have now, mmh, I'll elaborate on that
later, but we can harry them, force them to expend supplies and men." He turned over the top page, glanced
through the figures on the second.

"According to the Spiders, of the two thousand men in
his main army, two-thirds of them Taken foot-soldiers, the
rest his own men and recruits he's drawn in from the
Zemyadel and Halland. These last will be in the raider
bands, killing and burning, tough men, good fighters,
maybe not so good at planning. With the coms and the
Spiders spotting for us, we should be able to move supe-
rior forces against those bands and take out most of them.
It will be a bloody mess and worse destruction than you
can imagine, but we can't stop that."

He turned over the page. "Following one day behind
the main army comes the first reserve. Five hundred foot,
mostly Taken. One day behind them, a second reserve,
two hundred foot. Both sets with non-Taken herders, supply wagons, and spare mounts. Beyond that, he has most
of Cadander—always excepting the Harozh—to call on.
Barges on the river bringing food, mounts, supplies." Another page. "Spider seven has been watching and reporting for the past nine days; in that time, he's seen between
two and five barge strings a day moving upriver, average
string, three barges. Spider two reports barges also arriv-
ing up the Red Dan from Tuku-kul with ammunition,
mercenaries, a file of Sleykyn assassins. These last
haven't left Dander yet, but once they're in the field,

they're deadly fighters. They work alone, not as part of an army and according to Heslin, if you want to stop them, you've got a choice, a sniper with a longgun, good enough to make a head shot at maximum range, or a navsta you can afford to decimate, and I do mean decimate. Of those twenty men you'd be lucky to get ten back alive, I don't say whole. The new Web in Dander is watching them, there are plans to deal with at least some of them, but neither the Web nor Heslin are all that sanguine about success. We believe Nov means to set them at three things. The coms, the Marn and you, Osk. Fortunately, we have the meie Zasya Myers on watch here; the meien have dealt successfully with Sleykyn for centuries, so that's a worry we can defer. Osk, we need to get your miners into training as soon as possible; we haven't supplies for a siege, so we'll have to meet Nov in the field, try to cut them down, get behind them, and break their supply lines. It will help a great deal if we can divert their supplies to us, but you understand that in no way changes the situation. We can't wear a long war." He flipped the papers back, squared the pile. "That is the situation, O Marn."

"And Nov himself?"

"He's still in the Pevranamist, but the word from the source is that he will be leaving to join the army within the next three days; we suspect the Sleykyn will be leaving then, one at least as his bodyguard."

"Is there any chance of killing him?"

"Heslin and the Web are dealing with that. If it's possible they'll do it; if not, they'll let us know."

"Prak." Leaning forward, fingers laced on the shining wood, she looked down the long table. "I see several unhappy faces. Is anyone here under the illusion that Nov wouldn't march on you if I weren't here? Zdra zdra, I'm sure there are several of you without the courage to say it before the Mask." She pushed back the chair and stood. "Pan Osk, Vedouce and I will leave you and yours. I make this offer. We will withdraw from Oskland and leave you free to make peace with Nov if you so desire. I strongly suggest you talk to those who've fled Dander and Calanda before you make a final decision. Ask

Tingajil what happened in her family, why she had to
leave. Ask Vyzharnos Oram about the patch over his eye.
Ask Zatko of the guards. Ask Zisk the scissors grinder.
Ask any of those who were driven from their homes and
their family why they left."

Behind the Mask she pinched her lips together, fighting
back the anger that threatened to erupt in words that
would make the situation irretrievable. A deep breath, her
voice steadied, she added, "If you decide we should
leave, the weapons and stores we brought with us will go
with us." She beckoned to Vedouce and Zasya Myers and
swept from the room, leaving a loud silence behind.

Vedouce stood by the window as K'vestmilly had the
day Heslin announced his intention of leaving. She grimaced, looked away. "What do you think?"

"You took a chance."

"Did I have a choice?"

"Nik. That poison festering behind us would kill us
faster than Nov." He leaned against the wall; the gray was
thicker in his brown hair and the wrinkles from nose to
mouth had deepened to ravines. "They'll go with us.
They have no more choice than you had, though they
weren't willing to face that."

K'vestmilly sighed. "Until I rubbed their noses in it.
Can we hold out till winter? It isn't that far off."

"I don't know. That's the truth, Marn."

13. Serpents Dancing

The Weaver's Hall was filled with shadows and silence. Chaya sat on the floor by her loom, using the bench as a table while she tried to work out a pattern for the damask she wanted to start on her home loom. If she went home, she'd have cousins and neighbors dropping by to bring her little gifts and stay to talk endlessly; it was kind of them, but by the time the last one left, all she had strength to do was clean house and go to bed. Her honey month would be finished next week and life would go back to its ordinary round, but she wanted to be ready to set up, so she'd have a length of fine cloth for the Midsummer Weavers Fair in Mokadumise.

She had dozens of sketches in her notebook, flower forms, leaf forms, crystals, and anything that caught her attention when she had a pencil in her hand and a bit of paper—but nothing sparked when she looked at them. She was about to give up and go home, when the light strengthened and changed quality in the Hall and a ripple of harp notes cascaded around her.

She swung round.

At the end of the aisle between the looms a fuzzy oval of pale golden light shimmered above the dusty floor. As Chaya watched, a figure formed within the light, a woman seated with a harp. She wore a leather skirt that brushed against bare feet, a leather jacket with long fine fringes along the sleeves, fringes that swayed as her arms moved, her short strong fingers plucking the strings of the harp, a tune that Chaya had not heard before.

Into the shimmer of the light, the Hall snakes came and

other serpents, wild ones from the fields, until there were half a hundred of them swaying to the music.

They rose until they seemed to walk on the tips of their tails, wove round each other, twisting and untwisting in pairs with an urgency that left no doubt what was happening there.

The light dimmed and vanished, only moon and lamplight left in the hall.

The music faded with the light.

The serpents uncoupled and slid away.

Chaya sat without moving for several moments, then started sketching furiously.

>><<

The woman ran from the house, stood in the middle of the road waving her arms.

The house was a hovel, the oiled and scraped skins in the windows cracked and dry, the thatch so old even the roof rats had deserted it. It was out by itself, the village ahead too far down the road for the outlying buildings to show over the hedgerows. It had a garden to one side, a few wilting plants in furrows scratched in the hard, yellow-white soil. In a small shaky corral a cow stood nosing at straw in a manger, now and then licking at the grains of corn left on the bottom.

"Sekhaya Kawin, bless the Maiden for sending you by right now. There's a girl in here trying to have a baby and I don't know how to help her."

"Belitha, calm down." Sekhaya reached back of the seat, hauled her satchel from its cubby. "Lavan, take Joma to water and feed him something. We might be here a while." She kicked the steps out, came down from the wagon. "Tell me. Background first, then the signs. Snap, snap, you know what I need."

The midwife Belitha walked beside her as she headed for the house. "Name's Manzi, she doesn't know family, clan or totem, at least she's never said. Forest woman, I think. Never said that either. Just turned up one day and took to living out here. Poverty and general gormlessness. Scandal. Every man in the village has had a go at her, no telling who the father was of this one. It's not the first, but the others all died after a few hours, she buried them back of the house, knew enough to do that. Never a word to me or any woman in the village. I got a note left on my door yesterday morning, backhand writing, saying she was pretty bad off and would I go take a look. I suppose I could track him down, but I'd rather not. At least he had a little generosity, more than most of them. Very low energy when she's at her best, which she isn't, being half-starved. Irregular heart beat, both her and the baby. I've got her washed, brushed her hair, I've been keeping her warm, talking to her, trying to get her to work at . . ." She pushed the door open and the two women went inside.

Lavan unhitched Sekhaya's Joma, led him and his own mount to the watering trough. He was irritated at having another wait before they moved south again; he'd been impatient for days, though he knew traveling with the Herbwoman was safer and certainly much pleasanter than going ahead alone. Good food and a warm welcome from the villages they passed through. Footpads and riding gangs keeping their distance, attacking an herbwoman had consequences none of them wanted to chance.

Singing as he worked, an under-the-breath monotone that Chaya teased him about, saying it was like the drone of a courting mosquito, he unsaddled his horse, began brushing him down, combing out the knots in his mane and tail, laughing as Alegay leaned into him and whuffled with pleasure as the steel toothed comb scratched along his nape.

After he fed them graincakes and tethered them in grass and weeds beside the house, he pumped more water, scooped some up into one of Sekhaya's tubs, stripped and began scrubbing himself clean, washing away the effluvia from the day's riding. He worked soap into his hair and travel beard, sighing with pleasure not unlike Alegay's as he dug at his own scalp, then dumped a bucket of water over his head.

Dressed in his worn camp clothes, sandals on his feet, his boots upended over corral posts, he strolled around the house. The Forest was a dark line against the eastern horizon. He glanced at it, shuddered, and turned corners until he had that tumble-down building between him and the darkness.

He drew water and filled the washtub, set out towels and soap for Sekhaya, collected his blankets and groundsheet from the caravan, spread them out, and settled himself to doze away the hours until she'd be ready to move on.

>><<

It was late, near dawn, before the two women emerged from the hovel. Sekhaya stretched, moved across to the trough where Lavan had left her a tub of water, soap, and a towel. She glanced at the dark form stretched out by her caravan, smiled affectionately at him as she dipped the corner of the towel in the water and began scrubbing her hands and arms. "He can be irritating, but he's a good lad."

Belitha spread soap over her hand. "Not exactly a lad. Handsome man in spite of those whiskers. Who is he?"

"Journeyman silversmith pledged to my name-child. His Master died and he's hunting a new one. Bela, you might as well go home, you've got your family to take care of. I'll sit the day with this one; she'll live, I think. The baby won't. And if she keeps this up, next time. . . ." She shrugged. "Is there anything you can do?"

"The Dolman won't listen or do anything. Afraid of scandal. Even if I tell him what the men are doing is murdering her." She rubbed her arms dry, gave the towel back to Sekhaya. "I'll put the word around; it might help." She nodded to Sekhaya, then went trudging off into the darkness.

Sekhaya went back into the hovel, bent over the pallet. In the faint light from the nightlight she'd hung beside the window, the girl's face had a pearly quality; she might even have been pretty with a little more flesh on her bones and some animation. She lay on her back with her eyes closed, her shift lifting slightly with each long slow breath. The baby lay beside her, swaddled in clean clothes that Belitha had brought with her, a tiny, frail boy, barely alive. Sekhaya lifted him gently; he was so fragile even a breath would bruise him. She cooed to him, tried to give him a little warmth and love for the short time he'd be around to feel it, but there was no response.

She held him until he died.

When she took him outside to bury him beside the others, she was startled at how foggy it'd grown in the short time she'd been inside. This was the bottom of her Round and on the edge of the Drylands; even with the Forest as near as it was, the air was seldom damp enough for mist, let alone a blinder like this one where a hand outstretched was lost to sight. She sighed, got a better grip on the baby's body and knelt, groping for the spade she'd seen thrown down by the pitiful garden.

A cascade of harp notes came like drops of crystal water, the fog began to glow, the glow to open like an oval door. In the oval a woman sat with a harp, a leather skirt brushing bare feet, a leather jacket with long fine fringes along the sleeve that swayed as her arm moved, and short strong fingers plucking the strings.

"Halisan!"

The woman smiled at her, eyes sinking into nests of laugh wrinkles, nostrils flaring. The cascade turned to a lively dance tune.

A form thickened from the fog, an immense serpent with a woman's head and torso. The lamia held out her hands. "Give the child to me," she said. Her voice was deep and soft, like wind late at night after a storm. "I will take him home."

Sekhaya glanced at the Harper.

The Halisan image nodded.

"First, tell me this. Why this child and not the others?"

"They are all with us, we left the mounds to give the outcast solace if she would take it."

"I see. Is there anything you can do for her?"

"I will take her home when her time comes."

Sekhaya got to her feet, put the small bundle into the lamia's arms, then stood watching as she melted into the fog. As the light dimmed, Sekhaya called, "Come see me when you can, Halisan. It's been too long since we talked."

She thought she saw the Harper nod, then the light was gone.

Sekhaya shook Lavan awake. "Get dressed," she said. "There's toast and cha by the fire. We won't be stopping in Hintshifam for anything, you can stock up for the Drylands in Shillafam."

Before he could respond, she faded into the fog. He crawled out of his blankets, ran his fingers through his hair and stumbled for the pump.

>><<

Halisan the Harper reprised the chorus until the laughter died then went on with the list song, celebrating the guilds at the dinner.

> *Ah the poor weaver, tangled in twine*
> *bent at the loom sunlight and moonshine*
> *numb bum and sore spine*
> *crossed eyes and nose whine*
> *tring ling a ling ling, ling a line line*
>
> *Ah the poor scrivener, tangled in law*
> *sipping his substance through a long straw*
> *whipsaw and crabclaw*
> *scapegoat and cat's paw*
> *tring ling a ling ling, ling a law law.*
>
> *Ah the poor scrivener, ling ling a law law. . . .*

She bowed to this year's host, the Aide to the Scrivener Guild, sat back, and began playing soft background music through the laughter and applause.

* * *

As the meal was winding to its close, Hibayal Bebek glanced down the line at the faces of the Guild Aides, listened to the noisy talk moving down and across the table. It was going very well and he was pleased. And the outcome of this evening pleased him even more. He beckoned to one the scrivener apprentices who were doing duty as servants for the evening. "Bring in the brandy and the glasses. You remember your instructions?"

"Yes, Kos Bebek."

When the apprentices were lined up behind the Aides, each with a bottle ready to pour, Bebek stood and clicked his fork against his water goblet. "As a fitting tribute to the work you've all done the past year, let me pass on a gift from a grateful trader, a case of Santakean brandy." He smiled at them, a more natural smile than the usual tight grimaces that he wore on his face. "I doubt there's one of you who's not heard of that. You have it now to oil your ears and get in a giving mood for the speeches you all know are coming." He gestured to the apprentice at his elbow, waited till the brandy was poured, a finger's width of dark amber fluid. He took the glass, tapped it with the nail of his forefinger to make the crystal ring. "To the slopes of Santak and the treasure they hold."

Much later, in his attic shrine, Hibayal Bebek sniffed and swallowed. "Miser'ble hubbugs, simp'r 'n mince, kiss arse, snigg'rin at me. 'A coom in an' they stop talkin', know wha' that means." He took another gulp of the brandy, drooling part of it from the corner of his mouth. "Sssso p'lite, al'aysss ssso p'lite. 'S insult. A wanna slice th' lyin' grins offa them, a wanna make 'em hurt."

The Glory shimmered above the geode. *Belovéd, they are nothing, they are dream and shadow. WE are the true alive, WE honor you, hold you in OUR arms. Grieve not, Belovéd. They will learn. WE will teach them when the time is ripe. Come, Belovéd, put out your hands, take ME, bathe in ME. You will dream, but only of what is to come.*

He stretched out trembling hands, touched the Glory,

moved into it, felt the terrible LOVE pour into him. Terrible and wonderful, warm as his mother's blood splashing over him.

Curled up on the mat before the low table, he eased into a deep sleep filled with dreams of might-have-been and will-be.

14. Hard Landings

Hedivy swam up from the monsters that had haunted his sleep and realized that the swaying had stopped. He was no longer in the rope cradle, but lying on a hard cot with an old woman bending over him, a slight figure with fine wispy white hair wound in smooth bands around her head; the lines in her face were shallow, but there were thousands of them, as if she'd pasted cobwebs on her skin. Her eyes were the faint blue of winter lake ice; they were serene, even detached, but there was an edgy amusement in them.

"You've been very ill," she said. "Don't try to move."

"Who are you? Where . . . ?"

"Ah, yes." She turned her head, and he saw for the first time that there was another woman standing a half step behind her, a much younger woman with an eerie, alien beauty. "One wishes, Makalaya," the older one murmured, "that they would surprise us sometime with a new sort of question when they wake."

"Kieli, you're confusing the poor man." The younger Makalaya moved closer, lay her cool hand a moment on Hedivy's brow. "The fever's gone, that's good, but he's still very weak. I think he should sleep."

"Not till we can get some tonic down him. He needs strengthening."

Itchy with impatience as the women talked above him, ignoring him, Hedivy tried to reach out and catch hold of the old woman, but he was too weak to lift his arm.

"Now now, lad, just you lie quiet. Makalaya, lift his head so I don't pour this down his neck. Drink this like

the good boy you are and I'll tell you all about us. That's
right. That's splendid. I know the taste is not all that nice,
but you'll feel better when you finish. The name you can
use for me is Kielin, it means Wisewoman, yes you do
know that, don't you. Clever man, you are. The name for
my companion is Makalaya which is tree spirit. We are
Halathi from the Forest and being held prisoner here by
the Qilimen, there are more of us, you'll meet them later.
Good, you've finished it all. Sleep now. We'll talk again
when you wake."

>><<

For half a day Serroi watched the dark line on the horizon grow higher and develop detail.

The driver stopped about an hour after noon, tossed
food and torn paper through the bars, used his shortgun to
motion her back, and filled a pannikin of water for her.
The black cowl was pulled forward to hide the man's
face, his hands were concealed in heavy black leather
gloves, the robe covered the rest of his body; all Serroi
could make out was that he was short and seemed stocky
rather than fat. He must have been boiling in all that
black, but he showed no sign of it.

As she had every day, Serroi folded her arms and
glared at the driver. When the water was poured and the
man moving off again, she said for the thousandth time,
"Where are you taking me? Why are you doing this? I am
a healwoman of the Biserica, you'll bring the wrath of
meien and gyes on your head if you don't release me."

As he had every day, the man ignored her, watered and
fed the team of vezen, took his own meal behind a bush
and stayed there for twenty minutes, then reappeared,
climbed onto the driver's seat, and started the wagon
moving again.

Serroi inspected the scraps of paper, but they were only
bits of newsprint from Bokivada and told her nothing.
She used them for the purpose they were given to her,
tossed the waste over the side of the wagon and devoted
the last of her water to cleaning her hands. Then she settled into a corner of the cage and dozed. The cage bars

were steel rods big around as her thumb, set close together, running through the steel top and bottom and welded in place. Her arms were thin, her hands small but they wouldn't fit between the rods and there was nothing useful within reach anyway. The small grate she'd been pushed through, unconscious, besides being padlocked, had a thin steel chain wound tightly about its edges, binding it in place so firmly she hadn't a hope of dislodging it. She could just touch the wire beneath the cage that bound the ends of the chain together after it passed around a steel hook, could feel the twists put in it by a pair of pliers, but the ends had been snipped down to the last twist and only results she got from her efforts at trying to work them loose were lacerated fingertips; the chain stayed taut, without enough give in it to let her try fatiguing the metal.

She arranged herself as comfortably as she could and watched the dry land changing gradually to pasturage with clumps of trees that grew more and more frequent. They'd been the only ones on this road since she'd wakened, but she began to wonder as the land grew lusher if they'd begin meeting others using it.

She wrinkled her nose, rubbed at the eyespot between her brows. *The human steambath up front hasn't made any mistakes so far. Wonder what he'd do about that?*

As if he'd read her thoughts, half an hour later the driver looped the reins around a cleat, turned. He had a large black bulb in one hand with a horn protruding from it. He squeezed and a familiar dust cloud shot out.

Serroi tried holding her breath but her nose tickled furiously, she sneezed—and was gone.

When she woke, the cage was covered with canvas pulled taut and tied to the stakes that lined the sides of the wagon. The back end fluttered out enough to let her see a portion of the road and show her it was still day, the front end hung flat against the cage. It was the first time the driver had left anything where she could reach it, but there didn't seem to be much she could do with it.

About an hour later, the driver began singing, a loud, raucous, and exceedingly scurrilous song. For a moment,

Serroi wondered if he were drunk, then she heard the clop of a horse's hooves and understood.

No matter how loudly she yelled for help, the driver's powerful, growling voice would cover hers.

Maybe. She sprang to her feet, waited until the rider was passing them, thrust her fingers through the bars and jabbed at the canvas, yelling for help as loudly as she could.

Whatever he heard, the rider just kept riding, the sound of his horse's hooves fading rapidly into the distance.

Serroi sighed, settled back in her corner. She'd called kamen to help her and nothing happened. Called to her children. They never came. Perhaps there were none here. She'd tried taking hold of the driver's mind and sending him to sleep, but he was too far from her and too alert. So all she could do was wait and try to remember her old training; no matter how tight things got, eventually there'd be an opening that would let her move.

The road started to darken. Must be near nightfall. She expected the driver to stop as he usually did about this time, but the wagon kept rattling on.

Leaves whispered around her, the air felt stiller and closer, the sound of the vezen's hooves changed, grew duller.

The wagon stopped. It shifted and creaked as the driver got down. He unhitched the vezen, led them off somewhere, came back, and began unroping the canvas.

As the cover slid off, there was an odd sound that rose and fell around the wagon, like a flock of birds twittering. As Serroi stood blinking in the faint starlight, she saw a ring of figures in the shadows under the trees around the small glade; they were murmuring and chirruping, pointing at her, swaying, some of them doing a sort of dance. The Shimzeys she'd seen so far had been shades of brown from milky kava to deep bronze, but these were like ghosts, hardly any color to them.

One of the taller, sturdier figures, a man in a tunic and trousers of unbleached muslin, broke free and came to meet the driver. Without speaking, the driver pointed to the front of the wagon, then drew his shortgun and held it ready. The pale man rummaged under the driver's seat, found a bolt cutter and started for the back of the cage.

The driver brought his gun up, waved Serroi to the far side of the cage and kept her pinned there while the pale man cut the chain and the padlock, unwound the chain, and slid the grate open. He stepped back and waited.

At the impatient jerk of the gun, Serroi went to her hands and knees and crawled through the opening. As she swung down from the back of the wagon, the pale man's hand snapped out, closed around her wrist, then slid away, leaving a paper strip sealed around it.

"I am Liqebemalah, shaman of the Halathi, my clan is Lamite, my totem the vula serpent." The pale man pressed his palms together, bowed over them.

"I am the Healer Serroi." She frowned at the white strip about her wrist, then at Liqebemalah. "I was brought here a prisoner; I want to know why."

Liqebemalah bowed again, spoke with the same grave formality. "I cannot tell you that, Healer, because I do not know why, only that we must keep you with us."

"Why?"

"I cannot speak of that here. You will be told later, I swear it on the head of the vula." He touched the segmented pendant in the center of his chest, a stylized, coiled serpent carved from some dark wood. "Come." He walked away.

Serroi raised her brows, then tried to turn. She couldn't move. She reached down to jerk the paper bracelet off. Her fingers slid off it as if it were glass; she tried again and again. Distracted by this, for a breath at least she didn't notice she was following Liqebemalah like a sheep on a leash.

She tried to break free, but her body wouldn't obey her. It was the oddest feeling, there was no pressure, there was no tugging at her, it was as if she willed that following even as she was fighting against it.

She looked back. The driver was throwing the canvas over the cage again, a squat, dark figure hard to separate from the night. The man hadn't said a single word the whole length of the drive and now that it was over, he was still silent and detached. *I don't know anything about him. I suppose I never will.*

She relaxed her fight against the shaman's leash and trotted behind Liqebemalah, her short legs making it hard to keep up. The Halathi were all around her, flitting among the trees, watching her and chattering among themselves, though not loudly enough for her to make out the words. They were a small people, with very fair skin, almost no color in them, with fine flowing hair ranging from a lemon yellow to the white of thistledown. They reminded her of Honeydew, though they had no wings and their bodies weren't translucent, but those shocks of fine, pale hair and the delicacy of their features were much like hers; they moved through the forest with a grace and ease that caught at her heart.

She looked up, caught glimpses of great arching limbs interlaced high over her head, moonlight filtering in woven streams through openings in the canopy. A small tan beast spread arms and legs, snapping open the membranes between them, and glided from one branch to another. Nightbirds she didn't know sang to the moons or each other; one glided down so close the fur on its wings brushed her cheek.

It's beautiful here. Peaceful. There's no way I can stay here. No way. . . . The paper band around her wrist burned her for an instant, then cooled again.

"Is everyone where you come from little and green?"

Serroi rubbed her thumb across her eyespot. "Nay. I'm a tribe of one."

The ring of Halathi girls giggled and poked at each other. The one who'd spoken the first time composed herself, and spoke again. "You didn't have a mother and father?"

Serroi winced. Even after all these years, it still hurt that her parents would have given her up to be killed as all misborn were if Ser Noris hadn't bought her first. "Yes, but they weren't like me. I was a sport and pinched off. Ahwu, that was a long time ago. What's your name? If you don't mind my asking. I don't know your rules."

The girls crowded together and whispered, the first

speaker getting vehement about her protests. She pushed the others away. "I am called Lele-isi, it means Flower-friend."

"It's a lovely name, Lele-isi. As beautiful as the place you live in." Her hand moved in an arc, taking in the giant trees and the delicate, almost colorless plants that grew around their roots.

"Aaaah." The sound passed round the arc of girls.

Lele-isi leaned forward. "You like it here?"

"Oh, I do. But I'll have to leave again. And nay, I don't mind you telling your elders that. I have promises to keep, and I will keep them." She put a light stress on *will* and felt the band nip her again.

Several of the older women brought her bowls of food and water; they shooed away the girls, smiling back over their shoulders at her to let her know it wasn't her that caused this, but the fact that it was dinnertime.

When she finished her meal, she sat with her back against an immense root, watching the camp resolve itself for the night. Sheets of gauzy material that looked about as strong as a spider's web were pegged down, then lifted into shape by poles that the Halathi seemed to have carried with them though she hadn't noticed them before. In minutes the campsite was cocooned with tents and most of the Halathi had vanished inside, except for a few of the elder women still cleaning up after the meal and half a dozen of the men seated around a fire apart from the others, passing a long pipe from hand to hand.

"Healer."

She turned her head, got to her feet when she saw it was one of the elder women.

She smiled shyly. "I have brought you some blankets. It will get cold toward morning."

She returned the smile. "Thank you, Mother."

"Ahwu, you are a courteous child. I'm sorry we have to do this. I can't talk about it, though I can say that we have no choice." She pointed to the circle of men. "They will explain. When it's time. Sleep well, Healer Serroi."

They walked deeper and deeper into the Forest, the number of Halathi staying fairly constant, the individuals and small groups that left being replaced by newcomers. Serroi couldn't tell what prompted any of this; she knew too little about this culture, couldn't read the unspoken signals.

On the fifteenth day they came to a small lake, with houses built on stilts above the water. Liqebemalah took her to a house set apart from the others, stopped at the catwalk leading to it. "This will be yours, Healer Serroi. You arc free to go where you want, do what you want. Food will be provided as you need it, and anything else you need that we can find for you. There is only one limit. You cannot go beyond one day's journey from the lake."

"Why?"

"Will you invite me in, Healer?"

She grimaced. "Be welcome in your own house, Liqebemalah."

"Walk before me, Healer. It is our custom that the host step across the threshold first."

The room was comfortable with bright rugs and fine white gauzy curtains veiling windows without glass. There were no chairs, only large bright cushions tossed onto the splitwood mat by a low table with a handthrown cha pot, two handleless cups and a plate of iced cakes. A thin trace of steam rose from the spout.

When they both were seated, Serroi filled the two cups and Liqebemalah murmured a blessing. Together they drank a formal sip.

Serroi set her cup down, rested her hands on her knees and fixed her eyes on the shaman.

"Yes. It is time," Liqebemalah said. "The Grand Moon . . . what do you call him?"

"The largest one? Nijilic TheDom."

"Ah. The Grand Moon nears full tonight. When it was full the time before, Qilimen came over the mountains into the Forest. They broke the bindings on a Sacred Place, fouled it in every way, and took those who dwelt within away from there. They took our Dreamers away from us, though they did not kill them or hurt them in any way. The trees know that. Our Dreamers are hostages somewhere in Qilifund and if we allow you to escape, they will die in ways I cannot twist my tongue around, though we were told in clear detail. You have told our daughters you have promises to keep. I say to you, Healer, you have nine lives in your holding and if you throw them down, their pain and their death is yours also." He rose. "Think on that, Serroi."

>><<

The burly man kicked at a cat and slammed his toe into the wall as the cat flashed away. He swore and limped on along Tavern Row, a jagged street that ran past the warehouses fronting the wharves.

Adlayr sat in a heap of rags by the steps leading into a tavern, a bottle beside him, his face blurred in a mask of stubble. Through half shut eyes he watched the man coming toward him. Wem Wozem, half-Shimza half whoknew, muscle for hire with a virulent hatred for cats.

For two weeks Adlayr and Honeydew had haunted the Row. Hidden in Adlayr's rags, the sprite sniffed about for the auras of the men who'd taken Serroi. In this time she'd found five she was sure of, with Wem as the leader of the pack. Adlayr had followed him for three days now, waiting for an opportunity to take him, but he was flush with money and never alone. Until tonight.

It was about an hour before sundown, the time most Bokivadans ate supper, so the street was empty except for strays like Adlayr, a whore or two drifting from tavern to tavern, and a few sailors starting early on a long wet night before they shipped out.

After Wem limped past, Adlayr gathered himself to follow him, relaxed again as he crossed the street and went into one of the taverns. He settled himself to wait, sipping at the water in the bottle.

Wem came out about an hour later with a woman on his arm and two men laughing loudly at the things he said; they moved down the street, went into another tavern. Adlayr shifted along the street, shifted again when they moved again, smiling when he saw the entourage was reduced to just the one woman.

Sometime around midnight, Wem staggered out alone. Adlayr flitted after him, followed him until a turn in the street cut them off from view. As Wem reached an alley between two dark storehouses, Adlayr closed in, brought his sap down hard before the man realized there was someone behind him.

Wem Wozen woke in dusty darkness, froze as he heard a large beast panting near by, and smelled cat. As his eyes cleared and grew accustomed to the dimness, he saw a black shape stretched out on the floor, saw eyes catching the little light from cobwebby windows high in the wall and flickering red at him. He scrambled backward, hitting the wall, but before he could claw himself up, the sicamar rose, leapt, knocked him over, and drew its wide rough tongue up the side of his face, ripping off skin as it passed. He fainted.

Adlayr pulled the slide on the dark lantern, turning the beam onto Wem's face. He emptied his bottle over Wem, bent down and pinched his earlobe, then stepped hastily back, gun in hand. "Stay where you are."

"Who you? Wha's . . ."

"You snatched a friend of mine. I want to know what you did with her."

"Do'n know what 'ch talkin' about." Wem's eyes were sliding from side to side, the whites glistening in the light from the lantern.

"You know. I'll ask again in a minute. I won't ask a third time, there won't be enough left of you to answer." He shifted. The sicamar slammed into Wem, knocked him flat; this time the big cat licked the other side of his face, a rougher scour, taking an ear and part of his scalp.

Adlayr shift to man form and stood in the glow from the lantern. He grimaced, spat out part of Wem's ear.

"Urk." Wem's face went green. He swallowed, started to raise his hands to his face, forced them down. "Wha are you?"

"You don't want to know. Where did you take my friend?" Adlayr ran his tongue across his teeth, watched the white start to show around Wem's eyes. "Either you answer or I go after a couple of others I've got my eye on. They should babble like old ladies once they get a look at what's left of you."

The trax landed on the roof, shifted. Honeydew was tucked into a niche in one of the building's chimneys; Adlayr squatted beside her, out of the wind. *Got it, Honey. You picked the right one, ei vai, you did. It was his lot took Hedivy, too. He didn't know for sure, but he gave me all the rumors he had. Serroi's in a cage on her way to the Forest, I don't know why. Hedivy went way south into the swamps of Qilifund.*

Serry in a cage? Honeydew giggled. Sil lee, Serry won't stay there. She sobered. Serry first?

Asha, Honey. Wind's bad up here, can you hop aboard if I switch? This city's going to be jumping in a little while.

Honeydew can do.

A gibbous Nijilic TheDom was high, spreading pale white moonlight across the land as the trax swept in a wide circle around an abandoned farmstead. A macai was drinking from the trough in the corral behind the tumbledown house, two more were in the shed, folded up on straw, sleeping with that relaxed completeness that healthy macain managed in every kind of weather and condition. The trax spiraled lower, circled again; he couldn't see any disturbance about the place, the clews he'd left were all intact. *Honey, you awake? I'm going to land. Hang on.*

His neck tickled as she stirred and shifted her handholds, his ears twitched with the shrill whistle of her waking squeal.

Honeydew do.

He strode into the house with the sprite on his shoulder, took a lamp from inside a box with most of the slats kicked in, lit it and set it atop the box, lifted the door he'd left lying flat and propped it in the doorway. *Ei vai, Honey, I need rest and food right now. We'll get started in the morning. Wem gave me the area, but I'm going to depend on you to find Serry for me. Honeydew can do?*

The sprite launched herself from his shoulder, heading for the nest he'd made her in the corner of the room. She looped over, rolled, looped some more, her version of physical giggles, then dived for the woolly nest and wriggled around until she was almost covered. She lifted a tiny arm and waved. Honeydew can do.

A week later, leading the spare macain and following the fragile figure of the sprite, Adlayr rounded a bend in the road and saw the vast dark stretch of Forest.

>><<

The month at sea had nearly kicked Mama Charody back to a sleeping root. A thin, deeply wrinkled ancient, she clung to Treshteny's arm and tottered off the boat between her and the manHorse. When her foot hit the pavement, she sighed and straightened, color returning to her face. "Ahhhh, that is good." She chuckled as Doby grinned at her, dancing about her in his relief. "I could kiss the earth. You'll never get me on an ocean again, I don't care if it is faster."

Treshteny laughed and pulled the bandage off her eyes. She blinked at the sudden confusion, but found its familiarity comforting; she was back to herself, the self she'd known for the thirty years behind her. She straightened her shoulders and draped the scarf around her neck as she walked beside Mama Charody, her eyes fixed on the manHorse striding before her, going she didn't know where.

15. Worse and Worse

The waitress looked over her shoulder at the Sleykyn, lowered her eyes and walked away; she wasn't young or especially pretty, but her body was firm and slender in the right places so he drank his beer and watched her glide about the room, knowing she was aware of him wherever she moved.

He bumped the glass on the table and she brought him another beer. When she bent to take his coin, she murmured, "I want you to hurt me."

He said nothing and she went away. The room was crowded, most of the drinkers Nov's men. He watched her laugh and flirt with them, moving away from grabs with a fluid grace that excited him. When she brought him his next beer, he said, "When?"

"I get off at midnight. Hour after." She slipped the coin in her apron pocket and went away to answer another summons.

The negotiations continued as the evening wore on, a word or two at a time; he let it go on, enjoying the game.

"How much?"
"Five silvers."

"You haven't the face for 't or the youth. One."
"Three."

"Two."
"Done."

* * *

"What do I get for it?"

She looked at him, eyes heavy-lidded, hardened nipples showing through the flimsy white cloth of her blouse. "Anything you want," she said, her voice slow and husky. "Anything."

"Where?"

"First farmer's landing, Calanda side. Shack there. An't much, but it's private."

He dropped sail, looped the painter over a bitt, and with a powerful twist of his body swung up onto the landing where he stood tense, listening. There were few trees about the shack, some patches of brush, but Nijilic TheDom was high and nearly full, the trees were sickly and hadn't the leaves to hide a sniper, nor was there cover anywhere close on this side of the river.

The door to the shack opened and a fan of faint yellow light spilled out. The woman stepped into the light and stood waiting, naked, hands out and open.

He moved closer. "Is anyone else there?"

"Yes," she said.

"What!"

"An old friend of mine, to take care of me when you're finished. She's a granny, no threat to anyone, and she knows how to keep her mouth shut."

"Tell her to come out where I can see her."

The woman moved aside and a small shabby figure limped out, a tiny hunchback with stringy white hair. She bowed to him, went to her knees with some difficulty, and crouched there, waiting.

"You. Move away from the door." When the woman was out of the way, he bounded across the intervening space, glanced in the shack. It was empty except for a lamp on the floor, a pallet with blankets, a pack in the corner and a tray with a rope, a small whip and a jumble of other instruments. He left the door and loped round the shack to check all sides; the silence was profound, even the nixies silent in the river. He turned the last corner, reached for her.

She backed off, nodded at the kneeling granny. "Coin first, give it to her."

She paused in the doorway, leaned back against him, his armor dimpling her soft flesh. "Would you like my hair down? Most men do, it's very long."

"All right, all right, do it."

When she'd taken down the bands wound about her head, she caught a fistful of her hair, rubbed it against his face under the mask, strands of it coiling up, clean, sharp perfume in his nose, softness brushing across his eyes. "You can use it," she murmured, "throw me about, strangle me with it. . . ." Her other hand came round suddenly, but, half blinded by the hair, he didn't see it in time to react; it slapped against the eyehole of his mask.

His hands tangled in her hair, jerking her down with him as he fell; she felt a shudder, then another, then he was still.

The old woman took the long pin from the Sleykyn's eye, rubbed it clean on a bit of cloth and stabbed it through the strap on her fake hump, hunted through his armor, retrieved his purse, and slipped it into a pocket in her skirt. "There's gonna be trouble 'bout this'n, Jasny."

"Get his feet, I'll take his shoulders."

They carried him from the shack to the end of the landing, dropped him on the decaying planks. Jasny pulled his mask off, tossing it into the river. "Nixies, come along, we've got a new playtoy for you."

The water bulged with nixy heads, glistening arms thrust up and waved; she could hear their glubbing voices, though she couldn't understand what they said. She put her foot against the Sleykyn's shoulder and shoved.

He rolled into the water; the nixies seized him and drew him under.

Jasny buttoned the shirt, tucked it into her trousers, then knelt to roll the blankets into a bundle. "I know,

Fletty. Nov's kryshes saw me talking to him. But I've got no family here," her mouth tightened, "at least, none left. So that won't be a problem. You should be safe enough, the few who've seen you with me won't be talking about it." She straightened her back, sat on her heels. "There's scissors in the pack, come cut my hair for me."

"Jasny, your beautiful hair. . . ."

"It's no use to me now, just in my way. Come, Fletty, I can't see the back of my head, so I'd just make a mess."

The steel of the scissors was cold on her neck, the long black strands fell in a pool by her toes. She felt nothing. Since she woke from her raging fit after Bakory brought back her son's gnawed finger, she'd walked around as if scooped out inside and sealed in glass. Killing the Sleykyn was no more satisfaction than any of the others she'd gotten with the pin, but the planning gave her something to do, some way to fill the empty hours. She'd thought about walking into the river, but that seemed like giving them the ultimate victory and she had enough hate left that she wasn't willing to do that.

Fletty brushed gently at her neck, grunted as she bent to pick up the discarded hair. "What y' going to do?"

"Go east. Oskland. Keep up the hunt." She shook her head, fluffing out the shoulder length hair. "My head feels so light." She got to her feet. "Tell Sansy and the others what happened and warn them to keep their heads down the next few days."

"The other Sleykyn, they'll be sniffing after you. You know the stories."

"Let them." She smiled. "Our dead friend left us his boat, kind of him, mh? If they can trail on water, they're better than I think. There's a brisk wind coming from the south, it'll blow us back to Dander faster than we came and I'll be well away before they miss him."

The rider slid off his macai and ran into the tent; he showed his badge to the Trivud Throdal, started speaking at the same time. "Raider band heading for Chibanyx.

Macai mounted, half chovan, half wharflik, thirty strong. Scouts ahead and to the side, chovan whistle talkers."

Throdal grimaced. "Pek! Spojjin' chovan. That the only band out?"

"Nik. Two more, same mix. Pointed to Jeninyx and Azaranyx. Messengers sent their way, left when I did. I'll stay till you close with them, in case they change direction. Nov's lot know about the coms, they'll maybe be hopin' to take us off guard that way. The spiders will watch and let us know what's happenin'."

With their whistle talkers busy as mobbing rooks, the raiders burst through the boundary hedges and into burnt out fields, plowed and still soft. The village itself was a collection of blackened hulks, the well filled with stones.

The chovan leader tossed a loop over the neck of the guide, kneed his macai into a rocking gallop; he rode whooping through the ghost place, the body of the dead man jerking and bouncing behind him; the rest of the band followed, cursing and howling their disappointment.

Whistled warnings brought them to a stop, they split into five smaller bands and starred out from the center, riding for the nearest cover.

Three navstas converged on them, pressing them back and back, seventy-five to their thirty, shooting as they rode, the drills that Throdal had run them through over and over paying off as chovan, citymen, and their macain went down. Some of the chovan got clear and vanished with practiced skill, but most of the band died fighting, taking as many with them as they could.

Throdal sat his macai and looked over the bloody field with its wounded and dead. He lifted his hand. "Clean them out," he said, "anything usable. And remember. No prisoners." He brought his hand down. "Go."

>><<

"Spider one to Mountain. Go."

"Mountain here. Go."

"Things have been crazy around here, Purgers breaking

into places all round us, banged on our door every night the last four nights. One of the Web offed a Sleykyn. She got clear, too, she's heading your way. Jasny Zarcadla, a Zemyadelin, tall, thin, short black hair. Turn her loose and she'll do some good for you. Questions? Go."

"How's she comin'? On foot? Go."

"Riding. We lifted a macai for her, a racer from Nov's own stables. Bad news from the Harozh. They've got their backs to the mountains, facing a horde of Taken Tribes, getting hit everywhere. The terrain's on their side, it's hard to mount a wide-front attack and the Tribes aren't working together, at least not yet, but the Harozhni are getting pushed and they can't take in any more folk runnin' north. They'll send those that get through the Majilarn across the mountains to scratch out a living how they can in the fish villages on the Stathvoreen. They don't expect you to send help their way, they just want you to know how things are. Go."

"I'll pass it on. Maybe the Marn will come up with something. If she does, we'll relay through you, Spider one. There's still no change on direct calls, the dead spot between here and Ankhold hasn't moved. What's coming into Dander, Red Dan, Yellow Dan? Go."

"We've been getting between ten and twelve barges a day up the Yellow Dan from the Bezhval and the Zemyadel—food, men, and mounts." Greygen checked his notes, glanced at Sansilly who shook her head, nothing stirring. "One thousand five hundred fifty-three barrels of salt and smoked meats, seven hundred barrels of fruit juice and pulp, three thousand sacks of grain and tubers, two thousand bales of hay, eight hundred men, all Taken, sent to train at the Base Field, two hundred macain, ninety-five horses. By the way, the Web has managed to penetrate the warehouses without alerting the guards, and we're gradually pulling out and storing as much of the food as we can without leaving obvious holes. Red Dan, traffic's down to one or two barges a week, bringing in weapons, all of them. They don't go into the warehouses any more, but straight to the Pevranamist, into the cellars there. We've got sources inside the walls, but none we want to waste on siphoning out a few weapons, we need the information more. Couple of things to add. Our best source in the Pevranamist says Nov has been trying to buy some coms, but there aren't many of them out of ruling hands and them who have them won't sell and the Biserica has turned him down flat. Second thing. The little False Marn is having a miserable time. She hates the whole business, but between her father and the Enemy, she hasn't much room to move. Our source thinks its possible she'll try to kill herself one of these days; the source wants to know if you'd like us to help that along. Go."

"I'll pass that on and let you know. Anything else? Go."

"My own situation is getting very shaky. One of the Purgers is trying every way he can think of to get me thrown out of here. Me being in the chair has saved me so far, makes me hard to transport, but I have a feeling that's not going to last long. Just letting you know. Out."

>><<

Fletty worked her way along the walk, picking up scraps as she moved, stuffing them in the sack she was dragging, using the short handled besom to sweep the planks clean. Out in the street, the flagellants danced and beat at themselves, crying out their unvarying chant, "Kazim, kazim, kazim."

She was a scruffy shadow, essentially invisible as she did the work that earned her a few pennies from the Temple funds and gave her the workpaper she needed to keep her small dark room in the Mid-Dander warren. She watched and listened as she swept, counting riders and wagons, noting who they were, what the loads were, listened to conversations as men moved past her, and altogether swept up a surprising amount of information for the Web.

A hand fell on her shoulder; she stiffened, fear shutting her throat, then she dropped back into her public role. "Wha wha wha?" she quavered, "gotta sweep, gotta sweep, I din' do nothin', gotta sweep." She twisted her head around, mouth slack, eyes dull. It was a Purger she

didn't know, a skinny youth with pimples flaring like
small fires across his face. There was another one, an
older one. Him she didn't know either.

The young one sneered at her, turned to the other.
"This piece a nouzh?"

"He say bring 'er, we bring 'er. Wanna argue with
Him?"

They put her in one of the drunk cells in the Chitelhall,
went away grumbling.

Fletty sat hunched over on a filthy cot. Ravach was
coming for her and from what that pair of notneys said,
the Dancer himself was interested. She looked around,
sighed. Miserable place to die in. The sigh turned to a
soft mirthless chuckle. Dead don't care where they lie.
She curled up on the cot, gnawed at her wrist until blood
spurted across her face. Ignoring the pain and the revolt
of her stomach, she dropped her forearm over the end of
the cot so she'd drain faster and bit into the second wrist.

>><<

"Spider one to Mountain."

"Mountain here. Go."

"This is my last call. We're going to be evicted day after tomorrow, my wife and me, sent south to work on
some Bezhval farm. They've got Purgers all round,
watching us, they search us each time we go out to make
sure we're not taking coin we're not supposed to have. I
can't leave the com here when we go, I know they're going to take the place apart; I'll destroy it, drop the pieces
down the drain. We'll be going out over the roof tomorrow night; even so I don't want to take any chance of that
lot getting hold of a com should they land on us. The Web
is getting hit, they picked up one of the women, took her
to the Chitelhall, but she killed herself before they got
round to questioning her. Two or three other families are
being whipsawed like I was. The rest seem safe enough
so far, except they can't get out much any more, ordinary
folk aren't supposed to leave home except to go to work
or get food, though if you're tokened to Glory or you're

one of Nov's oslicks, you go where you want and when. They closed down the schools yesterday and the parks, parents were warned to keep their kids inside, any that's out will be corralled and sent south. They claim they're trying to get hold of the streetliks, stop their thievin' and traitor's acts. Questions? Go."

"Someone taking over from you, Spider one?"

"Spider two. She's still clean and will move out of the active Web. I've talked with her, given her the com setup, she'll start reporting tomorrow, coordinating the Web. Way things are, she probably won't be able to give you much. Source in the Pevranamist says Nov has calmed down the Sleykyn, talked them into going after the Marn as the one really responsible for their companion's disappearance. They haven't found his body yet, but they've seen nixies playing in his shape, mocking them, so they know he's most likely dead. Zdra, without Nov around, that source won't be providing near so much. Any word about the False Marn thing? Go."

"Prak. Marn says we're not that desperate yet and besides, it probably wouldn't change anything. So leave the girl alone, let what she does be her own choice. You coming our way? Go."

"We haven't decided yet. The news we've been getting, not that it's much, it says the Travasherims are fairly quiet. We've talked about heading up there and getting something organized, the Harozh being closed and I imagine you could do without a couple more mouths to feed. Go."

"One minute, the Marn's come in, let me tell her. . . ."

Greygen sighed. Sansilly and he were seated on the bed, close but not touching. He reached out, caught hold of her hand, held it against his thigh. "Do you really want to keep going, Sansy? We could pass through the mountains and settle on the Stathvoreen until this is over."

She snorted, didn't say anything, just dug her fingers into his thigh.

The Marn's voice came through the com. "Greygen, you there? Go."

"Here, O Marn. Go."

"I'm going to ask you to do something very difficult

and very dangerous. I want you to think very carefully
before you answer me. You spoke of going into the
Travasherims. How do you mean to do that?"

"Two other families from the Web will be coming with
us, their situation nearly the same as ours. One of them is
from the Shipper's Quarter, men in the family been
bargeveks since the first Marn. There's an empty barge
tied to the southernmost wharf, we'll liberate that, using
the nixies for cover, they're active every night doing
some mischief or other; we'll take it down the Yellow
Dan to the last Tower, move from there into the mountains. We should get away clean, but if not, almost all of
Nov's mounted guards are in the army or training the new
men, any he sends after us will have to fight to take us,
we'll capsize the barge if that seems likely and drown before we're taken. Go."

"That fits in better than I expected. Greygen, I want
you and Sansilly to go to the Biserica for me, tell them
Marnhidda Vos needs what help they can send us, weapons and otherwise, and any fighters who are willing to
come into a desperate situation. Tell them about the
Dancer and Mother Death. Tell them it threatens even
them; perhaps not now, but the time will come when
they'll face what I face, if we don't stop it here. Tell them
what you've seen in Dander and Calanda."

There was a pause, they heard her draw a breath. "You
may be worried about how to pay for this. If you can get
to Tuku-kul, I've been in touch with my mother's friends
there. These blесséd coms, they'll reach that far at least.
I wish they'd reach to the Biserica, but that's not possible.
The Fenekel will do this as a business transaction, a loan
to be repaid with interest, though they will not interfere in
any other way, not even to send a message themselves,
and I had to talk myself hoarse to get this much. Tell that
also to the Prieti Meien, if you will, please.

When you reach Tuku-kul, go to House Hekkataran,
ask for the Malkia Hekkataran. She will give you the
money you need, get you on board a ship you can trust
that will take you to Southport. Once you're there, you
should be safe enough. Will you do this for me, for
Cadander, for yourself? Don't answer now. Talk it over

with Sansilly and when you've decided, call us back. You know your own strength; if you don't think you can do it, there is no shame in that. You've already endured more than many. We will wait here for your answer. Out."

Greygen looked at Sansilly. She nodded. "I need to be doing," she said. "Something that means something."

He drew his finger along her nose, touched her lips with it. "Sansy, my Sansy." When he spoke, his voice was halting, husky; it was hard to say words he felt so deeply, almost as hard as leaving these rooms they'd lived in all their married life. "I was blessed," he cleared his throat, "blessed the day I met you and blessed every day since." He touched the call button.

"Mountain here. Go."

"We've decided. We'll go."

16. Diffusion Increases

Chaya Willish hummed as she wove; she'd been working for an hour and was deep in the rhythm of the guildcloth, simple weaving, the unbleached threads lifting and falling, feet on the treadles, the shuttle flying back and forth, clack and click, thump of the beater bar, the sounds of her work melding with that from the other looms, the footsteps of the Weavemistress Iduna Yekai walking the aisles, checking tensions and the evenness of the weave, stopping an apprentice here to correct a problem, tapping another on the shoulder in praise, shadow falling across Chaya's work, slipping off, falling again, as Iduna moved up and down between the looms. Chaya was in her deepest work-trance, everything right, present in the body, present to the weave, not a thought in her head, nothing but the weave. . . .

The door crashed open and jolted her awake. A man came walking in. He wore a white robe that covered him from neck to wrist and ankle, held a wide leather strap in one hand and knife in the other; his head was canted back, his eyes were blank. "Kazim," he chanted and crossed his arm over his chest, bringing the strap down on his own back. "Kazim." He took a step, struck at himself again, another step. A woman dressed the same way appeared in the door behind him. "Kazim," she chanted and struck herself with a similar leather strap, a look of ecstasy on her face. After her came another and another until a line of five men and three women were moving down the middle aisle between the looms, dancing in eccentric spirals, chanting that enigmatic word.

Round and round they danced, side to side, striking themselves, striking at the looms, the straps cracking like whips; round and round they danced, the naked knives darting out, slicing at the warp threads. When they reached the end wall, they changed the chant to a loud wordless cry, swung round and stood with arms out, mouths open but silent.

The man who led them lifted his arms, turned his head side to side; in the bright light pouring through the tall windows, his eyes were the color of butter, white and iris alike. "The Glory comes," he boomed, "bow down to the Glory." He waved the knife over his head, brought it down fast and hard, stabbing it through the palm of his other hand, but when he drew it clear, there was no blood, no wound, not even a mark. "Kazim," he chanted, "kazim, kazim."

He led his followers down the aisle and out the door.

Catilu, the newest apprentice, looked at the slash across the warp that she'd spent hours getting just right, the Weavemistress standing over her and making her start again and again until she got the proper tension in all the threads, the twists and tangles gone. Hours of tedious effort and only an inch of cloth woven, and that wasted now. She walked round the loom and stood touching the ends, just touching them and gulping and trying not to cry.

Chaya sighed and went to her. "There's no getting around it, babe, we've got to clear this out and get you started again." She grinned, ruffled the girl's exuberant curls. "Count it as just one more practice. You should've seen the messes I made of my first weaves. Where's your scissors? Let's cut away the bit you did get done. You keep it for your memory box, it's good work, see how nice and smooth it is." She laughed. "And look, Catilu, the black one's come to cheer you on." She pointed at one of the Hall snakes; he'd slid from his hole and reared up, his head swaying back and forth, his red tongue flickering. She blew him a kiss which started Catilu giggling. A moment later they were both kneeling and cutting away the strip of newly woven cloth.

* * *

The other apprentices rushed to the doorway and stared down the street after the Chanter's Line.

"Where'd they come from?"

"I dunno, I never seen any of them before. You, Mazzy?"

"Na, I been to Gwelefam an' Sikanafam an' Yaysifam and I never seen that lot. 'Specially not that crazy man. You see what he DID?"

"Glory? What'd he mean by that? Gaaah, my belly went knotty when they started with those knives. I was figurin' first the warps, then us."

The Weavemistress clapped her hands loudly several times. "Get back to work. We've got a mess to clean and you've got quotas to meet. Let the Headman and his Peacers take care of them, it's none of your business."

Harlo, who was the most restless of the apprentices, lingered behind the others; he took another look out the door, made a face, and shambled toward his loom. "An't," he said.

"What?"

"The Peacers. An't gonna take care of them. Not showin' nose, none of 'em."

The Weavemistress strode to the doorway, looked out, said a few sharp things under her breath. She pulled the headscarf off, smoothed her hair down. "Like I said, there's quotas to make. Get those warps cleared and restrung. I'll be back with a swatch of Peacer hide if they don't start tendin' their business like they should."

Lavan Isaddo rounded a clump of trees and saw a wagon rumbling toward him. Despite the heat, the driver was covered head to toe in black, black gloves on the hands that held the reins of a spindly pair of vezen that kept plodding along as if they'd fall over if they stopped. He was singing, a raucous bawdy thing Lavan remembered from a visit to the Traders District in Bokivada.

Lavan winced as he got nearer; the man wouldn't know a tune if it exploded in his face, all he knew was LOUD. The noise came close to drowning out the creak of the axles and the thumps and noises from whatever it was under the canvas. He rode on past, curious about that load, but too impatient to reach Hubawern to indulge that curiosity.

The road was deserted, every day hotter than the last; he took to riding at night when the alkali surface seemed to glow in the moons' light, the white dust blowing from Alegay's hooves like smoke from a ground-hugging fire. There was water and browse along the way and he fed Alegay corncake and grain from the saddlebags, tubers he dug in the cool dew of the morning, but by the time he turned north along the paved road that met the dryland ruts, both he and the horse were in need of a rest.

Built on a bend of the river, Hubawern was a town rather than a village, considerably bigger than Hallafam, with more traffic passing through it every day than Hallafam got in a year. It had a small waterfront, a warehouse and a ferry you could summon by ringing an iron bell. There were oil lamps at the corners of a square ringed with shops and around the fountain in the middle, and others on posts along the side streets. The square was filled with people though the sun was an hour down, some walking about, some playing skittles on a smooth spot near one of the lamps, some seated at the tables of a cafe that were spread across the walk into the square, the miniature lamps on the tables glittering like stars in the dusk.

Leading Alegay, Lavan limped along the street to the square; he was too tired even to be hungry. He caught hold of a boy running past him, asked, "Where's the traveler's hostel?"

" 'Tother side the cafe." The boy pulled loose and went whooping after his friend.

This village was accustomed to travelers. The folk in the square made way for him and his horse without comment or much curiosity.

The hostel was a small neat building, painted white as in every village, but this paint was new and shiny, enamel not whitewash, and the stable behind it was clean, with fresh straw and grain for the horses. He gave Alegay a good workover while the horse ate, brushing him down, combing out his mane and tail, even scrubbing his hooves. He scratched the big sorrel along his belly, especially where the cinch had been, digging his fingers in, laughing aloud as the horse leaned against him and made the little squeals that signalled extreme contentment. "Ahwu, ahwu, you can get all fat and lazy now, the hard work's done for a while."

After his bath, he was too restless to sleep so he went out to the square, settled at a table and sipped at a mug of kava while he watched village life swirl around him. *I'm going to like this place, I think. It's not moribund like Hallafam. I've got to get Chaya away from there, all those snoops, family looking down their noses at me. Chaya love, I've been a rat, worse. I know it, but everything was rubbing at me. If it goes well tomorrow ... Guildchapter won't want to let Chaya go early, she's one of their best weavers ... but maybe we can make a trade, if there's a chapter here or close by ... depends on tomorrow. ...*

In the morning Lavan stood before the door to the house built on a knoll overlooking the river. He brushed himself down, straightened his tunic, glanced at the sample case resting against his right boot, swallowed and lifted the knocker; he hesitated another breath, then brought it down with a heavy double tap. It was a cool, clear morning with a few wisps of cloud in the west, drifting in from the Channel. The garden around the house was running wild, but there were cascades of flowers everywhere, filling the air with their perfume.

Nothing happened.

He waited what seemed like an eternity and knocked again.

"Hang on, hang on, give a body time to move."

The voice that came from inside was low and growly; Lavan expected a much larger man than the white-haired gnome that opened the door and peered up at him. "Who're you? What y' want?"

"You're Casil Kinuqah?"

"Yes, yes, what y' want?" White eyebrows like woolly caterpillars wriggled impatiently and the yellowed mustache bulged with the pursing of his lips. "I got water on to heat, gonna boil over on me, you don't get to it."

"The Herbwoman? Sekhaya Kawin? She told you about me. I am Lavan Isaddo, clan Dashiliva, totem salamander, guild silversmith."

"So you finally got here. Come in. Come, come." Casil shuffled briskly away, not bothering to check if Lavan were following. "We'll look at y' stuff in the kitchen, you don't mind. Don't matter if you do, it's where we're goin'."

The kitchen had the neatness of a good workshop, everything the old man would need to make his cha laid out like a line of tools on the counter within easy reach of the stove. The whistling kettle was puffing out threads of steam and bouncing on the grate above the coals. "Sit y'self at the table, ne'mind there's only one chair. Been used to doin' for m'self since m' wife went, then Kubalm got that kuq'n fever. Only needed one chair, so that's all I kept in here."

He set the cha to steeping, then bustled about getting down another mug and saucer, rinsing them off and wiping them dry, cutting slices from a new loaf wrapped in a clean white cloth, getting out a plate with butter and a jar of honey.

He put it on the table with the neat easy moves of a longtime craftsman even though age had stiffened his stubby brown fingers. "If you'll fix me a slice or two, I'll be back in just a minute, I like m' butter thick and crust to crust."

"Hah! Good way to start the morning. Na na, friend, keep y' seat. Should we come to terms, we'll do this turn and turn about, but till then you are my guest, Lavan Isaddo."

When the table was cleared and polished clean, Casil bustled round to Lavan. "Let's have your hands. I want to see and feel 'em."

Lavan sat squirming with embarrassment as the old man washed his hands and dried them carefully, prodding at them as he worked, checking the nails, the conformation of his palms, the elasticity of the joints.

Casil nodded, tossed the washcloth into the basin with the plates, and hung the towel up. He pulled out the chair he'd fetched in and sat down across the table from Lavan. "So. Show me your pieces."

Casil turned the last of the pieces over and over, feeling every inch of it, bringing it close to his yellow-brown eyes, holding it at a distance, tilting it through varying angles. It was a brooch in the shape of a crescent moon with a catseye set below the center, Lavan's prize, in his mind the best thing he'd done, elegant and simple.

Casil set the brooch on the velvet showing board. "It's good work. You haven't gone for the obvious or the flashy in any of these pieces. You won't find a quick sale, but the people who know what they're looking for should be willing to pay premium for these. You have weaknesses. I think you know them. You're still feeling for line and you have a difficulty with negative space. You've countered that rather nicely with unusual forms and some interesting color choices. I'm not young ..." his soup strainer mustache twitched over a quick grin, "but I'm healthy and m' Da went only two days short of his hundred. So, should you want to take the chance, I'm willin'. Standard day wages and I'll see about locating what you need for your masterwork."

Lavan relaxed. He'd liked the old man from the beginning, and everything that had happened since had increased his desire to work with Casil. "Thank you," he said, struggling to keep his voice steady. "These last years ... it's not been easy."

"I expect not. Any problem about moving down here? It's a long way from y' folks."

"Haven't got folks except for an old cousin. Lost 'em in the kujuneh plague, last time the kuj swept 'cross the plains. I'm promised to a woman up my way. She's a weaver, just made journeyman. But that's a problem we'll have to work out ourselves. In any case her uncle, he's clan head, won't sanction a marriage yet, he says he has to see me settled first."

"Ahwu, families, families, if there's trouble to make,

they'll make it for you. How'd you get here, ride or by boat?"

"Rode. I've got a horse."

"Stable out back, han't been used in a while, you'll have to clean it out, get in some straw and such. There's a pump back there, don't know how well it works, froze a couple winters since last I used it. If it's broke, I'll get it fixed. Where you staying?"

"Hostel."

"Pho! I'll show you your room and the workshop, then you go get y' things, hmm? Na na, I'm wrong. Let's both go up town, see the scrivener, and swear the oath. That suit y'?"

Lavan grinned. "Suits me fine, Master."

"Haaaah! That sounds good. House's been a smidge lonesome." He pushed his chair back and shuffled for the door. "Had a daughter," he said over his shoulder, "she married a trader from the Bikiyafund. Only time I see my grandchildren is when the family comes to Bokivada for the Quatrafest. Outlived most m' cousins and their kids don' know I'm alive. Ahwu ahwu, no point complainin'." He turned down a short narrow hall and started up the stairs at the end. "Your rooms 'll be at the back of the house, look down into the garden and past that to the river. There's a Munga tree for shade, it gets a bit sweet in the bloomtime, but that's Spring and we get plenty of rain in the Spring, so you won't be stifled up there. There's a bathroom down the hall and a cistern on the roof." He grinned at Lavan. "Be your job, journeyman, to keep it filled."

Lavan stood at the window of his bedroom looking down at the moon-silvered river. It'd been a hard day and a long one, but he was settled, the oath was sworn. Signing the papers when they were drawn up was only a formality. On the desk behind him was an unfinished letter to Chaya; he was too tired to finish it, but there was no rush. In the morning he'd find a Wandermonk to carry the letter to Hallafam, then start his work with Casil. He'd gotten a quick look at the old man's current pieces when Casil took him through the workshop, but even a glance

was enough to send his blood beating in his throat.
Maiden Bless Sekhaya Kawin. Casil wasn't just a Master, he was one of the Great Ones. He stretched, yawned,
looked from the bed to the desk, and decided to finish the
letter after all.

>><<

Hibayal Bebek glanced out the window; his offices
were in the west end of the Scrivener's Hall and the
clouds piling up over the Channel were a spectacular boil
of gold and shell pink as the sun slid down behind them.
He was signing the last of the papers on his desk and applying his seal ring to them when he heard the sliding
knock of his aide.

"Come."

Phomben edged past the door. "There is a man who
says he must see you. He won't give me a name or any
hint to his business. He said to tell you Mount Santak."

A muscle twitched at the corner of Bebek's eye. "I'll
see him." He squared the pages he'd finished, pushed
them across the desk. "Take these and put them in the
case for the next Wandermonk that comes by and send
the man in." He frowned. "Wait. Do you have any of the
brandy left?"

"Yes, Master Bebek. I am to give the Wandermonk a
drink before he leaves?"

"As always. Now the visitor."

"He's got a heavy bag with him. Will you want me to
make him leave it outside?"

"Na na, it's all right. Send him as he wants to come."

The man was broad and squat with reddish highlights on
wide cheekbones and yellow-brown eyes; his hair hung
loose to his waist like a fall of black water. As he crossed
to the desk, his walk was eerily silent with the suggestion
of a hunting sicamar.

He lifted the bag onto the desk, the muscles bulging on
the arms left bare by his heavily embroidered dalmatic; he
stepped away, sat in the client's chair, his big hands resting on his knees, the loose trousers falling into graceful

folds about his legs. "If you will open that, Glory's Child, and see what lies within." His voice was a soft rumble as big as he was, filling the room without effort.

Bebek undid the clip and spread the top.

The bag was filled with coins. Bebek reached to the bottom and brought out a handful, spreading them on the desk before him. Gold coins, some so ancient they were almost smoothed flat. He looked from the bag to the coins, then to the visitor. "I see. What is the purpose of this?"

"You are to build a House for Glory. You will need to acquire land and permissions, workers and materials." He tossed an envelope on the desk. "I was given these names you can use for cover; any one of them will certify that you are acting as agent, if the question comes up. And there will be more gold as it is needed."

"Who are you?"

"A Hand of Glory. You will see others as the Glory spreads through Shimzely, you are Glory's Favored Child." He bowed his head onto crossed hands. "Bless me, Glory's Child, touch me and bless me."

After the man had gone, Hibayal Bebek took more coins from the bag, a handful at a time, piling them in stacks of ten, old gold, new gold, shiny, sharp-minted coins, ancients clipped and worn, some with stains spreading across them like varnish, piling them across the wood until the desk top was covered, five hundred piles of ten coins each. Five thousand gold. He took a handful of the coins, smoothed his thumb across them, closed them in his fist, shook his hand, and listened to them clank.

He shook himself out of his daze, opened the door to the strongroom built into the wall behind him, transferred the coins except for a half dozen he dropped into his belt purse, locked the door, and went home.

17. Attack and Defense

The Forest was a dark line on the horizon, vanishing into blue to the north and south. Adlyar stopped his macai on a rise and looked along the line. "Murd! It's one thing to see it on the map...." He pulled the long pin from his hair, shook his braid down, wound it into a tighter knot and skewered it in place.

Honeydew wriggled in his shirt pocket, stood and stretched her wings. *Stopping now?*

Just a break, not camping, Honey. You get any feel for Serry yet?

She climbed from the pocket and jumped; her wings caught the air and took her into a rising spiral that left Adlayr grimacing as her search ran like a rasp over his brain.

She made a small disgusted sound and plunged down, landing on his shoulder. *Adlee, Serree in there, Honeydew can feel her, but it's funny, like a buzzing on top of her and sometimes she's there and sometimes Honeydew can't feel her at all.*

What about the people who've got her?

Adlee, there's something, but I can't say what. Like ghosts. Shivery. 'Fraid. Maybe kinda friendly, too. Weeeird, Honeydew don't know what they are. Adlee, how come the cherts push Serree all the way out here?

Don't know, Honey. Might's well get back in the pocket and go to sleep. Be a while yet before we get close enough to really start looking.

The day was nearly over when they reached the tall trees on the fringe of the Forest. Adlayr pulled up again in a glade created by the fall of one of the giants to storm or disease, slid from his macai, looped the reins over a stub on the dead tree, and lifted his wrist to his pocket. *Honey, I'm going hunting, you'd better wait here. Come.*

She crawled out, perched on his shoulder, grumbling under her breath.

Honey, I can smell a blooming plum off to the north a short way, you go eat something, sweeten your temper. He chuckled as he began undoing the ties on his tunic. *Might be an hour or two, Honey. Depends on what I come across.*

The sprite worked her shoulders, pinched a bit of skin on his neck. You be careful, Adlee, this place is weee-ird. She powered herself into the air and went looking for the plum tree he'd mentioned.

The sicamar gave a chuckling yowl and loped off into the Forest.

The small fire built by the hollowed section of trunk near the root pad crackled and popped, throwing red onto Adlayr's face. Stretched out on one of the dead roots, Honeydew glowed like ruby glass, her translucent wings shimmers of vermilion and gold. Adlayr lifted his head, scanned the darkness outside the fire. "I heard something. . . ." He listened, shook his head. *I can't touch anything out there now except some small-lives rooting about. Honey?*

The sprite swung her legs around and sat up, blinking drowsily. Honeydew feels lots of lives, hot hot hot hot. . . . She waved her arm through an arc, then stretched out again, yawning. Wild things 'n people too, silly folk, mad at somethin'. A sigh shook her whole body, then she settled back to dozing.

"Snoopers." Adlayr rested his hands on his knees, his eyes on the darkness under the trees. "Ei vai, let them watch."

As he moved deeper and deeper into the trees, a growing number of the Forest folk gathered about him, murmuring, hostile, the ring thickening and tightening but never quite closing, leaving a bubble of emptiness about the intruder that moved with him—the pale folk in it hurling words where they wouldn't put their bodies, hushed words, never shouts, words packed with rejection and an implied threat.

> *go awayyyyy*
> *we don't want you heeeerrrre*
> *the forest is ours, you don't belong here*

Honeydew flitted about, ignoring all this. The Forest enchanted her. She spiraled up to the high limbs, ran along them, one after another, went diving off again with the soaring furries, played giggling tag with the birds—and chattered, a cascade of words that never stopped, didn't matter if anyone was listening or not.

> *go awayyyyy*

... like home, Honeydew budded on a tree like this ... smelled like this 'un, looked like this 'un ... aaaaaahhhhhhhh. ... It was a long wail of pure joy as the sprite went tumbling and looping through the air in convoluted, intricate aerobatics.

> *we don't want you heeeerrrre*

With a quavery sigh, she landed on Adlayr's shoulder and went on talking. Honeydew is happy, Adly, happy, happy, happy, like coming home, Adly, Honeydew had not so good times when Honeydew was little, Honeydew was diff'rent, Adly and Serree know 'bout that, but Honeydew had lots of good times, Honeydew had friends, li'l people with bird wings bigger'n Honeydew but not much, they call themselves Shapsa.

> *the forest is ours, you don't belong here*

Shapsa childlings and Honeydew play games 'n chase each other. ... She sighed, a long, body-shuddering breath. Then there was the Bad Time. The Mountain goes bump bump bump and spits fire on Shapsa places and Shapsa and sprites, the little 'uns, and birds and furries go running, it does that lots of times and everyone runs 'n everyone comes back when Mountain grumps to sleep again, but this time the Trapper comes and catches Honeydew and Ryol and K'ritsa and kills lots the other Shapsa.

> *go awayyyyy*
> *we don't want you heeeerrrre*
> *the forest is ours, you don't belong here*

She fell silent, nestling close to Adlayr's neck and clinging to his hair, dozing until the shadows under the canopy thickened, the macai hooted protest, and Adlayr began making camp for the night.

Talking in a steady streak the sprite flew in circles over Adlayr's head as he hobbled and fed the macai, then took the waterskins to the stream he'd smelled out. . . . Honeydew don't know what they think they doin', sittin' there gogglin at Honeydew and Adlee and the macs, silly silly. . . . She flipped through a lazy loop, fluttered ahead, came back. Tika and Honeydew used to play touch-and-go in moonlight like this, one two three count and go, touch knot on chak'i tree, touch second zad'ya nest, touch first yarma bud, count an' touch and first in wins and when ol' mountain go bumpa bump, Ryol and K'rista and Tika and Honeydew go to Dozh'de Falls 'n fly through when creek hiccups. . . .

Do you have to go hunt, Adlee? As she watched him strip and fold his clothing, Honeydew's mosquito voice went higher and higher in her distress. Honey don't like them out there, they scary, they want to hurt Honey and Adlee. Honeydew don't want to be left all alone.

I need fresh meat, Honey. I can go a while on dried and trail rations, but it weakens me. Not a good idea right now. And you can't come along. You'd just get lost, you know you would. Anyway, I thought you liked the Forest.

Honeydew do, Adlee. Honeydew not scared of the Forest. It's them out there, 'cause they stop that noise 's afternoon. They just sitting and staring at Honeydew and Adlee. Honeydew think they getting ready to do something.

Adlayr moved his eyes along the ring of pale forms out in the darkness, the forest folk staring back in eerie silence. *Not much we can do about it, Honey. We'll give it one more night, I'll go after one of 'em tomorrow morning, see what this is all about.*

>><<

A low moan flew round the ring of watchers when Adlayr shifted and those in the ring in front of him scrambled hastily away as he loped toward them. Honeydew heard his laugh-yowl and giggled. It always seemed to surprise them when he shifted and came at them, as if they hadn't seen it the night before and the night before and so on. The sprite heaved a sigh, her tiny body shuddering with it, then she fluttered upward, looking for a comfortable crotch where she could curl up and get some sleep till Adlayr got back.

Honeydew woke some time later, sweating with terror though she didn't know why. She rolled onto her stomach, eased her head over the curve of the limb, and peered around, trying to find what had frightened her so much. The night was very still, no wind, no small-lives rustling about. And the watchers were gone.

Adlee's been gone a looooong time, she told herself. Hours and hours ... no moonlight left. And this place is like Honeydew's place, baaaad things all round. She pushed herself up and sat kicking her heels against the satiny bark. Honeydew is tired, Adlee's got teeth and claws and he knows how. . . . Nay, she yelled at the night. Honeydew won't sit like a stupid lump. Honeydew will find him.

She flew through the darkness, weaving back and forth across the line Adlayr had taken when he left camp, teased on and on by the faint sense of something way out at the limit of her reach. It didn't *feel* like Adlayr, but it didn't feel not-like him either. It was very confusing. She darted toward it, concentrating so fiercely on keeping hold of it that she didn't notice when the link with Serroi vanished.

After what seemed an eternity she swooped panting to a branch and knelt there, trembling as she looked down at a black sicamar growling over the body of a zimza, head turning in threat at the three lewah standing a few yards away, the spines over their shoulders erect, their black lips draw up from their dagger canines. They were constantly changing place, shifting side to side, long thin legs moving with an angular meticulousness, as they tested him with feint after feint, edging closer, trying to goad him into a charge that would let at least one of them get behind him.

Honeydew chewed her lip. Anything she might try could tip the balance the wrong way, so she waited.

The boldest lewah made a mistake and dodged in too close, got too far from the others. Before he could retreat, the sicamar was on him, powerful jaws closing on his neck. He whirled the lewah off its feet, snapped it around. Even in her tree Honeydew heard bone crack. A second later he was crouched over the zimza again, black tail switching, mouth open in a silent roar.

The other two lewah backed into the dark and a moment later Honeydew heard the pat-scratch of their feet as they headed somewhere else as fast as they could move.

Giddy with relief she fell off the limb and went swooping down, chattering as she swooped. Oooooh, Adly, that was marrrrvelous, Honeydew just about chewed her fingers to bone, but oooooh. . . .

The sicamar whirled, snarled, and swiped at her, barely missing her as she scrambled frantically away, driving her wings as fast as she could. Ad leeee. It's Hon eeeee.

As soon as she was out of reach, the sicamar went back to gnawing at the carcass.

Honeydew flew in circles high above him, trying to feel into him; she'd never had trouble before—whether he was sicamar or trax he was still Adlayr, calm and cool and funny. What she felt now was blood-hunger and beast, except . . . way down under that, like a faded perfume, there was just a hint of Adlayr. A hint that got fainter the harder she tried to get hold of it.

She fluttered wearily up to a branch where she rested a moment, then gathered herself and mindscreamed as loudly as she could, SERREEEE, HONEYDEW NEEEEEEDS YOU, ADLY NEEEEEDS YOU.

There was no answer.

As far as she could tell, she was screaming into darkness with no one out there to hear her.

She crouched on the branch, watching the sicamar that almost wasn't Adlayr crunch bones and gulp down hunks of bloody meat. It's them, it's those krofkrof watchers.

They're doing it. SERRREEEE. SERRREEE. HONEYDEW
NEEEEDS YOU. SERREEEEE.

She beat a tiny fist against the bark—if she left him
here, she'd never find him again, but if she didn't find
Serroi and get her here to fix him, he'd sink into the beast
and never ever never come out.

In the end she decided to stay with the sicamar and
keep calling. Serroi was out there somewhere, maybe she
was trapped or something, but as soon as she heard, she'd
come. Honeydew knew that as well as she knew her
wings.

She found a crotch higher in the tree, padded it with
leaves, curled up to wait and watch. And send out her cry
at lengthening intervals as the night passed and her energy wore down.

>><<

Hedivy opened his eyes a slit. The room was empty. A
soft light filtered through the splitwood blind on the single window and the door was open a crack, held there by
a pair of stones. Like the walls of this clinic—its purpose
and arrangement seemed similar to those back on
Cadander, so he thought of it as a clinic—the door was
constructed from lengths of heavy bamboo laced together
with cords and varnished over to make light, strong panels colored a mid-amber that shone with a cheerful bright-
ness in the steamy sunlight that filtered through the blind.
On the table beside the bed someone had put a heavy
stoneware jug and basin, a slim, black-glazed vase with a
branch from a blossoming tree rising from it with an elegant simplicity which he knew enough to recognize but
had no feeling for. Aside from a bamboo chest pushed
against the far wall, a three-legged stool, and the cot he
lay on, there was nothing else in the room.

He could hear voices in the distance, men and women
chanting something, he didn't care what, the important
thing was how far away they were. He listened for sounds
nearer at hand, but all he heard was the tap tap of the
blind as an erratic breeze pushed it about.

He threw off the sheet and swung his legs over the side

of the cot. His head swam for several breaths and there was a twinge or two from his leg, but the fever was gone. He brought his foot up, rested it on his sound knee, wincing as the wounded muscle protested. He worked the leg carefully, lowering it, bending it, twisting it until a thin layer of sweat lay over his body, sticky and persistent.

Outside, Kielin called to someone, laughed at the answer, and came briskly up the walk; by the time she set foot on the ladder of the stilted house, he was stretched out again, the sheet drawn over him, his head turned from the door, his eyes closed.

She looked at him and her mouth twitched. "That's too much sweat for a sleeping man."

He turned his head and looked stonily at her, saying nothing.

"Unhappy?" When he still said nothing, Kielin snorted. "I liked you better when you were raving. Little man, the trees tell us the Qilimen are coming. We don't have much time to get ready, so climb down off that snit and listen to me."

"I'm listening."

"Mp. What we decide to do for you depends on you."

"I will not be answering questions."

"Nor will I be asking the kind you mean. Do me the courtesy of hearing me before you shut down." She folded her arms, frowned at him. "I have the feeling that many lives, honest lives, depend on your silence."

He thought that over a moment. "Yes," he said finally.

"It is Wa'heykaza you fight. Mother Death is your name for her, or so I believe. You also call her the Enemy."

Another long pause. "Yes. Her?"

"So it appears to us. Do you know the Qilimen?"

"Nik . . . nay. I know almost nothing of Shimzely."

"Almost. That means Bokivada?"

"Yes."

"Then you will not know that the Qilimen who serve death have given themselves utterly to Wa'heykaza."

"If they serve death . . ."

"Wa'heykaza is not death, so your name for her is misleading. What she is . . ." Kielin shook her head. "We've been puzzling about that, but we have no answer yet. Never mind. It is the Qilimen that must concern us."

Hedivy pushed up, carrying the sheet with him as a barrier between his private places and the old woman's too-knowing eyes. It didn't matter that she'd washed and cleaned him when he was in fever, he wasn't sick now. "That's all you want to know?"

"Ahwu, we guessed it, but we needed your words to confirm what we knew."

"And if I lied?"

She smiled at him, ice-blue eyes twinkling, "The day you can lie to me, Hedivy Starab, is the day I drown myself. And no, you didn't spew all that out in a fever rant; mostly you were cursing your father and pleading with your mother to get both of you away from there."

He turned his head so he couldn't see her, his hands closing so hard on the sheet that he tore it.

"Ahwu, to the important thing. You can't run, Cadandri. There are guards all round this island who know the swamp out there better than you know the wharves of Dander. They stay away from us because we make them uncomfortable, but that won't keep them from netting you and hauling you back. I'd let you see for yourself, my skeptical friend, if there were time and your leg were up to it. We have something else in mind for later, when we're ready, but right now we want to throw you back into deep fever. It won't be pleasant and you'll no doubt be saying things you want no one to hear to some very ugly people, but don't fool yourself you could stand up to the Qilimen; between drugs and pain they'd empty you before the day's out. Will you trust me enough to drink what I give you?"

"Why are you doing this?"

"You have companions and they'll come for you. What saves you, saves us."

"How do you know about them?"

"The trees tell us; they babble continually about the one called Serroi, even here in Qilifund where there's no one to hear them." She lifted her head, seemed to listen. "Decide now, Hedivy Starab. The one who watches has seen them with his body's eyes."

After a quick glance at her, he fixed his eyes on the floor; he was floundering and he knew it and he hated it. He didn't understand people like her, except to suspect she most likely would opt for what she saw as the greatest good—which might mean drugging him and handing him over, ready to talk. On the other hand, she hadn't really needed to warn him about the Qilimen or ask his consent, he'd been chugging down her noxious brews for days now—if she had just handed him the glass, the stuff would be down his throat already. Ask his consent? Couldn't bring herself to betray him without his cooperation? He swore under his breath and held out his hand. "Give it to me."

It was dark when he surfaced enough to know who and where he was. A soft hand muffled the first sounds he made and Makalaya stooped down until her mouth was inches from his ear. "Guard outside the door," she whispered, her breath hot on his face. "We don't want him in here."

The shadow bending over him went away; over the thunder, the sudden sound of rain beating on the thatch and against the side of the house, he heard the clink of stoneware. Her hand caught his, closed it around the mug, then she helped him sit up so he could drink without dripping down his neck. The water was elixir in his arid mouth.

When the mug was empty, she eased him down, crossed the room and opened the door. He could see her teeth gleaming after she pulled the door shut and turned back. "He's gone under the house to get out of the rain," she said. "If you want, you can talk. Quietly, of course."

"What happened?"

She perched on the stool beside the bed, folded her hands in her lap, smiling again. "Nothing much," she murmured. "The Gazingey—if you don't know it, that's what they call their questionmen—he tried to make you answer him, but didn't get anywhere. Mostly you just stared at him, muttered, and sweated. After you started going on about tattooed snakes, he left." She muffled a giggle behind a hand. "You hurt his feelings, poor thing.

Qilimen don't like snakes, playtime is hunting them down
and torturing them."

"He'll be back."

"That's what the guard's for. To make sure we bring
you round and tell him when it happens."

"I've got to get out of here." He tried to sit up, but the
drink, whatever it was, had drained his strength until he
was almost as badly off as he'd been when the Qilimen
had brought him here.

"Hush now. Don't worry." Her hand was cool on his
shoulder. "We've got a plan. Relax and go back to sleep.
We'll take care of you."

>><<

Serroi leaned on the back rail of the house, looking out
across the lake as Lele-isi and her friends set tiny candles
in leaf boats and slid these onto the water where the evening breeze blew them along like captured stars. She
could hear the young women's laughter and a word or
two in their light, rapid voices, the liquid splats as fish
broke the surface after bugs, the sleepy twitter of birds.
The lake village was lovely and peaceful, the Fetch had
left her alone, no dreams, no waking visions, she'd slept
well, eaten well, lazed away days that slid past almost un-
marked. Adlayr and the others would be looking for her,
she knew that, but seldom thought about them. All thinking seemed to be an effort not worth making.

She sighed and straightened. Nine lives if she moved
against the constraints and broke free. How many lives if
she didn't? That she had no answer to that troubled her
more and more in spite of the sweet stillness of this place,
a stillness that seemed to drain all energy from her mind
and body.

Inside the house Liqebemalah was waiting for her. He
bowed, put a small jar on the table, placed two horn flagons beside it. "It is the Anayanga, Healer. The time of
New Wine. The Clans of Chihi Qakaza send you this taste
of our halaberry wine. I ask that you be great-hearted and
drink a health with me."

"I believe you when you say this isn't what you wanted, Shaman. I'll do it."

The flagons were small and delicate, the horn scraped until it was translucent enough to read through, set in a base of dark, tightgrained wood. He poured a little wine into each, less than a finger's width. It was a dark rich red and thicker than she expected. She touched her flagon to his. "Health and happiness," she said.

"Health to your and yours, Healer. May you find what you need."

She took a sip of the wine; it was tart, perhaps a little too sweet and strong enough to send heat through her as it slid down her throat.

He emptied his flagon, set it on the table. "You will hear drums later this evening, Healer. Though it gives me pain, I must ask that you stay within. These things are private with us."

"I hear and understand."

He bowed again and left.

Serroi yawned, stretched. She stood a moment contemplating the jar. "Why not," she said aloud and startled a laugh from herself at the sound of her voice.

The flagon filled, she wandered into the bedroom and stretched out on the blankets, her head and shoulders resting on the pile of embroidered pillows.

The drums started a few breaths later, joined by another instrument that produced a low hoom that seemed to vibrate in her bones. She sipped at the wine and listened, enjoying the distant concert even more when the male and female voices joined in.

>><<

Lele-isi smoothed the white robe along the sleeping woman's body, glanced up as Liqebemalah came in. "Why? She wears the kalis." She touched the white paper bracelet still sealed about Serroi's wrist. "She couldn't do anything you didn't want her to."

He touched Serroi's arm, pulled his hand quickly away. "The little one is calling her and she would have heard before morning. Nothing would have kept her from answering, Lisili. Not the kalis. Not you nor I nor anyone. We had to stop her while she still trusted us. She seems so tiny, so like a child, you forget how dangerous she is."

>><<

Treshteny followed Yela'o who was trotting close to the manHorse walking silent ahead of her, Mama Charody and Doby at her side. The manyness was back, but now that she knew she could make it come or go whenever she wanted, she greeted it like an old friend; letting Mama Charody lead her, she sneaked glances at the people jostling past them. Shinka-on-the-Neck was bigger, louder, dirtier and apparently more dangerous than Dander and Calanda combined, because a large portion of those she looked at had winding sheets in their immediate future. She looked until she grew weary of it, then closed her eyes and drifted along.

A growl snapped her eyes open; the street was dirty and the buildings mostly boarded up. Except for the men around them, half a dozen hooded thugs, no one else in sight; two of them held shortguns aimed at the manHorse.

"You, woman, take hold of that kid." The biggest man pointed a finger at Doby. "What's wrong wi' you, you some kinda mushhead or somefin?"

The manHorse turned his head, nodded at her.

She took Doby's hand and followed the jerk of the man's finger, leading him away from the others into the middle of the street. He clung to her, silenced again and shaking with terror. Yela'o was squealing and dancing with anger, but he, too, followed the manHorse's lead and stayed with her.

She blinked, looked full at them, and sighed. "Don't worry, Doby. It'll be over in just a minute."

He stared up at her.

She nodded. "Like the chovan," she said.

The man ignored them, stabbed a finger at the manHorse. "Shuck outta that pack and drop it. Good. Now. You'n granny there, you get on you knees and crawl outta here."

Mama Charody chuckled, spread her hands. "Kamen, come!" she cried, "Stonebrothers, come!"

Nothing happened.

"Crazy ol' ... on you knees, I wanna see you crawl, granny."

Charody put her hand out to the manHorse. "Help me down, friend, these knees are old and creaky. Slow and steady, slow and steady." He stared at her a moment, then did as she said.

The minute her knees touched the cobbles, the street jerked apart beneath the thugs, dropping all but one of them into a chasm that seemed to have no bottom, then it crunched together. A head bulged through the cobbles. Is that sufficient, sister? We are few as yet in these strata, though more of us are born as the Mother moves South.

Quite sufficient, brothers. Maiden Bless and may your numbers increase as you desire. She got to her feet with an ease that belied her age and weight, laughed at the silent grumble in the manHorse's bearded face, and turned to the last of the thugs who stood gaping, too terrified to move. "Shoo. Go way. Tell your friends to leave us alone or they'll get the same. Or worse."

He gobbled some formless sounds, then took off running.

Mama Charody chuckled, stretched, and shook herself. "Pick up the pack and let's get going; I can smell green and damp earth, so the edge of this rat warren can't be too far away."

18. Dissolution in Cadander

When Jasny heard a spatter of shots ahead, yells, squeals from macain and horses, she turned her mount and angled across a smoldering field of shen toward one of the boundary hedges and the trees that grew there.

She looped the reins over a low branch of a big, old kerov, stepped from the saddle into the crotch, climbed as high as she could and set the longglasses to her eyes.

One group of men was shooting from a stony ridge beyond a hedge that was smoldering and sending up streamers of thick yellow smoke, the others were in a clump of trees, a grove of javories and brellim. As she watched, half a dozen of these crept from the grove, swung into the saddle and began a wide circle, heading around to get behind the men on the ridge.

Who was what?

She scanned the riders, focusing on the faces, but she found nothing familiar in them; they might be Osklanders, they might be anything.

Though it was hard to see clearly through the smoke from the hedge, she kept scanning the ridge until the wind picked up for just a moment, giving her a fair look at three faces; two of them meant nothing to her, the third was one of her husband's cousins from Brojit in Zemyadel. He'd run from his farm to get away from a whip-mad Rodin and the Web had passed him on to Oskland.

She watched until the riders moved out of sight, then scrambled down the tree, flipped the reins loose, and urged the macai into a quick walk. When she reached the grove, she dismounted and moved into the shadow under the trees, silent as a shadow herself as she glided from cover to cover, locating her targets, the men left behind to keep the ridge's defenders pinned in place. Three of them were up in the trees, two were on the ground, standing behind the trunks, using them as shelter and as support for their longguns. She slipped a stiletto from her boot, ghosted toward the man closest to her, matching her steps to his shots. Taking the last steps at a run, she drove the blade in and up, piercing his heart. She caught him as he slumped, eased the longgun away from him and posed him with his shoulder against the tree, then went after the next man.

The nearest of the treesitters caught a glimpse of her and shouted, but he was late, she got the blade in and out and was rolling away when he shot at her; the bullet burned a crease in her buttock, she felt the hit but no pain, not yet. She scrambled around a tree, slipped the knife into her boot as she rose on her knees, then unsnapped the holster flap. Because he'd had no boys, just her, her daddy'd taught her how to shoot when she barely reached his belt. That was years ago, but Greygen had given her some spare ammunition and she'd practiced a few shots on her way here. She eased around the tree, squeezed off two shots, and smiled with satisfaction at the yelp that followed. She might not have killed him, but she'd put a crimp in his self esteem.

The wounded man started yelling. "Jaddo, Ludz, the notney's got Tenk and I don't hear nothin' from Dool. I think the spros's over 'hind that tree next to where Tenk was. Get 'm."

Jasny shoved the gun into the holster, snapped the flap down and faded toward the outside of the grove, slipping from tree to tree, keeping low, listening to the yelling and other noises behind her, ready to dive if they started shooting.

Spros's gotta knife.
Dool's eatin' dirt.
So's Tenk.
How you, Boud?
Shoulder and leg, get me outta this prokkin' tree.

Get down y'self, we goin' afta him.
Jaddo, you pizh, get me down, I'm leakin like a . . .
Forget it.
Jump, Boud, we busy. . . .

Thugs, she thought contemptuously, couldn't find a
cowpat on a tile floor. She ran for the next tree, felt a
blow on her shoulder, a burn across her thigh, flung herself into a roll, then scrambled from the grove. One arm
useless, she pulled herself into the saddle and kicked her
macai into a run as two men burst from the grove.

She rounded the trees before they could get set to
shoot, urged the macai into a full-out run across the field
toward the hedge, screaming, "Chirro, Jasny, Chirro
Chirro, it's Jasny, they comin' behind you, they comin'
behind you. . . ." She kept it up, focused so intently on the
men ahead of her she forgot the others.

Until she felt a blow in the back and saw red spraying
across the macai's neck growths.

Everything slowed and the world slipped away from
her. . . .

When it came back, she was stretched out on the
ground, Chirro bending over her; she could see the worry
in his face and wanted to tell him it was fine, she didn't
mind at all, but she couldn't make her mouth work, then
she forgot as the numbness faded and the pain seized hold
of her, wiping away everything else. "Hurts," she managed. His face wavered and then there was nothing.

>><<

Greygen worked his knees, got to his feet. "It's time,
Sansy."

In the light coming through the cracked shutters her
face looked pale and she sat stiller than he'd ever seen
her. They were in the kitchen, the packs on the floor beside the table where they were drinking a last cup of cha.
After a minute, she turned her head slowly, her eyes moving over things that added up to most of her life. She
reached out, touched the stoneware cha pot Husenkil had
made for them. She pushed the chair back, picked up the

pot, and crashed it to the floor; without a hitch in her movement, she stooped, lifted her pack, got her arms through the straps, wriggled around till it settled properly, then stood glaring at him. "Zdra, what you waitin' for?"

On the attic floor of the warren where the cheapest, flimsiest rooms were, they moved swiftly and silently over the worn drugget, keeping close to the wall to avoid creaking boards, turned into the lavatory and went out the window onto the fire ladder, moved from that onto the flat roof. The buildings along the street shared common walls and moving from roof to roof was more tedious than dangerous, though they had to remember to stay away from the front where they might be seen.

Prah Strojny the bargevek was waiting in the stockyard at the back of a leathershop that was closed because the owner and his entire family had been shipped south. Greygen helped Sansilly off the ladder, moved stiffly to Prah; his legs were sore, he wasn't used to this much climbing about. "How's Mosec doing, he going to make it?"

"He sent his oldest over with a bit of bread Malry baked. Note inside. Said to wait till tenth watchbell. If they weren't at the meet by then, they couldn't get away. With kids that young . . ." Prah shrugged. "It was always iffy, you know that."

Greygen rubbed a hand down his side, nodded. "How long you been here?"

"Twenty minutes, maybe less. It's been quiet out there," he nodded at the gate leading into the Valley. "No sign of trouble."

There was a hiss, a knocking on the ladder. A head popped over the roof edge; a whisper dropped to them. "Purgers. Marching along t' back street."

Prah waved and the head withdrew. "That's Herec, my eldest. If we're quiet, I don't think they'll look in here. But we better move by the wall and get ready."

The minutes dragged past. Greygen closed his fingers tight on Sansilly's shoulder and stopped breathing as he heard booted feet marching down the alley, but the Purgers kept going, turned onto the street and marched off, heading north toward Steel Point.

Greygen drew a shuddering breath, heard the others start breathing again, heard the boy on the roof flip over the edge and slide down the ladder to join them.

Prah led them through the streets to a Market Landing, rowed them across the river and took them through the maze of lanes at the edge of the Shipper's Warren to the back of another deserted shop where the rest of his family was waiting.

The watchbell in the Temple tower began sounding. Donggg, donggg, donggg.

As the third stroke died, a man's head appeared at the top of the fire ladder, a half-rotten pole with pegs pounded into it.

Prah knocked twice against the wood, then twice more. The head withdrew, then a woman appeared, eased over the edge. While the man steadied the crude ladder, she started down.

Donggg, donggg, donggg.

Sansilly hugged Malry, patting her arm. "Gonna be fine," she said.

Malry's mouth twisted into a rueful smile. "Sansy, you don't change." She gripped hands with Besah, then turned to pluck her youngest off the ladder.

Donggg, donggg, donggg, donggg.

By the time the echo from the last of the strokes died away, Mosec and his family were in the yard with them.

"Purgers ransacking Shipper's Warren," Mosec said, "Didn't seem like they were ever gonna get out."

"Don' matter." Prah snapped his fingers; Besah and Malry began getting their children in line. "Plenty of dark left."

With Prah leading because he knew the alleys and byways in the Shipper's Quarter and Greygen and Sansilly bringing up the rear to help with the children, they ghosted through dark and silent streets.

A soft whistle hardly louder than the wind.

The children faded into shadow, crouching at the base of the wall, their arms over their faces.

A second whistle, three pulses a little louder. A long lean form stepped from an alley. "Seven." He spoke swiftly, softly, his words chasing each other with barely a break between them. "It's all clear ahead. There's a barge in from the Bezhval, the bargeveks are trying to get it unloaded, but the nixies are spooking the horses and generally giving them fits. We liberated some longguns and ammunition from the Training Ground, dug out some stores for you, that's all in the cabin. Greg, take this." He held out a belt pouch. "It's the coin Fletty lifted from the Sleykyn; we figure you can put it to use, to say true, we don't dare in case the notney marked it some way. Maiden Bless all of you, may you get where you need to be."

He was gone without waiting for a response.

While the women were hustling the children into the long low cabin, Greygen crouched by a bitt, watching the upstream show. One of the horses went overboard, dragging several of the ladesmen with him. It screamed and went under, the men struggled a moment longer, then they, too, were gone.

"Greg, it's time. Shodd the bow tie and come aboard."

With Prah at the tiller, crouched low so he was less likely to be seen, and young Herec in the bow reading the water for him, the barge slid away from the wharf and drifted out into the middle of the river. No alarm sounded. If anyone saw them, the loose barge could be attributed to to nixy mischief.

Once they were clear of the city, Greygen and Mosec got the mainsail and the jib up and were lying flat on the deck when the barge reached the junction with the Red Dan. Prah eased the barge round the bend and with a strong following wind, it picked up speed, slicing through the dark water, smooth and steady.

"Bend ahead, five rets, Tower showing over trees." Herec's voice hadn't changed yet and the high notes cut through the creaks and groans from mast, sail and rigging and the howl of the wind. "I see a light, top windows."

Prah took the barge as far as he dared from the north bank, but the moment they rounded the trees, Greygen saw a dark figure leaning from a widow, the cone-shaped hailer held to its mouth, heard the hoarse yell, "Who goes?"

Pray cupped his hands around his mouth. "Dosta Smyka bound for Tuku-kul!"

"Say again."

"Dosta Smyka. Tuku-kul."

Silence. Greygen grimaced. "He's not buying it, Prah."

"What we thought. Yeah, there it goes."

The alarum gong boomed out, the deep brazen notes filling the space beneath the clouds.

Mosec patted a yawn, jacked a bullet into the chamber and sat with the longgun on his knees. "Wonder how long it'll be before we've got company?"

Greygen frowned. "Don't know, Mos. Prah, send Herec below. This won't be any place for a boy."

"Can't. Need him. Been gettin' him ready for apprenticin', teaching him the Dan. You and Mos, you good men in a fight, but you don' know nothin' about riverin'. We hit a sandspit or a snag, we might's well jump in an' swallow water."

"I brought some of my tools, maybe I can cobble together some sort of shield . . . any suggestions?"

"Yeah. Don't. Just make a target outta him and fool with the balance and wind. With the barge this light, she can be cranky. Shootin' starts, you and Mos send it back at 'em, shake up their aim, yeh?"

"Yeh."

For nearly an hour the barge slid along out in the middle of the Red Dan, Herec occasionally calling snag, shoal, bend. The clouds blowing up thickened, the wind driving the barge along at a good clip grew heavy with damp.

Sansilly came on deck and stood with her arms folded on the top of the cabin. "Was goin' dippy shut in down there. What's happenin?"

Greygen eased his hand under her wind whipped hair, rubbed the back of her neck. "Right now, nothing."

She slid her arm around him, pulled him tight against her, then shifted around so she was leaning against him, looking up at the inky sky. "Gonna rain. What'll that do?"

"I don't know." He raised his voice. "Prah, this storm coming up, what's it goin' to do?"

"Wish we had more ballast," Prah yelled back. "Sansy, you better go warn the others, we gonna start dancing in a bit. Get a bucket ready, it really gets twisty, you gonna have some green faces down there."

"Tower bend coming, six rets," Herec sang out, "I see light on water."

Prah swore, said, "Not s'posed to be anyone there. Herec!"

"Huh, Da?"

"What'd I tell you if there's trouble?"

"Keep belowside and 'hind jib when I gotta be up."

"You do that or I'll skin you good, you hear?"

"Yeh, Da."

Sansilly came back on deck, Besah only a step behind her. "Malry's gonna keep the kids, this round; we worked a system out, two of us up, one down." She glared at Greygen, then at Prah. "We not gonna be left out of this, none of us, you hear? Bes is gonna reload for us, me, I'm Harozh, I was shooting verks time I was two. Been a while, but it's not something you f'get."

Greygen caught hold of her shoulder. "You will stay down, Sans, if I have to knock you on the head, you're goin' to stay low."

She chuckled. "No fear, I'm not gonna be makin' orphans outta our boys." She punched his arm. "And don' you do, either."

The wind dropped, turned erratic; the barge slowed and started giving Prah fits as he tried to do three men's work at once. Greygen left shelter behind the cabin, crept on hands and knees toward him. "Prah. Give me the tiller, you handle the sail."

The bargevek growled, then nodded. "Hold her where

I got her, 'less I tell you move her." He stood, holding the
tiller steady while Greygen took his place, then set
Greygen's hands on it and began hurried work with ropes,
lowering the sail halfway down the mast, tieing reef knots
to pull it taut again, winching the boom around a little.
He kept talking while he worked. "You know angles?"

"On wood."

"Angles be angles. I say north two, you turn tiller north
two degrees. North meaning toward north bank, don't
matter 'f we goin' straight west or not. You can do that?"

"I can do that."

"Good. Herec," he called, "how far c'n you see ahead?"

"Water maybe one ret," the boy called back. "Bends
two three rets."

"Yell out what you see ever time you pop up, even if
'tis nothin'. You hear?"

"Yeh, Da."

The tip of Greygen's shoulder stung an instant before
he heard the crack of the longgun. "Shootin'!" He slid off
the bench, crouched beside the tiller, holding it as steady
as he could. The numbness wore off, pain shot through
him when he tried to move and he could feel a tickling
stickiness on the outside of his arm.

He heard the beat of horses' hooves, a clank, then a
series of scrapes and clanks; the barge shuddered under
him, fought to turn. Sounds of feet, shadows moving by
the cabin, vanishing round the end, more clanks, a
grunted curse, Sansy's voice. He clamped his teeth on
his lip to keep back the words knotting his throat. The
barge swung wildly for an instant, then settled. More
scrabbling noises, Sansy and Mos shooting at the tower
and the riders, and then they were round the bend,
shielded from the tower and the road by a long, narrow
grove of javories.

Greygen shivered as a small flurry of raindrops hit the
back of his head and dripped down his neck. "What was
that?" He kept his voice low, letting the wind carry his
words forward.

"Grapnel." That was Mos. "Tryin' to haul us in. Bad

throw, we got it off easy. Next time though, we an't gonna let them get that close."

"Sans?"

"I'm fine, Greg. Din't touch me."

"Prak, but I got creased. Shoulder. Already stopped bleedin' but I think while there's time, I better get it tied up."

"Saaaaa! Bes, where's that . . . good. You just sit still, Greg; Mos, you go hang onto tiller. I can see Prah needs about three more hands as 'tis."

Riders came pounding along the river road; they swerved out as Mos and Sansy started shooting, dropped off the levee into the fields beyond, but kept coming through the tall shem in the field, trampling the grain flat as they cut across the bend, trying to get ahead of the barge.

Herec dropped the minute he saw a flash, gasping as he heard the chunk as the bullet hit the rail. "Da," he yelled. "They up in front a us, shootin' back."

"Water?"

"No snags I saw, no shoal ripples, but it's dark out there."

"Hug the deck till we get past 'em. You hear?"

"Yeh, Da."

The rain came down as the barge reached the bend, flurries at first, then a blinding downpour. The storm shielded them from the shooters on the bank, but sent the barge into a twisty dipping dance. Mosec was the first to go under. Sansilly tried to hold on, but emptied her stomach overside, then let Prah half carry her to the hatch and shove her down the steps. Bes gathered up the guns and the clips and followed her below to help with the motionsick. If the riders were still following, they were riding blind and no danger at the moment.

"Snag comin', one ret ahead, south, no shoals north." The boy's high voice came broken through the storm.

The rain beat down, the wind howled, the rigging thrummed and creaked.

"Half a degree north, Greg, hold, hold, a hair more, that's got it." Prah's yell was hoarse from the strain.

The uprooted tree rolled past, a ghost of a battering ram coming out of the murk, the widest branches brushing against the side of the barge.

"No shoals, southbend two rets."

"Two degrees south, Greg, good, that's got it, now feel your way round the bend, let's see how you do, gotta learn sometime, this's good as any, just a hair more pressure, good, that's it. Even 'f you can't see bow, feel how she moves, feel wind, watch bank. Good. Good. Y' got good hands, working with that wood, I s'pose." Prah loomed from the darkness and the rain, touched Greygen's arm, vanished again as he went to tend sail.

The storm lasted the night, but blew away with dawn. When the strengthening gray light was strong enough so Greygen could see the river road again, it was empty. The riders had given up the chase.

Sansilly came up, white and shaken, a bucket in each hand. She emptied them overside, then leaned on the cabin roof and watched the road unreel. After a long silence, she turned to him and smiled. "We beat 'em again."

Prah chuckled. "That we did. How they doin' down there?"

"Malry gave out like me, but Bes was a tower. The kids're fine. Ferla had a bit of a problem, but she wasn't nearly as bad as us. You think we could stop a short while? There's some cleaning up to do." She kicked at a bucket, made the bail clank.

"No need to stop." After a glance at the sail and the river ahead, Prah whipped a section of rope loose from one of the neat coils lined up against the cabin's side, knotted it to the bail and dropped the bucket overside. He sloshed it about for a moment, drew it up, brimming with river water. "There's that un, hand me t'other."

When he finished with the second, he said, "Sansy, how you feelin'? Tired?"

"Fair. Nik. Why?"

"Would y' be willin' to go let Herec show y' how to read water, then send him down so he c'n get some sleep?"

"Zdra zdra, why not." She grinned. "Beats swabbin' vomit." On her way to the bow, she bent into the hatch, yelled, "Bes, your man's rinsed out the buckets 'n got us some clean water, come fetch."

Prah chuckled. "Greg, I was gonna send you down, too, but I think I'll wait on that."

Greygen yawned, moved his shoulders, wincing at the pull of the bullet burn. "Until it drys out down there, I'm with you on that." He glanced right and left at the fields of shen stretching flat and yellow out to the horizon on both sides of the river—wasn't a figure moving, man or beast, in all that space. "You really think they've given up?"

"Probably figurin' we not worth the effort. Nov'll sweep us in when he finishes with Osk and Ank."

"You ever think of coming to Tuku-kul with us? Might be safer, lots of chovan in the Travs."

"Weren't for the kids, I'd do 't in a minute. Trouble is, the Fenekel, they fine to people movin' through, but they won't let y' settle. And beyond that, too many ifs, 'f you know what I mean. Better to find folk we know and dig in with them." He smiled as his wife came up with a bucket and emptied it over the rail. "Bes, want more?"

"Nik, what I want is you go get some sleep. I'll watch sail a while."

The barge slid on without trouble through a day turned from gray to gold, shimmering with heat, the wind reduced to small, spaced gusts, like a beast sighing on the backs of their necks.

>><<

Tall and stately in her dress robes, the sun gleaming on the Mask, the meie Zasya Myers behind her, Ildas an elusive shimmer trotting in circles about them, K'vestmilly Vos walked the walls of OskHold, showing herself to her people, looking down at the teeming courts and the village lower on the river that filled the Hold's moat. There were people everywhere, Osklanders and others. On a flat beyond the orchards of the Hold navstas of recruits swerved and galloped to the yells of their vudveks. Children were gathered wherever there was a bit of shade, teachers taking them through their lessons, women were outside, sewing, spinning, washing, sweeping, taking their baking to the communal ovens, standing in clumps gossiping, old men were sitting about knitting or working in leather and wood. No one was drinking. Pan Osk had shut down the taverns and shaved the heads of every man or woman who got drunk in public and promised a session at the whipping post if they did it twice. There was grumping at that, but most people agreed with him. There were too many crowded in too small a space to let things get out of hand.

There were shouts as she walked, *Marn, Marn, Marn, Maiden Bless, Marn Marn Marn*.

She waved and moved on, waved again and again until her arm was weary.

Her face behind the Mask still damp from the water she'd thrown on it, the formal robes exchanged for a cooler tunic and trousers, K'vestmilly Vos came into the shadowy comroom, stood by the door listening as Camnor Heslin's voice came through quiet and clear.

Loneliness hit her like a blow beneath the heart. She wanted him in a way she couldn't put into words, a complex combination of sex and companionship and the need to sharpen her own wits against a mind quicker and more devious than her own—an all-over yearning that was stronger than any feeling she could remember, even her faded infatuation with Vyzharnos Oram.

I'm a fool. I threw away a jewel for trash. Irritably she shook off that skein of thought and crossed the room to stand behind Vedouce.

". . . got word from Trivud Stoppah, they totaled a squad of raiders, mostly citymen, lost seven men and one woman, Jasny Zarcadla, the one who killed the Sleykyn, she got it warning them the chovan were trying an ambush. Too bad. She killed two and wounded another before she went, would have been a good addition to our forces.

"Bad news—though it could be worse. Spotters missed one of the mixed raider bands, chovan and city thugs, they hit Trivud Shaten's force, caught them unprepared, slaughtered all but three who managed to get mounted and away. These three ran into one of the Spiders and when he heard what happened, he slipped up close enough to put a longglass on them, said the raiders went through everything there like a swarm of rats. Hunting for a com, he thinks. They took off, Spider six spotting them for Trivud Throdal. Throdal set up an ambush, hit them from three sides, took them down. No prisoners.

"The main army has reached the border, they're moving at a good clip, disciplined and steady. Mern the Fist may have the soul of a viper, but he's a good organizer, he's got scouts out, whistle-talking chovan, they keep him well informed about what's going on round the army. Nov has joined them with his Sleykyn, they're still with him, haven't broken away yet to go on their own, but we expect that any day now, so you better tighten security at the Hold. The Spiders have been warned to watch for them, but there's a danger now that we can start losing coms should a Sleykyn sniff out one of the spotters. The minute we get word the Sleykyn're gone, we'll send a warning and you should switch to the scrambler immediately. Any questions? Go."

Vedouce frowned, tapped the go button. "Supply trains. How vulnerable are they? Go."

"Mern's thought of that. The main supply wagons move in the middle of the foot forces, stay there when the army camps for the night. New supplies coming up from Dancer, they're different; the wagons are scattered along the whole distance and only have a few guards. Same for the herds of vul and spare mounts traveling with them. If you want, we could take some of the navstas from defense and send them back to capture those wagons; thanks to the Web in Dander, we have a clear idea of what's in each shipment, where the herds are and the numbers of guards with them. I'll send the list in a minute, but before I do, any questions? Go."

"No questions. Send spotters with coms to . . ." He stared into the shadows a moment, then spoke quickly into the com. "Trivuds Throdal and Stoppah so I can talk to them. I don't need the list, they will. That'll be six navstas, hundred and fifty men. I've just sent them some new trainees, so they should be up to strength. They can use the new men to escort the wagons back, herd the captured mounts, let the vul scatter. We haven't space or fodder for them. Go."

"Got it. Hold on a minute. . . ." A mutter and movement noises reached them. "Back. Coms are on their way. The Marn, how is she doing? Go."

K'vestmilly Vos leaned past Vedouce. "She'll tell you herself. I'm fine, just missing you, Heslin. Take care, will you? Go."

"Ah." There was a long silence, then Heslin said, "The heart grows fonder?" Behind the Mask she wrinkled her nose as she heard the laughter in his voice. "Vedouce," he went on, "is there anything else? Go."

"Nik. I'll be here waiting. Out."

Vedouce leaned back, closed his eyes, the weary lines in his face exaggerated by the flicker of the lamp. "Waiting," he said finally. "Chaos out there, everyone scuttling like cockroaches in the kitchen when you light a lamp. Trying to pull together a pattern. . . ." He shook his head and got to his feet; he went to the door, waved to one of his servants waiting outside. "Bring me a pot of strong cha with a couple of sandwiches. I'm going to be here a while."

19. The Contagion Spreads

Chaya frowned at the sketch, then at the diagram she was working out; she wrote quickly, then began checking her notes against the loom. Playing games with numbers was one thing, the actual threading of the loom was something entirely different.

She heard knocking at the front door, the bronze serpent coil striking against the bronze plate, sharp metallic sounds in a buoyant rhythm; she didn't recognize the knock, but the cheerful tattoo made her smile as she pushed the chair back and went to see who was there.

The Wandermonk was a cheerful plump man with smile creases around his eyes and mouth; he reached in his pouch, brought out a folded, sealed packet. "Letter, kos. If you be Chaya Willish?"

"Oh!" She slipped a copper ning from the receptacle pegged to the doorjamb and passed it to him. "Yes. That's me. Chaya Willish. Thank you. Would you like something to eat or drink?"

"Na, kos. But if you'll direct me to the fam hostel?"

"Of course." She stepped onto the porch, walked to the front steps and pointed "If you'll follow the path you came on back to the road, go north along it till you reach the Weave Hall, that's easy to find, it's the biggest building in the fam. Turn into the lane that runs beside it on the north side, follow that back, the hostel's at the end of the lane."

"Maiden bless you, kos." Whistling a cheery tune, thumbs tucked in his belt, elbows swinging, brown robe billowing around his ankles, the Wandermonk went off down the path.

The packet getting sweaty in her hand, Chaya went back into the house. She stood in the entrance hall staring down at it, at the familiar writing with her name and the directions for finding her. "Lavan," she said aloud.

She took the letter into the kitchen and set it on the table while she pumped water into a kettle, stirred up the fire and added a few more lumps of coal from the hod, got down her second best cha pot and the cha caddy and set it on the table.

She turned the letter over, looked at the seal, touched the yellow wax and sighed, then went back into her workroom, put her sketch and patternbook away, pulled the cover over the loom, centered the bench. By the time she'd finished all this, she heard the kettle whistling and hurried back to the kitchen.

She took a sip of the cha, held the butterknife against the side of the pot till it was warm, then slid it under the seal, turned back the flap and took the letter from its cover.

Chayacici

It's done! We've sworn the oath. He IS an old old man, but he's strong and vigorous despite that and O Chaya, he's a Great One, his designs, so strong and simple they make my heart sing, it's only been a day and what I'm learning, ah my love, WHAT I'm learning, what I'm GOING to learn!

This is a pleasant town and it is a town, not a village, more than three times as big as Hallafam. It's on the river and boats are going by both ways almost every day; people pass through here heading in a dozen different directions, peddlers, Wandermonks, players, pilgrims, and more. You'd love it here, Chayacici, always something new happening and the evenings are warm and no one goes to bed before midnight, they're in the square, dancing, playing games, talking.

You should see the workshop, Chay. He's got
tools I've never even heard of. Zok was a good
man and a better technician, but Casil Kinuqah
is an artist. He set me to working on a ring he'd
designed. Some Familyhead in Bokivada sent
over this big stone, an oval tourmaline an inch
long and half an inch across, very intense color.
He's got this gold bar which is a very pale yellow,
some sort of impurity, I imagine, though I don't
know what it is. The design is an elongated
flower form with a hint of leaves, very simple,
very abstract, the balance between metal and
stone is so perfect—ahhh Chayacici—I wish you
could see it! And he's going to let me do everything, just gave me the sketch and said go to it.

Chay my cici, my isaganah, I miss you terribly.
I've been a fool and worse, taking out my fears
and worries on you. I was so scared, cici, after
three years of NOTHING, I thought I'd never be
more than a boot-about journeyman and I'd lose
you in the bargain because your uncle would
never agree to us wedding and loping off with
you, ahwu, you know what that would mean. But
never to run my fingers through your soft brown
hair, never touch your . . .

The knocker on the front door beat an imperative summons. Chaya started, swore under her breath (her father
used to clout her when she used those words, tell her that
he didn't care who she heard saying that, she wasn't to
bring filth under the family roof, so even now she never
said the words aloud though he and her mother had been
dead five years). More knocking. Thump ka-thump.
Heavy and demanding. She folded up the letter and went
to answer the door, smoothing down her hair as she
moved, checking her apron to see if it was clean enough
for company. *Ahwu, ahwu, keep your hair on, I'm coming.*

Two women stood on the porch, smiles tacked on their
faces, looking nervous but determined. Neighbor wives.
She didn't know them well, but she'd played with their

kids when she was a tadling herself. "Kos Hobsa, Kos Vivin, be welcome."

She waited for them to tell her what they wanted, but they took her greeting for an invitation and walked past her into the house.

During the next two hours she was startled, then amused, then increasingly irritated as they scolded her for living alone, fighting with her uncle about it and just about everything else in her life, then settled to worry at her, trying to get her to join the Glory, help them build a House for the fam. They ignored her when she said she followed the Maiden, brushed that aside, calling it habit, nothing more.

"Come to the meeting, Chaya, you'll see, let the Glory touch you. . . ." Hobsa's broad face flushed, her eyes glowed. "You can't know what it's like unless you're there." She stretched out her hand, closed it around Vivin's. "Isn't it so, Viv, isn't it truly so?"

Vivin's eyes were glazed with memory. She nodded, the tip of her tongue sliding over her lips. "Like nothing else in the world," she breathed. She blinked, freed her hand, and leaned forward, her eyes fixed on Chaya's. "You must come."

They both stared at her as if they were willing her to agree with them.

She kept her temper, even managed a small smile; they were her neighbors and she'd have to live with them. She stood, spoke with an unaccustomed formality to put a wall between her and them. "I thank you for your concern," she said. "This has been most interesting, but I must remind you that I am beginning work on my masterproject and I have only the hours after I finish my quota of cloth at the Weave Hall." She waited, still smiling though her mouth was feeling more than a little strained. "If you'll stay a moment, I'll fetch a little something to add to your House fund. Nay, nay, 'tis my pleasure."

She shut the door after them, slipped the bar into its hooks as if that could keep out the craziness. For a moment she stood with her eyes closed, shaking with anger, remembering the Glory marchers who'd slashed their way through the Weave Hall. Vivin and Hobsa didn't mention that. Nay, not a word.

She shivered, went to the kitchen, and pumped water into the heater, then filled the heatbox under the tank with coal and got a small burn started, using the bellows to nurse it until it was strong enough to keep going. She wanted a bath to wash away the slime those women had poured over her. In her agitation she worked the bellows too vigorously, blew the fire out, and had to start again. They'd spoiled Lavan's letter for her, she'd been so happy at the happiness that burned through every word, the weave pattern was slowly taking shape and she'd been happy at that. Now....

With the fire going well and the water beginning to heat, she got to her feet, hung the bellows on its hook, and went to wash her hands at the sink. She glanced at the table, the cha pot, the cup—and the letter. With a shiver, she went into the kitchen garden and began pulling weeds. It was nearly sundown, heavy black clouds low overhead, a threat of rain in the air, so she ended up pulling nearly as many foodplants as she did weeds, but by the time the valve whistle blew on the water tank, she felt a little better.

>><<

"... I was so angry, Lavacece, I couldn't even finish your letter then. I had a bath and took it to bed with me, wishing it was you, do you remember...."

Lavan smiled but skipped the next part and continued reading the letter aloud. He was sitting on the grass in the back yard, Casil Kinuqah was in an old wicker chair under the Munga tree. The sun was low on the horizon, the garden filled with the drowsy hum of insects and birdsong; the breeze off the river was cool, tickling at his hair.

The letter went on to tell of the attack on the Weave Hall, asking if he'd seen anything like that and did he remember Sekhaya's tale?

"I've found the pattern I wanted, Lavacece. Remember

how I was fussing about that? I saw the Hall serpents
dance with a lamia one night when I was working alone
there, you know how it is when you make journeyman,
people won't leave you alone, they mean well, but there's
no way you can get anything done. If you come back for
the Thazayyaka Fest, I'll show the pattern to you, I think
you'll like it. I'm working hard at charting the design, I
should be able to start threading the loom in a month or
so. It's going to be a brocade so even the trial piece won't
be done for months; it has to be seven ells long and as
perfect as I can make it, but if I get it approved and I do
the masterwork as well as I think I can, in two years I
should be free of obligation. I thought I was going to be
sad at leaving this house and I was rooting around for
ways not to, but Hallafam is going strange on me, starting
with when Iduna Yekai tried to rouse the Peacers to collar
the Gloryfolk and get them to pay for the damage they
did; they told her to go away and stop interfering with the
pious doing their religious duty. Can you believe that,
Lavan? If things keep up that way, I'll be happy to go. In
any case, I want to be with you, I'm so lonely without
you, love. . . ."

Once again Lavan stopped reading. He folded the letter
and tucked it into his shirt. "She has her uncles and cousins there, but I don't know how much use they'd be. I
don't know what to do, Master."

Casil stroked his mustache, the curving yellow-white
hairs flattening under his fingertip and springing back.
"Sounds like she's not worried enough to leave yet, won't
want to before she makes master. I'd say give her slack,
you know how hard it is without that c'tificate. Hmm.
This nonsense is spreading like a plague, had a letter
from m' daughter day b'fore you got here, weird thing,
way out on the east coast she is, but she was goin' on
like those women in that." He waggled a finger at the paper in Lavan's hand. "Worried 'bout m' grandkids." He
shrugged. "Not a thing I can do."

"Shouldn't somebody do something?"

"Who?"

"The Arbiters at Mokadumise? Why not them, don't

they train the Servants of the Maiden? And isn't this an attack on Her?"

"What could they do and who'd listen? We aren't like other folk, Lav, no Mucky tellin' us do this, do that; got a problem, clan or guild they settle it. They can't, you call the Arbiters and have a whale of a time arguin' a couple of years 'n they settle it. Used to be I liked it that way." His mustache spread as he grinned at a memory. "Fun watchin' it, good drunk aft' they settle." His nose twitched. "An't fun now, this lot. I seen 'em, got all the juice squeezed outta them."

They stared at each other a long minute, then Lavan folded the letter, shoved it in his shirt. He swung round, drew his knees up, draped his arms over them, and sat watching the sun go down.

>><<

Sekhaya Kawin scowled at the shopkeeper. "What?"

A sheen of yellow in his eyes, the tall thin man shook his head. "Nothing, Herbwoman. I don't sell to outsiders. Be best for you to leave Karafam."

"How can I leave without travel food for myself and my horse?"

"That is not my problem. Must I call the Peacers?"

"What's wrong, Kato Yosets? You know me, I've been by here a thousand times. Outsider?"

"We neither of us're what we were, Herbwoman. Only reason I say anything is 'cause I know you. Leave Karafam and don't come back again." He turned his back to her and began rearranging boxes on a shelf.

When she went out, there were at least fifty people on the fam's single street, a street that had been empty a moment ago; they were staring at her, their faces closed against her.

She yanked the tether loose, coiled it onto its harness hook, climbed onto the driver's seat and took up the reins. "Amb'h amb, Joma. Ch'ka ch'ka. That's a good horse. Nay, hold back, cece, we won't give 'em the satisfaction. We may be goin' but we goin' at our own pace."

Joma's hooves were loud in the heavy silence, klip

kalop klip kalop. There was a faint squeal in one axle of
the van; she hadn't noticed it before and made a note to
find the problem when next she stopped. As they creaked
out of the fam, shifting from pavement to packed dirt,
Sekhaya went over memories of the last several fams
she'd visited. There'd been a few stares, some hostile
looks, but nothing like this.

Usually her visits were breaks in sameness for the fams
on her round, an occasion for parties and meetings; she
carried news from fam to fam, who was wedding whom
and what the quarrels were, who had jobs to offer, what
places were open for new apprentices, widows looking
for husbands, widowers for wives, a hundred bits of this
and that. Twice a year she made the round, spring and
fall; this year the news she carried had dwindled to a
trickle, then not at all as she came south and turned the
bottom curve, but she'd thought that was because she was
late this year, what with Chaya's celebration and finding
the Master for Lavan, but maybe that wasn't so. Maybe
all the fams would be going like this one. She wrinkled
her nose at the thought.

Joma ambled along, content to dawdle if she was content to let him; the hedgerows were high and overgrown,
the drainage ditches between them and the road were
choked with weed, some of it high enough for the horse
to snatch a mouthful of green as he plodded along. Food,
she thought, it's going to be a problem, not so much me
as him. She frowned at the sorrel's flicking ears. Can't
count on the next fam being any different. Maybe I
should cut across the fields, go back the way I came. I
hate to abandon the other fams, if they aren't gone weird,
they'll be expecting me. Still, I could look in on that Forest girl. If she's still alive.

When Joma reached a place where the hedge turned
brown and skeletal, a man stepped through the gap.
"Herbwoman." His voice was hoarse, barely louder than
a whisper, and there was a desperation in it that woke
prickles along her spine. "Turn in here, please. Quick. I
don't think anyone's watching. Please, my little girl. . . ."

He ducked behind the hedge, brought out a board,
placed it across the ditch, repeated with three more boards

until he had a bridge wide enough and, she hoped, strong enough to bear the van; she didn't like the thought of getting stuck this close to Karafam, but if a child was really sick. . . .

When she was safely across, he lifted the planks and flung them behind the hedge, scraped and scrabbled with his hands to smooth out the marks that the boards, the wheels, and Joma's hooves had left on the banks, using a bit of dead hedge to sweep away the last of the sign. He stood stiff and straight a moment, listening with an intensity that told her better than words how terrified he was, then he wheeled and ran past her. "Follow me." The same hoarse whisper.

He angled across the field, a pasture without grazers, no doubt because of the gap in the hedge.

She wondered about that gap. Hedgebrush was tough, it could even survive several years of drought and come back strong and it didn't have any diseases that she knew of. Something had certainly killed that section, though. Not fire, more like some kind of poison. She sucked her teeth, shook her head. *This world is getting crazier by the hour.*

The man climbed the bars of a gate, balanced an instant on the top one, looking anxiously about, then he jumped down and swung the gate open for her.

He led her though a tangle of lanes, stopped her by a grove of Munga trees. He stood looking up at her, sweat glistening on his face. "Herbwoman, would you please leave that," he put his hand on the side of the van, "in the trees there where it won't be seen? I'll send my boy with corn and hay for the horse. Thing is, I've got neighbors and if they see. . . ." He squeezed his shoulders, his eyes fixed on hers, the pupils wide with fear. "They'll call the Glorymen and. . . ."

"Show me the best way in and don't fuss, hmm? I'll be glad of the food for Joma, my supplies are low."

The house was small and dark, one room with a kitchen behind a dividing wall and a sleeping loft. The little girl was on a pallet stretched beside the hearth, a rushlight in a wooden holder by her head, her mother sitting beside her holding her hand, the same sweaty tension in her face as there'd been in her husband's, the same fear darkening her eyes.

Sekhaya touched the mother's shoulder. "Put some water to boil, will you? I'll be setting herbs to steep as soon as I see what this is."

The man came in, pulling the door shut. "The boy's gone. He'll stay with the van to keep an eye on things."

Busy probing the child's neck and armpits, Sekhaya said, "Thanks. No one round here would help?"

"Nay. We havena gone to Glory and. . . ."

"And they won't help outsiders."

"Yeh. M' wife, she was daweyth taught, so she's strong for Maiden, and me, I don' like that lot. Bonjjin' lackwits." He moved his shoulders. "Been thinkin' about moving to Fundasendle, got a cousin there, told 'im what's happenin' here, he says none a that thuv up there. M' wife, she din't want to go, all her kin's here, then Hallie, there, got sick. . . ." He sighed.

"This looks worse than it is," Sekhaya said, "just a bad case of kuy fever. She must've got bit by a tick. I'll leave you some kweel powder to dust round the house." She lifted the child's head, began feeding her the infusion, cooing to her as she turned her head, trying to get away from the bitter drink. "Coom, coom, Hallie luv, drink it down now, you'll feel better, coom a coom, that's a good baby."

When the mug was empty, she eased the girl down, drew her finger along the soft cheek, chuckling at the sleepy murmur. "Day or two and you'll be out pesterin' your brother again, and don't try to tell me y' din't. I did, we all do 't."

She got to her feet. "I left two packets of herbs in the kitchen along with a sack of kweel powder. Brew one up round dawn in a mugful of water, give her the last round sundown, dust the powder in the bedding and round the house." She put her hand on the man's arm. "Do you know about the fams north of here. Have they gone the same way?"

"Sablerfam got it 'fore Kara did. They come down on

us. More'n that I dunno." He looked at his sleeping daughter, his face tightening. "We han't got money, Herb-woman."

"Maiden's Honor, man. Better days to us all." She squeezed his arm. "Stay here, I know the way."

The boy came from the shadows. "Hallie?"

"She'll do fine in a day or so, just a nasty tickbite. You watch out for yourself, you hear? And take yourself home, more'n time you were in bed."

He nodded without smiling, ghosted into the trees as if he'd had a lot of practice in silent walking.

She stroked Joma's muzzle, dangles on the bridle clink-ing musically as he pushed his head against her. "Have yourself a good feed, cece?" She clicked the bit into place. "Marchin' time, Joma. Mp, tired as I am, I think I'll walk a while. It's east for us, old son, and hopin' there's no cousins of yours out there, you do get chatty, m'love, if there's anything horsy on the wind." She snapped the tether into the bridle ring, slapped his shoul-der with the ends and moved off with him, eyes swivel-ing, ears alert.

>><<

Hibayal Bebek sat naked in the windowseat in the dor-mer window, his feet on the cushions, a brandy glass balanced on his stomach, a bottle on the ledge beside him. In the street below, the flagellants were snaking down the street, their white robes bloody. There was a new thing about their scourges; the leather thongs on the end had bits of glass and steel sewn into them. They tore the flesh now when they hit. He groaned as he watched them, watched the sweet red flowers bloom on their backs and thighs, grew hot and hard as waves of their ecstasy rose to him, closing around him, calling him. "Let me go," he said, "Please. Let me go."

Nay, Belovéd, the Glory whispered to him, each word a kiss, a lick of the tongue. *Nay, Child, we need you held apart. We need you seen as impartial agent. You serve us, truly you do, with a service greater than any of those.*

Reach out your hand, Belovéd, touch us, take us within you, let us show you how splendid you are.

He turned his head from the window and looked at the table altar across the room. A mass of yellow light, thick and heavy as butter, floated, pulsing and throbbing above the geode. He stretched out his arm and watched with detached interest as the light drifted from the stone until it touched his fingers, then changed form and slid like oil over his hand and up his arm, gradually sinking into his flesh.

A moment later the familiar pain burned in him, terrible and wonderful. At the height of it, he came in an orgasm more explosive and intense than any he'd known before, even his first times when his uncle beat him, then beat him again for messing his pants, every thought blown away, body and mind merging with the universe.

He woke sometime later, flat on his face on the grass mat before the altar. He put the embroidered cover over the geode, staggered from the attic room, locking the door behind him. There was no energy left in him and little strength, but he forced himself to pump water for a cold bath and eat a dry sandwich while he waited for it to heat. These days he worked from the moment he opened his office door until long after sundown. All the "brothers" the brandy had made for him sent their business to him and on top of that there was the House business. He'd managed to get the clearances he needed and demolition was beginning on the property he'd purchased. There were the architects' plans for the House itself, he had to look them over, talk with the men, choose one of them and that wasn't easy. He'd tried asking for help in this, but the Glory wasn't interested in details, just the House built as soon as possible.

And the Maideners were starting to cause trouble, asking too many questions, daweythies hanging about. . . .

He swallowed the last of the sandwich, washed it down with a gulp of water, then went to take his bath.

20. Changing Configurations

The dawn sunlight shone through the scraped shell plates that were the windowpanes, touched Serroi as she lay unconscious on the bed. Lele-isi sighed, got to her feet, cramped from her long vigil. She looked down at the tiny woman, shook her head. Such a little scrap. And nice. But Liqebamalah knew about these things and he said she was dangerous to the Halathi. She sighed again and went out to the kitchen to set the water heating for her cha and Serroi's bath.

Salda-mai came in when she was fanning alive the fire in the stovehole. "Sa-sa, Lisi, what you want me to do?"

Lele-isi grinned at her. "Fetch in some water, ho?"

"You. Laaaazy." Salda-mai caught up the yoke buckets, turned in the doorway. "Any idea when this is going to be over?"

"Maybe you could get it out of Liqebamalah, he wouldn't tell me."

Singing a mim-chant under her breath, Lele-isi pounded lamva seeds into a paste for the broth they were going to trickle down Serroi before they bathed her. She didn't notice the stiff silence spreading around her until it was broken by a heavy dragging sound. She set the mallet down, crossed to the kitchen door, and froze as she found herself staring up into the face of an immense lamia.

Great glowing eyes swept over her, then the lamia dismissed her and moved on. The serpent body was thick as a small tree; muscles bunched and rippled under skin patterned in vertical stripes of muted browns and ochers, moving her across the room with surprising speed.

She went into the bedroom.

Lele-isi gulped, eased past the twitching tail and fled from the house, nearly knocking over Salda-mai as she toiled from the lake with the water she'd gone to fetch.

"Lisi, what . . .?"

"You didn't see her?"

"Who? You mean the Healer woke and got away?"

"Nay, the lamia." Lele-isi bit her lip, looked from the isolated guest house to the others in the village. "Um . . . I don't know . . . Salda-mai, I'd better stay and see what . . . um . . . go wake Liqebemalah, tell him. . . ."

She stopped as Salda-mai shrugged off the yoke and grabbed her arm. "What?"

"Lissss. Look."

The lamia came huge and stately from the house, swaying and slithering forward, the body of the sleeping Healer in her arms. As soon as she moved from the walk and touched earth, a green glow gathered under the white robe, spread the length of Serroi's body, then boiled free, exploding outward, filling the air above the lake, the space inside the ring of trees, then streamers of green spread beneath the trees.

>><<

The sicamar was curled in the crotch of a smallish tree at the rim of a glade, relaxed in his day sleep. Honeydew rested above him in the top of the same tree; she'd stopped calling because her head hurt and she was so tired she couldn't even sleep, just curl up in the nest she'd made for herself and wait for the sicamar to move on. She was miserably unhappy, there was no one to talk to, no one to snuggle against, and there was nothing she could do about any of that unless she wanted to abandon Adlayr and the thought of doing that squeezed her heart.

The sicamar lifted his head, snarled and leaped down from the tree. He reached the center of the open space and stood there, tail twitching, ears laid back, a low hiss thrown from the back of his throat.

Honeydew launched herself, flew out to hover above him, trying to see what he saw.

A shining green mist was sliding through the trees, filling the space beneath the canopy, racing along as if it were blown along by a galeforce mage wind. It slid round the glade, but didn't seem able to enter it.

The green throbbed. It seemed to sing to her, to call her.

Honeydew hesitated, then fluttered cautiously toward the trees. She put out a hand, snatched it back, touching the green only long enough to get a taste of it. Serroi? SERREE!!!!

The answer came, not in words, but in a finger of mist that reached toward her but stopped before it touched her and waited for her reaction.

She hovered, thinking furiously, looking from the finger to the sicamar who was turning and turning, yowling in fear and fury.

With a panting cry, she plunged into the green, winding it around herself. Using every bit of strength she had she drove herself down toward Adlayr, dragging the green with her.

The sicamar reared up and swiped at her. Force surged through her and she was stronger and faster than she had ever been, she swooped around those lethal claws, turning and turning until he was switching ends so fast even he couldn't keep it up. He landed wrong and as he was scrambling to his feet, she got past and slammed down on his neck, sinking her hands into the thick black fur. . . .

He screamed in fear and denial, twisted around to claw her away. . . .

And collapsed on the torn up turf of the glade.

The sicamar faded.

Adlayr Ryan-Turriy lay comatose and naked, facedown on the dirt.

>><<

The guard was sitting on the landing, legs dangling over the edge, body draped over the rail, snoring and mumbling in his sleep. Kielin tapped Hedivy on the

shoulder, touched her finger to her lips, then pointed
down.

She joined him on the ground, took his arm. Without
speaking, she led him along a narrow footpath along the
spine of the island, stopping him when they reached the
ring of stilt houses where the rest of the captives were
housed. "The Gazingey is coming," she said. "He's bringing his herbman to look at you, so there's no point in dosing you again. We have to hide you."

He looked around. The island was a wart of dry ground
surrounded by muck and scummy water, patches of thick
reeds, gnarled trees with thick, bottlebrush foliage and
moss beards dripping from every branch. Eyes followed
him from the water, glistening in the persistent twilight;
in the distance he could hear splashes, squeals, bird
squawks and the beating of wings. A huge pointed head
dipped beneath the foliage, swayed back and forth a moment, then pulled back into the deep shadow. Dull gray-
green coils slipped and slid along the limb as the serpent
moved back to the trunk. He shivered, swung round to
face Kielin. "How?" he said. "I can just about see across
this place and, shaky as I am, I could walk it end to end
in less than half an hour. You want me to go off in a boat
of some kind?"

"Nay, Hedivy Starab, nothing like that." She patted his
arm. "We have our ways. Come along, trust us, haven't
we done well by you so far?"

He shrugged and followed her to the edge of the ring
and one of the largest trees on the island. The trunk was
the color of vomit, the bark pale and slick. It was at least
five feet across and looked as if half a dozen trees had
sprung from seed so close together that they'd grown into
each other. The lowest limbs were huge and put down
subsidiary trunks to support their weight. Roots rayed out
from the trunk, thrusting up knobby knees at irregular intervals. Thin pale vines wound round the trunk, dripped
in complicated loops from the branches adding their limp,
nearly colorless leaves to the long dark green fingers of
the tree's foliage. She led him into the shadow, pointed to
a mat plaited from reeds.

"Sit there," she said. "You'll find water, some yenko

fruits, and a packet of sandwiches on the other side of that root knee. I'll be back in a moment."

"What's going on?"

"I'll tell you when I return. Just be patient. Everything will be fine, I promise." She turned, looked over her shoulder, one gray brow raised quizzically. "I never promise lightly, Hedivy Starab."

He watched her walk off, as unhurried as ever, wondering if she ever got flustered like ordinary folk. His leg started aching, so he eased himself down, reached over a root, and poured himself a glass of water. It was going to be magic, he could smell it; turned his stomach, just the thought of it. He rubbed his hand across the stubble that was getting itchier every day, no sharp edges for prisoners. His beard would be coming in red, it always did, made him look like a clown with his hair such a different color; he hadn't much personal vanity, but there were limits. He touched the trunk, smoothed his hand down it, feeling bumps like pimples in a slick surface, but when he looked at his hand there was no exudate so he leaned back and sipped at the water, wondering what fool thing this lot of woolly heads was going to try on him. Funny woman, Kielin. To look at her you'd think she was sharp, no flies on her, then she'd say something weird and you'd wonder what the dreck was goin' on.

There was a creaky slithering sound over his head. He looked up, flung himself away from the trunk, the glass flying from his hand to crash against a knee. He rolled up, glared at the boy standing beside Kielin, a grin nearly splitting his thin face in half.

The boy circled round him, stepped over a root and reached up to cuddle the huge lanceolate head against his. "It's only Luhida, she doesn't eat anyone we don't tell her to." He shrugged out of a pack woven from reeds, then squatted on the mat where Hedivy had been sitting.

Hedivy bent, swatted grit off his trousers; when he straightened, his face was back under control. "I don't like snakes."

Kielin hmphed. "Like or not like, we need her. Go back and sit down and stay as calm as you can. Be best if you could go to sleep."

"Sleep!"

"Try it. You might find you prefer snoring to being bored to stone just sitting there. Mithel has a way of turning the eyes away from things he doesn't want people to see, but they have to stay a certain distance off to make it work and that's what Luhida's for. When the Qilimen look in here, they'll see Mithel alone with his reed work and they'll see Luhida's loops and her head swaying over him and they won't come closer."

"And that's it?"

"Others of us are posed here and there in trees and on the ground, working alone at small projects, so Mithel won't be odd in this. Nothing to catch the eye or start a question in those ravers' minds. So go sit yourself down and relax, Hedivy Starab. We've tried this on smallthings and one another and it does work." She started to leave, turned back. "But don't talk to Mithel. He needs to concentrate and he can't hide the sound of your voice."

"I hear." With an unhappy squint at the snake, Hedivy moved back to the trunk and settled on the mat beside the boy. He shivered but didn't move as Luhida's forked tongue flicked out, touching his face and hair; after a minute he closed his eyes, leaned against the trunk and tried willing himself to sleep.

An hour later Hedivy woke as he heard voices near the tree, cracked an eye and saw Kielin walking past, a short broad man beside her dressed in black, every visible inch of his skin—even the scalp of his shaved head—tattooed in an intricate interlacing of symbols, each with its own color; his features seemed to melt and flow with each movement of his body. Tattooed in the same way but with a different meld of colors, a taller thinner man followed them, silent and grim.

". . . still weak," Kielin said, "but he's in his right mind and his appetite's come back. I haven't seen him since early this morning, but I doubt the fever's returned."

"Is or isn't, the Dahun demands to see him."

"Ah."

"You will explain his condition to the Thomo and. . . ." The voice faded as they moved out of sight. Hedivy closed his eyes again and settled to wait for the explosion.

A faint green mist crept through the trees; it had a fresh, clean smell, unlike the dank mold-ridden air that drifted off the swamp. Hedivy glanced at Mithel.

The boy's eyes were wide; he reached out, took hold of Hedivy's thigh, his grip strong enough to be painful. "Do you see it?"

"Yeh." Hedivy kept his voice low, the word a thread of sound which he hoped was lost in the rustle of leaves overhead. "What is it?"

"Don' know. It has the feel of . . ." The boy stroked the head of the serpent which had come down to rest on his shoulder. ". . . of her," he said after a moment. "You know. Your friend."

Hedivy remembered then what Kielin had said, the trees were talking of Serroi; it'd sounded like nonsense, but he couldn't figure any other way they could've heard about the Healer. And peculiar things did happen round that woman. And that green stuff did have something. . . . "Yeh," he said. "Her."

"Ahwu, you'd best sit back so I can strengthen the shield to where it was."

"Yeh." A howl from the direction of the clinic hut. "Hear that? I'd say he's ticked about something, wouldn't you."

Mithel grinned at him, then set a finger to his lips.

Hedivy nodded, leaned back and closed his eyes. That prokkin' snake was still swaying there over the boy's head and the less he looked at it, the less his stomach churned.

Qilimen guards came racing from the swamp, driving their dugouts up onto the sandy sides of the island. They swarmed over the island, nosed into every possible hiding place as if some hollow or tree branch would magically produce their quarry. Several of them went gingerly into the maze of secondary trunks, shied at the snake, yelled at the boy weaving baskets and backed out again without coming close. As the hunt continued, the hunters grew red-faced and their eyes glazed over, then one by one they sank to the ground and lay there like logs.

Kielin came running. One of her eyes was nearly closed, a bruise darkening around it, another bruise purpled her throat. When she spoke, her voice was hoarse. "Mithel, Hedivy, come. Everything's changed. We're leaving here now."

Mithel stroked the snake's head, murmured to her.

Her tongue flicked out, touched his mouth, his ear, then she poured away, massive coils shifting with the ease of water flowing.

Hedivy shivered again, came to his feet with an enormous feeling of relief. The green left the air with the departure of that snake, though it still had that smell in it like mountain forests which he'd never much liked. He was a lowland man and proud of it, though it was certainly better than the miasma of the swamp. He stretched, strolled from under the tree to stand looking down at one of the Qilimen guards.

The man's eyes were open, staring up from a mask of tattooing that covered his brow and the upper part of his cheeks; his nose poked up pale and untouched, adding a touch of absurdity to a round plump face.

"What bit him? You?"

"This," Kielin said, moving a long thin hand in a closed double curve. "The green."

He rasped a hand across his stubble. "I thought it went away."

"Ah. You don't see it?"

"Did. Don't now."

"Hmm. While Mithel's shield was working, I suspect. The green is still with us, Hedivy Starab." She caught him by the wrist. "Hurry. I don't know how long we have."

By the time they reached the beached dugouts, the other hostages had loaded them up and launched them; there was a man standing with a pole at the back of three of the canoes, Makalaya stood in the fourth. Two women and a boy were seated among blanket rolls and lidded baskets, space left for Hedivy, Kielin and Mithel.

A few beats later and they were gliding off into the swamp, the polers working with easy, quick thrusts that propelled the dugouts with a speed and control that surprised Hedivy and gave him some hope they were actually going to break loose.

Now and then when sunlight broke through the moss and leaves clotted overhead he saw something like a faint green serpent, a sinuous length of colored light that seemed to beckon to him, but most of the time he sat with his hands on his knees, staring ahead, willing the polers to get on with this, get them out of here, onto solid ground where he could feel like a man, not a sack of mush being hauled along by someone else.

Two hours later they broke from the trees into clearer water, a reed swamp buzzing with insects, the channels between the clumps of reeds nearly choked with bright red blooms floating on the water, huge green pads with bright-eyed lizards jumping and darting about, eating those insects. The dugouts slowed. The polers were tired and shoving through that mass of vegetation would have been difficult even if they were fresh, but they worked their way onward, first one then another taking the lead, pushing the plants aside.

They held line with tenacity and a touch of desperation, guided by the green that Hedivy could no longer see but knew must be there, struggling to get through this featureless place before their guide left them. On and on, lift and shove, bodies working like machines, the polers drove the boats. On and on. . . .

"Ahhhh." Makalaya's voice. She was in the lead with the lightest of the canoes. "It has gone," she cried. "Gone."

Kielin clapped her hands, the sound cutting sharply through the thick air. "La lee lah," she chanted.

> La lee lah   the others chanted.
> Ma yah lah
> Yah kah thah
> Ham' thee nah.

The chant went on and on.

The dugouts slid on and on through the clumps of reed and water flowers.

On and on.

In the swamp behind them, drums started up.

Hoom hoom hoom. A steady beat like a heart throbbing. Hoom hoom hoom.

At first the sound was only a breath on the wind, but it grew louder and louder until it threatened to drown the north-seek chant.

As the sun slid behind the dark smudge of the swamp, the lead dugout rounded a reed island and broke into a river. The man poling it shouted a warning, fought his canoe around and shoved it along the bank until all of the canoes were free of the swamp and there was an upslant of solid ground to their left.

Hedivy stood looking north at mountain peaks sketched in blue and white against the blue of the sky. "That's where we have to go?"

Kielin nodded. She stood beside him, stroking the bruises on her throat, purple and black with streaks of red. "Those are the peaks of the Isisu Khat. The Forest lies on the far side of them. Once we reach that, we'll be safe. Your friend is there."

Behind them the beat of the drums grew louder and more urgent. Kielin handed Hedivy the cane she'd brought, then went to help unload the canoes.

>><<

The trees shivered as dryads were born into some of them, as fauns budded from the tips of branches and dropped to the forest floor; out in the lake the water boiled and a head broke surface, a woman's face with watergrass for hair, a twinned tail, the sections supple as eels, undulating behind the head, a siren translucent as glass, insubstantial as a mirage. Water snakes came from the reeds and swam in celebratory circles around her.

Adlayr stumbled from the Forest, Honeydew fluttering above him. He saw the great serpent body, saw the sleeping healer in the lamia's arms, shouted, and ran toward her.

The lamia shifted her grip on Serroi and thrust out a hand.

It was as if she'd slapped him, slapped with enough force to throw him off his feet.

You leave her alone, you. Serree din't do nothing to you. Go 'way. You don't need to be here, go 'way. Honeydew zipped up to the tree tops then dived at the snakewoman, her wings driving her as fast as she'd ever gone, her lips curled back from her teeth, her tiny hands clawed.

The lamia ignored her, shifted her grip once more, and laid a long forefinger on the eyespot throbbing between Serroi's brows. *WAKE. IT IS ENOUGH. WAKE, O MOTHER.*

The glow faded, the flood of greenness stopped as if a tap had been turned. Serroi groaned, sighed deeply, moved her hands. The lamia eased her onto her feet and steadied her while she emerged from the drug and the Shaman's sleep spell.

Adlayr picked himself up and limped forward, Honeydew spiralling down to land on his shoulder.

The lamia smiled at them, eyes glowing with feral laughter, then she nodded to Adlayr, dipped in a kind of curtsy to Honeydew, and went glide-slither back into the shadow under the trees.

Out in the lake, the siren keened a high note and sank beneath the water, the swimming snakes diving with her.

Serroi opened her eyes, swayed and put out a hand. "Gah. I'm weak as a kitten. Adlayr, give me a hand, will you?"

When she was on her feet, she looked around at the pale folk who'd come running from the village, at Adlayr, Honeydew. "So. What's been happening?"

>><<

Treshteny gasped and dropped to the ground, huddling into as compact a configuration as she could manage with her long arms and legs. Her eyes were squeezed shut, but that wouldn't keep out the memory of what she'd seen, the earth itself dissolving into unstable mist, as far as she could see, in every direction. Chaos. No place to set her feet. Nothing the same from one breath to the next.

"Change," she moaned, "change change change. . . ."

Her mind's eye saw . . . exploded open and out out out farther than she'd ever looked, ahead and before all mixed, vision merging with vision, impossible to comprehend it all, impossible to keep it in her head except for short concrete things that tied in with this journey, she emptied her head in a spate of words, emptying herself of the confusion so she wouldn't have to think about it when the premoaning fit was done.

And it was done. At last it was done.

She cracked an eye, snapped it closed again.

The earth was still flowing and dissolving, changing . . . the change slowing a little so she felt a throb in it like the beating of a heart and there were solid bits that kept their shape.

When she felt her own hands begin to change, her body to slip and flow like the earth, she fainted.

The sky was coral and gold when she woke, the sun a red sliver in the west. She lifted her head and saw that they were moving along a road beside a wide canal, no one else in view, the cultivated fields beyond the road and the canal were empty except for a few pastures with grazers in them. The manHorse was Horse again and she was tied on his back like a sack of grain. She wiggled around and made some noises.

Untied and on her feet, she looked back along the road. The city was below the horizon behind them, a faint glow from the streetlights still visible. The earth was solid again, though it pulsed with a life force that wasn't there before; she could feel the energy coming up through her feet, coursing through her veins. "I'm hungry," she said, an understatement of some magnitude; she wasn't merely hungry, her body was crying out for food.

Mama Charody wrinkled her face. "We'll stop at those trees up there; looks to me like a traveler's rest. You want to walk or ride?"

"Oh, walk. Yes. I want to walk." She stooped, undid her sandals, and took them off. For a moment she stood, wriggling her toes in the dirt, feeling her face flush with a pleasure she hadn't known before. With a laugh, she snapped her fingers to Yela'o, then went racing ahead with him, on fire with what the earth was giving her.

Treshteny emptied her mug and sighed with satisfaction. " 'Twas a lovely meal, Charody. You have a way with stolen greens." She giggled, leaned closer to the fire, letting its warmth play over her face.

"If I didn't know better, I'd say you were drunk, Treshteny Falladin."

"Perhaps I am. Don't you feel it?"

"Zdra, if you put it like that, I do. What did you see?"

Treshteny wrinkled her nose. "Too much. I don't remember. Didn't you listen?"

"Zdra, I did. For what good that was. Too much babble, too many words tumbling over each other. Tell me what you remember."

Treshteny sighed. "Confusion. A terrible, insatiable yearning. I don't know who or what. But that was on everything like a bad smell that gets into your house and you can't get it out. A war. People fighting, hating, so much hate. . . ." She scrubbed at her mouth as if it were a taste on her lips. "A fire mountain and a sense of ending. Oh. And south. We have to keep going south. That's all that stayed behind."

Charody glanced at Doby curled up in his blankets, sleeping. It'd been a long day for all of them and he was only a boy; he'd barely kept awake long enough to swallow some supper. "War," she said, shook her head. "He's had enough of that."

"Shouldn't you leave him with someone?" Treshteny grimaced, stretched out her hand. "Pay no attention to me, Charody. What do I know?"

"I would leave him, Seer. Were his life a hair different, I'd do that in a minute. Did you ever try to nurse a bird with a broken wing? Nik? I suppose they wouldn't let you. Sometimes the body's whole before the mind's ready to fly." After a minute she shrugged. "What comes, comes."

21. Attacks

The sun was cracking the horizon in the east when the barge turned toward the levee where the Last Tower stood, a burnt-out hulk starting to collapse in on itself. With Herec at her shoulder, watching to see how well she'd learned, Sansilly swung the anchor up and dropped it overside. She smiled with pleasure as it caught, then hurried to the other side for the second anchor as Greygen butted the barge's bow into the soft mud of the levee.

Prah swung over the rail and reached up for Mosec's youngest, a one-year-old who was crying and cranky in the cold, dry morning air. None of them, children or adults, had gotten much sleep this whole trip.

He waited as Besah helped Ferla over the rail, gave her the baby, then reached for the next youngling.

Greygen stood beside Sansilly, his hand on her shoulder, watching the line of walkers vanish over a low rise, appear again on the next hillock. They turned and waved a last time, Mosec and Malry, Prah and Besah and the children, then moved into the trees clustering over the lower slopes of the foothills.

"Zdra, Sansy. . . ."

She made a face at him and moved to the windlass. "Let me know when you're ready."

"You're sure?"

"I'm not sure of anything except I want to do this."

"Let me set the jib first. We'll be taking it slow as we can." He tried to smile at her, found the smile coming more naturally as she ostentatiously spat on her hands and took hold of the pin. "Zhag deep and cloud high," he shouted, shook his fist at the sky, then unwound the jib's halyard from its cleat.

Washimin's Chasm—a millennium and more ago on the orders of Marnhidda Bar, the Norid Washimin had cut a canyon through the mountains, slicing heartstone in a deep, double curve. Caught between those slick stone walls the water raced and roared in a demi-twilight, the sun too low to reach in and touch it.

Sansilly stood in the bow singing at the top of her voice. Her words came to him broken on the wind, but he heard the energy, excitement—joy—in them and knew what she was feeling. This barely controlled whirl through a slot in the earth was terrifying, but it boiled in his blood like bubbles in a sparkling wine.

Time passed. There was more light, then the light dimmed. His body ached, his ears had gone numb with the noise, his eyes burned, but the exhilaration didn't go away.

Nijilic TheDom was low in the west, a fat crescent resting on a layer of clouds, when the barge slid from the canyon into a wider, slower stretch of water. Greygen eased toward the east bank, Sansilly threw the anchors overside and lowered the jib.

They leaned against the cabin and looked around at the dark shapes of the land, then they clutched at each other and laughed till their sides ached.

>><<

"Valk to Mountain. Switch to scramble, now! Sleykyn are out. Repeat, Sleykyn are out. Go."

"Noted, Valk. We pass it on. Say about Cut-out. Go."

"Stoppah hit the end of the supply train, collected half a dozen wagons; they're coming your way guarded by ten men, along with the wounded not fit to ride. Five men so far, that's all. The numbers were on our side. He's perched in the same spot with the rest of his men, waiting for the next shipment. Throdal's looking over the second

reserve force, the one with two hundred of the Taken, and
when the ground's right, he's going after them. We have
to know how the Taken fight, what we have to do to put
them down. This is eating power. Expect short reports
from now on. And take care of the Marn! Out."

>><<

Throdal eased away from the knot poking him in the
back, settling the longglasses again.

The Taken marched with easy strides across the trampled ground. They were silent. There wasn't any joking or
the half-serious grumbling he was used to from his men,
but they weren't sheep. Swearing because he'd expected
to see a more mechanical movement, something clumsier,
he lowered the glasses and wiped at sweat that was burning his eyes and fogging the lenses.

He cased the glasses, swung out of the crotch and went
down the tree until he was hanging from the lowest
branch. He dropped to the ground and trotted to the hillock where his aides were due to meet him.

"I counted three scouts, if you could call them that."
Weslev jabbed the pointer at the map drawn in the dirt.
"Here. Here. Here." Three dots a hand's width ahead of
the circle representing the army. "Not chovan, or Taken.
Hired men from the look of them. Slouchin' in the saddle
half asleep. 'S clear they don't expect trouble." He
handed the stick to Vuthal who drew a line at the rear of
the army, moved back, and tapped a line of dots into the
dirt.

"Supply wagons keep lagging behind." Vuthal set the
stick on his knees. "Last night it was a good two hours
after camp was set up that wagons got there. They're
gonna be even later today. Drivers are Nov's enforcers,
lazy notneys. Say we can hold the attack to mid-
afternoon, we could probably take the wagons without
alerting the forces ahead. Given no proggin foul-ups." He
thought a moment. "Or do the army first, then take the
wagons. Either way's good enough." He handed the stick

to the third man, son of a farmer who'd grown up on the edge of Oskland. "Given a good lay of the land."

Marud nodded. "This is how she goes. The Border country's mostly the same as you all seen so far. Hedgerows and groves, land rolls a lot, some ravines, but not too many, some rock thrusts, not too many a those. They keepin' to same line t'others took, same reasons, easiest walkin' and there's water enough to keep 'em happy."

He smoothed a space a double handspan ahead of the army circle, drew a line straight east from the circle. "Say this is a half day's march on. Stone ridge here." He drew a second line slanting away from the first. "Groves here, here, here and here." Dots from the stick forming a rhomboid shape below the ridge line. "Berryvine all through them, thick, good cover for hob and jillik, this is Rodin huntin' country, why the vines an't cleaned out. Rip you apart you tried to march through it, so they'll get squeezed an' tail out some. We could maybe put some shooters in trees, but I'd keep them near the edges, orwise they won't be able to move either. Those vines they been growin' for Maiden knows how long and they got thorns could rip the hide off a bull vos." He drew a long oval touching the ridge line, put a small circle in the far end of the oval. "This is meadow, that other's a bobri pond, lot of seepage from the dam so the ground's dry near the ridge and really mucky down t'other end." He touched the west side of the oval. "Brush, mostly hadank, miserable stuff, too low to give much cover and made to trap your foot, break your leg. Some rock, some tall grass." He passed the stick to Throdal. "That's the best lay I found and it has this goin' for it, the rate they're goin', they'll get there 'bout 'n hour 'fore sundown."

Weslev scowled at the map. "Yeh, but we'd be attackin' into the sun."

Marud shrugged. "Depends on how it's set up, where we hit 'em at."

Vuthal nodded. "Say the scouts keep noddin', we could have a force waiting round behind one of those groves, take 'em in the rear, same time snipers cut down on them from side, 'nother force waitin' there 'hind that ridge, get 'em from the front 'n side as they get mashed from that corridor 'tween groves."

Throdal scratched his chin with the point of the stick. "There's two hundred plus Taken there, don't know how they're goin' to jump. Could be all two hundred turn and come at the men behind. Can't put more'n thirty-five, forty back there. If there's no runnin' room. . . ."

Marud took the stick, tapped the pond circle. "Need to stay away from this side, too mucky. He tapped the first of the southern groves on the south. "There's some brush, enough to give a little cover, not enough to threaten a horse's legs or a macai's. Rough ground, lots of rocks and some sand, but it's still faster going for rider than a walker. You could get round the grove, hit them from behind again, take off, lead them down the channel into the meadow, cut off, and let the shooters on the ridge take over." He waved the stick over the scrawled map. "We're gonna find out how well they shoot at movin' targets, for sure, zdra, for sure."

The Taken in the reserve force kept to the beaten path left by the first two groups of men, marching more slowly than they had in the morning, but moving steadily along in that silence of theirs. When they reached the first of the groves in the rhomboid, the mounted commander yelled an order and they shifted from ten abreast to five, making the change so smoothly it was like a dance, almost without breaking stride. With the commander riding at the head, the column began snaking past the grove.

A whistle.

Snipers in the trees on either side started shooting.

Riders came round the grove, sat their mounts across the path, and shot.

Hit in the shoulder, the commander spurred his horse into a belly-to-the-earth run out of there. The back ranks of the Taken who were still on their feet swung round, returned fire. Half of these started trotting toward the riders, dropped to their knees after a few yards, and fired while the others caught up with them and ran past in two files, leaving the middle open. They died and the Osklanders died, horses and macain went down.

The front ranks moved forward at a trot, one man on each side of the column dropping to a knee and raking the trees with return fire. When these were killed, others took their places.

A whistle.

The riders collected the wounded and the dismounted, fleeing round the trees and out of sight.

The rearguard Taken swung round again and went trotting to join the others.

On the ridge Throdal watched the wounded commander ride out onto the meadow, scat across it and plunge into the brush. "Haldar, stop him. I don't need to talk to him, so it don't matter how you do it."

Haldar grinned, swung into the saddle. "That one, I won't even take his ear for smoking." He snapped a finger at the string of ears hanging from the horn, making them scrape across the saddle skirt.

"Thought I told y' to put those away somewhere. I see 'em again, you're gonna be polishing so much leather, you'll wear your tongue to bone. You hear, cousin?"

"I hear, cousin." Haldar grinned again, sketched a salute, and patted his macai into a low fast lope, angling downslope to intercept the horse and rider.

The Taken came at a quick trot past the last of the southern groves. Their longguns were unslung and ready to fire, but with no one shooting at them, they slowed as they hit the meadow, spread into their usual formation and went marching along the trampled ground left by the armies ahead of them.

Chewing on the whistle, Throdal watched through his glasses as they emerged, his nostrils flaring as he spotted limps and blood splotches. Tongue clicking in the rhythm he'd learned as a herdsman in the Harozh, he counted them off, grimaced at the result. Around thirty gone. There should have been more. *Proggin' tight-fisted. . . . Won't give ammo for practice, what can y' expect?* He made a note to commandeer any guns and ammunition as he could lay his hands on. *Yeh, and send a man to Stoppah to say same. Mp. Stragglers out. Time to go.*

He blew a long note on the whistle and grunted with satisfaction as he heard a spattering of shots coming from the groves, followed a steadier crackle from the men stretched out on the ridge.

>><<

"Valk here. Throdal withdrew from attack with fifteen dead, twenty-seven wounded, four serious enough to send home with the supply wagons he collected from this lot. Five macain dead, three released as unridable. Five horses dead, two wounded seriously enough to be shot, four turned loose. Killed seventy-one of the two hundred Taken, plus scouts and commander. Four horses and a scatter of weapons seized. No prisoners.

"Taken are quick, maneuver fast and smooth—it's like their heads are connected. Tell Vedouce to watch out for that. Can't go for the leaders and expect to stop them that way. They will keep coming no matter how badly they're wounded, dangerous if they've still got a hand and half a working leg; head shots are best, a chest shot might put them down, might not. Arterial hit, they tie on a tourniquet and keep coming. Anything else, they ignore and keep coming. And they're better shots than we expected. The best edge we have is speed. We're going to have to do a lot of hit and run. The coms are vital. Otherwise, we'll be fighting without any direction and half or more of what we do will be wasted. Saa! Talking too much. Out."

>><<

Leaving Zasya Myers by the door, watching warily, with Tingajil following silently behind her, lute in her hands, K'vestmilly Vos walked down the line of the wounded, touching them, stopping to talk to a man here, a man there, taking a blinded man's hand and letting him feel the growing bulge of her child.

"You fought for her," she said and felt the hand warm

and trembling through the cloth of her robe. "For all that is to be." She touched his cheek under the bandage, laid his hand on his chest, and moved on.

When she'd greeted them all, she stood in the doorway, Mask heavier than it had been since the day she put it on, though she was glad of it because they couldn't see what was on her face. "Tingajil," she set her hand on the singer's shoulder, "will sing for you. Ask her for what you want to hear."

As K'vestmilly and her guard followed the nurse down the hall, she heard the first notes of "River of Blood" and shuddered. "I hate that song," she murmured.

The nurse smiled and patted the Marn's arm. "They love it because it's their lives."

"I know."

Vyzharnos Oram wiped at the sweat on his face, leaving behind streaks of printer's ink. "Broadsheets," he said. "Some of the paper Stoppah sent east. Pan Osk had it brought round, said you said we could use it better than him. Thanks."

K'vestmilly Vos unrolled the sheet, looked at the heading and smiled behind the Mask. "The Hungry Eye?"

He grinned. "Sees all, knows all, tells a lot of it." He looked at his hands, wiped them on the handiest rag. "War news, names of the wounded, tributes to the dead, this'n that from the families, recipes, gossip, questions from the readers." He sobered. "We put in a report about the Sleykyn and a warning not to try stopping them, just get the word back fast as possible. There'll be a lot of eyes watching, Marn. And you shouldn't be walking about alone like this. Not even here in the Hold."

"So Osk tells me. I'm not alone. The meie's in the hall." She set the sheet down, watched it snap back into a cylinder. "Each one of these you put out, send a copy to my office." She let her hands smile for her. "Not to censor them, I trust your good sense, Poet. As I trusted your father. If I'm going to be so hemmed in I can't move, I'll need something to break the monotony."

* * *

K'vestmilly Vos stood at the window of her tower suite looking down over the chaos of the Hold and the teeming slopes around it. There was a touch of sadness in her because a small glow had died. Vyzharnos was handsomer than ever with that black eye-patch giving him a rakish, do-down-the-devil look, but the heat he'd woke in her was dead as yesterday's lunch. Nice man, reasonably intelligent, a bit of a radical and once this was over, the kind to make trouble for her. If the Sleykyn didn't break through, if Vedouce could hold back the Taken, if and if and if. . . .

Heslin, oh my Hes, I wish you were here. Did you know how bored I was going to be? Scared, confused, driven, busy every minute, but bored, bored, bored! I need you. I need someone to talk to without this proggin' Mask. Double mask, ivory and custom. Mama, you were right. They need the distance, they need the mystery . . . they . . . that's everyone, all of them, even Osk. He rules this place where his Family's been for Maiden knows how long, but even he needs the Mask and the Marn. I can't take the Mask off and just talk to him. Oskliveh! I miss your sharp mind, Hes, I miss the arguments. I miss you. . . .

She dipped a handkerchief in a glass of water, patted her face. It was a midsummer afternoon, hot and still, the air felt used up, stale. High as she was, inside these thick stone walls, the heat was oppressive. She didn't want to think about what it had to be like for those people outside the walls, living under canvas. She moved impatiently, knocked the glass from the sill, squatted to pick it up.

A loud thunk.

She squatted where she was, hand pressed against her mouth, staring at the crossbow bolt sunk into the soft wood of the ceiling.

>><<

The Dancer sat cross-legged on the altar below the transformed statue, now the Glory smiling benignly across the newly laid down mosaic of immolation, her arms outstretched in welcome.

Motylla stood in the yellow circle and scowled at him. "What you want?"

The pastoras who'd delivered her to the Temple gasped and dropped to their knees, banging their foreheads on the stone.

The Dancer spoke. "Go. We wish to be alone with our servant."

"Slave," Motylla growled. She'd gotten beyond caring about what she said when her mouth was her own. Nobody listened to her, so what did it matter?

The pastoras glided out, their soft chant lingering behind them. Kazim, O Glory, kazim. . . .

"So what you want?" Motylla clasped her hands behind her to hide their trembling, stood planted, feet apart, her short sturdy body stiff with defiance.

"Come to us, our servant, commmme."

"You want me, fetch me."

The Dancer slid off the altar and came toward her, the yellow light flickering around him. When he stood just outside the circle, she could see he was little more than a skin bag filled with bone and that buttery light. "Give us your hands," he said. His lips didn't move, his eyes weren't looking at her, weren't looking at anything.

He's a puppet, she thought, *with the light pulling his strings. He's dead.* She swallowed, blinked, then shuffled away until she reached the far side of the circle. When her heel touched the silver line, she felt a burning, a pain so intense she hesitated. . . .

and he was in the circle with her, arms snaking out, bony hands closing tight on her shoulders. . . .

she tried to scream. . . .

she tried to move, to run. . . .

the Glory closed around her, oozed into her, filling her with pain, such pain. . . .

fire burning away what was left of will and being. . . .

Motylla-not looked down at the discarded husk, grimaced, and stepped from the circle. A gesture and the thing was ash and dust on the drafts that blew across the floor. Pulling the Glory around her, she climbed onto the altar and *summoned* HER servants.

22. Fear

Chaya Willish heard the knock at the front door, swore under her breath, and set the thread cone on the table beside the warping board. Ignoring the impatient thumps that followed, she wrote down the number of turns she'd completed, wiped her hands, and smoothed her hair before she left the workroom. She did not want company. She particularly did not want the company she suspected was waiting on her doorstep, more neighbors come to preach at her.

"Uncle Seko?" She blinked, startled to see him smiling benignly at her, his wife behind him with two of their elder daughters. She stepped aside, moved her arm in the invitation arc, and said, "Be welcome."

When they were all seated in her parlor, she said, "If you will permit, I'll put water on for cha."

"No need, Chaya niece. Come and sit. We have serious things to talk about."

A cold knot forming in her stomach, Chaya perched on a straight backed chair, folded her hands in her lap and waited.

"We have arranged a marriage for you, Chaya niece."

She drew a long breath, tightened her fingers' grip, said as mildly as she could manage, "I am already promised, Uncle. You know that."

"That clan-reft loser? Nonsense. Forget him."

"He has found a new master and will be a master himself within the year."

"How do you know this, Chaya niece?"

"He has written it. I can show you the letter."

"HE has written? Ahwu, I think we can dismiss that bit of brag. Nay, niece. We forbid you to think of him any longer. You will wed as we tell you and your husband will be Shangwe Koxaye, clan Axara, totem Iewah, Grand Pastora of the Glory."

"Nay," she said, fighting to keep her voice even. "I will not." She knew the name, knew the man; he was the one who'd led that invasion of the Weave Hall, he was the one ranting in the fam square, his followers seated around him, echoing and adoring him. Sucking in more and more of the fam's people. Not the Weavemistress. The thought brought an easing in the stiffness of her face. Iduna Yekai had marched up to Koxaye and demanded compensation for the damage he'd done to the cloth in the Weave Hall, her voice riding over his, attracting a muttering crowd outside the ring of his converts. To get rid of her, he snapped his fingers and one of his handmaids passed over a purse. The Weavemistress marched off to scowls and cheers and passed out the coin the next day to her weavers so they could pay for missed quota.

Seko Willish kept talking as if Chaya had dreamed the words that came from her mouth. "The Dolman has come to Glory, praise be to Glory, he will officiate at your wedding one month from this day, Chaya niece. You will spend the month in preparation, readying yourself to greet your husband; your cousins Kahlin and Lobyl will move in with you to help in the purifications and the gathering of your goods for presentation to he who will be your lord and protector." He leaned forward, a smile on his face, but none at all in eyes like gray pebbles. "We will do everything necessary, Chaya niece, it will be our gift to you. You will not need to leave this house until it is time to meet your husband before the ambo of the Dolman."

The chill moved out from the knot in her middle, filling her with a dread so strong it drowned the anger building in her. She passed her tongue across dry lips. "I have a duty," she managed finally. "As a journeyman I have a quota of weave to fill; otherwise there will be fines and a delay in my release."

"The Pastora Koxaye has been most generous. He has bought off this year's obligation. Any weaving you do henceforth will be for your children and your man."

"Though you have denied the tie, courtesy demands I write to Lavan and tell him of this."

"There is no need. We gave a letter yesterday to a Wandermonk; it informs Lavan Isaddo that the connection is to be severed and he is no longer welcome here."

How dare you! she screamed at him, but only in her mind. Seko Willish was clan head and she was bound by his will unless she could call council and protest it. Ordinarily she would, but now she was afraid. How many of her kin would be Glory-taken? She didn't know, but from what she'd seen in the fam, she hadn't much to hope from them. *The Arbiters,* she thought, *get to Lavan and then to the Arbiters and the Guildmistress.* Until she could get away, better they didn't guess how much rage was building in her. She kept her eyes fixed on her hands and said nothing.

Seko Willish stood. "That is most proper, Chaya niece. Kahlin and Lobyl will stay with you now. Phuza," he nodded at his wife standing silent beside him, "will send their clothes and other supplies across and," he smiled again, again the smile did not touch his eyes, "cloth for your wedding robes which you will begin working on this evening. I will be by to see how far you've got this time tomorrow. Glory be yours, Chaya niece." He walked out, his wife trailing behind.

While Chaya began preparations for the evening meal, Kahlin and Lobyl went snooping through the house, prying into everything. She gritted her teeth as she heard them in her workroom, opening drawers, knocking things about. They'd always been jealous of her; they were big, clumsy girls with neither charm nor gifts to take the place of charm and she had a strong suspicion that Kahlin had a passion for Lavan, though he never gave her any notice except to get away from her as quickly as he could in courtesy when she came giggling over to him.

Chaya stirred up the fire in the oven, set the casserole to heating, and looked through the larder for some strips

of salt meat, noodles, cheese and dried herbs to stretch
the small dinner she'd prepared for herself, once more
swearing under her breath and apologizing to her father
with every other word. She didn't know how she was going to stand it with that pair of jailors watching her every
move—for she had no illusion as to why they were here.

They moved out of the workroom and went thudding
upstairs. She scowled. *They wouldn't invade her bedroom,
even they wouldn't be that.* . . .

A door opened. Bathroom. Another, Guestroom. She
could hear their feet clumping about the room, hear
the thump of something falling. Out again. She heard the
board that always squeaked outside her door. Heard the
door open and feet going inside. "Bodj!" She went running from the kitchen, fury wiping away calculation. The
thought of that pair touching her things. . . .

As she reached the door, she heard them giggling.

When she jerked it open, she saw Kahlin had Lavan's
letters and was dividing them with Lobyl.

"You skents, those are mine." She sprang across the
room, tried to snatch the letters away.

It was an ugly fight, hair flying, teeth tearing, clawing
fingernails, elbow rams, shrieks, screams. They were bigger, but she was angrier and more focused. She got the
letters from them, went running from the room. When she
reached the kitchen, she thrust them into the fire, went to
the sink, and splashed water on her face, then leaned on
the cold stone, panting and crying.

She heard them moving around her bedroom, pulling
drawers out, dropping them on the floor, smashing her
water carafe, throwing her books down, getting back at
her by fouling her things. She looked at the noodles she
had thought to fix for them and felt like dashing them to
the floor. She didn't. It'd be as stupid as they were to take
her anger out on silly noodles.

She opened the oven, took the cover off the casserole
to let the crust brown, smiling tightly at the good smell
filling the room. If they wanted supper, let them cook it
themselves. They weren't guests, they were making that
quite clear, so she saw no reason to treat them like guests.

She set out an iron pot to cook the noodles, matches for

the fire and moved the coal hod onto the counter beside the pot grates where they couldn't miss it, then went to the back garden to pick greens for a salad. It was clear what she had to do. Lull them for a few days, let them think she'd bowed to the will of the clanhead. Not meek, nay, they wouldn't expect that, that'd make them suspicious, but starting the dress and keeping her mouth shut around her cousins. Then find a horse and go south fast as she could manage. Look for Sekhaya on the way, but most of all get to Lavan and go with him to the Sanctuary and the Arbiters. The betrothal had been done properly, the papers signed, it was sanctioned by her father, with the proviso that Lavan have his Master's papers before the wedding took place. Didn't matter what Uncle Seko and his lot did with the copies here, there were others at the Archives in Mokadumise. With Lavan swore to a Master again, the Arbiters would have to deny this other marriage. They'd HAVE to. Stupid Koxaye, buying her year. It meant she wouldn't be an absconder when she ran, there wouldn't be a blot on her record; that would certainly help with the Arbiters.

She washed the greens, made a dressing for them, took the casserole from the oven, and sat to eat her supper, ignoring the crashes and other noises over her head.

>><<

Lavan looked out his window to see a boat tieing up at Casil's landing. He leaned on the sill, watching the bargemen helping two women ashore, wondering if it was another commission. One of the women had white-streaked black hair and a long black cloak with a fur collar, the other was much younger and more poorly dressed.

"Siffy!" Casil Kinuqah went stumping across the yard, white hair fluttering in the breeze. He hugged the older woman, then stepped back. "What you doin' here? What about the kids, is there trouble?"

"No trouble. Can't I visit my own father without some song and dance about it?"

"Nay, of course you can. You're looking marvelous, Siffy. Life is treating you well."

"I've come to Glory, Fa. It's made a wonderful difference. But we'll talk about that later." She looked over her shoulder. "See that everything's there, then pay the men, Rudli." She turned back. "You said you had a new apprentice, send him down to fetch the baggage in, will you, Fa?"

"He's a journeyman, Siffy. In his last days, so treat him like the Master he'll be soon enough, you hear?"

Her lips compressed in a thin line, the woman nodded, then marched into the house.

Casil watched her go, his shoulders slumping.

Lavan leaned out the window. "Master, I'll be down in a minute. Be happy to help."

Casil looked up, his mustache spreading with his smile. "Thanks, Lav."

Siffana Kinuqah took against Lavan the minute she saw him. She treated him with icy courtesy and worried at her father to get rid of him while she was trying to convince him to go home with her so she could take care of him and his grandchildren would get to know him. The house was filled with tension, Casil turned cranky, snapping at Lavan every time he opened his mouth, telling his daughter to leave him alone and let him make up his own mind.

"Show me that thing." Casil coughed, clearing his throat, blew his nose, then jabbed a knobby finger at the roll of parchment that held Lavan's sketches for his masterwork. His rheumatism was worse and he was starting to have trouble breathing; he looked twice as old as he had when he opened the door to Lavan that first day.

After Lavan unrolled the parchment, the old man studied the newest of the designs, made since Lavan had started work with him, a wide armlet pierced and hinged. He tapped it with a stiff finger. "This is good. You ready to start?"

"I could do the projections, I don't have the materials."

"Light the lamp and come over here."

Casil led Lavan to the strongroom, unlocked it, and went inside to unlock the inner drawers. He was out again

by the time Lavan had the lamp going and reached the
door.

"Go in, choose what you'll need—gems, gold and silver."

"I can't pay. . . ."

"Don't matter. I'll worry about that when there's time
for it. Hurry, I want this done before she gets back."

Lavan went in without saying anything more; there was
nothing he could say that wouldn't make the old man feel
worse.

He set his choices on the workbench, a large black
opal, two smaller emeralds, two plates of gold, a coil of
fine silver wire.

Casil nodded. "Good. You always had a good eye for
color. Here's what it's about, Lav. Siffy isn't goin' to
leave without me and the way things are now," he shook
his head, "ahwu, 'tisn't goin' to get better. Put your other
projects aside, I'll finish them, give me an excuse to hang
on. Siffy's like her Ma, a good eye for the coin, she'll
ease when I tell her if they don't get finished, I have to
pay back the fees. You concentrate on your masterwork.
I han't got a doubt you can make it good, Lav. I'll send
for the Guild valuer, 's a good thing Bokivada's so close,
and we'll have you a Master's papers before the month is
out. You got anything to say?"

Lavan shook his head.

"Then you get busy on it now." He closed his hand
over Lavan's shoulder, squeezed hard, then went to close
the locks on the strongroom.

The next days Lavan spent in the workroom, eating at
the bench, leaving only when his bladder forced him,
sleeping when he couldn't keep his eyes open. Perhaps
because of the pressure and the hurry, perhaps in spite of
it, the gold yielded to his tools like a cat to a caressing
hand, the silver inlay flowed with a grace he'd never
managed before. On the thirteenth day, he gave the armlet
a last polish, set it on the viewcloth, and knew he'd never
done anything as good before, perhaps never would
again.

He looked at it a moment, stretched and yawned, suddenly so tired he could scarcely keep his eyes open. It was still mid-afternoon, but he left the workroom, went upstairs, and fell into bed.

Casil Kinuqah set the armlet on a viewing stand in the light pouring through one of the workroom windows, walked round it for an overview, then took it, ran his thumb along the nearly invisible line where it was hinged, opened it, holding it close to his ear, inspected the slide cover of the tiny hinges, went over every inch of inlay, the setting of the jewels, weighed it in his hands, judging the balance.

He set the armlet back on the stand and stood contemplating it for a moment longer, then he turned to face Lavan. "It is worthy."

Lavan began breathing again; despite Casil's good will and encouragement, the old man was an artist and he would never betray that. "And now?"

"Now I go into town, see the Valuer, get the paperwork started. Tomorrow you put on your best and we'll go swear the oath."

"Master, I. . . ."

"Hush, lad. You've had a hard time, but you've come through. While I'm in town, finish the wedding bracelets, see the cistern's pumped, it was gurgling last time I washed up. If m' daughter wants anything, do 't for her, favor to me. I'd like some peace about the house for a while."

The night after Lavan was certified Master, Siffana Kinuqah by her father's command made for Lavan Isaddo a celebratory dinner. It was a silent one. Lavan was still dazed by the suddenness of it all, Siffana was annoyed, Casil Kinuqah was merely tired.

"Ahhh, that was a fine meal, Siffy, you've got your mother's touch with a bird." Casil Kinuqah patted his mustache with the napkin, laid it beside his plate. "Master Lavan," his eyes twinkled as he put a light stress on the *master,* "will you walk to the landing with me?"

"Certainly, Master Casil." Lavan's voice was hoarse,

but this wasn't the moment for clearing his throat. Siffana Kinuqah's mouth was a blue line again and it wouldn't take much for her to start digging at him.

They walked in silence through the back yard and down the path to the river landing. Casil leaned on a bitt and stroked his mustache, frowning at the moonlit water. After a minute he said, "Lav, I've done something you're not going to like."

"With what I owe you . . . ."

"Nay nay, forget that. We've got on well, haven't we?"

"Yes. From the beginning."

"Never had a son. Had apprentices. You're the best of the lot, you know that?"

"Nay. Thanks."

"You don't thank a man for telling the truth. The day I had you start the masterwork . . . ahwu, something happened. A Wandermonk came by. You were out back cleaning the stable, so you didn't see him. He gave me this." Casil thrust his hand inside his shirt, brought out a packet; it'd been opened, stuck shut again with a patch of new wax. "It was for you, but I opened it. Nay, wait, it's not from your Chaya, the sender's name is Seko Willish. I saw that and had a bad feeling, so I broke the seal and read it. 'Fore I give it to you, I want you to understand why I did what I did. Tonight I'm going to tell Siffy I'll go with her. It's my grandkids, I've got to try . . . ahwu, that's not your business. I knew you'd want to be off and I thought you should have your Master's certificate first." He held out the letter. "Before you read it, let me say this. From what you've told me about your Chaya, if this is what she wanted, she'd write you herself. Go secretly, Lavan, and if she's being coerced, break her loose and bring her here. I put the house in your name when I was getting the armlet valued; there's no way I'll be back so you might as well have it. I don't know how much good it'll do, the way things seem to be going, but Hubawern is still a free town and with the river here, you'll have more choices than you would inland."

>><<

As Joma went jogging along the meandering road, Sekhaya lifted her feet onto the splashboard and leaned back, happier than she'd been in days, though that didn't say much. Shillafam had welcomed her as it always had, though the Dolman was surprised to see her back so soon. There were a few households where the doors were shut against her, but nothing like the fear and hostility in the fams on the other arc. "What's going on, Joma, old friend? What's happening to us? And why hasn't someone done something." She laughed as his ears twitched. "You're right, old friend. Who would do it and what would they do?"

She'd read about other lands, places with kings or some kind of central rule, but she didn't really understand why the people allowed such a thing to happen. Shimzeys wouldn't go for that. Maybe Qilimen, but who knew about them? Right now, though, it'd be nice to have someone who could take a look at what was happening and say this has got to stop and then go ahead and make it stop. She thought about that a while, wrinkled her nose, and shook her head. One of those cures that's worse than the disease. "Ahwu, Joma friend, we'll stop and see how Chaya's getting along, then I think we head for Mokadumise and Arbiter's Hall."

She laughed at his twitching ears. "Ahwu, I know, Jommy. Heat and bugs and grass and sicamars lying in wait." She pushed sweaty hair off her face, sighed. "Maybe that man was right, maybe we won't even bother with the Arbiters, just roll cross Sedli Pass into the Sendle, I don't know anyone there, but I can't live this way."

"Sekhaya Kawin." The woman stood close to the hedge where it opened on a narrow lane, shadow falling across her face. "Turn in here. Quickly."

"Belitha?"

"Yes. Hurry, will you? If anyone sees us. . . ."

Swearing, Sekhaya backed Joma a few steps, then turned him into the path. There was barely enough room for the caravan between the overgrown hedges. She pulled him up, waited until Belitha climbed up beside her, then started him moving at a slow walk. "Just keep going?"

"My house is by those trees up there. We'll go there."

"They've taken over here, too?"

"Not completely. In town, yes. If Brabby hadn't seen you and told me, ahwu. . . ."

"It's hardly been a month."

"I don't know how they do it, it's like kujuna fever when it's on a roll. First there's one, maybe two, then the whole place goes. Stop a minute. Let me down and I'll get the gate. Keep on going round the back of the house. Brabby's waiting, he'll get feed and water for your horse. You come on into the house, there's something I have to show you."

The room was dark and prickly with the smell of salves and infusions. Belitha led her in, eased back a curtain to let leaf-dappled light play on the face of the sleeping woman. "I gave her futhong so she could get rest and forget what happened a little while." She spoke in a low murmur. Even so, Chaya stirred; she didn't wake, but the hand outside the blanket tightened, then loosened again. "She was raped and beaten, left in a ditch. No serious hurts, not on her body. Her mind, ahwu, we'll have to see."

Sekhaya took the wrist, checked Chaya's pulse, probed her body as gently as she could. She straightened and followed Belitha from the room.

Belitha filled a cup with hot strong cha and pushed it across the table. "It was thieves. They took her horse and anything else that might bring some coin. The man who found her laid her at my door and took off. She said it wasn't him, they threw her in a ditch and ran when he came."

"When?"

"She said it happened just before it got dark yesterday. I washed her, put her in one of my nightgowns and got some soup down her. She was half starved, been riding for days, too afraid to go near fams or farm houses, so she was out of food and worn to a nub. Something else, she was fussing herself about getting pregnant, wouldn't rest, so I gave her kawiss, sat with her till I was sure she'd handle it, gave her the second dose this morning. I'd meant to put her to sleep, but with the kawiss I couldn't. So I held her, sang to her like she was a baby. A bad night, but we got through it. Ahwu ahwu, what the world is coming to."

"Why was she running? Did she tell you?"

"Clan head was forcing a marriage on her. Some Mucky in Glory. Cousins in the house acting like jailors, Uncle over to make sure she stayed put. So she ran, soon's she could. Packed some food, stole a horse, and took off; she was going to find Lavan and appeal to the Arbiters. Ahwu ahwu, Sekha, I'm glad to see you. She stays here much longer, I'll have the Peacers on my back."

Sekhaya nodded. She sipped at the cha, pushed the cup across for a refill. "Bela, I thought Cekers were content with the way things were, it always seemed that way when I went my rounds. Of course, I never spend much time in one place, not enough to get to know that many people. What did I miss?"

"I really don't know, Sekha. Folk round here, they're getting *something* out of those Glory meetings. They're bored, I think. Restless. There's something missing and they don't know what it is. They go, they get churned up and it feels good, and they go back to get that feeling again and by then they're Taken. I'm afraid of it, Sekha. I'm afraid if I went, it'd Take me, too. I've got my share of that restlessness."

"What are you going to do?"

"The Forest, if it gets too bad round here. Some Halathi came here when Manzi died. You remember, the girl whose baby died." She sighed, drank some cha, wrinkled her nose because it had gone cold. "That was a week after you left. They took her body away, left me a passthrough token, said if I needed sanctuary, I'd be welcome. Said the trees don't like Glory and won't let it in." She got to her feet, emptied the cup into the sink, and set more water to boil. She stopped by the sink on her way back to the table, looked out the window above it, and went stiff. "Sekhaya, get your name-child, take her to your van. Hurry. Brabby's just signed me the Peacers are coming."

A thin, nervous boy was waiting by the back door, dressed in dark clothes with heavy leather gloves on his hands. He glided into the grove at the back of the house, leaving her to follow as she chose.

He took her to a tangle in the middle of the grove, a mix of bushy saplings and old blackthorn vines. Some of those vines were planted in shallow boxes; he dragged them aside to make a path she could carry her burden through, hurried ahead of her to show her where the van was. Still not speaking, he helped her get Chaya inside.

The jolting had broken through the effect of the drugged infusion; Chaya was starting to wake, to make sounds. That bothered the boy. He chewed his lip, glanced at Joma who stood drowsing over a water bucket and pile of corn, then up at Sekhaya crouching in the back door of the van. "The Peacers are riding macs. He won't whicker at them, will he?"

"Any horses around?"

He shook his head. "Farmers have mostly vezen. Don't eat so much. I've got to go. You better keep her quiet. They'll be out here sniffin' round, but the thorns should keep 'em off." He smiled at her suddenly, touched his hand to his brow, and hurried off.

Sekhaya pulled the door shut, eased past the pallet, settled herself, and took Chaya's head in her lap; gently stroking the girl's face she sang a child's nonsense song in a whisper, a song she used to sing to tadling Chay to make her giggle. "Old man bagpipe, he live 'n a hole, trinkee trankee hoot a hoot, eat his meat in a bambee roll, kinkee kankee toot tee toot. . . ." As the song went on and on, she felt Chaya relax and drop back into the futhong sleep.

Sometime later she heard voices, stiffened when she felt the van shift as Joma moved restlessly. He stayed quiet so she relaxed a little. She couldn't make out the words, but she recognized Brabbal's voice; from the sound of it, he was being very polite. *This is loathsome, teaching our children to lie. Ahwu, where's it going to end?*

The voices faded.

She sat in the darkness inside the van, listening to Chaya breathe and waiting for word she could move.

In the anteroom outside the High Meeting Room of the Scrivener's Hall, Hibayal Bebek sat rigidly erect, ignoring the others called to wait here with him. He wore his newest black trousers and tunic, had his hair smoothed tight to his head; his only ornament was the silver seal ring on his left hand.

The Guild masters and mistresses were inside, an extraordinary meeting called to chew over the inroads of the Glory and to decide what to do about it. Bebek knew all about it; the Guildmaster of the Silversmiths had the discretion of a spring flood and spilled the agenda into the ear of his Aide, a 'brandy brother' won secretly to the Glory.

"Master Bebek."

Hibayal Bebek stood, shook the creases from his trousers, and followed the page into the Meeting Room.

The revolving presidency of the Guildmasters had fallen on the shoulders of Eleni Lusika of the Weavers. She sat at the head of the long, ornate table, the others ranged along the sides. The page took Bebek to the foot of the table, then left the room through a side door.

Lusika leaned forward. She was a big woman with wide shoulders and strong square hands; her abundant white hair was braided and woven into a crown atop her head, increasing her force though she didn't need it. She spoke slowly, her deep, mellow voice soft and confiding, meant to draw him in and make him complicitous. "Master Bebek, this is an inquiry into the cult that seems to be taking over our land. Since you are involved in the building of what looks to be its motherhouse, we will be interested to know what you can tell us about the organization."

He rested his fingertips on the table, set himself to be grave and austere, the incorruptible that his reputation made him. "I am ah disturbed by the ah implication that I should be willing to discuss my clients' affairs without first gaining their consent."

"This is a Guild matter, Master Bebek. If you require it, I will direct your Guildmaster to ask the questions."

He contemplated his reflection in the polished wood, his mouth set in a stern line to hide his enjoyment of the scene. When he had his voice in order, he raised his head. "That ah will not be necessary. I do not ah approve of convenient fictions." He cleared his throat. "Although I can tell you very little, I fear. I am merely the agent selected to handle the matter of acquiring the land, recording the deed, and obtaining the building permits from the clan that holds the district where the edifice is to be erected. Further, I was to select the builder and oversee the process so the client will be given full measure for his money. I was, of course, informed as to the nature of the building. It is indeed to be chief among the Houses of Glory. The reason this information was provided is simple, it was necessary for the choosing of the proper builder and instructing him in what would be required of him. The sole contact I have had with the ah cult is through the man who approached me and who is providing the funds as needed for the construction and ancillary matters."

"And this man is. . . ."

"Nachal Cazuko, clan Uzach, totem windhover, guild papermakers."

"Have you any further information about the cult?"

"I have none. As to the physical representations that will be present in the finished structure, I have scale drawings and notes which I will show to any accredited representative of this board. I prefer that these do not leave my strongroom, but will bow to the decision of the board."

Eleni Lusika nodded. "We thank you for your frankness, Master Bebek. Sometime later this afternoon I will come myself to view these materials. You are quite right to limit the exposure of your clients and your business. Good day."

Hibayal Bebek bowed, turned, and walked from the room, holding himself rigidly erect so the laughter fizzing in his blood would not burst out and betray him.

23. Circles and Southings

Serroi reached for the cha mug, jumped as a crooked wire of green lightning snapped from the mug to her finger. She grasped the mug firmly and sipped at the cha while she listened to the argument going on between Liqebemalah and Adlayr. The gyes wanted to go after the hostages, get them out, and then go looking for Hedivy who was somewhere in Qilifund. Liqebemalah kept saying, no no, you'll get them all killed and yourself, too.

Honeydew perched on the knob on the cha pot's lid, wings waving slowly back and forth as she looked from face to face, her black eyes sparking with impatience.

As Serroi set the mug down, the side of her hand brushed the table and the wire lightning zapped her again. "Saa! That does it." She banged the cup on the table, glared as the others turned to face her. "You're butting heads and getting nowhere. I want to know things I'm not hearing. One. Where are they? Two. How do you know and how sure are you that your knowledge is accurate? Three. Why haven't you sent a force to fetch them back? Four. Are you ordered to keep me inside the Forest, or are you simply forbidden to let me return to the coast? If I crossed the mountains into Qilifund, would that be taken as negating the agreement? Five. Have you received any orders about Adlayr and Honeydew? Six. If so, what do you intend to do about it?" Ignoring the prickles of force, she slapped a hand on the table. "Give me answers. Short and to the point, please."

Liqebemalah scowled at her. "You have no understanding of our lives, Healer. Short and to the point, pah! A short answer is a lie because it ignores too much. And what right have you to order us about?"

"I might ask what right have you to keep us prisoners? I won't because you can't. Not now." She brushed her hand across the smooth polished tabletop, then lifted it a few inches and held it, watching the wires of lightning snap between her palm and the wood, then slapped it down with a sharp cracking sound. "I'm not sure what would happen if you laid hands on me, but I don't recommend it. Answer me, if you please."

Adlayr Ryan-Turriy got to his feet and moved to stand behind Serroi, arms crossed, waiting.

Liqebemalah stood, bowed to Serroi and left.

Adlayr stretched, grinned at Serroi. "Started something."

"Maybe."

"Think you'll get your answers?"

"At the moment, I don't really care. I'm tired of this place, this business. I want to find Hedivy, drag some answers from his sources, and kick off from this miserable island." She pushed back her chair, looked round the room. "Tsaa! Pretty prison, but prison still." She charged out the door and went to stand on the shelf behind the house, leaning on the rail and looking across the lake.

Honeydew fluttered out, perched on a post, kicking her heels against the wood. *Serry got lots and lots of childlings this time.*

I suppose so. She sighed. *I'm beginning to feel like a pregnant squid.*

Honeydew giggled and winked at the siren who'd surfaced out in the middle of the lake and was swimming about, crooning to the water snakes wriggling around her. *We going into Qilifund?*

Oh, yes. I'll ride this out a while longer because it'd be better to go with agreement than without, but Hedivy's ours and I'm not going to let a clutch of wizards or whatever do away with him.

Adlayr leaned out the door. "He's back, Serroi."

* * *

Liqebemalah sat on the bench, hands resting on his knees. "We have agreed to answer your questions, Healer. Insofar as we are able."

"Yes?" She wasn't going to relax the pressure until she actually got answers she thought were reasonably accurate.

"One. Our people are on an island in the Grand Swamp, not far from the mountains. Two. The trees have told us. You of all people will know the worth of that. Three. While we can hear the trees in Qilifund, our ties are to the Forest, we don't know whether our defenses would work on the far side of the mountains. We are not fighters, we live in balance with our people and our home; if there are disputes, the Halathi Arbiter holds a talk circle until the problem is worked out. Qilimen deal in death every day. Four. We were told to keep you inside the Forest until someone came to collect you. It is possible we might stretch the definition of Forest to include trees on the far side of the mountains; however, all equivocation would have to end at the edge of the Swamp. Five. No one has said anything about the Change man or the Sprite. Six. You're right, we can't constrain you, we can only ask that you do not endanger our Dreamers." He fixed accusing eyes on her and when he spoke again his voice was heavy and filled with implication. "Who are as much your children, Healer, as the dryads, fauns, and others who have come alive in our Forest. The trees tell us it was your coming that woke the Dreams in them." He folded his hands. "All that is inadequate, truth lost with what has been stripped from the bare statements."

"At the moment I'm not interested in truth however defined." Serroi's irritation sharpened her voice and put more bite in her words. "That's an argument that would use up both my lifetimes without getting anywhere." Honeydew fluttered over to her, landed on her shoulder, and patted her, her tiny hand tickling like a fly on the cheek. Serroi smiled, comforted, and spoke more sedately, but with no less determination. "We're going to Qilifund to retrieve a companion the Qilimen have as prisoner. Will you help or hinder us?" She managed another smile. "Or ignore us."

Liqebemalah's pale eyes moved to Adlayr then back to Serroi. "Let him go. You stay here."

"Nay. There's been too much scattering. I won't let it happen again."

The blood rose in the Halathi's face and he wouldn't meet her eyes. He was silent a moment, then got to his feet. "We will take the third road," he said and left the room.

Lele-isi came an hour after sundown. "I was hoping you'd be awake," she murmured when Serroi opened to her knock. "Look, Healer, our crowd'll be with the others tomorrow, we have to, you know. I'd go with you if I could, spite of them, but if any of us sets foot on the far side of the mountain, the Qilimen will know it and that's baaad. Tobenjo did a map for you, Kanta-re and Salda-mai have got the gyes' weapons and stuff from where the jawin hid it, and we collected food and like that. We had to sneak it, the jawin would've stopped us if they knew." She frowned. "They know something they're not talking about. You can see it in the way they look at each other." She shook her head. "Don't know. Doesn't matter, I suppose. Kanta-re and Salda-mai will mark the trail you should take and cache the things along it. The map's just for in case something weird happens." She caught hold of Serroi's hand, her eyes filled with tears. "My mother is with the Dreamers, Healer. Be careful, please. And bring her back to us."

The sun was not yet visible over the treetops and dew was still beading every surface when Serroi and Adlayr left the house and walked into the village, Honeydew perched on the gyes' shoulder, one tiny hand clutching at his braid. The Halathi they met turned their backs and stopped talking. Near the edge of the trees Lele-isi was waiting to see them leave. She turned her back like the others, but her fingers were twiddling behind her, a tiny wave of farewell and good fortune.

The Forest was open and filled with greenish light from the sun filtering through the canopy—and silent, the only sounds the faint rustle in needles on branches a good fifty feet over their heads. No birdsong, no barks and squeals from small-lives. Nothing.

Adlayr tapped Serroi's shoulder, pointed at a white blotch clearly visible against the smooth red-brown bark of one of the giants, a bit of papyrus glued to the trunk to mark trail for them. After a few more steps they could see another glimmer of white at the edge of visibility. Though the ground was already tilting up, the going was easy, but more than a little eerie because of the silence and the sense of waiting.

That silence stayed with them till long past noon, when they were well into the mountains. As she walked, Serroi kept waiting for the Fetch to brush against her, call to her, do something, anything. Nothing. No sense of Its presence. That should have been comforting, instead it left her increasingly uneasy, wondering what it was she didn't know.

As the day darkened toward night, one of the men strode ahead of Hedivy and the rest of the Halathi, breaking way through the tallgrass, stirring up swarms of biters and thumping the ground with his staff to chase off the snakes and vermin that nested in there. Makalaya and the other two men followed him, widening the path. Kielin walked beside Hedivy, keeping an eye on his leg and how he was handling it. When he tried to move faster, she wrapped her hand around his arm and pulled him back as if he were a fractious horse she was keeping under control. He glowered at his feet, ground his teeth as he stumped and swung along, grimly fighting off the weakness the fever had left in his muscles and the growing pain from his thigh.

TheDom was up early and broad enough yet to light the way for them, so they went on without stopping after the sun went down, squeezing as much distance from the day as they could. Then the clouds began thickening across the moon's face and Kielin called a halt.

The Halathi Dreamers tugged Hedivy into the middle of the patch they'd trampled in the grass, made him sit on blankets and not touch the earth, then they danced in a circle round him, hand in hand, whispering words that fell into his ears and out again without any pause between.

At a signal he didn't catch, they broke apart and Kielin came to poke his leg.

"What was that about?"

"We don't want visitors in the night."

"If you could do that, then why . . . ?"

"Why were we prisoners?"

"Yeh."

"It's a subtle thing, Hedivy Starab. In the beginning they surprised us, after that they stayed too close. Take your trousers down, I want to see the wound."

"It's fine, you don't have to fuss."

She flicked a finger at his hand, stinging him a little. "Don't play the fool with me, foreign man. Or with yourself."

His mouth in a grim line, he unlaced the fly and slid the trousers over his hip, pushing the cloth down to uncover the puckered puncture wound.

She touched it lightly. "Heat. I was afraid of that."

He grunted as she drove her thumb into the muscle around the wound and hit a sore spot.

"Not as bad as it might be. I'll have a fomentation ready in little while. You won't like it, it's going to be very hot. You can pull that up now, if it makes you feel better." She moved away and stood in a huddle with Makalaya and the other women.

Mithel left the boys and came to squat beside Hedivy. He didn't say anything, just watched Hedivy lace up his fly and shake his shirt down.

Hedivy scowled at him. "Huh?"

"Where you from?"

"Zemyadel."

"Where's that?"

"North a here."

"You don't talk much."

"Nothin' to say, why talk."

"I never been out of the Forest. Tell me 'bout the Zem . . . Zem . . . that."

"Left it when I was younger'n you. Farms and such."
Mithel blinked at him. "How come you went?"

"My business."

"Oh. Sorry. Where'd you go?"

Hedivy bent his knee, drew his leg up, straightened it,
repeated the actions, working out the stiffness that had
come back when he stopped moving. "City," he said.
"Dander."

Mithel moved his lips side to side, wiggled his brows.
"I've never seen a city," he said finally. "Tell me 'bout
it."

"Lots of people, lots of noise. Get hungry a lot. Get
beat up till you big enough to do the beatin' yourself."

Mithel made more faces as he considered this, but before he could ask anything else, Kielin was back with a
steaming bucket. "You go tend soup a while, young Mith,
and let the questions rest."

Kielin used a short stick to bring a steaming clot of
rag, stewed leaves, and less identifiable slop from the
bucket; when she slapped the mush over the wound,
Hedivy clamped his teeth together and stared past her at
tufts of grass seed black against the sky.

She chuckled. "Oh, yes, you're a tough one. No doubt
about that." She used another rag to bind the poultice in
place. "Makalaya, time."

The younger Halathi brought him a mug of something
that smelled like the mess on his leg. "It's for the poison
in your blood," she said, "like the poultice was for the
flesh."

He took it and kept staring at the grass while he gulped
the noxious liquid down.

Makalaya smiled at him. "Good," she said. She took
the mug and handed him a twig that smelled like liquo-
rice. "Chew on that a while, it'll take the taste away."

The drums started again.

Two of the men knelt, facing each other, eyes closed,
heads bent and touching; Kielin and Makalaya knelt also,
facing each other, hands moving in swift curvilinear ges-
tures.

Hedivy spat out frayed twig slivers, wiped his mouth. "What's that for?"

Mithel scratched his nose. "Lookin' for us. They know we around somewhere, just not where."

"And them?"

"They nudging the phthatha away from us." Mithel picked up a bit of fluff from a seedhead, blew it off his fingers, blew again and sent it arching toward the grass. "Softly softly, no-bo-dy feel a thing."

Hedivy grunted, picked up his bowl again and scrapped out the last of the tuber stew. He'd had time to think and wasn't happy about any of this; they didn't have a weapon among them except a chipped stone knife one of the men had produced. He drained the juice from the bowl, took a drink from his watersac. *Deadhead, you didn't even think of collecting the guards' guns and bringing them along. Proggin' jekker, that's you, worse than Turkl the Peabrain.* He cleared his throat, spat. *Zdra, must a been that proggin snake took m' mind off m' business.*

A worm of suspicion turned in his mind when he looked at these woolly heads, a suspicion that said it was them, they didn't want the guns along so they didn't let him think about them. He watched the Halathi intently, was so short with his answers to Mithel's endless questions that the boy went off, and finally curled in his blankets to snatch what sleep he could.

After a few hours into the next day, they'd left the grass. The land began rising more sharply, clumps of trees and brush mixed with areas of thick groundcover, some vines, some of it short stiff grass with spines that could cut like needles. Now and then he heard the drums again, but there was a questioning note in them as if they'd lost focus. He dug his fingers in the incipient beard that was collecting dust and itching like five days' bad luck. *Proggin' magic.*

By nightfall they were in the fringe of a forest, trees all round them.

Kielin probed around the pink, puckered scar. "No heat, good. Does this hurt?"

"No."

"Ahwu, you haven't done yourself damage this day. Tomorrow will be more difficult." She pushed at the strands of white hair straying into her eyes, got to her feet. "For all of us." She listened a moment to the drums. They'd changed again, gotten louder and more insistent. "They're pushing at us. I don't know. . . ." Her shoulders slumped and her eyes looked bruised.

"Mp." Hedivy pulled the laces tight, tied them off. "How long before we're into your Forest?"

"Xosa Pass is two days off. If they've gotten this close, they know where we're headed. They'll send a force round to wait for us."

"And?"

"I don't know." She walked away.

Hedivy sat watching the others get the camp set up. They were all tired, on the ragged edge of falling apart, even young Mithel was subdued. He brooded about the drums and what Kielin told him, ate what he was given, and watched the Halathi go through their enigmatic maneuvers. He was angry and humiliated, shamed by the stupidity and carelessness that had put him into this mess in the first place. *Twice. Not once. Twice! Stepping in it and rescued by someone else.*

Kielin came over to him and stood looking down at him. "Whatever you're planning," she said, "don't do it."

He looked past her, said nothing.

"If you step outside the circle, you'll have that lot," she waved her hand toward the rumble of the drums, "you'll have them down on us before the night's done."

He glared at her. "The guards had guns."

"The guns were bound to them."

"What?"

"Have you ever seen chinin trained to lures?"

He looked away. "You know I have."

"They have men called makkhan who can smell out the marks they put on things. We didn't have time to unmark the guns and taking them would have brought a makkha straight to us with no need to search for traces."

"So it's wait here, lick arse and beg to stay alive or do the same at the Pass?"

"Not quite, foreign man. We're in Forest now and these trees, this earth is ours." She grimaced. "Ahwu, almost ours. Go to sleep, Hedivy Starab, and keep your plotting for places and people you understand."

Churning with resentment, Hedivy watched her walk off. He'd run his own life since he was nine. Didn't matter how he had to scramble or what he had to put up with, it was him in control; even going with Oram was his choice. He could have run, started up somewhere else. Now he was as useless as he'd been when the Qilimen were carting him through the swamp in that hammock. More than useless. The half-formed plans for taking control again that had been floating in his head were air dreams. He rolled himself into his blankets and willed himself to sleep, but he couldn't will the nightmares away, dreams from the old time he thought he'd forgotten.

Under the trees the slope was steep enough for the cane to be more bother than it was a help. Hedivy considered tossing it away, but it was the only thing he had approximating a weapon so he hauled it along and distracted himself by figuring how to sharpen and fire-harden the end. A short staff . . . he knew a thing or two about stick fighting . . . with a good point on the end if he got a shot at a throat. . . .

As they passed through a meadow and the sun hit him full for the first time, he wiped his sleeve across his face, scratched some more at his beard, then went stumping on after the others, eyes on the ground, looking for a pebble to put under his tongue so he could forget about the thirst that was turning his mouth to a washboard.

A loud squawl brought his head up.

A black trax was circling overhead.

He straightened, waved.

The trax dipped a wing, squawled again, then took off.

He stood looking after it until Mithel came scrambling back to him. The boy stood with hands clasped behind him, watching the trax vanish into the clouds. "What's that?" he said.

Hedivy shook himself, began trudging up the steepening slope to where the trees began. "Trax," he said.

"I KNOW that." Mithel trotted ahead of him, switched round so he was climbing backwards, moving with an ease that irritated Hedivy. "I shoulda said who."

"Friend." Hedivy grabbed a handful of the aromatic branches, used them to pull himself up a tough section, the whippy limbs bending and creaking, but not breaking away even when he put most of his weight on them. "Help's comin'."

Half an hour later the trax was back. He swooped low over Hedivy, arced up and around, came back and dropped the longgun he clutched in his talons, then went racing away toward the Pass.

Hedivy caught the gun, the weight of it slapping with comfortable familiarity into his hands, the bulletsac tied to the trigger guard swinging against his gut. He smiled and began untieing the sac from the guard.

Mithel came running back. "Lemme see, huh? Lemme see."

Kielin caught him by the arm to drag him off. Over her shoulder she said, "What saves you, saves us. Remember?" She scowled at the boy. "Leave him alone, Mith. This is his business."

Hedivy smiled again. His business. Yes. He shook the strap loose, slung the longgun over his shoulder, pulled the sac open, and began shoving bullets in a clip as he climbed up the slope, his body moving easily now, aches and weakness forgotten. *One thing you could say about the gyes—he might be as woolly headed as this lot, but he knew when you needed a gun in your hands.*

He caught up with Kielin, walked beside her. "Can you find out how many Qilimen are waiting for us?"

"Seven." She chuckled at the expression on his face. "The trees."

"You telling me trees can count?"

"No. We can."

He brushed at his face as if brushing away cobwebs. "And you know where they are."

"Oh, yes."

"And you can show me."

"No need. Your friend will take care of them."

"Huh."

>><<

Serree, Adlee say he see ohhh eight ... nine ... ten folk climbing up the mountain ... last one, it's Hev ... limpin' along like he hurt or somethin' ... Adlee say no guns, no weapons, just folk climbin' mountain and back down below, Qilimen, lots and lots and lots of Qilimen, spread out all over the place, got drums, bangin' on them, he don' know why ... saaa! more Qilimen sittin' in trees ahead of Hev and the Dreamers, waitin' for them, Adlee thinks ... the Pass, that's where they are. Where Honeydew and Adlee and Serree gotta go. Got guns and lookin' ugly. Adlee says he wants to take his longgun and drop it to Hev, just in case, he says.

Tell him I think it's a good idea, Honey, and he should come back right now.

After his supply run Adlayr dropped to the ground in his usual awkward, stumbling touchdown, choreographed to Honeydew's giggles. He got to his feet, brushed the dirt off his face, and took the trousers Serroi passed to him, talking as he began getting dressed.

"Hev is lookin' better now he's not just a passenger. I could tell he was feelin' low." He hopped about, got his second leg in the trousers and ran the laces round the hooks, shook his head as Serroi held out his shirt. "I'm probably gonna have to fly again, no point in it."

Serroi set her hand on his arm, held him still a moment. "You're all right?"

"Easy in, easy out," he said, but wouldn't meet her eyes.

Serroi shifted her pack, started walking. "How far to the Pass?"

Adlayr caught up his pack and moved after her, Honeydew settling on his shoulder, her hand tight on the long

braid that went past his neck and hung down his chest.
"We're closer on this side than the Dreamers are on
theirs. I'd guess from how they're moving, it'll be at least
a day and a half before they get into the Pass, we should
reach our end sometime round tomorrow noon. It's a
winding gorge, looks like a river ran through it, then the
land rose and cut the water off. Thirty, forty stades long.
Take at least ten hours to walk it, probably longer. The
Qilimen are waiting about five stades inside. Narrow
place, with walls too steep to climb, a cliff on the west
side. They've piled rocks up along the edge, can shoot
through gaps, rake the pass for half a stade on either side.
Two of them are up trees with longglasses, the others are
sitting round under the trees, eating, talking, hanging over
a fire that smells like the Biserica infirmary, snuffin' up
the smoke. Longguns layin' about, some kind I haven't
seen before, double barrels with a round can-thing where
you'd usually see a clip. Two drums hanging from one of
the trees. I get the idea, the minute they see the Dreamers
they start bangin' those drums, then they hold the Pass,
kill anyone they can. Wait for the rest of the Qilimen to
get there."

Serroi trudged along for several minutes after he finished. "How many?" she said finally.

"Seven. What you thinking?"

She snapped thumb against finger, watched the green
lightning jump. "Remember the spy in Govaritil?"

"The one in the wall? The one you put to sleep?"

"Him." She moved her shoulders. "I don't know if it'll
work, but the way things are, ei vai, it's a chance. If we
wait till we're close and their attention is on the Halathi."

"'S mountains. Probably got kamen from you pulling
me loose. Why not call and let them tromp the Qilimen?"

Serroi shivered. "Nay, I can't."

"Why not? If an army of the Qilimen popped up and
started shooting at us, wouldn't you call for all the help
you could get?"

"Yes, but," a wry smile twisted her mouth, "I'll make
killers of my children, but not murderers."

"Mm. Doubt they'd care a lot. They're stone, not flesh,
it wouldn't be like they're mashing their own kind."

"Ei vai, say I don't know what it would do to them. You want to leave stonemen with a taste for blood this close to the Halathi?"

He wrinkled his nose. "Probably not a good idea."

When they were well into the pass, Adlayr flew another sweep, came back to squat beside Serroi. "Two of them are rolled in their blankets, sleeping. One's on watch, up a tree, drum on his lap waiting for Hedivy and those to get well inside the pass, another hour, I'd say. The other four are sniffing smoke. Want me to take the rope up?"

"Yes." Serroi closed her hands into fists, opened them again, watched the faint glow rolling like sweat over her skin. "I'm ready."

Honeydew perched on a rock, her wings shimmering in the sunlight. She was silent and tense, listening to Adlayr as he circled over the torpid Qilimen.

Serroi was stretched out on her stomach, her head on her crossed arms. The sun was hot on her back, sweat was trickling into her eyes and she was uncertain about what would happen. So much she couldn't control.

Serree, he ready.

Good, tell Adlayr to take out the man in the tree the minute he reaches for that drum.

Adly know that, Serree. He say you do yours and he do his.

Serroi smiled, turned her head to rest her brow on her arms. Holding the image of the Qilimen as a focus, she brought forth from the ancient stores in her mind the command set she'd learned from Ser Noris, shaped the force that flowed from her, and sent it through the earth.

Adlayr swept in tight circles above the scattered trees at the top of the cliff, his eyes on the man sitting in it, though he glanced now and then at the four swaying over the fire.

When he saw them go still, then fall over, he plummeted toward the tree, shifting to sicamar as he reached the top branches, plunging down to land on the Qiliman's branch, a black paw ripping out the man's throat. He shifted again, man this time, straddled the limb, clutching at the corpse, gulping in air until the dizziness and nausea from the double shift went away.

"Murd, what a. . . ." He grimaced at the shaved skull in front of him, intricately tattooed in purple, red, and green. "Time, gyes. Get to work."

He dropped and began moving among the sleepers, tieing their hands with the short lengths of rope he'd prepared beforehand.

>><<

When he saw the trax, Mithel broke from Kielin and ran to join Hedivy. "He's back."

Hedivy grunted.

The trax spiraled downward until he was head high, then turned and powered along the winding path. He swooped up, repeated the plunge and low flight, then hovered above them.

"I think he wants us to keep on going," Mithel said.

Hedivy ignored him and went stump-swing forward, leaning on the cane, the longgun tucked ready under his arm, resentment boiling in his belly. It was more of the same, he couldn't do anything on his own, no struggle, no need to be clever; that green bitch had done it again, all he had to do was keep walking. *Like this lot of woolly heads smiling all the time with the sense between them to draw a breath and not much more. Chased by a clutch a stumblefoots coon't find arse at noon. Stumblefoots that could still catch up with them. Green bitch probably thought of that, too.*

When he rounded the bend, he saw the Healer and the gyes waiting for them. At the same time the ground started shaking. He looked back. The cliffs were falling in, huge sections of rock cracking loose and tumbling down to block the passage. Mouth clamped in a grim line, he stumped on. *Healer bitch did it. Like I thought. Why'm I here anyway? Why'n zhag 'm I botherin' with any a this? Sh'd go back t' army and fight like a man. Proggin' magic.* He nodded at her and walked on past, heading for the Forest and the nearest way back to Bokivada.

>><<

Mama Charody heeled the macai that Horse had charmed out of a field for her and Doby into moving faster, caught up with Horse, and touched Treshteny's arm, waking her from a pleasant dreamstate.

"Yallor's just over the horizon, timeseer, we could be there before nightfall. Is there any reason we shouldn't camp now and leave passing through till tomorrow?"

Treshteny wriggled in the hammock of Horse's back, waking Yela'o who squealed protest then jumped down and went trotting ahead along the road. She looked vaguely around as if she'd find the answer in the grass and trees or the plants in neat rows in the fields on the far side of the road. Yela'o and Mama Charody were as solid and single as always, the macai was a blur of shapes, fetus to skeleton, Doby the same, the ground was crawling, wet and dry at once, gravel ghosts flying where Horse and macai might be going to kick them—but it was all ordinary, nothing strange ... until she focused on the road ahead where Yela'o was cavorting, hitting at stones with a stick he'd picked up somewhere.

The thin gravel was swirling, flying off as if kicked by dozens of hooves; dust boiled up, subsided a little, boiled again. The disturbance diminished abruptly by a stand of trees, though small poufs and jumps continued on to end at Horse's feet. She looked away.

"Zdra?" Charody's deep voice was impatient. "What do you see?"

"I see the road and it seems to me that horses' hooves are stirring it up. A lot of horses. Or maybe not."

"Where is this?"

"All along, far as my eye reaches. It lessens near those trees ahead."

"As if we meet another force there?"

"Or not."

"And you feel no warning?"

"Except in a premoaning fit, I only measure what is before me. And the premoaning comes when it will, not when I will it."

"Then we'll camp and see what happens."

The girl on the tall black gelding sat easily in the saddle, looking down at them, a half smile on her face. Behind her the dozen guards stared into the distance, visibly not-listening. "My name is Zayura," she said. "My father is the Galyeuk. The Healer's Children told me you were coming."

Treshteny blinked at her. Among her phase-images was a pale child with a twisted leg. She nodded, understanding what the girl hadn't said. "And you came."

"I came." She swung down from the gelding, tossed the reins to one of the guards and walked past Treshteny and the others into the shadow under the trees, moving with a vigor and ease that made the timeseer smile.

Charody took Treshteny's arm and with Doby trailing behind followed the girl into the grove.

Zayura shrugged and a small green creature crept from her pocket to perch on her shoulder, a horned and hoofed mouselet like a miniature Yela'o.

Yela'o snorted and squeaked at the mouselet who squeaked back at him.

Zayura ignored them. "I know why you travel south," she said. "I want to help."

Charody tugged at an ear, twisted her pleasantly ugly face into a clown-grimace, then sighed. "Most commendable, but we'll be taking it slow and easy and keeping our heads low."

"I know. But I've brought clothing, blankets, and a supply of food for you. And some gold, not enough to weigh you down, but you might find it useful now and then. And I mean to escort you through Yallor. I know my Yallorese." A flash of white teeth and dark eyes twinkling. "I'm sure you could squelch any trouble, but if you want to keep your heads down, it's better you don't have to."

She stepped close to Treshteny, took the seer's hands

between her own. "Look at me, timeseer. Tell me what you see."

"It's better not."

"Tell me."

"There's nothing certain. Do you understand that? I see possibility, not fact. A tapestry with dangling threads that could make a hundred pictures."

"Tell me."

Treshteny freed herself, reached out for support from Charody, closed her hand about the older woman's arm and focused on Zayura—stared a long moment at the images spreading before her like glass playing cards overlapping so that no image was totally clear—stared and fainted.

A moment later she was looking up into the girl's frightened face. She smiled, shook her head. "Nay, it wasn't what I saw, it just takes me that way. Help me up, will you?" When she was on her feet again, she said, "Are you sure you want to hear this?"

Zayura compressed her lips, then nodded. "Yes. But alone, if I may."

Mama Charody held out her hand and the mouselet jumped onto her arm. She snapped her fingers to Yela'o, nodded to Doby and led them out to wait beside Horse.

"Kuyu, tell me, timeseer."

"There were three threads of roughly equal strength. In the first strand, two or three years from now, your father has you strangled because he's got you pregnant and if that crept out, it's the one thing that would bring him down. In the second strand, a year or two from now, you kill him, run and find sanctuary at the Biserica, live out your life there contented, even happy. In the third strand, a few months from now, you slip away from Yallor and follow us south to the place where we meet the Enemy and you either die there or are badly hurt, I don't know." She drew a breath, let it out in a long sigh. "And remember, a new starting point would change all this. Tomorrow's possibilities might be quite different." She grimaced. "I told you it's better not to look."

Zayura's eyes were wide and dark, her face at first drained of color, then she was blushing furiously and couldn't meet Treshteny's eyes. She turned her back. "What you've seen. . . ."

"T'k! Families. My twin brother murders people. He's dead and he's trying to make a whole land dead like him. You do what you have to and keep the carnage down if you can. What do you call that little mouselet? My son's Yela'o."

Zayura cleared her throat, spat. After a moment she turned, her face a smooth mask. "The faun's your son?"

"Oh, yes. The only one I'll ever have. He's enough. I see him single and he stays with me till I'm dead."

"That's a curse you have, not a gift."

"Oh, nay, I wouldn't say that."

"His name's Laret and he's got a score of kin that run about my garden."

"Yes. Born when Serroi straightened the bones."

"That's what they say. They've taught me some interesting things."

"That's good."

"Yes, the Healer did more than fix my leg; she woke a talent or two that will surprise folk one of these days."

Treshteny smiled.

Zayura nodded, a short, sharp jerk of her head. "I'll think on what you've told me. The thing now is to get all of you safely and quietly through Yallor. Shall we go?"

24. Attack and Counterattack

K'vestmilly Vos crouched by the window and stared at the bolt that had long since stopped quivering. She was panting, rapid shallow breaths that sounded very loud in the quiet room. For the first time she was aware of how many windows the room had, six casement windows, all of them cranked wide to get as much breeze as there was, slatted inner shutters pinned back.

Light. So much light.

She could see everything in the room with astonishing clarity, the gleaming parquet floor, the tapestries that hung from the walls to block drafts, the chairs and the daybed, the writing desk, the small tables scattered about, some with lamps on them, some with piles of books and rolls of the broadsheets the Poet had sent up, the pierced wood screen with its overly ornate carving pushed up against the wall beside the door, the duvokin skins tossed about as rugs, their plushy ocher fur with chocolate brown stripes making bright accents on the dark wood tiles of the floor.

A bead of sweat slid into her eye and burned there. She blinked and woke from her paralysis. Careful to keep her head below the sill, she eased onto her hands and knees, worked her skirt out of the way, and crawled across the room; when she reached the door, she shook her clothing into place and started to reach up.

She snatched her hand back, called, "Zasya, unlatch the door and give it a push, but stay away from the opening."

"Marn?"

"Yes. Did you hear what I said?"

"Ei vai, I did. Here goes."

As soon as the opening was wide enough, K'vestmilly scrambled out and got to her feet; for several breaths she stood leaning against the wall, eyes closed, then she said, "Keep low, look to the ceiling on your right."

The meie knelt, eased her head into the room. A moment later she was out again and on her feet. "How close?"

K'vestmilly drew her sleeve across her face. "If I hadn't stooped to pick up a glass, that bolt would have gone through my neck into my brain."

"Maiden Bless. Wait a moment." Before K'vestmilly could protest, she went through the door. After a few minutes of scrapings and squeals, slams and jars, she was back out. "You can come in now."

The shutters were drawn across most of the windows, the screen had been moved to cover the window the bolt had come through. Legs still shaky, K'vestmilly moved across to the writing table and sat in the chair behind it.

"I took a look," Zasya said. "I think he was in those trees by the tent villages just outside the walls. Crossbow's quieter than a longgun, different kind of sound, not so threatening, and with all that noise down there I doubt anyone noticed a thing. No point in having a look, by now he's long gone."

"Sleykyn?"

"Who else."

"They'll be trying for the Hold next, won't they."

"If they're not already in."

"Zhagdeep, I never thought of that!" She flattened shaking hands on the table. "What . . . ?"

"Ildas is on guard outside. Sleykyn won't get near him without my knowing."

K'vestmilly slid her hands off the table and cupped them protectively over the slight bulge of the child. She stared past Zasya and when she spoke, it was more to herself than to the meie. "I've never been so frightened in my life, not even when my mother died. I was angry. . . ." She shook her head. "I've got to think . . . what do I do . . . what would Heslin do . . . ahh! Zasya, I've got to get to the printshop."

"Why don't you have the Poet come here?"

"Nik." She wrinkled her nose. "Politics, Zasya. I'd have to call Osk up first and he won't like what I mean to do. Better to set it going before he finds out."

"Ei vai then, you'll need to wash and Mask."

"Wash?" K'vestmilly pulled her hands up, grimaced at the dust smears. "I suppose my face. . . ."

"Mh."

They moved quickly through the halls, Ildas running before them, Zasya beside K'vestmilly, handgun drawn and ready. K'vestmilly ignored the stares she got, let Zasya do the watching and went over what she wanted the Poet to set his mind to. It should be a variation on the campaign Heslin arranged when her mother was killed, getting the word out far and fast, so Osklanders and exiles both would be looking for the Sleykyn, turning the Osklanders' unease at all these foreigners invading their place away from her, onto the Sleykyns' heads, doing what Heslin called a double dip. Not that she was going to explain any of that last to the Poet or to Osk himself.

Her appearance in the doorway brought the hubbub to a sudden stop. Vyzharnos came hurrying across the room, wiping inky hands on a rag. "Marn?" There was a touch of uncertainty in his voice as he glanced from the Mask to the meie standing with a shortgun held down at her side, but ready to fire.

"I've got something I want you to do for me immediately, Poet. Can you do it?"

"We're setting up to print tomorrow's sheet. We could get started right after that."

"Nik, Poet, it can't wait for that. The Sleykyn are here. I was nearly killed a short time ago. Crossbow bolt through my window. It missed me only because I happened to stoop at the right time. I want the story in the sheet tonight, along with a reward for anyone who spots a Sleykyn. You worked with us after my mother was killed. You know what to do. Do it fast."

Vyzharnos grinned at her. "Haven't told Osk yet, have

you." His voice was a thread of sound that barely reached
her ears. He spoke again, more loudly. "You got it,
Marn." He swung round, shouted, "Marl, Jink, pull the
wagon report, we'll fit the attempt story there, kill the re-
cruit box, set up another box in its space for a reward notice, change the surround to double wide. Telesny, get
your boys in now, have 'em ready to run before the hour's
out. Zeks, grab a pad 'n hit the office, I'll be with you 'n
a minute." He looked over his shoulder. "Anything more,
O Marn?"

"Send me a copy when you've finished. I don't need to
approve it, but I'd like to see it."

"You got it."

In the hall again, K'vestmilly lifted the Mask, wiped
the sweat from under it. "Now we go find Osk. Saaa! this
is going to be a rough one. I wish Heslin were here. Or
even Vedouce."

>><<

In the sleeping section of his command tent, Vedouce
leaned over one of the maps his artists had compiled for
him from older charts and the written reports Heslin's
scouts had sent in; the sheet of paper was mounted on
softwood, the location of the navstas marked by paint-
dotted press-pins so they could be shifted when necessary.

There were scattered farms on both sides of a creek almost wide enough to be a small river, which ran in a shallow arc through the foothills. Fields enclosed in hedges,
most of them centuries old, tough and thorny. Scattered
groves and individual trees. Rocky upthrusts with clumps
of grass, croppeys reported to be swarming with snakes,
all poisonous and easily irritated. The farm buildings
were burnt and deserted, the animals driven deeper into
the mountains, away from the raiders.

During his march on Oskland, in village-farm pods
much like this one, Mern the Fist had kept his supply
wagons in the center, while he divided the Taken into columns of four by fifty, each headed by half a dozen
mounted fighters, spreading his army out over a wide

area, marching them through the winding lanes with the chovan whistle talkers before and behind, riding scout, keeping the columns in touch, weaving a web of sound that Heslin reported as even more effective than the coms.

Vedouce frowned. No one he knew could read those whistled sounds, but it was clear they meant trouble for the Marn's Army. More trouble. Despite the rotation of greeners into the veteran navstas striking at the raider-bands where they got some experience under fire, most of the Osklanders that made up a good half of his army were unblooded and he couldn't be sure how well they'd stand once the fighting started. He'd scattered his veteran navstas over a wide arc, using the croppeys, the ruined villages and groves as ambush points. It was a thin arc, but he'd chosen this place to make the most of what he had and Merk had just passed through those other hedgerow-farm-village sections and might be less likely to look for trouble. Throdal was following as closely as he could without making contact, Stoppah was instructed to remain in the rear and keep the supply line cut until the last moment, then bring his men to join Throdal.

"Tuhl General."

"Come."

His aide Spalyr ducked past the flap. "Valk just called in. The army's still on the same line, no sign the Fist is expecting trouble. Valk says we should see advance scouts around one hour on."

Vedouce stood. "Good, much longer and the men's edge would've gone off." He moved past Spalyr, into the main chamber of the tent. "Tou, get your runners moving, I want those scouts taken out. Spal, get back to Valk, tell him to go on clear, we know where all the coms are. I want everything he can give you on the enemy."

He nodded at Korchil, who was seated at the common map, shifting the markers to lay out the new data from the spotters. "Spal, did you alert Throdal yet? Good. I want him ready to go when you send word. Zdra. One hour. Where's Merun?"

"I sent him and the others to get the team hitched up and the gear stowed. We can strike and clear out of here inside of ten minutes."

"Good." Vedouce straightened; he lifted a hand as if he raised a glass. "The Marn, tuhlveks."

"The Marn."

The rider flashed by, tossed a stone-weighted wad of paper to the Vudvek Zatko, vanished around the grove on the way to the next navsta.

Zatko shook the stone out and flattened the scrap of paper, ran his eyes over the lines written on it. "Hurb, get ova here."

"Yeh, Zat?"

"Chovan comin' to look us ova. You'n your cousin Val, you go whistle huntin', eh? Duch says two of 'em heading through trees down by stream. Whip, rope, knife. No shootin', we want Nov's Deadheads walkin' nice and peaceful into our lovin' arms."

Hurbay grinned, turned away with a one finger salute. He swung into the saddle, hit his cousin on the arm and set his macai to a fast walk.

Riding beside him, Valban fished in his pocket, pulled out a silver coin, balanced it on his thumbnail, "Call for whip?"

"Go."

"Y' got it." He flipped the coin, caught it, slapped it on his wrist, kept it covered with his hand. "Call."

"Mask."

Valban lifted his hand, grinned. "Bridge. Whip for me, knife for you."

"Zarker notney, you got that strib trained."

Valban pursed his lips in a silent whistle, an exaggerated innocence on his round, guileless face. "Zdra zdra, jus' luck 'n good looks."

The two chovan were riding warily, one of them half a length behind the other, the eyes of both scanning the trees and ground ahead of them. They were small wiry men, their dark greasy hair tied back with leather thongs; one had most of an ear torn off, the other was missing two fingers on his left hand.

Hurbay wrinkled his nose, but didn't move a hair. *Not so pretty as jelen, they weren't, but as wild and skittery.*

The first one rode by under his limb, his rancid odor
rising thick enough to choke a vep. *One . . . two . . . three,
go!* Hurbay launched himself on the second rider as Val's
whip closed round the throat of the leader and jerked him
from his horse.

The chovan was slippery and strong as an eel; the creak
and shhp from the tree gave him warning enough to free
his feet from the stirrups and twist around, knocking the
knife from Hurbay's hand. They hit the ground hard, the
chovan underneath but far from out of the fight, kicking
and squirming, rolling Hurbay over, going for his
throat. . . .

And collapsing as Valban drove the knife up into his
brain.

After his cousin jerked the knife loose, Hurbay flung
the corpse off him.

"Gah! What a proggin' stink." He got to his feet,
brushed the dirt off his trousers. "Rather a month sloppin'
out stables than dancin' again wi' somethin' like that.
Phah!" He looked around. "Yours?"

"Broke his neck. Bit a luck there."

Hurbay grunted. "Next time, I get the whip."

"Toss for it."

"No proggin' way, cousin. I'm tired a that pet strib a
yours. Let's collect those horses and get back to Zat, see
what else he's settin' up for us."

Vedouce stood frowning down at the map as the reports
came in from the spotters watching the army of the Taken
counting off into columns, the huge supply wagons and
their eight orsk teams plodding along in the center. And
reports from the vudveks of the navstas telling of chovan
dead or unhorsed and on the loose with trackers on their
tails. He'd had luck there, none of the scouts had got
close enough to see the navstas in ambush and nothing
had got back to the Fist, at least not yet. All it'd need was
one look for anyone smarter than a slug to know what
was waiting for the Taken. Half an hour, forty-five minutes, it's all he needed, the Fist would be committed to
the lanes and the trap would spring.

On this map the markers were thumbnail sized cubes of

wood with felt glued on the bottom, each marker representing a navsta. Heslin's voice was an intermittent murmur through the com as he collected reports, collated
them and relayed them to Spalyr. Spalyr called the
changes to Korchil who brought the map up to date.

Touhan was on the far side of the tent, taking reports
from his runners, noting them down. His time for changes
would come when the armies engaged.

As the minutes ticked past, Vedouce watched the
woodchips crawl across the painted paper ... from the
lanes about the last village, across the open ground held
in common with its plantings of dry-reap shem and mountain ryzha. . . .

"Could be trouble," Spalyr said suddenly. "No warning's got back yet, but the whistle talkers with the army
are getting agitated. Valk thinks it's because they're not
hearing answers from the scouts. At least, not so far." He
listened a minute then started reporting directly what he
was hearing. "There's a lot of riding back and forth, arguing with the men around the Fist. Nov's there, he asked a
question or two, don't know what or the answers he got,
but he's looking impatient and the aides are shooing the
chovan away. Nov and Mern are talking now. Army's
breaking into columns, moving into the lanes ...
Zhagdeep, whistle talk coming from our way, one of 'em
got through ... army's not stopping, though, or pulling
out of the lanes ... men are swarming over the center
wagon, unloading something ... slings, Valk says. Like
the toys kids use but bigger. Leather loops around four
feet long. The Fist must have had men practicing in secret, or we'd have known about it. Valk is not happy
about that at all ... he says he's seen Krymen using them
against ships ... worse'n portable catapults, he says ...
they're unloading something else ... round things ...
Valk says he thinks they're those bombs that blew up half
Dander ... he says get the word out, get your men ready
to move fast ... should probably put your best shots in
trees with orders to sit quiet till they see the slings start
whirring, then get as many of them as they can, men or
slings, and a lucky hit or two might blow the bombs before they're thrown, cut them down with their own weap-

ons . . . prak, they know you're waiting, that's sure, but they're not stopping, not trying to find better ground . . . nik, they're moving faster, coming at a trot."

"Tou, pass the word. Now. All of that. Go on, Spal, let's have the rest of it."

"Valk says Throdal's just come through. There were some whistle talkers back his way, but they're gone now like they melted into the ground. He wants to know, should he start moving up and what about Stoppah? Leave him for the reserves?"

Vedouce glanced at the map, rubbed at his chin. "Have Valk tell Throdal to move up slowly, no contact yet; he's to hit the rear ranks only when he hears the shooting start. Stoppah can move this way, but keep his distance. I want his men in reserve in case the Fist starts falling back. Forget what's left of the Taken reserves . . . nik, cancel that. Tell him to leave a spotter watching them, let us know if they start moving faster. Unless that happens, we'll leave them be for the moment."

In the tree he'd chosen, straddling a broad limb with the trunk between him and the lane, Hurbay watched the Taken march forward, coming up the lane at a trot that didn't seem to leave them breathing hard. Easy, fluid movement, nothing like the mechanical dolls he'd seen once when he was a tadling and a player's troupe passed through the Harozh. According to Zatko, they knew what was waiting, but they came on without a change of expression. It made him shiver, even though he didn't know any of them. He was glad of that, it'd be terrible watching a friend who'd turned to a Deadhead running at you. Though his navsta was mostly Harozhni veterans from the gritz war with a few Oskland miners to make up the numbers, he had family who'd married south and there were Dander men in other navstas; as he waited for the signal to fire, he wondered if any of the Dandri were looking at brothers and cousins and neighbors. It was an ugly thought.

He rested his longgun on a handy branch stub and began tracking his man.

The horn blew and he shot; the man didn't go down,

there was blood on him, but he kept running. Hurbay
swore, put a bullet through his head and found his next
target. All around him the others were shooting, some
Taken were going down, but too many of them just stumbled, then came on like Hurbay's had done, came on and
started shooting back, the bullets cutting through the
leaves, searching out the snipers in the trees, Hurbay
heard a yelp, saw Helfer drop, riddled before he hit the
ground, there was a sting alongside his own head, his ear
started dripping blood, but he ignored that and the other
shots that came his way and concentrated on those bobbing heads, no slings yet, at least none in sight, he was
disappointed about that, he wanted a bomb, he could hit
it before it flew, he knew that, he wanted to hit it,
he wanted to see the meat fly and if Nov was around, he
wanted to see him ripped up like his sister, under his
breath he spoke to them down there, he sang them a
name, his sister's name, she'd married a bargevek and got
smeared across a building's wall when one of those
proggin' zhagballs blew. He could smell the burnt powder
and the bullets were getting closer, more than one of the
Taken were shooting at him now, but they couldn't see
him, only the drifts of smoke from the longgun and he
had the trunk between him and most of them, the longgun
was getting hot, it burned his face when he set his eye to
the sight, but he ignored that too . . . *head, get them in the
head, easy now, close enough, it was like shooting nest-
lings.* . . .

The horn blew again. Regroup, retreat.
Cursing with frustration, Hurbay dropped from the tree,
ran around the thicket where his mac was tied, vaulted
into the saddle and took off.

Gun trainer Mult clung to his perch and watched the
Taken stream past below him; he didn't look at their
faces, there were too many chances he'd see something
he didn't want to. That wasn't what he was here for anyway. He sucked at the sinta lozenge and looked dreamily
into the distance, the stump of his left leg tucked under
his knee, the pain from the metal in his body hanging

around but unimportant. Vudvek Vlet had warned him
that the chance of his getting clear once he started shooting was so thin a spider couldn't walk it. The thought
drifted through his mind now and then, but the sinta insu-
lated him as much from fear as it did from pain.

Thom and Benno had woven a kind of nest around him,
leafy branches that would hide him from anyone riding
below; that was Harozh for you, anything to do with
hunting they knew it. And they'd be back to look for him
once the battle was done. If they could. Him or the pieces
of him the explosion left behind.

He heard the constant crackle of the longguns, screams
from macain and horses, howls, yells and curses from his
side, nothing from the Taken, heard the horn call the
navstas back, then the creak of the wagons following the
Taken into the lane, brushing the hedgerows, breaking
enough of the twigs that the eastering wind brought him
the acrid scent of the sap. The lanes wandered around the
edges of the fields, someone said once that back in
the dreamtime when Cadander was being assembled, the
farmers got a macai drunk and cut the lanes where he
wandered. It wasn't true, of course, but it was a funny
thing to picture.

The lead orsks came round the hedge, their horns sawn
short and capped with wooden spheres. Mult rearranged
the thongs he'd tied to screening branches, but it wasn't
yet time to pull them down. Not the first wagon, Vlet
said. It'll be the second. Look for a black crate, or they
might have covered it again, they use a brown-drab quilt
to wrap round it.

He watched dreamily as the long wagon appeared, the
box resting on leaf springs, the iron tires chewing at the
ruts, turning the hard pan into white dust. As the wagon
passed under him, the dust billowed high into the tree,
coating the trunk and leaves, the wind bringing the finest
grains to plaster across his face. He closed his eyes,
leaned against the trunk and waited.

More distant now, the crackle of gunshots started again.

Below him there were riders in the lane, they were
looking up into the trees, he could hear them talking and
he smiled as they rode on without a suspicion anyone was

watching them. He recognized Pan Nov on his favorite
Black, Mern the Fist riding beside him. *Ride slow, you
pair of notneys. Ride slow so you end up riding the blast.*

Thom and Benno. What a pair, they were, two boys
barely old enough to be starting beards, but they knew
their blind-building and the Taken would already be
learning the quality of their shooting.

The team leaders of another hitch of orsks came round
the bend in the hedge, slab-sided beasts with blotchy
brown and white hides, horns bigger around than a man's
wrists, sawn off near the quick and capped with wooden
balls painted a bright red, but so covered with the white
dust they were pink except in the streaks wiped clear by
hedge leaves.

Mult slipped his longgun free of the sheath, one of the
rapid-firers collected from the enemy, settled it across his
lap, pulled at the thongs to bend the branches down, tied
them off when he had a clear shot at the lane.

The second pair of orsks appeared, the third, then the
wheelers and front of the wagon, the driver sitting
hunched over, lines draped through his fingers, his aide
standing beside him, feet apart, whip looped up and waiting to snap. As the rest of the wagon appeared, Mult saw
a large bale sitting in the middle of barrels and chests, a
dull quilt roped round it.

Mult brought the gun up, eased his finger through the
guard, settled the stock so he was comfortable, stroked the
twin triggers a moment until he was satisfied by the aim,
then began shooting as fast as he could into that bale. . . .

The world opened up. . . .

The air was sucked from his lungs. . . .

Heat boiled up around him. . . .

The tree shuddered . . . began to lean away from the
lane. . . .

Then there was WIND. . . .

FIRE. . . .

A NOISE . . . opening like a flower. . . .

then nothing. . . .

>><<

That-which-was-not-Motylla sat on the altar leaning against the sculpted legs of the Glory, yellow light running like melted butter over and around her.

The light stiffened around her like arms clasping her. It lifted her, rushed her through walls that turned to mist before her—like the wind, swift and invisible, she flew across the land, drawn to a flash of immense force, moth to fire. . . .

>><<

Thom's mouth gaped in a silent yell as he saw the sky go yellow, then a blue stain move across the yellow, not sky blue but brighter, gaudier. The blue closed in on itself and became a great sphere rolling toward him. And the NOISE came with a roar of hot wind. . . .

A giant girl's form moved inside that sphere, gliding through the trees, the false Marn with the false Mask.

The Taken poured from the lanes.

The horn sounded charge. Thom wrenched his eyes away from the image, kicked his mac into a belly-down run, handgun and sabre ready for the shock when they hit the enemy.

>><<

The vach herd was a shimmer against the lowering sky, the Majilarn on their rambuts like dark dots along the edge of the mass of beasts with their long silky hair almost the same color as the Grass.

"Shoal off right bow two rets ahead," Sansilly called back, then leaned on the rail behind the screen of ravelings. When they got into Majilarn country, Greygen had teased open some rope and nailed a thick tangle of fibers along the top of the rail, taking it high enough to hide the head of anyone looking through the small gaps in the snarl. It wouldn't stop a bullet, but it's harder to hit what you can't see. She scowled at the men riding toward the river on their rambuts, horned beasts with split hooves, a medium brown on the upper body and legs, the brown streaked with dark red stripes, stiff stubbly manes as red as the stripes. "Stinking notneys, go progg a vach and leave us alone."

This was not the first herd they'd passed, nor the first band of Majilarn. Sometimes the Majilarn ignored them, sometimes they attacked. There was no telling which sort these would be until. . . .

"Greg, those riders coming at us, they're waving longguns. You want me to heave the anchors?"

"I see 'em, Sansy. Keep down, will you? Not yet, wait till we're past that shoal, hmm, and a bit farther round this bend. Way we have to go here, they might be able to get too close. Better to keep moving as long as we can."

Sansilly divided her attention between the river and riders racing toward them; she dropped on her knees when she heard the crack of a shot. A moment later a bullet tore through the ravelings, hit the far side with a faint chunk, and tumbled onto the deck.

Another shot.

The barge wobbled.

"Greg!"

"I'm all right, Sansy. Bullet burn on my shoulder, that's all. Same shoulder as before, too, send them to Zhagdeep. The shoal, am I missing it?"

Sansilly scrambled to the bow, popped her head up for a quick glance at the river. "A hair more to the east; you'll miss the sand as you go, but I'd say a bit more room would be a good thing. Not too much, I can see those glide lines Prah warned us about, I think this proggin' river's got a flooded bar there."

Greygen chuckled. "Thread the needle, Sansy?"

"You be careful, you hear. Keep your head down." She bobbed up a moment to look through the ravelings, saw half a dozen Majilarn riding at a trot along the bank, keeping even with the barge. One of them must have seen her shadow because he whipped his gun up and clipped a curl from her hair as she ducked below the side.

Sansilly crawled back to the bow and crouched there, keeping low until she had to look to make sure the barge was missing the sandbar; even so she never put her head up twice in the same place.

The Majilarn followed with grim determination, silent

and lethal, shooting at the slightest glimpse of a target. Or whenever they felt like it.

"Deep water," Sansilly cried, "one ret at least." She crawled to the bow anchor. "Ready, Greg."

"One minute. Mainsail down first."

She heard thumps, then the creak and hiss of the pulleys and the halyard. A moment later he called, "Ready. Count it."

"One . . . two . . . over."

The barge glided on a few lengths before the anchors bit and jerked it to a halt.

There were angry yells from the bank; one of the riders tried to force his rambut into the river.

Watching through the ravels, Sansilly grinned as the beast squealed protest, tried to hook his horns into the rider's leg, then started switching ends. "Go," she whispered. "Dump him." She sniffed with disappointment as the Majilarn regained control. "Too bad."

He sent the rambut trotting up the bank, shook his longgun at the barge, then went riding off, the others following.

Greygen checked the tiller lashing, then stretched his legs out, moving carefully because his joints had gone stiff. Sansilly came crawling back, took his legs across her lap and began gently massaging his knees. He smiled at her, then leaned against the steersman's seat, closed his eyes. They sat in a companionable silence for several hours as the barge swung from its anchor cables and the herd ambled south.

When the last rider vanished over the horizon, they winched up the anchors, raised the sail and started on again, moving around the last of the broad, deep bends in the Fenkaful, the end of the long voyage in sight, Tukukul only four days off, no more Majilarn, no more chovan trying to kill them; all they needed to watch for now were the treacheries of the river and the barges heading north.

25. Running

Belitha came through the thorns an hour before dawn. She knocked at the door in the back of the van, handed Sekhaya a mug of hot cha when she dropped to the ground. "How's Chaya?"

"She's gone into natural sleep, should be waking with the sun." Sekhaya sipped at the cha, sighed with pleasure. "Ahhh, that's good. Do you any damage? Peacers, I mean."

"Turned out my chests and closets, stuck their noses everywhere, that's all. And left a watcher sitting in a tree. Brabby spotted him, but the sklink can't see the grove here from where he is. He's mostly watching the lane."

"Will they be back later?"

Belitha shrugged, but didn't say anything.

"Then I'd better get moving." She frowned at the cha. "Could I pass round your stable without that watcher seeing me? Head toward the Forest, then circle back behind him?"

"Why circle back? Remember what I told you about the Forest Token? Brabby and I've spent the night packing. . . ." Belitha turned away. "I hate this . . . this is my land, my house, it's been in my family since before time . . . Bror moved in with me when we wed . . . he's buried there by that tree where your horse is, under the thorns . . . Maiden Bless . . . family, phah! They've gone to Glory, all of 'em . . . almost . . . even my daughter, she married the butcher and her and my grandson . . . they keep worrying at me . . . not baby, he's too little yet, but with his mother like that . . .there's no one to stand with

Brabby and me." She moved her shoulders, swung round to face Sekhaya. "You don't need to worry about the watcher, Brabby will take care of him. But come with us anyway. You know how bad it's getting in the Cekefund. Once we're in the Forest, maybe there's a way to get a message to Lavan. It'd be better for Chaya, she was pretty badly torn and there's always the chance of infection."

Sekhaya drank the last of the cha, held the mug cradled in her hands. What Bel said was true, far as it went. The Forest was close and safe, but what would they do after they got there? She ran a hand through her hair. Chaya told Belitha she'd planned to reach Lavan and go with him to the Arbiters. If there was anyone doing something about this creeping disease of the soul, it'd be them. She sighed. "No, Bel. Maiden bless you and Brabbal and give you what you want, but Chaya's my name-child and I think I should help her finish what she started. I got this far, I can get back."

Brabbal came gliding around the house, his face pale in the starlight, his eyes dark with anger. He laid the longgun beside the driver's seat and pulled himself up beside his mother. "Got him."

Belitha caught his shoulder, squeezed it, saying nothing. A moment later she turned to Sekhaya, who was standing a few steps away from the loaded wagon, watching and trying not to let her anger show, anger not with Bel but with those who made this necessary. "You might's well go the way you came. If you aren't coming with us, no point in adding extra miles to your travel. Maiden Bless, Sekhaya. Let us know how it goes. If you can." She slapped the reins on the horse's rump, started him moving without waiting for an answer.

Sekhaya shivered as she passed a tree with a huddled knot high in it. *Lies and death. Children killing. I don't understand any of this. I don't understand why. . . .* She thought about Chaya inside the van, lying restless in a dream-ridden sleep. What those men had done to her name-child, that was horrible but almost natural beside this other thing. *It's like these people are taking an option on the air so that you breathe by their permission.*

She turned onto the main road and sent Joma forward at a jog trot, meaning to get as far as she could before the sun came up. It was a quiet night, filled with the small peaceful noises she'd loved all these years on the road, the sounds and smells and fugitive loveliness that made her journeying pleasant as well as necessary. For an hour or so she let herself forget all her troubles and exist in the now.

When there was pink in the eastern sky, she turned into a farm lane, slowed Joma to a walk, and began thinking about a place where she could camp for the day. The farms were stirring, the milking already begun, teams were heading for the fields to mow, plow and plant. Several of the men glanced at the van, looked away and went about their business, no welcome, no stopping to chat which was the way it'd been before. At least they weren't actively hostile.

"Ahwu, my Jommy, when we reach that grove up ahead, I'll give you some water and corn, but you're going to have to keep going, old friend. We'll take it slow and easy and hope there's no one sniffing after us."

There was a scrabbling behind her. She looped the reins around a cleat and let Joma go on as he would, went over the driver's seat and through the curtains in time to catch Chaya before she got the back door open. "Kazi, m' kaz, it's Sekhaya, you're all right, it's just me. . . ." She locked her arms around Chaya, holding her close and murmuring in her ear, paying no attention to what she was saying, knowing it was the voice that was going to reach through her name-child's panic.

Chaya went limp and began crying, a gulping, dry-throated grief that had nothing childlike in it.

With the van creaking along, Joma pacing steadily onward though there was no one guiding him, Sekhaya sat on the pallet, holding Chaya, rocking her as if she were a baby, singing to her, talking to her, helping her work through the horrors and back to a precarious calm.

* * *

"You just stretch out and relax, kaz, I'm going to see where we've got to. No no, don't move. Better to stay inside in case someone's following, hush now, I haven't seen anyone, but the field workers are out and they can answer questions. That's good. See if you can catch some more sleep. It'll help the time pass."

When Sekhaya stepped over the back of the seat and settled on her cushion, she saw they'd left behind the grove where she'd planned to stop, but there was a greenish haze on the horizon which looked to be another. "Ahwu, Jommy, good horse. We'll speed up a little, shall we, and this time, I promise you, we really will stop." She uncleated the reins, clicked her tongue to shift him into his jog, and tried to ignore the stares from the fields.

The grove was a traveler's layby with a table, benches, and a well with a trough for horses and other draft beasts. Sekhaya pulled the wooden washtub from beneath the van, filled it from the well and set up screens around it. When she turned around, Chaya had unfolded the back steps and was standing on the lowest, one hand closed so tightly on the door jamb her knuckles were white with the strain.

Sekhaya smiled. "Bath for you, Chay; it'll be cold water only, but plenty of soap. Belitha packed pads and tape for you and I've put them along with a jar of antiseptic cream on the stool. If you need help, yell. I'm going to make us some breakfast, then we'll see how we do."

Chaya managed a wrinkled smile before she vanished inside the screens.

Sighing, Sekhaya fetched wood from the crib beside the well, got a fire going inside the circle of rocks, put on water to heat for cha, and started peeling tubers for a stew. The silence behind the screens except for the occasional splash bothered her, but unless the sounds stopped altogether she thought it better to let Chaya do for herself, get back some control over her body. She started singing as she worked, a comfortable old song that came as easily off the tongue as the skin off the tubers. "The wake-gong is a silver cry," she sang. . . .

The wake-gong is a silver cry
Rising in a rosy sky
Waking souls from ease-ful sleep

The work-gong is a brazen call
Crying out to one and all
You've chores to do and vows to keep.

The noon-gong is a golden uir
calling to the midday fare....

She broke off as Chaya came round the table and sat
stiffly on the bench beside her. "Think you could cut up
some onion for me? There's not a stew worth eating without a bit of onion in it."

Chaya worked silently, peeling the bulbs then quarter-
ing them, setting them on a tin plate when she finished.
"Where we going?" she said finally.

"Ahwu, I thought we'd go find Lavan and then the Arbiters like you told Bel you were going to do."

Chaya's hands started shaking and the color drained
from her face. She set the knife down carefully; even so
it clattered against the plate. She got to her feet and went
to sit on the back steps of the van, her hands limp on her
thighs as she stared out past the trees.

*Idiot! You know better. Calling Lavan's name when she
hasn't even got herself together, let alone her and him.
Ahwu, leave her be for a while longer, then we'll see....*
She tipped the onion into the pot with the shreds of dried
meat, chopped-up tubers and the rest of the ingredients,
added water, and hung the pot from the hook above the
fire. "Keep an eye on the stew," she called. "I need to fill
the water barrels."

Sekhaya took her blankets and stretched out beneath
the van to get what sleep she could before nightfall.
Chaya was walking around under the trees, touching them
as if she saw a strangeness in them, though they looked
like ordinary shade trees, yeshes with their lacy char-
treuse leaves, pulas with their gray bark and huge arching

limbs and the whispering muthis, their dark green leaves
hanging from fine, limber threads, brushing against each
other at the least hint of a breeze, a few stray conifers
adding piquancy to the mix. Sekhaya yawned, tied a black
scarf about her eyes, and wriggled around until she was
comfortable; after the long sleepless night and the tension, she had no difficulty in dropping off.

She woke in twilight to hear Chaya talking to someone.
"But if you're just born, how do you know?"
A rustle in the leaves.
"Because your mother gave it to you, though she doesn't
know she knows. Who's your mother?"
Rustle.
"I don't understand. Who?"
Rustle.
"But if she's trying to stop this. . . ."
Rustle.
Sekhaya rolled from her blankets, got groggily to her
feet, pulling the scarf off as she rose; sleeping in the daytime always left her feeling as if her head were stuffed
with rocks. She saw Chaya sitting on a bench talking to
a glimmer of green and gold that almost resolved into a
form that vanished as her movements disturbed it. "What
was that, kaz?"
"Dryad. There's a colony of them here." Chaya
brushed at her face, then looked down. A small black
snake was curled in her lap, its head resting on the arm
she hadn't moved. She smiled. "I found Wily and fed him
some of your milk powder. Palaia, that's the dryad, she
came to watch and she started talking to me."
Sekhaya patted a yawn and strolled closer. Shadows
from the trees brushed back and forth across Chaya's
face, making it difficult to read. It seemed to her there
was a slight flush on her name-child's cheeks, a glassy
glitter to her eyes; she didn't want her interest to be too
obvious, so she squatted to look at the snake. "He's just
a little thing. Will you bring him along?"
"You don't mind?"
"He can keep the mice out of my herbs." She chuckled.
"Earn him his milk powder." She leaned on the bench,

pushed herself up, brushing her hand against Chaya's arm. "Put him inside and see about heating some water for us while I collect Joma and give him some corn, will you do that, kaz?" The arm was warmer than it should be, but not enough to worry about, could be just the healing. *I'll slip some dullah in her cha, that should do the job.* "It'd help get us ready to move on."

Sekhaya watched Chaya make a face at the bitterness of her drink; to distract her, she said, "What were you talking about, you and the dryad?"

"Things. . . ." Chaya stroked the small black snake coiled on the table beside her. "How she came here . . . and . . . and something about the Glorymen. . . ."

"Mmh?"

"She was born a few weeks ago, just about the time my uncle had his bright idea. . . ." Her voice trailed off.

Sekhaya sat with her hands quiet in her lap, her eyes on the flicker of the fire.

After a moment, Chaya went on, "She says the Glory gets stronger each time a dryad or a being like her is born. She's afraid of it, it made her shake just talking about it. Her mother is a focus bringing back . . . she called it xaleen . . . I asked her what that was, she said life force . . . magic . . . those are all words for it . . . whatever it is, it was gone, but now it's cascading into the world and . . . and one of the things it woke was . . . I don't want to talk about this anymore, thaz."

"Ahwu, that's all right, Chay. Finish your cha, then we have to pack up and get going."

They moved west across the plain, traveling at night until they got well into the grasslands and away from the thickly settled areas, then Sekhaya turned sharply south, heading for the Wastelands Road with its wells and laybys.

The dullah had no effect, so Sekhaya changed to lulay. When that didn't work either, she went through her antipyretics, got no result from those, tried a tonic which seemed to strengthen both her name-child and the fever. She coaxed Chaya into submitting to an examination, but found the wounds healing without difficulty, no heat in the flesh, no suppuration, decided finally that it was a fever born of the mind rather than the body. The exam did accomplish one thing, it woke Chaya from her brooding silence and started her talking—not about the attack itself, but about what led up to it.

"Shanqwe Koxaye," she said, concentrated venom in the words. "Plague carrier. That's what Bel said to me, and it's the truth. Tickle yourself to orgasm running people's lives for them. Rope them round so they can't move, 'less you say so, that's the truth. Why he wants me, zhag knows. I threw in his face just looking at him make me want to puke, I told him if he touched me I'd find a way to geld him, I called him every filthy name I could lay my tongue to and his eyes started shining at me and he licked his lips and I felt like meat, I felt like he was going to sink his teeth in me right there. Uncle was getting purpler by the minute, but he didn't dare open his mouth. When I got home, he came by and was going to beat me, but that koxa sent a man by to make him leave me alone, told Uncle right there in front of me that the Grand Pastora. . . ." she spat out the words as if they were a foul taste, "wanted my skin soft and supple for the wedding night, I vomited on Uncle's feet, he wanted to hit me, but he went away instead and the man went away and took my cousins with him. When I opened the front door to go out, another man stopped me, and there was one in the back garden and they said I was supposed to stay in the house and get ready." She looked down as the small snake nudged his head against her leg, took him on her lap, and began stroking her forefinger gently along his spine.

"Uncle made me go to a meeting once. Almost the whole fam was there and farmers from way round, even brought their kids. I was going to be quiet, just sit there and let the nonsense go by me, but I saw Catilu sitting on the floor in front, looking up at HIM. . . ." Her mouth twisted and her breathing got rough. She went quiet for a while, her hands cupped round the sleeping snake.

The van jolted along over the rolling grassland. They

were alone under a sky that seemed closer and more huge than sky had ever been.

"Catilu was looking up at the koxa like he was the essence of her dreams; you didn't know her, thaz, she was Chocho the Baker's youngest daughter, he'd just this year paid her fees to the Weavers and started her at the loom. A baby and looking at Koxaye that way. I couldn't stay, thaz. I couldn't. I wanted to catch her by her hair and drag her out. I loathed him before that, but it was nothing to . . . I looked at Cat and I wanted to cry . . . no, I wanted to scream . . . I wanted to claw his eyes out, that miserable . . . I wanted to take that knife he played his games with and cut him . . . I couldn't sit there any more. I jumped up. Uncle grabbed at me, but Aunt Phuza stopped him. I ran. Out of the meeting hall. All the way home. I heated up some old cha and drank that. And went out back and threw up. And I knew if I didn't get away soon, I wouldn't kill HIM, I'd cut my own throat."

She went back to brooding.

The fever got worse after that.

A week later, water in one barrel down to scum on the bottom, the other with a few inches left, food nearly gone, Sekhaya drove round an outcropping of rock and saw the road she'd been looking for so anxiously. She glanced at the curtains behind the seat, moved her shoulders impatiently, and sent Joma down the incline onto the rutted hardpan. Despite the heat and the jolting, Chaya was inside the van, stretched out on the pallet, muttering to herself, dropping in and out of dream-ridden sleep. The best thing she could do for her name-child now was find a layby with its well, then spend a day or two there, resting, doing a wash, and making needed repairs. Maybe they were far enough away they wouldn't have to worry about Glorymen coming after them.

Once they were on the road, Sekhaya pulled Joma to a halt and climbed down. She turned the tap on the second barrel, tilted it to squeeze out the last drops and took him half a bucket of weedy water. As he drank, she scratched his nape, licked her own dry lips. "Ahwu, old friend, you've labored nobly, let no one tell you elsewise." She squinted into the sun, wiped at her eyes. "Almost night. No matter, we'll keep going till we find water. No choice about it. Now, now, that's all there is, you'll get splinters if you try to eat the bucket."

She looked through the curtains. Chaya's face was flushed and working, her mouth moving though her eyes were shut; Sekhaya couldn't hear what she was saying, but probably it was much the same as she'd heard before, Chaya reliving the rape, cursing her uncle and the Gloryman, calling to someone she called Mother, not her own mother, Sekhaya was sure of that. Wily the snake was coiled up, sleeping on her chest, undisturbed by her movements.

Sekhaya sighed, swiveled around, uncleated the reins, and clucked Joma into a plodding walk. Listening to his iron-shod feet clop-clopping steadily on the hardpan and the creak and rumble of the van, she thought about Belitha abandoning her home and running for the Forest. She thought about her own years on her rounds, moving from village to village, south to the edge of the Waste and the start of this road, north again, birthing children and beasts, dosing the sick, whether they had four legs or two, brewing tonics, possets, poultices for farmers and their livestock. Just enough change to be interesting, otherwise each year was much like another, amber beads with stories trapped inside. *I'm as bad off as Belitha. Nay, worse. Her land will still be there, my round is gone. Like someone wiped it away. A dozen years from now, no one will remember it was there, no one will remember I was there. Tsaa, I'm too old for this.*

Three hours later she came round a thick clump of brush and saw a pinpoint of red some distance ahead of her. Campfire. She passed her tongue across dry lips. "Q'lik! Ahwu, Jommy my friend, we keep going and hope that's not a clutch of Glorymen or bandits."

She halted Joma, leaned forward, calling out, "Hola, friends, do you mind if I join you? I'm somewhat short of water."

A woman's voice answered her. "Be welcome, kos."

There were two by the fire—a bearded man with pale eyes, heavy through the shoulders, sitting with one leg stretched out before him and the woman who'd spoken. She was small and slight, dressed in dusty white, with hair the russet of ripe apples, eyes an improbable orange. A trick of the firelight gave a greenish cast to her skin. Sekhaya blinked, but the odd color didn't go away.

The woman got to her feet as Sekhaya drove into the layby and stopped Joma by the trough. "Hev, give her a hand, will you?" She moved closer, stood smiling up at Sekhaya. "My name is Serroi, I am a healer of the Biserica."

Biserica? How odd ... why is she here? Unless the Biserica has gone to Glory ... ayee, that's a frightening thought. She dragged a dry tongue over cracking lips, considering how to answer the greeting. "I am Sekhaya Kawin, clan Watella, totem owl, guild herbalist. I've heard of Biserica healers, though I've never met one." She swung down, glanced at the man who was working the pump to fill the trough for the horse. "Are you for Glory?"

Serroi reached across to Sekhaya, caught hold of her arm; her fingers were smooth and small, but very strong. After a minute she took her hand away, moving it quickly around behind her as she stepped back. "Hardly. You needn't worry, Herbwoman. The Biserica is still Maiden's Ground and the Glory is the Enemy. She's tried her best to kill us all."

Sekhaya hesitated, then said, "There's a girl in the back of the van. She has a fever I've tried everything I know to break, but nothing worked. Would you look at her?"

The orange eyes danced with an amusement Sekhaya didn't understand. "I'll do what I can. Get yourself some water, I can see you need it." She turned her head, called, "Come on in, Adlayr."

A man walked out of the darkness, a longgun swinging from a big hand, a tiny winged figure riding on his shoulder; he nodded to Serroi and settled beside the fire.

"Gyes," Serroi said. "The sprite is Honeydew. Hedivy," she nodded at the man by the well, "he's a companion in our travels."

Sekhaya filled a tin cup with water and drank it, rinsed it out, refilled it, and carried it dripping cold to the back of the van where she pulled out the steps and unlatched the door. "Be welcome," she said, and stepped aside for the healer, sipping at the water while she waited.

Serroi knelt beside Chaya; when the healer laid her hand on the girl's brow, Chaya sighed and all that was clenched about her relaxed. Serroi straightened, sat on her heels and turned her head to look at Sekhaya. "What happened?"

"She was set upon by thieves, raped and beaten, left in a ditch."

"And you couldn't take her home."

"There were reasons. Is there anything you need? I can tell you what herbs I have."

Serroi got to her feet. "Nay. I'd like her brought outside, though. Call Adlayr, will you? He'll carry her gently enough you don't need to worry."

"If she wakes and sees a man. . . ."

"She won't, not till I wish it."

The sprite fluttering over Serroi's head, the Biserica healer shook out the blanket and laid it on the ground by the fire, then Adlayr went to his knees and lowered Chaya onto it. When he stood, he raised his wrist to the sprite, brought her back to his shoulder. "Are you sure, Serroi? They're bound to be listening for it."

"In this, I have no choice. Adlayr, I'd like you and Honeydew to go aloft. Give me a shout if either of you see anything coming at us."

"You got it." He went striding into the darkness, the sprite clutching at his braid.

Serroi raised her brows at Wily the snake who was crawling from Chaya's sleeve, moving up to coil above her heart. "Hedivy, would you see to the horses? Keep them quiet." To Sekhaya she said, "Things happen when I heal. I can't control it, nor do I know what I'll bring on us. It would be best if you could go on as soon as I'm finished here."

"The horse is too tired."

"Ei vai, I warned you." She knelt beside Chaya, lifted

Wily and passed him across to Sekhaya. "Hold him while
I work." She closed her eyes, set her hands on Chaya.

Sekhaya stared. Green light flowed from the Healer's
hands, spreading along Chaya's body, sinking into her,
spreading out and out in a shimmering sphere. . . .

The sphere touched her.

A sense of deep well-being filled her; she felt Wily stir,
felt his small life linked with hers and Chaya's.

Gayo flowers pushed up around them in an expanding
spiral, a year's growth in a single breath, their red blooms
unfurling at the ends of the long seed stalks, their perfume heavy on the air.

Moth sprites the size of her thumbnail were wrung
from the air like raindrops; they fluttered among the gayo
blooms, shining bits of moonlight given form and life.

The well shimmered, the stones of the wall round its lip
shone with the yellowing-white glow of the moons; a column of water shot upward a dozen feet, broke, and fell
back to fill the excavation and go flowing over the incan-
descent stones into a stream that wound among the gayos
and ambled off along the road.

Abruptly, the glow-sphere hiccuped.

There was a deep droning hummmmmm.

A figure formed within the light, a woman with a
leather skirt that brushed against bare feet, a leather
jacket with long fine fringes along the sleeves, Halisan
the Harper, standing there looking startled, her harp floating unsupported before her; she caught it before it fell,
scowled at Sekhaya, turned and saw the healer.

"I know you," she said. "You're the Mother. You're the
Well."

The green glow vanished.

Serroi sat back on her heels, her hands resting lightly
on her thighs, a distant look in her eyes, a force about her
that sent shivers along Sekhaya's spine.

Chaya slept, the fever flush gone from her face, the
muttering stopped, the tension drained out of her. Wily
stirred, fell off Sekhaya's lap and went gliding off to coil
again on Chaya's ribs.

Sekhaya got to her feet. She circled round the blanket,

stopped beside Halisan, nodded at the tranced healer. "Anything we should do for her?"

"No. Me, I could do with a cup of cha. Any chance?"

>><<

Serroi wrinkled her nose at the flowers and the new spring that was still flowing strongly, at the moth sprites playing over the water.

Moth sprites.

For an instant she was back in the Mijloc, riding with her shieldmate Tayyan to take Ward in Oras, another part of the world, another life. She blinked and the image was gone. With a sigh, she sipped at her cha and watched the others around the fire. Me, Hedivy, Adlayr, Honeydew, and now the Harper. What a crazy lot round this fire.

"Halisan the Harper." Hedivy spoke suddenly, his voice rough with that Zemya lilt to the words as if he half sung them, but out of tune. "A man named Nehod, he told me that he knew you."

"Knew is right. He vanished a while back."

The strengthening wind blew the gayo flowers about, wisps of dry clouds high overhead darkened the night. Moth sprites flew in and out of the firelight, chased away by Honeydew before they could hurt themselves in the fire. Sekhaya came from the van where the girl was still sleeping, a strong woman, but more than a little lost in the convolutions of this game. She poured a mug of cha and sat beside Serroi.

"How long will she sleep?" she murmured.

"The rest of the night probably. She was exhausted and the healing tired her more."

The herbwoman went silent, sat frowning at the fire and Serroi went back to listening.

Hedivy dug his fingers in the bright chestnut beard that covered the lower part of his face. "I had a question I was wishing to ask him. Maybe you can answer it."

"And maybe I will answer. Or not."

"Cargo of a certain kind came into Bokivada Bay and it was shifted to other ships, ones bound for Govaritil. The same will be coming these days, but sent to Shinka and across the Neck to Tuku-kul. You tell me. Who in Bokivada would know about this?"

"Cargo of a certain kind. That's somewhat vague."

"You know what I mean."

"I would like it specified."

"They were bombs and other weapons sent by the Enemy. Mother Death."

"Bound for Glory."

"You could say that."

"You want to find out where they come from."

"Yes."

"Hibayal Bebek. Clan Bambana, totem eel, guild scriveners. If anyone knows, he does."

>><<

Lavan was in his room, packing saddlebags for the trip to Hallafam.

Below him, in the backyard, Casil and his daughter were arguing about him. Casil had given up trying to get her inside and was shushing her and keeping his voice low so Lavan wouldn't hear; Siffana Kinuqah had no such inhibitions. Words and phrases drifted up to him as he worked: sucking parasite, layabout, foreigner, steal-from-your-grandchildren's mouths. . . . She had a voice like a saw when she got mad and no discretion at all. He began to understand why Casil had been so tired these past weeks, worn out keeping the two of them apart; pity knifed through him, distracting him for a moment from his worry about Chaya.

He folded his copy of his master's certificate, fitting it into his belt along with the gold coins he'd got for the armlet and buckled it on. The Valuer had been so taken with the armlet, he'd bought it on the spot; it was hard letting go of something he put so much concentrated effort into, but Lavan knew he'd never get a better price. He buckled the flaps down and hefted the saddlebags to check their weight, glanced round the room. *I was happy here.* He slapped the bags over his shoulder, glanced out the window a last time, froze as he watched half a dozen men come round the corner of the house.

Five of them stood like black scarvabirds while the sixth walked up to Casil and croaked, "We want the girl." He was a long thin man, with a patch over one eye and black leather gloves on his hands, leather so thin and supple that Lavan could see the wrinkles by his knuckles. Around his neck was a heavy silver chain with a rayed pendant hanging at the join of his ribs.

Lavan clutched at the windowsill, holding his breath. Glorymen. He'd seen more than one of them passing through Hubawern.

Casil scowled at the man, annoyed. "What girl? What are you talking about?"

"Chaya Willish, clan Linfaya." His voice had gone whispery; it sent chills walking the nape of Lavan's neck. "Read this." He drew a folded paper from his sleeve and held it out to Casil.

Casil took his time flattening the paper; he walked away from the man as if he needed the sunlight out beyond the shadow of the Munga tree to let him read the script. All this time Siffana stood silent, her hands folded before her, her head bowed as if in reverence.

Lavan felt sick. Why had they come here hunting for Chaya? Had things gotten so bad she had to run? How am I going to find her? Should I wait? Or take the Wasteland Road and hope to meet her?

Casil finished the letter, folded it back with small, meticulous movements of his hands, taking his time, playing the ancient. "Don't know why you give me this. Only woman in m' house is m' daughter, you can see for yourself she's no runaway girl."

"Where is the man?"

"What man?"

Siffana lifted her head. "He's in his room upstairs, Servant of Glory. Packing to leave, or so my father says."

"You are of the Glory?"

"I am."

"Have you seen a young woman about?"

"By the Glory I have not. But I can't be everywhere."

"Then we must search the house." He looked around

for Casil, but the old man had slipped away. "Will you permit, Glory's daughter?"

"The asking is all the permission you need, O Servant."

As soon as the six men and Siffana were out of sight, Lavan swung through the window, muscled himself onto the roof and edged along it until he reached the Munga tree. Behind him he could hear feet stumping up the stairs. A glance into the yard, another at the tree, then he jumped.

He brushed against one limb, caught hold of the next, rode it down, released it, caught another to stop his plunge, dropped to the ground and ran for the stable, the saddlebags slipping from his shoulder to hang over his arm, a shout following him as a Gloryman leaned from his bedroom window and saw him.

Alegay was waiting, saddled and ready, Casil holding the reins. The old man coughed, set his hand on Lavan's arm. "She is what she is," he said, sadness roughening his voice. "Head for town, you'll need food. Here. This should help." He pushed a money purse at Lavan. "It's yours, what you woulda earned if you finished the year. Find your girl, give her a kiss for me, and when you have kids. . . ." He took hold of Lavan's arm, his grip biting to the bone. "Go on now. 'Fore those gits come here lookin'."

Lavan shoved the purse down the front of his shirt, swung into the saddle. "Send a letter if you can. To the GuildHouse would be best." He nudged Alegay forward, taking him through the half open door.

Another yell.

One of the Glorymen was racing at him. He whooped and kneed Alegay into a run, slapped at the man with the saddlebags he still carried over his arm and made it round the house before the others got out the door.

He was beginning to relax when he heard a crack and felt a blow near the end of his shoulder. "Shooting?" He bent low over the horse's neck, called for more speed and went racing down the curved road, heading for Hubawern.

At the edge of the town, he slowed Alegay and glanced

over his shoulder. Two dark figures were riding after
him—moving at an unhurried lope as if they knew he had
no place to run. He rode on into Hubawern, feeling at his
shoulder. There was a hole torn in his shirt, not much
blood, though. It was starting to hurt and he cursed the
Gloryman who shot him, but it wasn't serious, a bullet
burn, that was all.

He looked back again. They were closer and slowing,
following him, but not trying to catch up. He shook his
head, wondering what they were about, then looked
around. *Lot of people about. Maiden Bless, I don't know
anyone here except Casil. Even the Valuer's gone back to
Bokivada. With that letter from Chaya's Uncle . . .
Zhagdeep! Do they expect me to lead them to her? Where
is she? Sekhaya maybe? Whatever I do, chances are it's
wrong . . . can't stay here and wait for her . . . not with
those sklinks hanging around.* He turned into a lane leading into a tangle of houses; Alegay was fresh and shying
at shadows, sidling and trying to get the bit. Lavan
ground his teeth as he convinced the horse to behave, the
effort sending pain pricks darting out from the bullet
burn. He wove through the crooked ways, moved through
someone's back yard, trampled a path through a kitchen
garden, went round a pole shed, past a clump of trees,
into another lane, eased back toward the main street when
he thought he'd lost his pursuers.

Probably wasn't worth the time and effort, they'd just
pick him up again when he started south. But he couldn't
be sure they weren't looking for a place to drop a loop
over him and use him for bait. *Set me out to graze and
wait till she comes up to me.*

All the studying he'd done. All the work. . . . *No one
teaches you how to kick an enemy's face in, how to turn
his ambition into ash. . . . Zhag! Who would've thought
I'd have to know?*

He turned Alegay into the accessway behind the stores,
twisting around at intervals to watch what was happening
behind him, breathing easier as he saw no signs of the
Glorymen. This didn't help his shoulder which was burning more every moment. He was going to have to get that
seen to, but at the moment what he wanted was the Farm-

er's Market; he need a packmule and enough supplies so he could cut across the Waste if he had to. *Yes, Wastelands Road, then north. Find Sekhaya if I don't catch Chaya. Yes. A longgun and plenty of bullets. I'll have to practice, I haven't hunted since I was a boy. A quarter of a century that's been. Almost. I wonder if you forget, or does it come back with a little practice? Like riding. . . .*

A gust of wind brought him the noises of the Market and the thick, acrid smell of dung. He eased in the saddle and kneed Alegay into a faster walk.

Hibayal Bebek smoothed the sleeves of his tunic, settled it down over his lean hips and followed the builder's agent into the building. His boot heels hit the stone with sharp clicks and the sound echoed back at him. It was late and the workers had gone home to supper and bed, the emptiness of the structure was oppressive in the flickering light from the agent's lantern.

Without speaking, Bebek moved close to one wall, running his hand along the stonework. The wall was smooth and cool under his fingers; he couldn't feel the joins. There was a lot of debris on the floor, stone chips gritting under his feet, but the carved band that ran along at eye level was finished except for the final polish, the dancing figures with the rayed face of the Glory repeated in infinite variety, each slightly different from the last. As he moved about the main chamber, then into the side chapels, the agent followed him, holding the lantern high so he could see.

Bebek spent an hour doing his inspection, then he strode out the door, stopped on the portico and waited for the agent; when he spoke, his voice was at its driest and most formal. "It is well enough, though the work has been slower than promised. Is there a firm date for completion?"

The agent's eyes slid away from his. "Hard to say. You want it fast or you want it good?"

"I want your employer to do what he is contracted to do. If I don't receive a satisfactory reply and soon, I will begin subtracting a percentage of his fees. Inform him. If he wishes to discuss this, he should come to my office tomorrow." He strode away without waiting for an answer.

Hibayal Bebek slipped the robe off, tossed it aside, and sat cross-legged on the mat in front of his attic altar. He used his teeth to pull the cork from the bottle, poured the dark amber wine into a stemmed glass. "It's coming well," he said. "I put a burr under Gaxumek's tail tonight. I'm reasonably sure the House will be finished by TheDom Dark. The Guildmasters are running round in circles biting their own backsides. The Aides are seeing to that, brandy brothers, yesss." He gulped down the brandy in the glass, filled it again, his head swimming pleasantly, his body so light it came near floating.

"Even the dawethies look confused." He giggled. "They stand there shivering when they watch the processions. Sometimes tongues start sliding across lips and their hands stroking along their bodies till they notice what they're doing and they run away." He drank more brandy. "Rumors running like fire about the Arbiters coming south, true enough, two lectors who were brandy brothers came by this morning to tell me. Sibukel the Observer, Okhelan the Decider. Be here by the end of the Dommonth. What do you want me to do?"

The amber light pulsed above the crystals. *You are doing wonders for us, Belovéd, forget the Arbiters, they have no power and our power is greater with every day that passes. Sleep, Belovéd, dream of a time when you will be one with all, cherished by all. Sleep and dream. . . .*

>><<

The reed marshes of the Dar stretched out to the horizon in the west. The Kirojens rose high and stark in the east, their black stone summits patched with glaciers.

Treshteny writhed on the stony road, moaning, drool dripping from her mouth.

The premoaning fit went on and on, more focused this time . . . a blackness like a hole in the air, crying out, de-

manding, hungry, sense of immensity, power spreading
farther and farther, growing stronger, anguished voice
calling ... *Mother Mother, claim me, come to me, touch
me. Why won't you hear me? Why. . . .*

Mama Charody helped her sit up, lifted a cup to her
lips so she could drink. The water was warm and tasted of
the skin, but her mouth was parched and her head throbbing; she gulped it down, smiled as Charody moistened a
cloth and patted it over her face, wiping away sweat and
drool. She reached up, caught the old woman's hand.
"Help me up."

When she was on her feet again, she looked out across
the Dar into the haze on the horizon. "There," she said,
pointing to the southwest. "It or she or whatever, it waits
there."

26. The Glory Goes Rolling On

The blue sphere rolled forward across the land, moving with the Taken army; where it touched, the earth blackened and trees, grass, birds and beasts died—everything but the Taken; they lived in and out of the blue like amphibians living in and out of water. Mern the Fist, Pan Nov, and the heart of the army were blown to ash in the great explosion, but the Taken were getting their orders from another source now. The chovan and Nov's thugs fled in fear or merged with the Taken, Taken themselves the minute the blue touched them. When the blue touched one of the Marn's Army, he Changed, turned on his kin, and marched with the others.

Warning them to keep clear of the blue, Vedouce sent his men against the Taken, attacked and retreated, attacked again and again.

The Taken that fell lay dead only until the blue light moved over them, then they rose up and marched on with the same disciplined deadliness they'd had when they were alive.

Stretched out on the croppey, Hurbay emptied the longgun, shoved in a new clip, began shooting again, dropping man after man from the northern wing of the Taken navsta advancing across the uneven field, trying to hit them in the head so they wouldn't get up and come at him again.

"Proggin' corp! I swear I got that'n twice before."

Stretched out on the other side of a pile of crumbled rock, Valban snorted. "They all corps, like shootin' fish."

The blue light rolled closer and closer, dead on the ground rose and came at them.

The cousins wriggled backward, ran for their macain, and joined what was left of the navsta as they headed for the next ambush point.

"Valk. Throdal here."

"Valk here. Go."

"We can't get near the Taken with that blue light around them and shooting into it is useless. We tried that, closest I can get to what happened is a lump of sugar in hot cha. What I want to do is Stoppah and I should go back and hit the reserves, try to take out as many as we can, keep supplies away from them. Go."

"Hold on, I'll pass that on to the General. Out."

"Valk to Throdal."

"Throdal here. Go."

"Vedouce says you're on your own. He'd appreciate your hitting the reserves as hard as you can, but stay alive and stay mobile. Anything else? Go."

"That bad? Go."

"Worse than you know. Out."

"Vedouce to OskHold."

"Hold here. Go."

"Call the Marn and Pan Osk. And quickly, please."

"Will do. Out."

>><<

Light coming through the loosened shutter slats painted gold bars on the parquet. The meie Zasya Myers lay stretched out on the daybed, catching a little sleep, Ildas a fiery glimmer by her feet.

K'vestmilly Vos sat at the writing table with the Poet's newest broadsheet spread out before her. Two of the Sleykyn had been discovered and mobbed, killed after they'd slaughtered a dozen of the people piling on them, the names of the dead listed in a box bordered in black with a black star by each name, heroes they were called.

K'vestmilly grimaced. More dead heaped on the reports of the dead from the army.

A light flickered on the com sitting by her elbow, the small yellow glow lighting the hairs on her arm; Pan Osk had insisted she have it so she could call for help if a Sleykyn got by his defenses and made it up the stairs.

"Marn here. Go."

"Heslin, Marn. Set 9 5 7. Out."

K'vestmilly scowled at the com, scratching in memory for what he'd told her, moved the tiny wheels until the numbers he'd given showed in the slots. "Hear me, Heslin? Go."

"I hear. K'milly, you've heard about the blue glow? Go."

"Yes. I heard Vedouce describe it."

"There's nothing we can do, Kimi. Three or four days, that's all you've got. Your veterans are holding, though they can only nibble at the edges and hope to slow the Taken a little. The rest are starting to run. Thinking about their families, I suppose. What I'm trying to say, I want you out of there. Take the meie and get across the mountains. It won't help anyone if you get killed. And the baby."

"You come here, then I'll leave."

"I can't, Kimi. I wish ... nik, never mind. Vedouce is going to call Pan Osk in a short while, give him the bad news. If Osk goes, will you go with him?"

"I'd have no choice, would I. Hes, things have changed. I've grown up a little, I think. I want you with me, I miss you so much, I miss ... talking with you ... laughing ... you said I wouldn't miss you in my bed. I do. Every night, I do. Take care, will you? I didn't know my father until this year, but the little time we had I wouldn't have missed for anything. I want my daughter to know her father from the day she opens her eyes. Please be careful. Out."

Mouth pressed in a thin line, she reset the com, then dropped her head in her hands.

>><<

The blue sphere rolled on, the gigantic image of the false Marn inside it taking a mile at a stride. As Vedouce's army melted around him, he drew in the hard core of veterans and retreated before that remorseless torrent, nipping at it in increasingly futile strikes. Each death seemed to augment rather than diminish the power of the light.

They backed into Oskheart, turned, and raced for the mountains across the empty fields, past the defenses abandoned half done, past the great pile of stone that was as useless against the blue force as a heap of marshmallows.

>><<

His people filing past below him, Zarcadorn Pan Osk sat on his horse high on the mountain slope and looked back at the Hold valley, at Oskheart. K'vestmilly Vos waited beside him, a cold knot in her stomach as she wondered where Heslin was, if he were even alive.

Its blackened path a mile wide and vanishing over the horizon, the blue glow-sphere ate through the trees and rolled toward the Hold.

The blue touched . . . ate into the stone . . . slowed . . . slowed yet further as if daunted by the weight of what it consumed. . . .

The sphere quivered. . . .

Unfolded. . . .

The sound reached K'vestmilly Vos.

Like the blast that killed her mother, multiplied many times.

A groan, a roar, a vast and spreading BOO OOO MMM that shook the mountains.

Her horse reared.

She fought it down, fought it back into control, her strength multiplied by her terror for the child she carried.

The ripples of the Sou ou ound faded.

She heard a groan from Pan Osk and looked again.

The blue glow was gone; the Hold was a pile of rubble in a valley of death, everything gone, burned to the ground, trees, crops, even the grass, were all of them ash.

The Taken stood in disciplined lines waiting to be told what to do next.

She pushed the Mask up, used her longglasses.

A small solitary figure stood on the highest peak of the shattered stone, a slight young girl with a Mask the twin of her own, the False Marn viewing her kingdom.

27. One Journey Ends, Another Begins

Sansilly glanced back at the barge. With the wind shifting the torchlight so erratically, it seemed to dance in the darkness. She reached out, caught hold of Greygen's hand. "It's kind of hard," she murmured. "Like leaving home all over again."

"Do you mind so much?"

"Nik . . ." She dragged out the word, sighed. "In spite of everything, it was a good time, wasn't it."

He didn't answer, just freed his hand, dropped his arm on her shoulders and hugged her tight for a long moment, then went striding ahead of her to the pole lantern that marked the end of the alley, stopping beneath it to peer down at a wrinkled sheet of paper he took from a pocket.

They hurried through the winding secret ways, empty and echoing, where the life of the city was inside, shut into lamplit, noisy courts behind high mud-brick walls, following the names of streets stamped high on those walls, spelled in three scripts, mijlocker, fenekel, and dandri. It was a trader's town and Fenek reticence gave way to market needs.

Near the outer wall they came to the many-towered House Hekkataran, a pile the size of a small mountain.

Greygen looked at Sansilly, drew a deep breath, then caught hold of the heavy bronze knocker and hammered it against its plate.

A man leaned out one of the gate towers, looked down at them. "Who goes?"

Greygen licked his lips, spoke the pass phrase the Marn had given him. "A servant of one the Healer healed."

"Heyo, you made better time than we thought. A minute while m' lazy 'prentice stirs his stumps and opens to you."

Sansilly leaned into Greygen, limp with relief and a rising pleasure; it'd been a long time since anyone around her had spoken with such open, friendly ease.

Three days later they stood in the bow of the trader, the towers of Tuku-kul vanishing behind them, their Fenek guards squatting at their ease with their backs against the cabin wall, longguns resting easy across their thighs.

The banks of the Fenkaful moved out and out until it seemed the ship floated on a sheet of silvered glass, each half-submerged tree with its mirrored counterpart growing downward as it grew up. There was no wind and the silence beyond the ship was profound, except for the low hum of the hordes of insects which only seemed to intensify the stillness. The men of the crew had dropped their songs and moved with a languid competence that was as reassuring as it was eerie.

The master was a burley Fenek named Biddiyai whose short cropped hair was sprinkled with gray and the occasional silver coil; most of the morning he spent up on the quarterdeck, leaning on the rail, smoking a pipe and keeping a lazy eye on his crew. When the sun was overhead, he stirred, came down the ladder and crossed to Greygen, tapped him on the shoulder. "Eat."

Greygen stirred, blinked. "What? Oh. Yes. Sansy?"

The narrow cabin was dark and steamy, the table a board on chains lowered from the ceiling, the meal a fruit and vegetable salad with fresh baked bread and a pot of cha.

They ate in silence for several minutes, then Biddiyai said, "Swamp's been quiet past few trips. Nev' can tell, though. I say hop, you get out the way, hmm?"

Greygen closed his hand on Sansilly's arm, squeezed it in warning. "We held off Majilarn, we could help with swampies."

"Could. I'll yell if I need you. Better keep hid till then. Feneks shoot Feneks, that's one thing. For'ners do it, could stir up more'n you or me, we want."

Greygen nodded; Sansilly sighed.

Biddiyai rubbed his hands together, smiling broadly. "Haya, now that's settled, we be in Sinadeen five days on, then 'tis a week to Yallor. And there we part. Malkia put it to me to get you a safe ship. I'll do that, an' Maiden see you safe to where y' got to go."

The passage through the Kul Marsh was smooth as the water, slow and stately. Twice someone shot at the boat, but whoever it was hit nothing and Biddiyai didn't bother reacting. They slid into the Sinadeen and a brisk, following wind sent them skimming across the end of that sea, getting them to Yallor in less time than it took to cross the swamp.

"Haya, Am'l, got some passengers for you. Malkia said to tell you, they friends of the Healer. They bound for Biserica."

"Pho!" The shipmaster's nostrils flared as he ran dark yellow eyes over Greygen and Sansilly. "Good 'nough for me, come on 'board. Won't ask y' names out here, but mine's Am'litho, Master, m' ship's the *Wanda Kajamy,* the sweetest little goer in all the Sinadeen. Jy," he roared, "get y' butt over here and haul that gear aboard."

TheDom was a waxing crescent low in the west, the Jewels of Anish overhead, the Dancers just clearing the horizon in the east, the moons touching the long waves with streaks and spots of silver.

"It's beautiful, Greg." Sansilly sighed. "Trouble is, I'm thinking about our boys and Tesar and Ankhold. I wonder what it's like up there now?"

Greygen moved his hand up and down her nape, smiling as she relaxed against him, almost purring; he took her hand and led her away from the rail. "We get to Biserica, we'll be doin' for our boys. Let's go down now, plenty of nights left for lookin' at the moons."

28. One Mystery Down, Another Ahead

Serroi rode back to meet the van, the sprite on her shoulder, clutching at her russet hair. Herbwoman and Harper were side by side on the driver's bench with the girl Chaya kneeling behind them, crossed arms resting on the back of the bench. They'd been talking but fell silent as Serroi lifted her hand to signal a stop.

Sekhaya pulled the horse to a halt. "What is it?"

"About three miles ahead there's a fight going on. One man on a hill, using a dead horse and dead packmule as fort, holding off four men; it was six, but it looks like he's already got two of the attackers, at least there are two corpses dressed in black. Adlayr thinks they're Glorymen. Halisan, you can bespeak the sprite, yes?"

The Harper leaned past the Herbwoman, a frown on her bony face. "Yes. Why?"

"I'd like you to take a look at the man, see if you know him. We have to decide whether to go round this trouble or mix in it."

"Is there a question here? If they're Glorymen. . . ."

Serroi moved a hand in a warding gesture. "There's no time. Will you do it?"

"Yes." The Harper lifted her arm. *Come, Honeydew.*

Honeydew walked up the arm to Halisan's shoulder, words gushing out in her mosquito voice. Honeydew can do, but 'tis hard, Halisan should help Honeydew, Halisan should reach, don't just take. Adlee he flying in clouds, he don't want no glorymen makin' target out a him, but he gonna go down when Halisan and Honeydew say they ready, so Halisan and Honeydew get a goooood look, but the look gonna be short, so

Halisan be on her toe ready to go, ay ya, Honeydew a poet,
yes. . . .

The two women closed their eyes and let the image
flow into them:

The wasteland was dust and heat, shades of tan
and yellow, the only greens visible muted by the dust
until they, too, were a neutral tone in this palette of
dullness. On a low, rocky hill a man was lying behind the body of a horse the same rust brown as his
shirt, shooting whenever he caught a glimpse of
black as the four attackers shifted from brush clump
to brush clump, trying to close in on him.

The scene shifted as Adlayr swung round, trying to
find the angle that would give the best view of the
face, then there was a dizzying fluctuation as he
swooped down.

The man looked up, startled, then slid from view as
Adlayr sped past him and powered up again, plunging
into the clouds.

Adlee say do you want more or was that 'nough?

"Enough," Halisan said aloud; she leaned back, closed
short, strong fingers about Chaya's wrist. "It's Lavan,
Chaya. If I've helped you in your search, Healer, and
you've said I have, then I ask your help in return."

Serroi ran her fingers through her hair. "There's a
layby an hour ahead of us. Sekhaya, stop your van there
and wait for us. And you'd best be ready in case one of
them gets by us. I don't think it's likely." She chuckled.
"Hedivy is feeling very sour about Glorymen and he
hasn't had a chance to shoot anyone recently."

The sudden dive of the huge black trax had startled
Lavan, but he was too busy to worry what it meant; two
of the Glorymen were trying to circle behind him while
the others kept him pinned down. He'd killed the first two

doing the same thing after they'd shot the horse and the
mule.

He'd left the road, seeking to break free of them, made
the mistake of silhouetting himself against the sky. Two
shots put him on foot, the third dug a furrow in the side
of his head. One bit of luck, they weren't much smarter
than he'd been, killing the beasts and giving him both
shelter and water. Should have creased 'em and. . . . His
eyes burned from the sweat dripping into them. He
rubbed his sleeve across his brow, grinding his teeth at
the pain in his shoulder, ducked as a bullet slammed into
Alegay's hindquarters.

He caught a glimpse of black and fired, smiled grimly
as he heard a yelp from his target. "Got you, bhasta.
Where's your mate . . . ah!" He shot again, swore when he
saw the brush quiver as the other one crawled away.
"Missed this time. Try it again, deadbone."

He heard a flurry of shots, frowned. None of them hitting near him. What. . . .

The black trax came plunging down, knocked him flat
and left him gasping in a gust of fecal gas, flopped
around for another second, then was a naked man rubbing
dirt off his face. "Someday I'm going to have to take the
time to practice those zhaggin' touchdowns." The man
wriggled round and stretched out behind the forequarters
of the dead horse. "You're Lavan, right?"

"Yes, but. . . ."

"Adlayr Ryan-Turriy, gyes, Biserica. Friend of mine's
out there feeling mean. Give Hev a couple minutes, he'll
finish off the Glorymen. Him and that knife of his. Saaa,
I never want him hating me like that."

"Biserica? Hev? What. . . ."

"Long story." He eased his head up so he could see
over Alegay's forequarters. "That does it." He stood,
cupped his hands about his mouth, yelled, "Serroi, we
need you. This un's starting a fever." He dropped back to
a squat, wiped sweat from his face. "Hot, isn't it? Mind
if I help myself to your water? Traxing always takes the
stuffing out of me."

"Nay, be free."

"Zhaggin' Glorymen." He picked the knots loose with

a fingernail that looked a lot like a claw, upended the bag, and gulped down half the water that was left. "Ahhh, that's better. Shooting a good horse like this."

Lavan thought he saw the gyes' teeth lengthen, go pointed, then change back—or it could have been the woundfever confusing him. With the tension drained away, he hadn't enough energy left to talk, let alone question what was happening.

He was nearly asleep when he felt a cool hand touch his face. He looked up at orange eyes set aslant and skin. . . . "Green?"

"I prefer to think it olive," she said, comfortable laughter bubbling in her voice. "Relax, you're not seeing things. My name is Serroi, I am a healer of the Biserica."

"Biserica . . . he . . . the gyes . . . he said. . . ."

"Eh vai, don't think about it. Close your eyes and lie back; we'll have you well again in just a moment. . . ."

>><<

Chaya stood in the road straining to see into the dust cloud rolling toward them; the Harper said Lavan was well and coming to meet her, but she'd believe it in her body only when she saw him.

A horse emerged from the dust, a gray with a whitish mane and tail; it was coming at a gallop, a dark figure bent forward, urging it on. Her breath caught in her throat and there was a swimming in her head as if she were sunk in the mill pond with the weir propped open.

The horse slowed as it came up to her; Lavan swung from the saddle and ran toward her, catching her in his arms, hugging her so tightly against him she couldn't breathe. When he spoke, there was a groan in his voice and his breath was hot against her ear. "Chaya, my cici, I was afraid I wouldn't find you."

He pushed her away, used his thumb to wipe dust and tear stains from her face. "Serroi told me about the thieves." When she went pale, he shook her. "Did you think I wouldn't want you?" His voice went soft and he drew a hand down the side of her face, the touch making her shiver. "Chay, don't you know me better? I'm not

whole without you; I haven't been since I was chasing
you round your father's workshop." He turned her half
around, dropped his arm over her shoulder, and walked
her back to the fire.

Sekhaya smiled at them and filled two mugs with hot,
strong cha. "Go sit in the van," she said. "It's the only
privacy you'll get for many a day."

>><<

Serroi glanced across the fire at the lovers and sighed.
So long since she'd felt that sweetness, that time when
two people couldn't get enough of touching each other
and tried to merge into one flesh even when they were
walking along or just sitting by a fire. If Chaya and Lavan
had had troubles before this, and she thought they had,
those prickles were swallowed in the joy of this moment.
She scratched at her nose and tuned back in to what
Hedivy was saying.

". . . about Bebek."

Halisan caressed the harp that stood beside her on the
blanket, short strong fingers sliding along the wood.
"Ahwu, I know what I've seen, nothing beyond I can put
in words. Bebek is a man who wears a mask to buckle his
boots. He has a reputation for rigid honesty, hard work,
and cleverness; for being someone you can trust with
your secrets, no matter what they are. Rumor says he has
a finger in almost everything that happens in Bokivada.
It's true enough. He doesn't have friends, only a lot of
people who owe him favors and are grateful he hasn't
called them in. He's not known for generosity. The word
is that silver wesils scream in pain before he'll let go of
them, but a gold only whimpers since it knows there's no
escape. He could be a secret drunk, though he doesn't
show it in the daytime. From the pile of bottles that the
rag man collects there, he drinks enough brandy each
night to float the merchanter that carries it to Bokivada.
And it is only him killing those dead soldiers, he never
has company. As I said before, he has no friends."

"Where?"

"He has a house in the Vitifunder district."

"Guards?"

"None. Doesn't need any."

Hedivy brooded at the fire for several minutes, then he looked up. "We need a guide."

"You're asking me?"

"Yes."

She smiled. "Since I already know all this?"

"Yes."

"You're an honest man yourself, Hedivy Starab. I'll guide you."

"Good."

"Something else I'll do. I've got a house in Freetown. Lavan!"

Lavan started, turned to look at her. "What?"

Chaya blinked, blushed, and straightened; she drew her knees up and wrapped her arms around them.

"Clan law doesn't run in Freetown. You and Chaya had better plan on spending a while there, let things calm down a bit before you try for the Arbiters. My house is yours as long as you need a place."

>><<

With the new horses and the new food supplies from Lavan and the dead Glorymen, they made good time along the Wastelands Road, reaching Hubawern five days on. They circled to the north side of the town, crossed the river on the Huba-ferry, and started east through the broken, hilly country around the Bay. With Adlayr flying scout, they rolled unchallenged along a wide paved road, past big country houses, neat and prosperous farm villages. Now and then they caught glimpses of flagellants in procession and in those villages Glory Houses were being built; people turned to stare at them as they rumbled past, but no one questioned them or tried to stop them.

Early on the third day the van reached the summit of a low hill and Chaya saw the city spreading out along the curve of the bay. She was astounded and a bit frightened. Hallafam had a dozen families, around a hundred adults if she counted the young ones near apprenticing age. She'd expected something like Hubawern with its thousand citizens and stream of travelers passing through, but nothing like what she was seeing. There had to be fifty, maybe even a hundred times a hundred living down along the bay, crowded together in narrow houses built so close there was almost no space between them.

She closed her hands tight over the edge of the driver's bench and focused on Joma's bobbing head. *What are we going to do? How are we going to live? We can't just land on Halisan and expect her to take care of us, it wouldn't be fair. . . .* She swallowed. Not only would it be unfair, chances were Halisan would get tired of them real fast. And then where would they be?

Lavan and Halisan were riding up ahead, talking steadily. She wondered what they were talking about, then she smiled. What Lavan had talked about for days now, most likely. How he could get a client list started and how he was missing his tools, he'd had to leave them behind when he ran from the Glorymen. He did remember to mourn with her the loom she'd had to leave and the design charts that were gone with the thieves, but he hadn't changed all that much, in spite of everything that'd happened. *Ahwu ahwu, I love him as he is and he loves me and what more can one ask?*

Halisan led them through narrow winding streets crowded with morning shoppers to the wall that shut off Freetown from the rest of Bokivada.

"Wih! Fanek, I see your ugly face up there. Open the gate, let us through."

The guard leaned out the window, grinned down at Halisan. "Ahwu, it's that string-picker again. Make me."

She help up a broad silver wesil. "See if your fingers can stick to this." With a sweep of her arm, she tossed it to him.

"Always said you had a silver tongue, Harper. Stand back while we wind 'em open."

Chaya shuddered as the gates clashed shut behind them. The sound had a horrible finality to it as if the thread of her life had been sliced through.

* * *

Halisan's house was at the northern end of Freetown; she had a tiny stable and a bit of garden—grass and a tree and a few flowers, nothing she couldn't leave if she had a long engagement or was due for one of her wandertours. It was a small house with two rooms and a kitchen on the ground floor and two bedrooms above and a bathroom on the floor above with a cistern perched like a wart in an angle of the roof, a well, and a workroom in the basement.

Chaya relaxed once she was inside. The house was smaller than hers, but enough like it to make her feel at home.

Lavan opened the door, drew Chaya into the room. "We've been talking," he said. "Lots of things could happen tonight. And tomorrow there probably won't be time. Chaya and I, we'd feel more comfortable if you'd say the words over us, Harper Halisan. Sekhaya can hand off, Chaya's her name-child, so that's all right. And ..." he looked round, his mouth trembling as he tried to smile. "And we'd like you all as witnesses."

The room shimmered with light, there were candles everywhere, in holders, bottles, anything that would let them stand and burn. On a small round table there were a pair of candles in silver holders, two slender glasses with stems that seemed hardly wider than a thread, half filled with a crimson wine, two crystal dishes filled with an oil that gleamed palely gold with a creamy lopha blossom floating in each, releasing its perfume as it sank into the liquid. A red silk ribbon lay folded between the dishes, a twig from the tree in the garden laid across it, three heart-shaped leaves sprayed out from the tip.

Serroi stood beside one of the candle clusters, smelling the aroma of the hot wax, the perfume from the flowers, quietly enjoying the color, the scents, and the feeling of happiness that was radiating from most of the others in the room. Hedivy was irritated at being included in something he thought of as moronic nonsense, but he'd kept his objections to himself because they couldn't leave the house before midnight and he had to fill the time with something. She ignored him. Adlayr was relishing his role as groom's friend. Sekhaya was feeling sentimental and a little sad, the ghosts of memory hovering about her. And Honeydew was watching everything with eager interest.

Lavan and Chaya stood on one side of the table, between them Halisan's Harp; their hands were clasped above it, the altar that would sanctify their vows. Halisan stood across from them, her hands pressed palm to palm before her breasts.

She bowed to Chaya, bowed to Lavan, reached between the glasses, and lifted the twig. "By leaf and by seed, on harp and hearth, I call you to witness the binding of two into one." She sang the words, her rich contralto filling the room. "Who presents this man?"

Adlayr stepped forward to stand beside Lavan. "I, O Harper," he sang, his voice a deep baritone with an edge of wildness, a touch of sicamar's growl. "I, gyes and groom's man, I present Lavan Isaddo."

The candles flickered and the flowers sank lower in the oil, their perfume drifting up and forming haloes about the candle flames.

"Who presents this woman?"

Sekhaya stepped forward, set her hand on Chaya's shoulder. "I, O Harper," she sang, her voice husky, her grasp on the notes uncertain. "I, Herbwoman and thaz, I present my name-child Chaya Willish."

The Harper lifted the ribbon; it flowed over her pale hands, the candlelight giving it a liquid slide like running blood.

Serroi watched with a growing sadness as the ceremony went on, the young faces so serious, so happy, the ritual distilled of generations of family life, a life she'd never known; her family had sold her when she was barely old enough to walk, she'd grown up alone with a sorcerer who'd alternately petted her and tormented her. The Biserica had given her a home, a tradition to belong to, but she only had that a few years, then it was gone. There was no place for her there now. *I have the children, though ... that's something ... maybe I'll get used to*

*them after a while ... if I survive this ... if we sur-
vive....*

"... Chaya Weaver, plait the threads of your two lives
into a ribbon like this ribbon I bind round your wrist.
Like it, but stronger still, so neither pain nor pleasure,
sorrow nor joy, will pull it apart. Lavan Goldsmith, I
wind this ribbon around your wrist, make of your two
lives twin bracelets bound with links of steel that nothing
may break them apart. Place the hands that I have bound
upon the Harp and swear...."

Serroi's skin began to tingle with prickles of power
flowing from the earth and air and swirling round her.
She could feel her hair moving. Their voices came to her
through a thickening air; she heard both speak but could
not fathom the words. She took a step, then another, saw
Halisan looking at her.

Halisan lifted a hand gleaming with oil, beckoned to
her.

It was as if Reiki Janja stood there, the flesh form
taken by that complex of forces that was the Maiden, as
if Halisan were Reiki Janja recast, reformed, brought into
the world again with the flow of magic.

Halisan took up the twig with its wilting leaves and
held it out.

Serroi took it, held it before her, saw it change, glim-
mering into gold and jade. Her hands moved on their
own, her body moved one step, another. She touched the
jade leaves to Chaya's hand, then to Lavan's, felt force
flowing from her into them. Her mouth spoke, another
Voice came through her. "Be blesséd, wait, and hope."

Clouds swept in off the Sleeve and it started to rain
around midnight. Adlayr flew a rope over the wall,
shifted, and tied it to one of the iron spikes that ran along
the top. He helped haul Serroi and Halisan up and lowered them to the ground on the far side.

When Hedivy was over with them, Adlayr coiled the
rope over the spike, took a deep breath and *shifted* to trax
again, fell off the wall, beat his way upward and listened
a minute to Honeydew, who was perched on Halisan's
shoulder, sheltering under the wide hood of the Harper's

raincloak, then headed south along an empty rain-splattered street.

Working with care, Hedivy broke out one of the sections of glass in the small window set high in the door. He lifted Honeydew into the opening, passed her the end of a cord, knelt and began fiddling with the lock.

A moment later Honeydew waved through the hole, then withdrew.

Hedivy grunted, finished with what he was doing. He stood, tried the latch. "Prak," he murmured. "Get ready." He tugged on the cord, there was a thumping inside as the bar lifted, then the door swung open.

He charged inside—then stopped, stood listening.

The silence in the house was thick enough to feel.

Serroi pushed past. "I'll take you," she murmured. She went through the door at the end of the entranceway, began running up the stairs built tight against the wall.

The legs and arms of the man sprawled naked on the grass mat were a mess of whip scars and burns, old and new, weals of keloid or red and festering; one arm was curled about a dark bottle, others were scattered across the mat, some of them still dripping from the neck. The stench of urine and stale brandy was so thick that Serroi started shallow breathing the minute she opened the door.

Hedivy started to push past her.

"Nay! Wait." She stepped inside to confront the yellow light like a blob of melted butter pulsing above the geode. *MOTHER! CLAIM ME! I AM YOUR FIRSTBORN. COME TO ME. TAKE ME INTO YOU!*

Serroi recoiled, loathing filled her; she looked at the filthy room, at the ruined man starting to mumble drunkenly and shove at the floor in the futile attempt to get up. Images of the dead and destroyed filled her mind, the cries of the angry and grieving rang in her ears. *NAY! YOU ARE NOT. I WILL NOT. GO AWAY. GO. AWAY.* Her body shook with the repulsion she felt, green force bloomed in her, exploded outward, driving the yellow light into smaller and smaller compass until it vanished.

Serroi shuddered, her knees nearly giving way as the

force drained from her. She looked at Bebek who was curled into fetal position, crying, not sobbing, nothing so vigorous as that, more as if his soul were melting and running out his eyes. The urge to heal nudged at her, but for the first time she could remember, it faded and all she could think was that she couldn't bear the thought of touching him.

She walked past Hedivy. "He's yours. I'd get him out of there, but that's up to you."

Halisan was sitting on a bench in the entranceway. Serroi settled beside her. She thought about asking the Harper a dozen questions, but they all liquefied and flowed away before she could get them into words. She wanted to say something, she didn't want to think about what had to be happening up in that attic, something she shared responsibility for because she hadn't even tried to stop it. "They'll be all right?" she said finally.

"Chaya and Lavan? Ahwu, I think so. There's my house, they'll stay there while I'm gone. Better to have someone there to take care of it."

"While you're gone?"

"I'm coming with you. You knew that; why else would you call me?"

"You do me too much credit. Know? I'm dancing blindfolded in the middle of swords and trying to avoid the edges."

"Well, sworddancer, you need a Harper to keep the beat and that will be me."

Hedivy came down the stairs, a heavy, clinking sack in one hand. "He's paying our fares."

Serroi stood. "I'd better go to. . . ."

"No need, Healer. We didn't touch him. He's still talking up there with no one to listen."

"Where do we go?"

"Mount Santak. And we'd better get started."

>><<

It was nearly dawn when Hibayal Bebek uncurled and staggered to his feet. He looked at the dull, cracked geode, wrapped his hand around it, with a loud, wordless yell, hurled it through the window. His eyes were dry. He was done with grief. Holding to the stair rail, he got himself down to his bedroom, took a cold bath, wrapped himself in a blanket, and sat in the front window, listening as the rain come down in slanting sheets it was too dark to see. He willed his mind empty, drove out every image that sought entrance with the iron discipline that had carried him through life this far.

The hours passed. The rain slackened, then stopped. The clouds began to tear apart. A few stars shone through, paling as the sun rose.

He stirred. Relaxed. He thought about killing himself. Something tough and cold in him pushed the thought away. He stood, threw off the robe, and stalked into the bathroom to shave and get ready for another day's work. Dreams were one thing, even if they tore your heart out of you, but work had a solid presence about it that kept you steady.

And there was a lot to be said for vengeance. Woe unto ye who have wounded me.

29. Vision

Treshteny jerked her head up, swayed in the cradle of Horse's nonflesh.

Mama Charody rode closer and reached out to catch her, but drew her hand back as Treshteny sighed and straightened. "What is it?"

"I heard the Enemy crying in an anguish beyond telling. I felt emptiness and anger unfold over the earth. Serroi has rejected her child and war has been declared."

DAW

Jo Clayton

The Dancer Trilogy:

☐ **DANCER'S RISE**   UE2567—$4.99

For centuries spell-imprisoned, Serroi at last escaped her bonds to find herself in a strange land where magic, long vanished, seems to be starting to reappear.

☐ **SERPENT WALTZ**   UE2597—$4.99

War, fueled by a mysterious evil force, is sweeping the land, stealing the souls of dead leaders and raising up armies of dead warriors to fight again and again. Only Serroi's powers can stand against this evil, but will she be able to use them in time?

The Wild Magic Series:

☐ **WILD MAGIC: Book 1**   UE2496—$4.99

Faan was a mortal, kidnapped by the mightiest of goddesses, and trapped in a war between gods. Could she learn to master her own powers before the rival gods destroyed her?

☐ **WILDFIRE: Book 2**   UE2514—$4.99

Faan embarks on a difficult and daring search to find her mother, refusing to remain a pawn in the deadly games being played between gods and wizards.

☐ **THE MAGIC WARS: Book 3**   UE2547—$4.99

When universes meet and the wild magic is unchained, will Faan and her comrades survive the chaos of a sorcerous war?

DAW

Mayer Alan Brenner

☐ **CATASTROPHE'S SPELL** (Book 1)   UE2357—$3.95
Someone was on a power trip—and far too many acquaintances
of Maximillian the Vaguely Disreputable (Max to his friends)—
were being unwillingly caught up in the sorcerous struggle.
Trying to free two people trapped in a wandering castle, Max
runs straight into a war between Death Gods, necromancers,
and a sorcerer/detective who becomes mortally ill whenever he
tries to cast a spell. With inept wizardry running wild, can even
the mighty Max avert the catastrophic doom rushing to meet
him?

☐ **SPELL OF INTRIGUE** (Book 2)   UE2453—$4.50
Resurrected by one of the gods, Fradjikan the Assassin had
his work cut out for him, spying on Maximillian the Vaguely
Disreputable, the Creeping Sword, the Great Karlini, and all the
rest—as they followed separate pathways which would lead
them into the midst of a god-generated plot to find and gain
control of a missing ring of power.

☐ **SPELL OF FATE** (Book 3)   UE2508—$4.99
Return again to Brenner's world of hilarious havoc. This time
trouble is brewing for mortals and gods alike, as Maximillian
the Vaguely Disreputable comes closer to solving the laws of
conservation of magic and toppling the gods' power base,
while the Creeping Sword, who still can't remember his own
name, is drawn more and more deeply into the fighting between
warring factions of the gods.

DAW

Laurie J. Marks

THE CHILDREN OF TRIAD

☐ **DELAN THE MISLAID: Book 1** UE2325—$3.95

A misfit among a people not its own, Delan willingly goes away with the Walker Teksan to the Lowlands. But there, the Walker turns out to be a cruel master, a sorcerer who practices dark magic to keep Delan his slave—and who has diabolical plans to enslave Delan's people, the winged Aeyrie. And unless Delan can free itself from Teksan's spell, it may become the key to the ruin of its entire race.

☐ **THE MOONBANE MAGE: Book 2** UE2415—$3.95

Here is the story of Delan's child Laril, heir to the leadership of the winged Aeyrie race, but exiled because of an illegal duel. Falling under the power of an evil Mage, Laril must tap reserves both personal and magical to save the Aeyrie people from the Mage's deadly plans for conquest—plans which if successful, would set race against race in a devastating war of destruction.

☐ **ARA'S FIELD: Book 3** UE2479—$4.50

For many years, members of the Community of Triad have been striving to make it possible for the four primary species of their world to coexist. Now, the sudden, ugly murders of many high-ranked Walker and Aeyrie officials have shattered all hope of peace. Caught in the chaos of imminent war, the children of Triad must discover who is playing this deadly game of death and somehow force them to stop—before their world erupts in a genocidal war of species against species.